I0763466

FAR FOREST SCROLLS

Hourglass of Destruction

Each change deposited in our life delivers us another uncomfortable notch closer to its inevitable end. The darkness verily whispers to all awake to hear the truth, giving birth to that uneasy feeling endured with each change of season, and, if we look up, squinting into the heartlessly honest embrace of the cold, starless night, we see the lonesome howl of eternity mouthing its silent scream, "There is no cure for your fragile mortality."

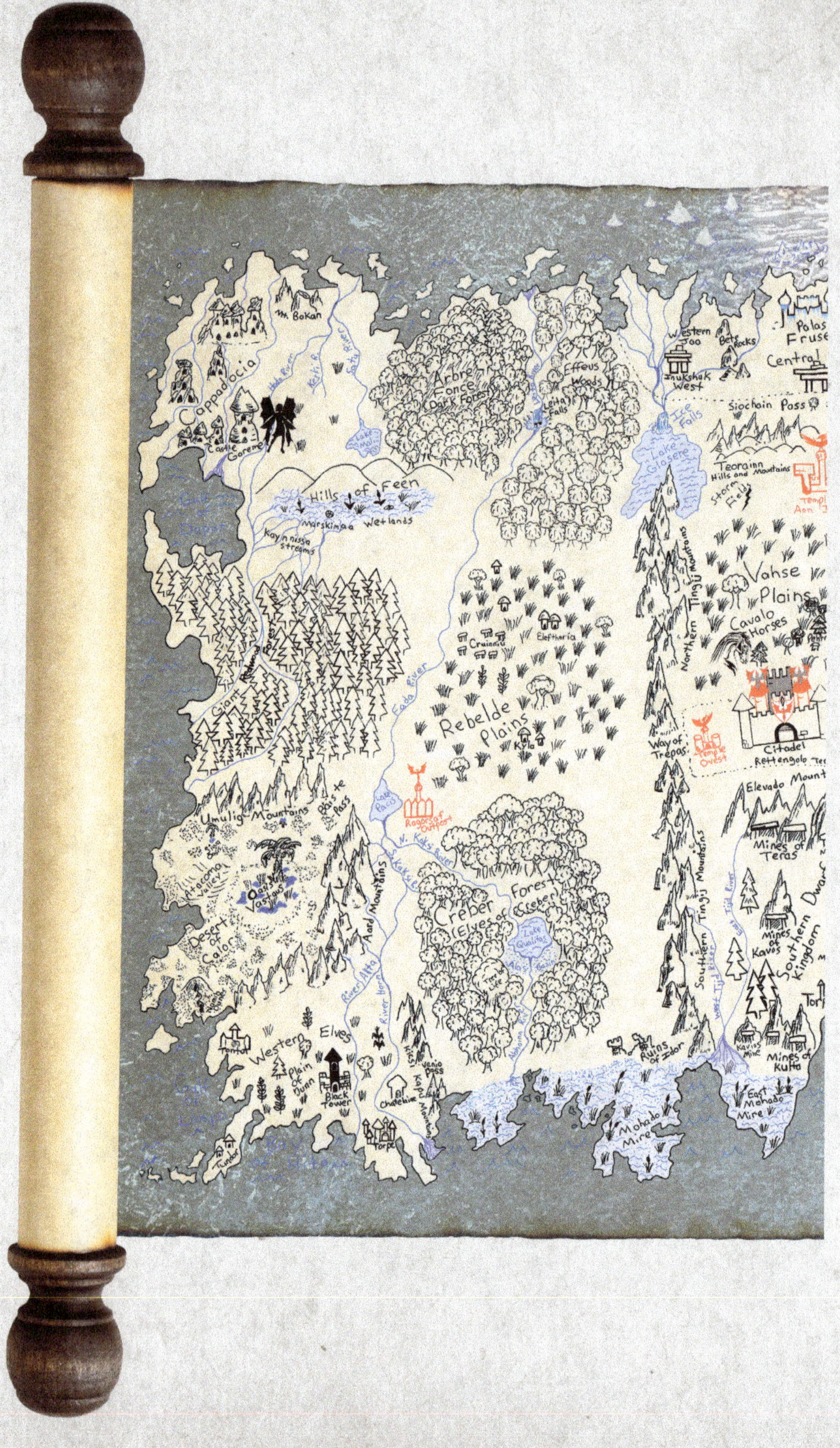

Mt. Bokan
Cappadocia
Castle Goreme
Hodo River
Keski R.
Satu River
Lake Mala
Arbre Fonce (Dark Forest)
Effeus Woods
Leita Falls
Western Joo
Bete Rocks
Polas Fruse
Inukshak West
Central
Siochain Pass
Ice Falls
Lake Glosere
Teorainn Hills and Mountains
Storm Field
Hills of Feen
Marskimaa Wetlands
Kaynnissa streams
Giant Redwood Forest
Eada River
Cruinniu
Eleftheria
Rebelde Plains
Kyla
Northern Tingiji Mountains
Vahse Plains
Cavalo Horses
Way of Trepas
Temple Ovest
Citadel
Rettengolo
Elevado
Mines of Teras
Umulig Mountains
Paiste Pass
Lake Pacis
Ragors Outpost
N. Kaks River
S. Kaksi R.
Atacama Valley
Oasis Vastaus
Desert of Calor
Aard Mountains
Creber (Elves of Forest Creber)
Lake Qualitas
Alas Basin
Tree of Life
Southern Tingiji Mountains
West Tijd River
East Tijd River
Mines of Kavos
Southern Dwarf Kingdom
River Alta
River Horn
Western Elves
Plain of Dunn
Black Tower
Chatelaine
Kiksi Kapu Mountains
Venio Pass
Torpe
Tundor
Ruins of Idor
Mohado Mire
Kavios Mine
Mines of Kutta
East Mohado Mire

Tebeotho Springs
Eastern Jaa
Inukshuk East
Nord
Jaa
Inukshuk Mitte
Koori Mountains
Northern Dwarves
Mount Honoo
Keha Haudella Volcanos
Storten Flower Fields
Anen
Kippe
Ruins of Murbh
Hino Mountains
Temple Ruins
N. Azul River
Haj
Ryba
Kala
Piscium
Isdo
Taiheart
Glan
Piscium
Pescore
Haavi
Miksi River
Pollen Lake
Toil Shaor
Cosan Bridge
River Vita
Liberum
Ager
Maotillo
Azul Delo River
Juopa Cavula
Dark Sea
Proliator Channel
Proliate Archipelago
Proliate Islands
Falcon Temple
Kissa Turkea Mountains
Temple Balia
Kovo Cliffs
Oroite Mountains
Jalokivi
Eluvies Delta
Cliffs of Karst
Torpen Sea
Isle of Hirmulisko
Dark Sea

The path to the Tournament of Flags has not gone well for the Knights and squires. Once the dominant military force in all of Verngaurd, the Knights have now retreated to three castles as their old nemesis, the Dark Warriors, have returned. Emerging from behind their castle walls, the Knights find a countryside covered in chaos and despair, crawling with enemies and the expansion hungry Proliate warriors. Verngaurd seems headed for a devastating civil war with suspicion and mistrust everywhere as the cycle of destruction, Na Cearcaill, is unleashed. Forced into a circuitous route the Knights find themselves haunted by strange creatures and magical beings. Book One ended with the Knights and squires fighting for their lives next to their allies under the shadow of the volcanic mountain chain that is the realm of the Northern Dwarves.

FAR FOREST SCROLLS

Hourglass of Destruction

BOOK TWO

Eternity sheds no tears as we deceive ourselves within the fraudulent bustling established inside the ordinary of each day, distracting our intellect from seeing, much less acknowledging, the small decay disseminating within us, and everything on all sides, as each tick of our life strides forward. The false façade of invariance blaring its lie from the world around us is simply a cruel, distracting trick fabricated from our deep desire for staticity. We sleep under the lullabic thought that how it is now, is how it was, and as it shall be, safely, and naively, relegating the laugh of eternity to the subconscious.

For more information and to view the illustrations for Book Two online please visit:
www.FarForestScrolls.com

Scrolls from 1000 C.E.
discovered during an archeological dig
in the Far Forest region of England,
the soul of this ancient fantasy tale
is reborn in your mind's eye.

Author: AAAA (Alpha Four) Illustrations: AAAA and Paganus
Scroll translation to English: Radek Novotny PhD Image Restoration: Altier Restoration

Library of Congress Control Number: 2019919074

ISBN (Hardcover, color edition) 978-1-7321499-4-6
ISBN (Paperback, black & white edition) 978-1-7321499-5-3
ISBN (e-book) 978-1-7321499-6-0

Book Two is represented by the rune of revolutionary change, Hagalaz—pictured here is the woodcarving found on the second of the timber chests discovered at the archeological dig within the Far Forest of England. Hagalaz denotes disruption, catastrophe, and unavoidable distress. For Verngaurd, and those you met in Book One, it symbolizes a seismic shift in the reality of world order rumbling through every facet of life as the mysterious time of Na Cearcaill ensues. {Aside about runes: The rune engravings found carved in the chests from Far Forest are from the Elder Futhark (the oldest runic script). The Elder Futhark is divided into three Aettir or "families," each one consisting of eight runes. Each Aett of eight runes is named for a god associated with the first rune in the family. Both Jera (from Book One) and Hagalaz (from Book Two) are from the second Aett known as Hagal's (or sometimes Heimdall since little is known of the Norse god of weather—Hagal).}

Seeing the truth and authentically understanding what is true are two indescribably different experiences. Our daily comforts spread a fog of numbing routine, shields of the accustomed cloaking us in the false warmth of the familiar, the insensible acts weaving themselves together until binding us within a fictitiously serene cocoon born from woven threads of the familiar.

Even tumbling within the world's massive times of change we struggle to see beyond our own insignificant moment, unable to comprehend the boundless ebony bookends of eternity, which do not even bother to acknowledge our insignificant time.

A sincere welcome back to the world of the Far Forest Scrolls. Return to its embrace, increasing (we humbly hope) your Wisdom of How to Live.

Table of Contents

Peractio: End of Book One • 1

Chapter One: Heroes Fall, Doubt Soars • 3

Chapter Two: Not So Festive Festival • 33

Chapter Three: Red Rising • 99

Chapter Four: Battle Begins • 159

Chapter Five: The Metal Hits the Scale • 219

Hardship and pain, forces that cannot be controlled—that is Hagalaz—that is existence. Often life mercilessly, and remorselessly, thrusts trials and adversity upon us, as it does upon those you met in Book One. A storm of adversity is upon them—all that is left is to see how they will deal with the travails...

Peractio

End of Book One

Laughing, the Watchers stood. "This is only the beginning of your end, fools!"

The three of them began chanting and vanished just as hordes of dragon flames engulfed the area. The dragons circled for several minutes to make sure the area was clear before landing.

The Dwarves dismounted, somberly standing over their fallen, and burning, comrades as the Knights and squires regrouped, cleaning off the blood and bird viscera.

"Thank you for fighting with us," Abhac said.

"It is we who owe you. Without your dragons, I fear we would all be dead."

"That was…unexpected…bizarre!" Abhac said, shaking his head.

Friar and Ritari recounted their previous run in with the Watchers and the minotaur.

"Bloody brain-sucking-spider-legged-birds, Watchers, and now minotaurs?" Abhac questioned. "The days keep getting stranger. I didn't think minotaurs existed."

"You don't have to believe in us for me to kill you!" a beast growled.

Off in the distance, an even larger portal than before swirled ominously as the thunderous stampede of hooves exploded.

"To your dragons!"

Figure 53: **Saatana Dragon.** *The largest of Verngaurd's dragons, the Saatana can be up to forty-five feet long. While unrideable, they can follow simple commands and be used in battle.*

The air cracked with a deep thunderous roar that shook the very ground.

Abhac laughed ominously as he turned towards his volcanic home, "Let them conjure whatever foul creatures from Ifrean they want. If they suffered under the Vioma dragons, see how they like our red!"

"Is that the Saatana dragon?" Lontas gasped.

The rattling of chains and a massive burst of flames rocked the sky as twenty Dwarf Dragon Warriors desperately struggled to maintain control over an immense red dragon. The monstrous beast seemed only mildly concerned with the orders being feverishly bellowed in his direction. Each movement of the dragon jerked the chains causing the Dwarves to surge forward, sometimes ripping them off the ground.

Figure 54: **A Saatana Dragon joins the fight.** *Twenty Red Dragon Warriors struggle to maneuver the giant dragon to join the battle.*

Chapter One

Heroes Fall, Doubt Soars

Scroll 1: Fettered by Gravity

"Vioma Warriors, get your hits in where possible, but stay out of the Saatana's way! Let the reds have a go at them!" Abhac yelled as the green dragon riders impatiently, and half-heartedly, restrained their dragons hungry for revenge and battle. "Knights, please hang back, our red Saatana is menacing and as likely to attack you as the enemy."

"Release and form lines!" the leader of the red Dragon Warriors yelled.

The Saatana dragon howled greedily as the chains binding it rattled to the ground. The ferocity of the red dragon conjured a look of doubt across the lead Watcher's arid face.

A shower of dragon flames exploded into the horde of advancing minotaurs. With no shields to protect them the front row of creatures were incinerated. Undeterred, the additional beasts bursting through the portal behind them jumped over the scorched corpses of their brothers before dropping down to three hooves and racing forward.

The rushing line of minotaurs leapt into the air, somersaulting and twisting to land hard on their backs with a loud groan: their heads towards the red dragon, and their knees bent with hooves pointing up. The next row of minotaurs through the portal vaulted forward, landing on the upright hooves perched over the anxiously coiled legs of the minotaurs lying flat. With a loud chant the minotaurs on their backs rapidly straightened their legs, hurtling their leaping comrades thirty feet high in the air.

The Saatana grabbed one out of the air, its sharp teeth instantly severing the beast in two, blood flooding the ground. He flung the shattered corpse in the air, knocking another minotaur off course. The others slammed into the dragon from above. Several massive hammer blows crashed into the dragon's head. Some minotaurs were flung off as the dragon tensed and jerked its muscles. Others managed to land, precariously balancing themselves on the dragon's substantial, but twitching back. They quickly unleashed massive hammer blows. The howling dragon turned and ferociously fluttered his wings to dislodge the attackers. As he did, a fresh host of minotaurs attacked from the ground. Some delivered hammer blows while others used the spear tip to repeatedly stab the dragon's underbelly.

Infuriated, the dragon roared, braiding pain and rage in his bellow. His thrashing tail smashed into several of the creatures sending them flying. His claws dug into others, easily ripping into the minotaur's flesh. The Aer Ridire riding the green dragons above shot bolts from their crossbows and cleared most of the minotaur from the red dragon's back. Several large bursts of flames from the green Vioma dragons removed most of the other horned attackers.

The Watchers began to chant and the lower portal to Ifrean closed as another opened high in the sky. Blue lines of magic coursed through the desiccated scar lines cutting their way through the Watcher's body as they conjured another, floating gateway.

Terror and pain flooded the face of the Watcher hovering in front as the red Saatana dragon flew upward with surprising speed, its massive jaws completely bisecting the stunned Watcher. A blue flash of brilliance and innumerable bolts of magical energy flashed out of the

Watcher's severed body, brutally shocking the dragon. A stunned look flashed briefly across the red dragon's eyes before they rolled back into his head. Both mighty wings and the dragon's body went slack from the enchanted shock. Gravity and the weight of the red Saatana dragon fused to send the listless body floundering limply through the air, forcefully hurtling to the ground.

The Watcher's eyes briefly looked down as his amputated hips and legs fell lifelessly next to the dragon on the ground. Strands of desiccated intestines waved in the breeze, desperate and dumfounded at the sudden change in milieu. Their forlorn gesticulations sent spasms of red blood and pure blue magic pouring downwards. The Watcher's four wings slowed as the supernatural sapphire veins languidly drained from his body. When they stopped beating, his top half fell to join his legs on the ground.

Smashing to the earth his dehydrated body burst into a cloud of dust which joined a flock of disconnected, blood soaked feathers. Softly falling, the wings fell with velvet gentility, lightly settling into the puddle of hushed black—the combination of his crimson blood and azure magic.

The Dwarves cheered as the remaining Watchers screamed in unrestrained rage. Collecting themselves, they resumed their impassioned chanting. The red-clad Dwarves hurried to their fallen dragon as the Aer Ridire moved their green dragons toward the remaining Watchers.

"Attack!" Abhac screamed. "These Watchers can be felled!"

The green dragons bellowed in anticipation as the green-clad Dwarves whooped their battle cry.

As the green dragons hurtled forward, the two remaining Watcher's eyes widened in dread while the cadence of their chanting sped up. As the lead green dragon moved within a few feet from them, the Watcher's conjured up a red, circular shield. A wry smile spread across their face as a crazed series of howls echoed forth from the newly conjured sky portal.

"Friar, let us in this fight!" Luchar screamed.

Friar hesitated, unsure of what could be coming through the portal. "For now, we wait, as requested by our Dwarf allies."

"But the Saatana dragon is out of the fight and is probably dead!" Luchar bawled.

"Wait, for now."

Luchar looked pleadingly at Ritari. When his captain remained silent Luchar used his axe to strike his helmet, and quivered in anticipation.

Before Abhac could utter any commands, a swarm of black figures whipped out of the elevated portal. A mix of scales and fur, the wolf-like head of the wyvern attached to a scaled body with two wings and two legs. Its tail ended in a brutal axe shape.

The first ones out abruptly tucked their wings in tightly and began to spin in a compact aerial roll. They disengaged out of the somersault right in front of the green dragon, using all of their momentum to send their tails whipping around, battering the axe-like portion of the tail into the head of the dragon.

The green Vioma dragon shrieked in pain as half a dozen of the axe-like tails of the wyvern bombarded its head and neck. The next

Figure 1: Watchers have summoned Wyvern from Ifrean. Distant winged cousins to the dragons of Verngaurd, they have two clawed hind legs and brutal, axe-like tails.

wave of six wyvern exploded out of the portal: three went towards the dazed green dragon's left wing, and three to the right as the Aer Ridire Dragon Warriors screamed commands at their stunned dragon. Using the sharp claws protruding from their back legs, as well as their sharp teeth, the wyvern clasped on to the dragon's wings, and then beat their own wings furiously.

The dragon howled in agony as his wings were stretched out mercilessly. The Aer Ridire dragon riders on his back shot several bolts at the attacking wyvern, but were soon set upon by newly emerging wyvern and quickly found themselves fighting for their lives. The original six wyvern returned from the backside of the dragon, again tucking into a tight aerial roll before unleashing fierce axe blows, empowered by centrifugal force, at the base of the dragon's wings where they attached to its body. The last of the blows on each side caused a grotesque wrenching sound as the tightly stretched wings started pulling away from the dragon's body. Muscles and ligaments stretched with sickening torment as the dragon's head flung side to side in agony.

Figure 2: A horde of wyvern are attacking a green Vioma dragon, sheer numbers overcoming their massive size disadvantage. Some wyvern are holding onto, and tensely stretching, the dragon's wings, while others perform aerial somersaults using their axe-like tails to slam into the base of the tautly drawn out wings.

The wyvern holding onto the dragon let go of the bloody, ripping wings to secure a more reliable grip. With a more anchored hold they once gain began to pull with all their might. The Vioma Dragon let loose a swarm of flames and several wyvern holding the left wing howled in agony as they dropped in flaming anguish. As soon as the flames subsided several more wyvern emerged to affix themselves to the wing and began to pull.

The dragon's wings started to detach with a nauseating tearing sound. It only took a couple of more hits from the gyrating, axe-like tails to make the wings completely avulse, sending showers of blood in all directions. Having lost the mastery of flight, the dragon's eyes, already burdened with agony, shot open in panic as its wingless body instantly became fettered to gravity while still convulsing in spasms of anguish. Blood flailed out in splattered cones as its body fell like a rock towards the earth. The small sinewy stumps, now ineptly wingless, beat impotently, managing only to disperse the blood surging out.

The green Vioma dragons that had been further back were fairing far better against the wyvern, using a mix of flames, claws, teeth, and bolts from their dragon riders.

Several wyvern had dropped down to attack the unconscious red Saatana dragon. The red-clad Dwarves would have none of it, instantly surrounding their dragon. Their fearsome Draak swords easily gashed through the wyvern's fur and cut deeply into its scale.

The remaining Watchers laughed as a fresh group of wyvern landed, slinking low to the ground and, with their teeth bared, surrounded the Dwarves protecting the unconscious red dragon. Letting out a fearsome wail, the wyvern thrust out their forked tongues. A green, viscous poison erupted from open tubes on either side of the tongues' bifurcation. The thick jade liquid hissed as it hit flesh and armor, a black gas sizzling out from the portions striking metal.

Any Dwarf unfortunate to have the toxin touch their skin began to gag and choke. Several fell to the ground, desperately clutching at their throats. Eventually their spasms ended a guttural sibilation. Those struck in the eyes had their muscles instantly convulse before their entire body succumbed to unabridged rigor. Their panicked eyes stared in silent desperation until their paralyzed chests could no longer supply oxygen to brain or body.

Dwarves hit with a smaller amount of the deadly toxin were thrashing in tonic-clonic agony. With the protective red-clad Dwarves dead or dying, the wyvern began feasting on the still insensate red dragon. Their sharp fangs and hind claws ripped and stripped the scales away before gorging into its flesh. The savage pain tore the immense dragon from its stunned slumber and it began to flutter. Several wyvern near its head stopped ripping flesh long enough to squirt their toxin directly into the dragon's desperate eyes, slit like nostrils, and mouth. Already weakened, the dragon's body shuddered before turning rigid—now an unwillingly compliant cupboard for the hungry wyvern.

"Defend our Dwarf brothers!" Friar yelled. "Knights only!"

Before the command had left Friar's lips Ritari and Luchar were already sprinting on their way.

Ritari thrust his spear completely through the back of the neck of a feasting wyvern. The beast let out a pathetic gurgle before crumpling to the ground. Unable to withdraw his spear in time Ritari switched to his broadsword and hacked at another of the beasts.

By this time Luchar had arrived and quickly decapitated the closest wyvern. Finally free to unleash his wrath, Luchar let out a horrifying noise, a mix of expectant laughter and repressed rage. The two wyvern closest to the Knights turned, extending their tongues through blood-filled teeth, complete with bits of dangling dragon muscle and sinew. As the powerful tubes began contracting to spit out their poison two arrows bisected each wyvern's tongue. Green toxin and a black mist exploded from the mouth of the injured wyvern.

Without turning around, Ritari made a quick wave of thank you to Lontas and Finn before cleaving one of the writhing wyvern's head in two. Luchar grunted while separating the other's head from its neck.

Sorea managed to fell one with a bolt from her crossbow right at the base of the wyvern's neck. The wyvern's body dropped like a rock, its pithed spinal cord no longer able to send impulses to the rest of the form.

As the Knights were making their way through the wyvern feasting on the red dragon and downed Dwarves, the two remaining Watchers began to shriek in fear.

"No! It can't be! He…is approaching!"

Scroll 2: Uninvited/Tragic Guest

With a loud whoosh a figure in white robes rushed through the portal which instantly closed behind him. A wyvern that was trying to cross through the magical gateway was cut in half as the doorway to Ifrean vanished.

The man, who had just exited the doorway, levitated above the field. He tilted his head to his left side and scrunched his face in exasperation, as if trying to make sense of the scene.

He wore a thin white robe, its hood resting over a thick leather overcoat. He had long brown hair and a scruffy beard. His wizard hat was cocked on his head, blocking his left eye.

He raised his hands and, without saying anything, all the wyvern instantly froze.

Luchar's eyes widened in unbridled joy and he quickly dispatched two of the closest gelid wyvern.

"Master! If we have offended you or done something wr…"

The Watcher was cut off mid-word as the levitating man's left hand slowly turned towards the now gasping Watcher. Slowly the arid trenches running down the Watcher's body glowed brilliant blue. After a few moments the sapphire magic turned into a thick vapor and flowed through the air until absorbed into the man's outstretched hand. Soon even the blue of the Watcher's eyes were drained of magic. The form of the siphoned Watcher held its shape for a moment before shattering into brittle dust and feathers, which indolently fell to the ground.

"You! Fat Knight!" the levitating man yelled to Luchar.

"Who you calling fat you bloody…"

"Stop killing my defenseless wyvern!"

Luchar looked up incredulously, he had taken the opportunity to slaughter five of the frozen wyvern.

"I am eternally honored by your presence, White Wizard," the remaining Watcher said, his voice quivering in fear.

A murmur went through the Dwarves, Knights, and squires as no one had seen him in Verngaurd before.

"Were my instructions mystifying? Was it confusing when I stressed avoiding encounters such as these?" the Wizard hissed.

"No. It's just…these…impertinent Knights were so…so…insolent…so disrespectful in the face of your…magnanimous glory! You see, it started when they killed a minotaur and…"

"Oh, I see," the White Wizard interrupted. "They killed a minotaur! So, then you simply took it upon yourselves to nearly drain my

Figure 3: The mysterious White Wizard appears in Verngaurd. Little is known about the ruler of the lands of Ifrean. He is rumored to be tyrannical and merciless.

Stymphalian Swamp by conjuring my beloved Stymphalian birds into battle?"

The Watcher's eyes darted from side to side, futilely looking for some way to escape. Seeing no possible route, he decided to answer. "Yes. You see, we thought they needed..."

"Oh, you thought?" the Wizard thundered. "You thought, did you?" he repeated, this time with a smirk. "Thinking, no. Obeying, yes!"

The Wizard tilted his head even further to the left and began to cackle. Instantly the magic from the last Watcher was siphoned into his hands until the Watcher's desiccated body drifted to the earth.

"Please, talk to our Veneficus," Friar said, having moved to the front. "There has to be a way for our two lands to live in peace. Surely this war will leave both of us decimated and the world destroyed."

At the mention of Veneficus the White Wizard's face contorted in rage. "Do not mistake my intervention at this time for compassion! Do not misinterpret my stopping this battle as a willingness to afford you any ultimate mercy. You will *all...die!* The simple reality is that *the* plan must come to fruition first. Do not let your pathetic minds confuse the fact that death is drawing you near, to smother you within the regenerative, pulverizing, and never-ending wheel of Na Cearcaill. Just...not quite yet!"

With a snap of his fingers the wyvern still alive disappeared. He raised his hands and chanted loudly. All the dead and dying corpses on both sides of the battle began to decompose at an extraordinary rate. Maggots, beetles, and other insects appeared by the thousands, speeding through their life cycles as generations fed, grew, and died on the tissue of the dead. Flesh and ichor liquefied, marinating into the already blood-soaked ground. The armor of the dead rusted, swiftly turning into a corroded dust. Eventually, even the bones dissolved and the deteriorated bodies sunk into the earth, with the dirt and rapidly growing grass hungrily devouring their substance. The Knights and squires squirmed as the previously trampled grass aggressively re-grew under their feet. All around them crushed flowers bloomed once more as the formerly burnt, trampled, and bloodied pasture returned to a pristine field.

An unpleasantly corrupt smile arched across the White Wizard's face, "It is not only abroad that you must look for the origin of your ruination." He paused, tilting his head to side before continuing. "I will leave you in peace, for now." Before they could speak, he too disappeared.

Abhac directed the green Vioma dragons down. He and the other Aer Ridire riders embraced and took stock of what had happened. There were no corpses to mourn over, no signs of the fierce battle that had just taken place.

"We can't even bury our dead," Abhac said to Friar.

Unsure of what to say, Friar averted his eyes, instead letting them brush against the peaceful, wind-blown beauty of swaying flowers and fresh grass all around them.

"Is this the new reality? Wyvern, Watchers, minotaurs, and the White Wizard?" Abhac asked, rhetorically, as he shook his head.

Gazing out upon the pristine flowers and fields, his eyes soaked in the beauty as both nostrils enjoyed a punching floral aroma, courtesy of a warm breeze. Swathed within such splendor it was hard to believe the grim battles they had endured against such strange creatures ever really happened.

"Two Vioma dragons, one Saatana dragon killed," Abhac said with genuine sadness, taking stock of the missing. "A dozen fallen Aer Ridire and all twenty of our dragon trainers slaughtered!"

Friar looked down, almost abashed at losing none of his Knights. *I should have sent my Knights into the fight sooner.*

"How can we perform our burial ritual, the obsequies, without bodies?" an angry Dwarf Warrior growled. "Not even their armor or weapons remain!"

"Body or no body, they will still get the honor of a full warrior obsequy," Abhac said.

"We are all deeply saddened by your losses. Dragon and Dwarf fought as valiantly and heroically as any warrior I have seen."

Abhac nodded in gratitude. "Their loses are ones we can ill afford. We will be doubling the already beefed up patrols of our lands. You are welcome to camp here for the rest of the day and night. I assure you, our dragons will have you covered!"

"A gracious offer we will kindly accept," Friar replied.

"I would offer you refuge in our mountains, but outsiders, even close allies, are forbidden from viewing our burial..." Abhac paused, despairing of having no bodies. "...I guess funeral obsequy practices."

"We understand and would not wish to disturb your mourning."

"Rest assured, I will inform our King and the blue dragon council of these strange events. I will return to check on you in the morning," Abhac said before turning and joining his brothers on their dragons.

Still a little stunned, the Knights and squires watched in silence as Abhac and the Aer Ridire flew towards their volcanic homes.

"I don't want them to leave," Lontas said. "Seeing them fly away makes me sad...and scared." His eyes darted anxiously in all directions, searching for strange portals or bizarre creatures.

Bellae squeezed his hand, "I don't want them to leave either."

Scroll 3: Lean Forward, or Fall Back

"Did you sleep at all?" Lontas asked as morning brazenly announced its intention to emerge by audaciously throwing out a thin orange band across the skyline.

"Not a bit," Bellae answered, hugging her mice friends, Grym and Borb. "I bet Cookie is in the main kitchen, cooking away..." small tears began to run down her face as her voice faltered with emotion. "I miss her, Liberum...everything!"

"Even the Tilkeri squad?" Lontas said, trying to put on a brave smile despite the homesickness pulling down on his spirit.

Bellae laughed and Lontas managed to avoid crying himself.

"This isn't at all what I expected," she sniffled, hugging her mice friends even tighter.

"I don't think anyone could have expected the slightest bit of what we have been through," Lontas said, looking to the early morning sky. "The dragons were noisy, flapping overhead all night. I guess their flying around should have made me feel safe, but it didn't."

"I know. To make it worse I could feel their anger. They are furious over the death of their friends," Bellae added, wiping away the last of her tears.

"Oh, you could feel their anger?" Jumeaux whined. "Well, I can feel the crap you are flinging heaping up around..."

"Get up and shut up!" Luchar yelled with wide-eyed fury. He had deep bags under his eyes as if he had not slept at all. Most of what he mumbled while walking away was inaudible. They could make out, "... better show up so I can kill more..."

Packing up the camp proceeded under a taut, silent fog complete with frequent glances to the horizon for any signs of portals, minotaurs, wyvern, or Watchers.

"The Aer Ridire!" Lovag cried out.

The sight of the majestic green Vioma dragons lifted everyone's spirits. The Knights on watch stayed at their post while the rest quickly gathered around the dragons as they landed.

"Good morning," Abhac greeted as he and his dragon riders dismounted.

"It is sincerely good to see you again," Friar said, gratefully clasping Abhac's forearm. "How were the ceremonies for your fallen?"

Abhac looked down, "Very odd with no bodies to return to the magma of the mountain, but all were well honored for their sacrifice. Again, I, and King Abernan, wholeheartedly apologize for not welcoming you into our mountains. Did you sleep well?"

"As well as one can after the day we both had yesterday," Friar answered.

"There is a peculiar tone to the air. I fear the strange days are not yet behind us."

"Unfortunately, I agree," Friar said. "Would you join us for breakfast?"

"We'd be honored," Abhac replied. His expression changed and he suddenly began laughing. "Speaking of strange, we had some pompous Proliator and an annoying Magician come by some weeks ago demanding we call you 'HK.' How do those fools think this stuff up?"

"I honestly don't know," Friar laughed as Bellae made her way to talk with the Vioma dragon, Soma.

"Where did you find that little marvel who can speak with dragons?"

"She is squire to Finn and possesses great talent," Friar stated.

"She is a pipsqueak who possesses a great talent to annoy!" Jumeaux snorted in scorn to his twin sister.

"Jumeaux!" Gimelli chided telepathically. *"She's your little sister, and she does possess amazing talent."*

"Possess? She's more of an abscess! That I will acquiesce as her pustules coalesce!"

"Jumeaux!" Gimelli steamed out loud.

He said nothing, but scoffed again, this time for the lack of appreciation for his humor and rhyming skills.

"Let's eat. Squires, get some food from the supply wagons," Friar ordered.

"Nothing like an abscess to ruin an appetite," Jumeaux said glaring at Bellae.

"Save your supplies. We'll get fresh meat. We've had a population explosion of fia asteikko. They are easy targets for our dragons," Abhac offered.

"Fia asteikko? Oh my!" Lovag said, his mouth watering.

"We would be honored," Friar said with a polite bow of his head.

Abhac approached Soma who was still conversing with Bellae. "You amaze me, squire. However, Soma has to get us meat for a hearty breakfast."

Focusing on the dragon he said, "Huun, Huun, Huun. Sivver fiasta. Herras fiasta unnoas."

"What did he just say?" Bellae asked Soma.

"He said, 'Up, up, up. Hunt fia asteikko. Bring it to me,'" Soma replied. *"These Dwarves are not very bright, but they are loyal to us."*

"These dragons are not that smart, but they are incredibly loyal and once we train them, they do a good job," Abhac said.

Bellae giggled.

"What?" Abhac inquired.

"Oh, you two just sounded alike, that's all."

"You really understand his grunts and bellows?"

"Yes."

"Well, ask him to let the other Vioma know the orders and hurry back. They should get four to six fia asteikko."

Bellae conveyed the commands.

"It's so much easier when you just talk to us. I wish you could stay," Soma said. He quickly relayed the message to the others.

To take off the dragons crouched low using all four legs and both wings to push their large bodies up. Once off the ground their powerful wings took over, beating the air mercilessly. Bellae, the closest, tumbled over from the forceful gust.

Once up off the ground she asked, "What exactly is a fee-steak oh?"

Abhac laughed, "Fia asteikko!"

"Oops, sorry."

"Don't be. They are horned beasts that live in the tall plain grass and bushes around the flower fields. They have armored scales and eight spiked tails that they use like whips."

Figure 4: The numerous fia asteikko living in the plains surrounding the mountains frequently provide sustenance to the dragons and Dwarves. Although fearsome creatures, they are no match for dragons.

Bellae had a hard time visualizing such an animal.

"Any hope we can keep her?" Abhac said, nodding to Bellae.

"Not a chance!" Friar replied aggressively, he quickly smiled to soften his outburst.

"Can't blame me for trying. Despite the tragedies of yesterday, we are glad you came north to experience the splendor of the Flower Fields."

Friar hesitated. "I cannot tell you how sorry I am…we are, at your losses. If we brought this trouble to you, I am forever contrite."

Abhac shook his head, "Not your fault. You did not conjure those vile creatures."

Friar nodded gratefully, "Thank you. We were most grateful for your help, and sacrifice. Despite the tragedy, I think we are all delighted to see the flowers you Dwarves maintain."

"They are beautiful!" Lontas admired.

"Really, Lontas? We should call you La-girly-tas who wants to see beau-tee-phul whittle phowers."

"Jumeaux, would you like to go set up for breakfast?" Ritari asked.

"No. Sorry!" he quickly added, his motivation to avoid punishment engulfing any fledgling heartfelt regret.

Bellae took Lontas' hand, "Don't let him get to you."

"It's thanks to your Knights that we even have the Storten Fields and the Saatana dragons," Abhac said, breaking the awkward silence.

"How so?" Gimelli asked.

"Eons ago, this field was held and ruled by the Kingdom of the Sprites. They lived in peace with us while maintaining the flower fields. The Proliators came and started killing the Sprites."

"I've never seen a Sprite. Have you?" Jumeaux asked sarcastically, implying he did not really believe in them.

"You don't see them because the ones who survived the attempted genocide fled to Cappadocia to live with the Fairies," Friar replied, ignoring Jumeaux's scorn.

"Why did the Proliators want to kill them?" Lontas asked.

"You must remember that back then the Proliators were little more than roving bands of marauders who plundered for a living. Their rise to a well-ordered military power is extremely recent, since just before the Dark War."

"It could have had something to do with the ugly, rocky place they call home," Abhac added. "The Proliators might have been jealous of the beauty and fragility of the flowers and Sprites. Anyway, they initially came to finish killing off the Saatana dragons that had come to our mountains to avoid extinction."

"What? Why?" Bellae asked.

"The Saatana Dragons used to live exclusively in the Proliate Isles. The Proliators drove them away, thinking they were full of what those radicals call 'evil fire!' Apparently the 'evil' dragon fire spreads death. They believe their god, Tallcon, brought the 'good fire' of life and rebirth. They also lusted after the thick, viscous naphtha that the dragons use to breathe their fire. We can harvest naphtha without hurting the dragons. The shortsighted Proliators would kill them and take the naphtha from the carcasses and then use it to make fire weapons.

"Dwarves have always lived in peace with the more docile Vioma and the highly intelligent Kirvella Dragons. When the Saatana were driven out by the Proliate, we took them in. Left on their own, they would have wreaked havoc on the surrounding countryside and it wouldn't have been long before they were hunted and killed by everyone, not just the Proliate.

"The Saatana were difficult dragons to train. The Kirvella eventually won their trust and then, slowly, over generations, we did as well. When the Proliate came to kill the rest of them, the Knights defeated..."

"You mean *demolished* the Proliators. It was an old fashioned pounding!" Luchar growled.

"You're right," Friar stated. "After those defeats at our ancestor's hands, the Proliate were absent from mainland Verngaurd until the Dark War. We must remember, victory yesterday does not guarantee success tomorrow. The Proliators have evolved a great deal."

"Their army is different—larger and more organized, but they are still causing trouble," Abhac declared.

Just then the wind's determined breath sent the flowers into a gyrating dance, coaxing an intense bouquet from their velvety petals. Also riding on the current of air was a barely audible whisper.

"Maigre!" Abhac called, recognizing the misty whiff of his wife's voice.

"Coming!" a fragile, swishing voice replied. If it had not been spoken in reply to Abhac's query you might have thought it was the flowers thrashing.

"When the Sprites were run off by the Proliate our Dwarf women heroically took over the honor of tending the flowers. My beautiful wife, Maigre, is a fifth generation horticulturist!"

After a slight rustling a dozen small creatures strode forward. They were incredibly thin and barely as tall as the medium length flowers. Their delicate arms looked like twigs. Their petite faces were rounded, almost as if they were meant to be plump like their male Dwarf counterparts. The only stout part of their figure was the long bushy mane germinating with a vengeance from their dainty heads. Their coarse locks were pulled back as tightly as the shaggy hair would allow and the shear weight of it made them lean forward slightly to keep from being thrust backwards.

You might have thought they were sick but for the fact that all the women had the same gaunt appearance, and, despite their hollow look, they seemed full of energy. Maigre waved a handful of pink and purple flowers with her right hand while her left struggled to carry a woven basket of pruned weeds and dead flowers.

Given their familiarity with Dwarf culture, Finn, Lovag, and Friar Pallium seemed undisturbed with their scrawny and diminutive stature.

They were the only ones.

"This is my wonderful wife, Maigre," Abhac said proudly. "Dear, this is Friar and the Knights from Liberum."

Bellae towered over the minute figure of Maigre as she quickly approached the petite Dwarf woman. "Hi, I'm Bellae. Those are stunning flowers!" Closing her eyes the young squire leaned in to enjoy the aroma. "I so love pink and purple."

"Hello, Bellae, and welcome to the flower fields. Pink and purple are my favorite colors too!" Maigre said, her smile broadening.

Abhac laughed. "I'm glad to meet someone who loves those colors as much as her! Our cave is..."

Jumeaux interrupted by clearing his throat loudly.

"No! Jumeaux, no!" Gimelli warned telepathically, her voice dripping with trepidation.

He did not heed her warning.

"You Dwarf guys should stop eating all the food and let your women have a little," Jumeaux chuckled to the icy and dismayed looks of the rest of the Knights.

"Jumeaux, what are you thinking?" Gimelli pleaded out loud.

Luchar growled, "Insolent boy!" He made a move to strike him, but Friar interrupted. "Luchar take this discourteous squire to the rear. He can be in charge of the setup *and* cleanup of our meal."

Luchar grabbed Jumeaux's arm and roughly led him away.

"A chiliad apologies for the boy. He has...an unusual sense of humor. Rest assured, we are all taken aback by the beauty of the women before us, and hope his punishment suites you," Friar said.

Abhac looked upset, but managed, "There is no charge for youthful ignorance."

Everyone laughed and the harsh tension slowly evaporated to a strained humidity as introductions were made complete.

Scroll 4: Red Warriors

"Please, join us for the feast," Friar beseeched the Dwarf women.

"No, thank you. We have work to finish before the suns get too hot," Maigre replied kindly, but the sting of the insult still hung about her expression and influenced her declination.

"It was nice to meet you," Bellae said, carefully hugging the fragile Maigre. Leaning in close, the squire whispered, "Do not let what my brother said offend you. You are as beautiful as the flowers themselves!"

"Thank you dear one. I sincerely hope to see *you* again, Bellae," Maigre said, emphasizing the *you* enough to imply Jumeaux was not completely forgiven.

"I would love that!"

"Good-bye!" Abhac called as undulating stalks of flowers swallowed the departing Dwarf women with barely a rustle under their negligible forms.

"How are things here in the Northern Kingdom?" Friar asked.

Abhac's smile vanished. "The red pestilence is all around us! After so many died defending Verngaurd from the Dark Warriors, it seems we traded a dark menace for a red one. The Proliate have the audacity to build massive castles they mockingly call 'temples' near the base of the Keha Haudella Volcanoes, to our east is Temple Palvoa. To our west is the immense Temple Aon Intinn."

"Have they made any moves against you?"

"Besides blatantly hemming us in? Not really. They do make repeated incursions into our lands, and have been doing so with increasing frequency. However, our neighbors have not fared so well," Abhac answered. "You would not even recognize the western Parishes of Piscium. Most have given themselves over to the Proliators and been forced to take their culture, worship Tallcon, and abstain from anything immoral."

"The Piscinians? They are fiercely protective of their lewd, sea-based culture," Ritari commented. "They are known more for pubs than piety."

"I know!" Abhac laughed. "The only explanation is fear of the Dark Warriors. The Proliate are exploiting this panic to spread their extreme cult, masquerading it as a protective religion."

"What of the Dark Warrior infantry?" Friar asked.

"We've heard of their attacks around us, but have never seen them in our lands. Other than the bizarre attacks we just suffered through with you, we have been left alone by everyone but the Proliate. They have the audacity to repeatedly enter our lands and accuse us of attacking Piscium. As if!"

"Why is the Dark Warrior infantry only attacking around you?"

"Maybe our dragons? Even before yesterday's battles we had started placing guards around the flower fields to protect the women, and Vioma riders make sweeps of the area.

"Some of the Kirvella Dragons think it's a conspiracy. The Dark Warriors create fear and the Proliate swoop in and take over other people's land."

Figure 5: A Dwarf and dragon hunting party fighting fia asteikko. Abhac has been on many such expeditions, but this time the dragons went by themselves.

Friar and Ritari exchanged a knowing glance. "We were thinking the same thing. In fact, we came across a village that confirms…"

A loud screech bellowed behind them, interrupting Friar. A few Knights drew their swords.

"It's just Soma," Abhac reassured. "We have hunted fia asteikko for centuries. They don't need us with them!"

Bellae muttered something that sounded like a disjointed chant. Seeing the confused expressions on everyone's face she realized it was in Ainmhi Caint. "Sorry, something's wrong with Soma. I sense pain… and he's flying strangely."

"Ah, he's just a peculiar dragon. Nothing new there," Abhac said dismissively.

"I'm telling you, I feel plenty of pain and lots of fear," Bellae insisted.

"We shall see," Abhac announced, a touch of worry entering his mind after the strange happenings of the day before.

As the dragon flew closer it became clear Soma was, in fact, weaving and twisting violently, nearly inverting at one point. The limp body of a fia asteikko thrashed viciously in his fearsome jaws.

"He's coming in too fast! Get out of the away!" Abhac yelled.

Everyone heeded the call except Bellae. She stood her ground and waved her arms. Soma's tormented eyes steadied as they locked on hers. Staring at her, he fought to control the weight of the fia asteikko carcass and land safely.

"Bellae, move!" Finn yelled in a panic.

"Steady, Soma! You can do this," she cried out.

Finn sprinted, picking her up he raced a few steps before he jumped, then rolled out of the way just as Soma crashed to the earth. His massive wings narrowly gliding over their heads. A stormy shower of uprooted flowers exploded in his wake covering them in a fragrant rainbow of blossoms. They brushed off pollen and petal as the massive dragon skidded to a lumbering stop.

"PLEASE, my Inion, be more careful!" Finn said breathlessly.

"But…he needed me!" she calmly said, as if being crushed by a dragon was worth the chance to help him. "Oh, and thanks, Finn."

"Don't mention it," he managed before sneezing loudly. Shaking his head he began scooping flowers off his body, before struggling to get the pollen out of the ruts of his thick skin.

Soma lay on his side, his chest heaving with irregular respirations. He had a spear sticking out of his neck and half a dozen in his wings. Green blood oozed from some wounds and gushed from others.

Bellae screamed and rushed to him.

"Why does it always have to be my poor right ear?" Soma wailed.

His right ear fluttered on one sickly, sinewy strand, now even more mangled.

"Oh Soma, that's not what you should be worried about," she said as tears blurred her vision.

"What? What happened?" Abhac cried out. "Fia asteikko don't throw spears!"

"Soma, what happened?"

Before Soma could answer Bellae, the other five Vioma dragons returned. Two of them carried the dead carcasses of fia asteikko. None of the others seemed injured.

"I managed to get this fia asteikko," Soma said, limply pushing the creature forward. The effort forced green blood to ooze out of his nostrils. *"These spears are a real drag on me. Get it? Drag-on a dragon?"* Soma coughed and blood spurted out over his teeth and around the embedded spear shafts.

"Quit joking! I'm too worried about you. Who did this?"

"The red warriors saw me fighting the fia asteikko and attacked!" Soma said. *"Tell the Dwarves that a few of the red ones are coming this way."*

Bellae immediately translated.

"Proliator scum!" Abhac yelled. "Go get the women from the field and escort them home immediately!" he instructed one of the other Dwarves. As that rider ran off, Abhac bellowed, "Zwerg!"

Short even by Dwarf standards, Zwerg sprinted forward. A rather straight brown beard framed his rugged face.

"You're our fastest rider, go get a Kirvella healer here now! Tell him we'll need a Vioma dragon sling and fresh Vioma to carry Soma."

Zwerg deftly mounted his Vioma dragon, shouting commands as they streaked into the air.

"The rest of you curs get ready for battle!" Abhac shouted. "Friar, we invite you to fight with us once again."

Friar nodded, "Always."

"Form up lines!" Ritari yelled. The Aer Ridire took up the flanks around the Knights centerline.

Abhac and Luchar began ranting angrily as they impatiently waited.

"Did your wife get out of the flower fields?" Lovag finally asked.

"What? Oh, yes. Thanks, Lovag. I saw the dragon carrying the women heading to the mountains," Abhac answered.

"Here they come," yelled one of the Northern Dwarves. Squinting, he sighed and rolled his eyes, "Lidenskap!"

"What's a Lotta-lice-n-cap?" Luchar growled.

"General Lidenskap of the Rutilus Obitus Sanctus Division," Abhac said scornfully.

"Stupidest name in world! What is that supposed to mean?" Luchar snarled, becoming increasingly agitated. "That Lice-cap guy and this

Rutilo-butt-kiss thing both sound like rare and highly infectious diseases. Maybe we should shoot them from this distance...to avoid the potential contagion. Eh, Finn?"

"Hold your arrows," Friar said firmly.

Abhac chuckled, "Rutilus Obitus means 'red death.' They are the Proliator's elite army in charge of defending their 'temple' fortresses and worshipers."

"I still think we should shoot them," Luchar stated sheepishly under Friar Pallium's scalding glare. "Just to be safe."

"Wait until you hear how he introduces himself! The all-powerful blah-blah-blah..." one of the Dwarf warriors started, but Abhac interrupted.

"Don't spoil it for them!"

"The Proliate are supposed to hate cavalry and yet, here they are riding horses like when they came to Liberum, and when heading to the village of Kippe!" Ritari exclaimed.

"They started using horses because of the rapid expansion of their territory. They still believe it's a sign of weakness to fight from horseback. Their silver divisions ride the nasty sprak beasts into battle," Abhac replied.

"So, riding an acid-spitting lizard into battle is manly enough for them, but not a horse?" Ritari laughed.

"Apparently."

"Zwerg's coming," Bellae said from the back.

He carefully guided his dragon down to a nimble landing. A blue Kirvella dragon jumped off the wooden carriage with a large bag slung over his shoulder and immediately began tending to Soma as several Aer Ridire began unloading a giant sling to attach to the injured dragon.

The six-foot tall blue dragon had a three-foot long tail and stood upright, fully clothed. Two small vestigial wings, useless for flight, fluttered fervently behind him. A few small spikes surrounded his face and kind, intelligent eyes.

"May I go translate for the Kirvella?" Bellae pleaded.

"Stay in formation," Friar replied, unwilling to put his prized squire in unnecessary danger.

Figure 6: The learned Kirvella Dragons co-rule with the King of the Northern Dwarves. Their vestigial wings are too small for flight, but they are known for their extensive intellect.

All four of the approaching Proliate wore red armor. Long spears jabbed menacingly into the sky, each bearing a fluttering pendant with a blood red image of a phoenix, representing Tallcon.

"Lidenskap is a total fanatic," Abhac said. "He will charm you in the day and cut you to pieces in the night. He's in charge of Temple Palvoa, but is incredibly ambitious. Rumor is his eyes are set on leading Temple Ovest near the Citadel, or possibly the entire Sanctus division," Abhac said.

"Good day. I am General Lidenskap," he said, taking off his red winged helmet. "Thanks to the magnanimity of the all-powerful Tallcon, who so generously, and personally, bestowed unto me, his humble servant, the sacred crimson sword of his sacred vermillion blood. Therefore, I humbly announce myself as Lidenskap, the bearer of the consecrated blood-red, and eternal, fire sword."

Figure 7: General of the Proliate army stationed at the Temple of Palvoa, Lidenskap is an ambitious and fanatically religious man. He is the only member of the Proliate to carry a blood red sword (rumored to have been bestowed by Tallcon himself).

Luchar pretended to snort awake, "Sorry, your diatribe lost me after 'magnanimity.'"

"I'm Friar Pallium of Liberum," he said loudly, hoping to cover up the snickering of the Dwarves and Knights. Lidenskap's vengeful gaze locked menacingly on Luchar.

Some Dwarves mumbled such things as, "Humble my arse!"

Turning to Friar the general's eyes softened, "Ah, I'm quite sure you meant to introduce yourself as HK. Old habits can die-hard. As such, a single such offense can be overlooked. Welcome to the territory protected by Temple Palvoa. All honor and praise to Tallcon who gives everyone life, and us strength!"

"These are Dwarf lands!" Abhac hissed angrily. "You have NO territory here!"

A smug smile spread across the general's face, as if trying to provoke them. His eyes twinkled with the pretentious tranquility of one speaking from a position of matchless power. The Magicians and Proliate not only controlled the Citadel, but innumerable strongholds throughout Verngaurd. "What brings you Knights this far north?"

"Visiting friends," Friar said, pointing to the Dwarves.

"A little holiday, then? How nice for you. We have far less pleasant business. We have been tracking yet another renegade green dragon that attacked a Piscinian village yesterday. We just came upon the culprit attacking an innocent Piscinian who..."

"Bloody Helvetti!" Abhac yelled. "Attacked a Piscinian, my arse! Our dragons were hunting bloody fia asteikko! Is your helmet covering your eyes or just squeezing your brain too tightly? You and your lot are a boil on Verngaurd!"

"Rude and vulgar Dwarf, not that I am surprised. You Dwarves are nothing if not predictable in your lewdness," Lidenskap decreed. He nonchalantly brushed the armor of his left shoulder as if sweeping away the Dwarf's pathetic comments.

"We, Dwarves? Do we all look alike to you? You are the mindless clones with your chants, base religion, and..." Abhac's ranting was cut short by a hand from Friar.

"I know it is hard to remain rational when your dragon was needlessly attacked while gathering food. Why don't you go check on his injuries?" Friar said.

His eyes still blazing with resentment and anger, Abhac reluctantly walked towards Soma.

"Thank you for restoring order, HK. They are an emotional bunch, those little Dwarves," Lidenskap stated.

"You do realize we are standing right here?" Zwerg demanded angrily. The enraged other Aer Ridire riders began moving forward, several Knights gently suggested prudence.

"Ah, so I see you are there," the general said dismissively. "So, HK, are you, perchance, heading to the Citadel for the Tournament of Flags after your little getaway?"

"We are," Friar said, grateful to have the subject changed.

"Would you like us to escort you through these dangerous lands to the Citadel?"

Taking a mental deep breath to remain calm Friar reminded himself anger is not helpful. "I think you shall find we are still quite capable of defending ourselves."

"Of course," Lidenskap replied. He then raised his right hand. One of the other Proliate immediately handed him a piece of parchment, which he passed to Friar, "Here is an invitation for you, and others of your choosing, to come witness a service honoring Tallcon before the Tournament. It is an exceedingly rare privilege for a disbeliever to be invited to the Great Temple at the Citadel!"

"I am grateful. I shall make every effort to be there," Friar stated stoically.

"Indeed," Lidenskap remarked, disappointed that Friar was not in awe of such an honor. "There is still the matter of dragons attacking the villages in Piscium. They endured enough agony from the Dark Warriors before we arrived. Once again they have asked us, the protectors of Verngaurd, to stop these senseless dragon attacks."

"We have never attacked a village!" Zwerg answered angrily.

"Did I say *Dwarves?* No. No, I did not. I said D-RAG-ONS!" Lidenskap answered contemptuously.

Zwerg gritted his teeth, "Doesn't it seem odd that these so-called "attacks" only started after you red birds showed up?"

In perfect unison, all the Proliators pointed their spears towards the Dwarf.

"This is neither the time nor place for this discussion," Friar stated calmly. "I assure you, the dragon that you attacked just left our side and brought back the dead fia asteikko you see before him."

Lidenskap looked critically at the injured dragon and the dead carcass. "This may be true in the matter of *that* particular dragon. However, the village of Sciocco was definitely pillaged yesterday and burned with telltale signs of dragons, and presumably their Dwarf riders."

"Lies!" several Dwarves yelled.

"I am one hundred percent confident it was a dragon attack!" Lidenskap declared.

"In my experience, one should avoid stating they are one hundred percent confident of anything," Friar declared.

"Confidence is strength! Also, and obviously, a giant green dragon is rather hard to miss."

"Over-confidence slides into arrogance," Friar observed.

"Enough!" Lidenskap declared. "There was a dragon attack on the village of Sciocco, and we are here to warn you Dwarves to stop them. Or we will."

A series of frustrated scoffs arose from the Dwarves.

"I look forward to seeing you in the Great Temple," Lidenskap said out loud, while thinking, *You ungrateful heathen!* Glancing menacingly at the Northern Dwarves he added ominously, "We will use whatever means necessary to defend the territory under Tallcon's rule!"

"I wonder, General Lidenskap, have you seen any unusual...creatures lately?" Friar asked as the Proliate were turning to leave.

Lidenskap did not hide his irritation, titling his head back in annoyance at the query, "You mean besides the disgusting attacks by their vicious dragons, breathing their corrupt fire?"

Friar, with various interjected details by others, recounted their strange battles.

Lidenskap's expression turned from uneasy skepticism to outright incredulity. When the tale finished the Proliate general looked down and gently rubbed his brow.

"This supposed battle happened here?" he finally said. "You mean dragons battled wyvern, minotaurs, and winged demons on this pristine ground with no evidence in sight?"

"I told you about the White Wizard's sorcery," Friar said, taken aback at Lidenskap's disbelief.

"The White Wizard? Here, in Verngaurd?"

"Yes…as I said."

"He shows up and 'magically' everything is cleaned up?"

"Yes. You know, he's a wizard, who does *sorcery*!"

"How conveeeeenient," Lidenskap drawled.

"Actually, it was absolutely *not* convenient in any way shape or form. Our Dwarf brothers had to perform their obsequies without the bodies of their fallen heroes," Friar answered as the Dwarves gathered around murmured their approval.

Lidenskap scoffed and half-heartedly tried to cover the disrespect as a cough. "Well, let me assure you, I shall immediately dispatch a most urgent message to the Citadel that all Proliate troops should be on high alert for mythical creatures with the good manners to clean up after their messy battles."

Several Dwarf warriors growled in outrage and began to close in around the Proliate who bristled back just as fiercely.

"Down Dwarves," Lidenskap said condescendingly. "We shall make our leave."

"No apology for heinously attacking our dragon?" Zwerg howled.

Lidenskap waved dismissively before mounting his steed. As the Proliate galloped away, a cloud of hesitation hung over the Knights, everyone pondering whether the trip could get any worse.

"Are they really that blind? How do they mistake a fia asteikko for a human, or a Dark Warrior attack for a dragon strike?" Zwerg seethed.

Friar paused. "There is *no* way anyone could make such a mistake without magical deceit." *There are dark forces tearing Verngaurd apart,* he thought helplessly.

"I hate to say I told you so, but this General Lice-in-his-cap and the other guys with the Rutey-tutey-us O-ridiculous disease are a bunch of fools. Apparently, they have all been turned insane and ill-tempered by dreaded sickness," Luchar growled.

Faint laughter rippled through the gathering.

"The good news is, that disease is easily cured with a little swipe from my axe."

Chapter Two

Not So Festive Festival

Scroll 1: Good-Bye, Hello

Concern carved its way across Abhac's face while he paced back and forth, anxiously watching the blue Kirvella dragon bark orders to Dwarves struggling to get the sling attached to his injured dragon Soma.

Luchar grunted and moved forward uncomfortably, determination barely overcoming his hesitancy, towards the worried Dwarf. The Knight slipped off his heavy helmet and leaned in to whisper, "In the end, it is the effort given in battle, and the honor with which we fought that will echo on forever. The last couple of days the Northern Dwarves and your dragons have fought with integrity and distinction."

Abhac nodded and smiled, understanding enough about the brash Knight to know such a sentiment would be painful to utter. "Thank you. We would be honored to fight with you any day."

Time sludged forward as the Dwarves struggled to secure the sling, punctuated by their grunts of effort and Soma's whimpers of pain.

"Hang in there, Soma. Love you," Bellae finally cried as four Vioma dragons carefully lifted their injured friend in a giant sling.

"You need anything?" Abhac asked, already strapped into the carriage of his dragon.

"Thanks, but we're set," Ritari stated.

"Safe travels. See you at the Tournament."

"We look forward to it," Friar said. "Hope your dragon pulls through."

The discouraged Knights watched the features of the Dwarves and dragons diminish to a small blur as they flew to their mountainous home.

"Lovag, can you help cook the fia asteikko that the Dwarves were kind enough to leave us? It seems a shame to waste the meat," Friar asked.

"Yes, sir."

"Go then! Quick as possible, I want to head out." Friar commanded.

Jumeaux glared at Friar after he had finished cleaning up from their breakfast.

"Thank you for your work, but do not disrespect anyone, ally or foe, like that again," Friar said. "Respect is the first branch of friendship, and the first step towards peace of mind. A calm mind is a stride towards peace within you, and your relationship amongst each other."

Jumeaux looked down at his sore hands and prune fingers from washing, preparing the fia asteikko, and then cleaning up, but he said nothing.

No one respects me! the young squire's mind shouted.

Seeing his angst, Friar turned, for they had more pressing business. "A-guard!" he yelled with surprising vigor. The advance guard quickly approached. "See to our water supplies."

As they rode off, Friar spoke again, "Ritari and Lovag to me!"

Once the three had moved out of earshot Friar sighed deeply. Stress and worry fused, teaming up to highlight his age. Creased and furrowed, he looked drained.

"I'm not sure our morale can take much more adversity." His words lingered questioningly, imploring them to contradict him. "Our reputation and ego have taken a pounding since our optimistic beginning. What now?"

"We should go south to Cosan Bridge," Ritari suggested. "With haste we may catch up to our fellow Knights." He turned and looked back to where Soma had been lying. "Staring at blood-soaked earth and destroyed flowers reminding us of the previous days battles is not helping anyone's enthusiasm."

"Lovag?"

"We should avoid Kippe and head north, skirting the base of the Keha Haudella Mountains."

"The volcanoes? Sounds like a recipe for disaster," Ritari countered.

While his Knights argued Friar had a flashback from what had become an all too disagreeable routine, his nightly visions. The one from last night featured Liberum crumbling under a Proliate siege. His eyes fluttered, exhaustion tugging at his will. *I need a good night's rest, for once.*

"We cannot fail," he mumbled out loud.

"What?"

"Nothing. What were you saying?"

"The Path of Takar leads over the two forks of the northern River Vita. It should be passable for the supply wagons," Lovag announced.

Ritari looked at Friar. "Should be passable? Seems like an unnecessary risk."

"Lovag, can the wagons make it?" Friar asked.

"Yes," he replied, but his head bobbed questioningly side to side.

"Let's try it, a change in scenery would be good for us and I honestly wouldn't mind having dragons patrolling the skies above us," Friar said, thinking of the devastation at the village of Kippe and the strange creatures they had battled. "I doubt we could survive another of those attacks without help from our Dwarf brothers."

Once the advance guard returned, they headed northwest towards the Keha Haudella Volcanoes.

"Lovag, tell us about this crossing through the mountains," Friar requested.

"As the two braches of the northern rivers snake down from Jaa, they run around, through, and underneath the mountains. There is a nondescript path north of the fork in the River Vita that leads over the river through a deep gorge in the volcanoes."

"Why keep it off the map?" Ritari asked.

"The Dwarves don't want the traffic. Plus, there are innumerable shallow, maze-like passages that dead-end. Most importantly there are magma vents that eject hot lava. If you wander across one of those, you are broiled alive," Lovag answered.

"Oh, okay. Broiled alive is a good reason. You should have started with that."

After setting up camp near the base of the mountains all but the night watch turned in early. Some were tired, others afraid of what tragedy might await them on the morrow. Everyone was hoping for a clean and favorable start.

"Gimelli, you awake?" Bellae whispered.

"Not on purpose," she said, rolling over. "What's up, Sis?"

"How do you stop seeing those villager's faces?" Bellae asked. Staring through Gimelli she saw their dirty and tattered clothes, and the desperation brewing within their cages. The hazy smoke of the burning village framed their emotionless faces and accusing eyes, casting a dull look of betrayal from their battered souls. The images of the mutilated animals created such a powerful memory her nostrils burned as if the rotting flesh were still close by.

Gimelli smiled out of uncertainty, and reflexively pushed Bellae's hair out of her eyes.

"That's a hard one. I'm not sure you can ever get rid of them." Gimelli paused. "Maybe we shouldn't. Friar told us to acknowledge and accept bad thoughts and images. The harder we try to suppress them, the more frequently they rise. Realize that bad things, including death, happen as a part of life, and it's not our fault."

"Is talking about death supposed to cheer me up?"

"Oops, sorry!" Gimelli laughed and quickly put her hand over her mouth to suppress the noise.

"Will you two cretins clumsily disguised within sister clothing knock it off?" Jumeaux huffed.

"Sorry J," Gimelli said, still giggling.

"The point is, you can curl up and let tragedy consume you, or you can stand up and fight to make the world a better place," she whispered. "That's what the Knights do, improve the world for everyone in Verngaurd. You control your attitude, creating a good one makes everything seem better."

"You know what would help my attitude?" Jumeaux asked sarcastically. "If you two would shut it and sleep."

"Nice, Jumeaux. I am trying to help our sister," Gimelli said telepathically.

"Sleep," he said sourly.

Gimelli smiled warmly at Bellae, who mouthed, "Thanks."

Sleep finally received Bellae into its heedless arms. The reprieve was short lived as something made her eyes bolt open. Unsure of how long she had been sleeping she turned to see Borb standing on his hind legs, nervously sniffing the air.

A horrifying noise fractured into her ears. Covering them until it stopped, Bellae stammered, *"What... what was that?"*

Borb's high voice cracked with uneasiness, *"Don't know."*

"Should I wake the others?" Bellae wondered.

"I don't think so," Borb answered. *"It's coming from inside the mountain."*

"Can't they hear it?"

"Apparently not."

Bellae cuddled with her mice friends and huffed, knowing it would be almost impossible to convince sleep to return.

In her mind, time, as it often does in a sleepless night, alternated between a constrained forward crawl and explicitly stopping.

Borb squeaked and Bellae jumped as another startling howl ripped them from a foggy soup of half-arousal, half fragile-slumber. Taking a deep breath Bellae looked at the stars and tried to relax.

"This is super fun!" Grym chirped. *"I would like to congratulate whomever chose this excellent spot for camping. Peaceful, restful, except for the minor detail of the blood-curdling screams..."*

"Bellae," a voice called.

Even though she was staring at the night sky a part of her had a flash of hope that it was morning and time to wake up and leave. It was Grym and Borb hissing and chattering that sent a shiver though her flesh.

"Bellaaaaaaaaaa!" the frightening in its familiarity voice drawled.

Closing her eyes and shaking her head Bellae thought, *Just when you think the night can't get worse.*

"It was worth a try," the specter said with a dry chuckle.

Bellae turned on her side and looked back to recognize the frightful face of a Nishi. The spirit's eyes widened in hatred and seemed to sink deeper into their recessed wells of animosity. Her hair floated and danced liked waves as she floated several feet off the ground.

"Not too late for you to follow me, you little rat-faced misfit, doomed to die in pain and misery. What do you say? Accompany me and endure only a sampling of pain and torture."

Tempting, Bellae thought. Briefly she contemplated rushing towards the ghost and hitting it with her forearm charm made from iron, obsidian, and neverita duplicate—the shark-eyed shell. That idea quickly vanished as she remembered her last major run-in with the Nishi. Her stomach lurched at the sickening *crack* as a possessed Bestilla had fallen and broken both her legs in the library. Suddenly, Bellae began laughing.

"What? You think this is a game? An early, relatively painful death is your best option! Agony is your future, yet you laugh?"

"Just thinking of someone funny," Bellae replied. Her exhaustion made the memory of diminutive, hunched, and beady-eyed Trelos, who helped forge her talisman, seem infinitely funnier.

"You die!" the specter shouted, floating quickly towards Bellae.

The squire quickly pushed back her sleeve and held out the iron charm which encircled her forearm. The Nishi stopped and mouthed, "See you soon…"

Bellae could hear the clanking of armor before she saw one of the advance guard Knights sprinting towards them.

The Nishi disappeared as he approached.

"What…what was that strange…light?" the Knight asked.

"An old friend," Bellae answered sarcastically.

The Knight shook his head in disgust. "Get some rest, squire, morning will come soon!"

Not soon enough, Bellae thought, wrapping her cloak around her ears and holding Borb and Grym tightly. She spent a fitful night anxiously waiting for first sun to rise. A few times she heard the night watch clink by in their armor or a green dragon fly overhead. While they made her feel better, it was not enough to allow restful sleep as the intermittent howls of pain and fury from within the mountain continued.

"Get up, sleepy head," Gimelli said, softly shaking Bellae's shoulder. "Looks as though you ended up sleeping well."

"Didn't you hear the howling last night?" Bellae asked, sitting up with bags under her eyes.

"Howling? No, and actually, you look really exhausted."

"What are you rambling about now, Bellae?" Jumeaux challenged.

"There was a screeching noise all night."

Jumeaux harrumphed.

Friar or the night watch will know, Bellae thought, standing up.

"Where are you going?" Gimelli asked.

"I need to find out what that was."

After a quick scan she moved towards Friar and Ritari who were talking to a handful of Dwarf Warriors in red armor.

Pushing back his bushy black hair one of the Dwarves continued, "Not sure what's going on with that dragon. He gets meaner every day. You may have heard his screeches last night. Some say his cave is haunted by ghosts that torture him, but we never see anything and the howling continues even though we have moved him several times."

"Bellae, this is Trenalai, a master dragon trainer with the Saatana Divisions," Friar said, looking directly at Bellae.

"Hello," Bellae replied, as all eyes turned towards her.

"How do you do?" Trenalai asked, surprised to see the young squire.

"Did you hear the howling last night?" Friar asked.

"Yes, I came to find out what it was."

"A troubled Saatana Dragon."

"With the Tournament just days away I am not sure what we will do," Trenalai stated. "He's one of the three dragons we're using for the Dragon Battle."

"Bellae could talk to it," Friar stated.

Her eyes lit up, *Yes! I need to talk to that dragon!*

"Out of the question!" Trenalai said indignantly.

"She's an Ainmhi Caint, and may be able to help," Friar replied calmly.

Trenalai looked impressed, but repeated, "It's still not possible. If you end up fighting him at the Tournament, the contact would look suspicious."

"Of course," Friar said, nodding in agreement.

Bellae stared at Trenalai, willing him to change his mind.

"We probably shouldn't bring it to the Tournament, but there are no choices for a replacement," Trenalai declared. "Good luck with your journey. We better get to work."

"Thank you for your time," Friar stated.

The Dwarves bowed and left.

"Did you hear anything useful last night?" Friar asked.

Bellae closed her eyes. "I only felt pain…and lots of anger. Why couldn't the other squires hear it?"

"I think being able to feel the dragon's emotions made it seem much louder to you. Why don't you go get some breakfast?"

Once Bellae had gone Friar wheeled towards Ritari, "I knew bringing back the Dragon Battles was an absurd idea!"

"Well, it just got worse for whoever has to face that shrieking dragon at the Tournament. Speaking of shrieking, Jumeaux is still having trouble. He's always angry and can't relate to the others," Ritari stated. "I broke up another fight last night."

"You realize who he sounds like?" Friar chuckled.

"Have mercy on us if he turns into a little Luchar," Ritari replied, laughing as well. "I can't fathom what you see in that boy."

"It's difficult enough to see the true self in those we meet. It's harder still to see the potential that lies within. Jumeaux has promise and, I believe, a role to play in the future."

Scroll 2: Forget the Girl Who Talks with Dragons?

"The rest of you, head out!" Friar yelled. "Hopefully the advance guard has found our path through and will check back soon."

"I don't want to go deeper into the mountain," Honey complained nervously.

"I'm not too excited about it either, especially after last night's howling."

Bellae stared anxiously at the giant ebony wall of rock towering to her right just as white clouds drifted into its side. The rocky surface appeared to absorb them, as if the volcano's steam was fed by gently drifting clouds instead of surging up as a pungent warning of the inconceivable heat and power lying within.

"These volcanoes are really active," Gimelli said, pointing to a summit spouting lava.

"Yeah, they have indigestion. The smoke is a burp, and the lava is puke!" Jumeaux laughed.

"Actually, Jumeaux, that's pretty funny," Scelto admitted.

The further into the mountains they travelled the more barren the ground became. Eventually they entered a true mountain pass and, for the first time, were walled in on both sides.

Lontas leaned in close to Bellae. "Did you see that?"

"Rocks? Yeah, pretty much all I can see!"

"I thought I saw our friend...from the cemetery."

Bellae smiled, "I knew I felt him watching over us!"

Or waiting to eat us, Lontas thought.

Bellae whispered to Lontas about the Nishi attack the night before and endured several minutes of an angry diatribe about waking him up next time.

"Okay, Okay, I promise!"

After several hours of weaving through cramped passages, the smoother surface of the middle Keha Haudella Mountains gave way to the irregular, almost serrated edges of the Western ones.

"Where's that blasted advance guard?" Luchar growled as they entered a relatively large mountainous courtyard. "There are four bloody paths! Which one do we take?"

"They should have reported back by now. I don't think we should wait for them," Ritari said.

"We should keep moving. Try the largest one?" Friar asked.

Lovag nodded and they entered the widest opening. After going in about ten feet a small puff of smoke drifted casually up from the trail ahead of them.

"Stop!" Lovag yelled. "Back up! Back it up!"

A loud pop was followed by a whoosh, as if air were being sucked into the mountain.

"Shields! Shields!" Lovag yelled.

As the others moved back into the courtyard Ritari and Luchar leapt off their horses and quickly moved forward. They locked their shields together just as an intense burst of flames ruptured up in front of them. The spray only lasted a moment, but the heat and steam lingered. The sizzling mountain rock hissed its displeasure at the impromptu broiling.

"We seriously don't want to go down that path," Lovag stated.

"You think?" Luchar growled, eyeing his scorched shield. He was feeling trapped and crowded by the stifling heat and formidable cliffs. The already stale air seethed after the vented magma escaped. "How often does that little freak show take place?"

"Well…" Lovag started.

"Don't listen to him! He's obviously led you into trouble and doesn't know how to listen to our mountain," the familiar voice of the Dwarf Abhac stated slyly. He had a wistful expression and seemed at ease among the barren cliffs that were his home. "Morning, Friar. I found these hopelessly lost Knights, whom I believe belong to you, roaming around aimlessly amongst our paths." He pointed to the contrite-looking advance guard just entering the courtyard from a small trail.

"What are you doing here, Abhac?" Lovag asked with wholehearted relief.

"Our scouts told me you were taking the path over the rivers, and thought you might need a hand listening to the mountain's advice. I guess I was right!"

"You hear the mountain's speak?" Luchar questioned doubtfully.

"The mountain just told you not do head down that largest path, didn't it? These mountain walls are stronger than any fortress and hum with life lessons."

"What lessons?" Luchar growled.

"Mountains enhance the soul, teaching hard work as they beckon us to climb to the top, and beseeching us to take a moment and enjoy life with the reward of unfathomable views."

"Just to be clear, you're still talking about *mountains*?"

"If you scream the mountain echoes an answer with reciprocating emotion and…"

"Very nice," Friar interrupted before Luchar could bark a derisive response.

"Finn," Bellae whispered.

The Elf smiled.

"Ask about Soma…please."

"You do it. Come on up."

By this time, Friar and Abhac noticed the commotion. Their stares made her blush. "I'm Bellae, squire to Finn."

"How could I forget the girl who talks to dragons?" Abhac said smiling.

"How's Soma doing?"

"He's a tough dragon. He'll be up causing trouble soon enough."

"We're all ecstatic to hear that! Now, how the blasted do we get out of here?" Luchar snarled, glaring angrily at the mountainous enclosure surrounding him.

"I'll lead you out," Abhac said, pointing to the first path they would need to take.

The Dwarf rode on Honey with Bellae and they moved to the front with Friar, Lovag, Ritari, and Finn.

"I know it has been said before, but let me once again declare how sorry we are for your losses in battle," Friar said.

Abhac looked down, "It has shaken us to the core, but we are ready if those vile creatures come again!"

"How's King Abernan doing?" Lovag asked.

"He grows impatient with the arrogant Proliators. He says they're like a nagging wife whose obnoxious family moves in for the wedding, then never leaves!" Abhac laughed.

"Everywhere I look I see a sinister shadow cast over all of Verngaurd, spreading mistrust and hostility under its dark shade," Friar lamented.

"The red scum Proliate are as much to blame as the Dark Warriors! They feed on the rampant fear and abuse their power to spread their faith!" Abhac seethed.

"Power is a responsibility that does not, by itself, corrupt. It only becomes dangerous when brittle souls, easily beguiled, wield it fraudulently," Friar said. "Frailty of the psyche is not a foregone conclusion."

Abhac scrunched his eyes skeptically, "Philosophize if you must, I'll stick with hating them and sincerely think you overestimate the resiliency of most of Verngaurd's inhabitants!"

"How are relations with Jaa in the north?" Ritari asked.

"Suddenly their attitudes have turned quite chilly. There are no temples to Tallcon in Jaa, but they seem pretty cozy with the Proliate all the same. Maybe they have an alliance with them, maybe not."

"Have you traveled to the Citadel lately?" Friar asked.

"Once you Knights left and it became infested with scurrying Proliate and Magicians, few of us made the journey. Then, once when the libraries closed everyone from our kingdom, even the Kirvella stopped going."

"The libraries closed?" Lovag screamed in aggrieved astonishment.

"What of the universities?" Friar asked expectantly.

"Gone and gone."

Silence settled on those in the column as they digested the memories of what used to be, while contritely wrestling with the current reality.

Friar let loose, "What has become of all the books and scrolls? What are they using those buildings for? Are there any schools left?"

Abhac regarded their concerned faces. "The Kirvella took some Saatana infantry and grabbed as many books and scrolls as they could. The Proliate destroyed the rest. The intimidating Saatana warriors made quite the sight, strolling back in full armor leading wagons loaded down with books!"

"Why wouldn't they give us a chance to rescue all that knowledge?" Friar asked rhetorically. "What of the other questions?"

"I don't know what happened to the university buildings. In terms of schools, you can study about Tallcon and their religion, train to become a Magician, or attend a Proliate military academy. Those are your options. Ah, here we are! That path will lead you out," he said, pointing to a narrow opening.

Friar and Ritari exchanged nervous glances.

"Our wagons won't fit through there!"

Abhac laughed as he dismounted. "It's wider than it looks. There's a human village on the other end, they're harmless and nice enough. They will be able to direct you from there!"

Lovag also dismounted, "Thank you, and see you at the Tournament," he said, embracing the blushing Dwarf.

Abhac deftly disappeared back down the mountain path, mumbling something about having to do patrol and the importance of personal space for Dwarves.

"If my siege engines don't fit through there I'll be livid!" Sorea grumbled.

"The trail isn't getting any wider. Let's find out," Friar said.

Initially, the narrow path was lit with ample sunshine. As they traveled further the walls rose progressively higher until only a thin strip of blue sky traversed weakly above them, useful only as a faint guide of upcoming twists and turns.

As they continued, the oppressive path of high walls constantly seemed to converge just ahead, giving the claustrophobic illusion the narrow trail was going to come to a dead end at any moment. However, the false point of termination moved onward at the same rate they did, which, at least in their minds, was incredibly slowly.

"Bellae," Lontas whispered.

She followed his trembling finger towards an arch high above the gorge.

"A bump on the arch?" Bellae questioned. A second look sent a chill racing through her. "I can feel him!"

"Keep quiet!" Luchar snarled, but looked up to where Lontas was pointing.

Abruptly the lump stood up. Two large wings unfurled and the creature quickly disappeared over the top of the gorge walls.

"Another Watcher!" Luchar cried out, grabbing his war hammer. "Arquero, your bow!"

"Can't be a Watcher. They have four wings, that creature only had two," Finn said.

"Was it a Kirvella dragon?"

"The wings were too large," Ritari replied, searching the sky. "Remember, Kirvella can't fly."

"If the Watcher's did open a portal in here, we would be obliterated," Luchar growled anxiously.

"Our friend *is* watching out for us, that won't happen," Bellae whispered.

Lontas rolled his eyes and shook his doubtful head.

"Six of you go ahead and make sure there are no surprises. Take note of the area outside the gorge as well," Friar instructed the advance guard.

"Our friend *is* watching over us," Bellae said, trying to convince her friend.

Lontas rolled his eyes again, but resisted the temptation to call it a demon.

Scroll 3: A Farmer's Face and a Joyful Embrace

"The path is clear all the way out of the gorge," one of the advance guard reported upon their return.

"How much further?"

"Five minutes. We encountered several harmless villagers who know the area and are helping with directions."

"Let's quicken our pace," Friar ordered.

The softest hint of fresh air tantalizing beckoned their nostrils, encouraging them forward. Soon, more light from the third sun was streaming into the narrow path. Once clear of the ravine, they took refreshing deep breaths before galloping towards the rest of the advance guard and several villagers.

"...clear the Hino Mountains. Then you would head diagonally southwest. The Citadel will be right there," a villager was saying.

"Thank you for the information, Svika of Bocht," one of the Knights said.

"You're welcome," Svika said. His face was well creased, stamped deeply with the appearance of one who lives under the authority, and unyielding strength, of volatile weather. "Here comes my daughter. She went to the town of Inops to get a dress. Vanalia!"

He has a farmer's unflappable face, Friar thought.

A girl of seven or eight came running towards her father. She was average height but thin and drawn. Her complexion was pale, and her delicate features sat dutifully in their exquisite subtlety. She had long black hair that was haunted by tangles and burdened by grime. Smears of dirt sat comfortably in prominent places across her face, history had taught them they were convincingly secure from fear of being cleansed. A chunky, ill-fitting dress hung upon her slender body.

"Beautiful dress," Svika smiled.

"Thank you, Daddy," the girl replied. "Do we get to go?" she asked with a soaring pitch of excitement.

"Looks as if we will have to wait until the next Tournament. It's only four years away," he answered in the unapologetic and patient tone known only to those used to bathing, with complete immersion, in disappointment.

"Okay," the girl said, although her eyes hinted at regret, her face revealed a surprising mix of enigmatic cheer and inexplicable optimism.

"What's the special occasion? A birthday, perhaps?" Friar asked, moved by their affection and tolerance for disappointment.

"No," she murmured in a barely audible whisper, she seemed to have just recognized the Knights and squires.

Her father spoke up. "We were thinking of going to the Tournament of Flags. My dad took me when I was her age…" He looked down dejectedly.

"We appreciate your help and directions," Friar said. Reaching into his coin purse he gave the villager several pieces of gold. "In recognition of your help. The conditions are that you go to the Tournament and cheer for us."

Svika froze, staring at the coins as if expecting them to disappear at the slightest movement.

"Does this mean we can go?" the girl asked.

"Yes!"

Sometimes the simplest of words can wield the greatest power, Friar thought as the two embraced joyfully.

"Thank you so much!"

"You're most welcome."

"Long ago I saw you compete at the Festival with my Great Aunt Dana."

"She was an amazing Knight!" Friar exclaimed, embracing Svika. As he did, the familiar fragrance of impecuniosity: sweat, toil, and dirt, deeply entwined themselves upon him.

"My name is Bellae," she said, moving close to the girl.

Vanalia insecurely pitched her head down, but curiosity compelled a hesitant gaze up to see Bellae from the modest safety created by the flimsy shield of her partially closed eyelid.

"Your new dress is nice."

The girl's smile widened, and sensing a refuge of kindness in Bellae, her head shot up. "Thanks!"

"Svika said the other Knights, having made it to the Citadel and found us missing, sent several rounds of scouts all the way up here looking for us," one of the advance guard said. "Apparently, they are worried!"

"I imagine so. That was a long trip through the mountain passes." Friar sighed, gazing at Phoebus, the third sun, quickly plunging towards the horizon. "There is not much light left in this day, we shall camp here for the night, I am sure the dragons will be watching over us. However, tomorrow we wake early and make haste."

"Would it be okay for Vanalia to camp with us tonight?"

Friar looked at Vanalia's father who shrugged his shoulders. He was still reeling from the gifts of gold and the opportunity it provided.

The radiance that comes from pure joy shone from Vanalia with such energy it compelled her grunge to appear less noticeable.

"Can Vanalia and her family ride with us?" Bellae asked innocently.

Friar exchanged anxious looks with the advance guard. Extra people would mean more mouths to feed and people to protect.

Svika looked down awkwardly. "It's okay. We'll be right behind you."

"Nonsense. A relative of a great Knight like Dana deserves an escort to the Tournament," Friar smiled, unsure of what he had just agreed to.

"Vanalia, you ride with me," Bellae said, reaching for the girl's hand early the next morning.

"All right then. We head to the Village of Bocht, home of Svika's family."

The Knights forged through the tall grass that made up the Vahse Plains.

"Finn, do you think we will see any Cavalo Horses like Crann?" Lovag asked.

"Unlikely, they stick in large herds and even have scouts to avoid contact with outsiders."

After a quick ride the slightly slanting outline of Bocht became visible.

"What is this shambles supposed to be?" Luchar growled as they moved closer. "They call that muck fortifications?"

"Do not insult our guests. That is the Village of Bocht and what suffices as their defenses," Ritari answered.

The village had a shabby palisade of sharpened wood trunks surrounding it. One lonely lookout tower leaned precariously next to a dilapidated gate. Within the meager watchtower a diffident boy stood languidly leaning against a rusting spear, his small nose wafting comically in the immense helmet overwhelming his diminutive head as he amateurishly played the part of guard.

"A litter of drunken kittens could storm this village and conquer it," Luchar rumbled in a low voice.

"Luchar!" Friar warned, as several Knights chuckled. "Upon completion of the Tournament we will help them fortify their defenses, and by 'we' I mean 'you'!"

Luchar grunted.

"Can you come with me?" Vanalia asked her new squire friend.

"Go ahead, Bellae," Friar responded. "The rest of us shall wait out here."

Svika came running out, waving enthusiastically, "Welcome!"

The two young girls joined him and the three proceeded through the neglected defenses of Bocht, Ritari moved next to Friar. "Why did you give them your own coins? I saw the list of goods you wanted to buy for your office at the Citadel."

Friar smiled at his captain almost patiently, as if explaining something to a young child, "The objects money can buy are temporary and provide the body with something it needs for but a brief moment. The joy and hope born from a simple of act of kindness, handing over my coins, can never be taken away."

Ritari nodded his head contemplatively. "Hard to argue with that."

"Acts of compassion always have an infinitely greater return on investment than anything monetary."

Bellae quickly realized the inside of the village fared no better than the outer defenses. Unorganized and shoddy dwellings surrounded a dirty courtyard littered with debris and weeds. The young pretended not to notice the poverty, the adults hurried about pretending this was a fine way to live, while an assemblage of the extremely elderly huddled with bent backs under blankets pretending not to be teetering precariously off the edge of the waterfall of death.

"In here, Bellae," Vanalia said, standing in front of a porous hut with an animal skin hanging discourteously over the entrance.

The dwelling was cramped and dark. Several rolled-up bed mats slumped idly on the dirt floor. There was a small central flap in the roof directly above a small fire pit. The only furniture was a rudimentary shelf holding a few pans severely battered by time and overuse. Vanalia smiled, her narrow perspective and familiarity with the hovel were so complete she did not think to be embarrassed.

Svika moved towards his wife with a cavernous smile. "I kept a secret from you last night. I told you Vanalia would sleep in the Knight's camp, but I did not show you these!"

Vanalia's mother began to cry at the sight of the gold and embraced her husband.

"It gets better. We ride with the Knights!" he exclaimed. "Oh sorry, this is Bellae, a squire. This is my wife, Koniena."

"Hello," Bellae smiled.

Koniena froze, wide-eyed. Svika soon joined her gawking.

"It's nice to meet you?" Bellae said, feeling uncomfortable under their fiery gaze.

Holding out a trembling finger Koniena pointed to the two mice peeking out of Bellae's cloak, "Mice! Get the cat!"

"This place is disgusting. Wait, why is everyone staring at us?" Grym wondered.

"They're not used to mice and humans being together."

"Are you singing to them mice?"

Bellae looked up to see the three villagers staring at her as if she had horns growing out of her head and a dragon tail swishing out her backside. "These mice are my friends."

"You're friends...with mice?" Koniena mumbled.

"Get back inside my cloak," Bellae prompted. They did so as the family continued to gawk. Eventually, they silently packed a few of their sparse belongings, occasionally stealing quick glances to see if any other rodents had made an appearance from Bellae's clothing, until finally the four made their way out of the village to the Knights.

Scroll 4: Big Changes

Back riding Honey, Vanalia quietly ruminated about Bellae not only having, but *talking* to mice.

"Uhm…so you can really speak to animals?"

"Yes."

Honey neighed nosily and Bellae revealed what Vanalia asked.

"What does she think you're doing? Trying to have a bowel movement?"

Bellae laughed. *"It's new and scary for her, that's all."*

"It sounds like you are singing, or something," Vanalia commented.

"That's what people say. For me, it's just talking."

"How did it happen?"

"I was born this way. Just like Lontas is super smart and Scelto was born to be big and tall."

After a moment, Vanalia smiled. "I guess it's pretty neat to talk with animals."

Early the next morning they were again moving south with the girls and Lontas settling into easy conversation, directing time to move past them swiftly. A faint rise slowly became visible in the distance. If you didn't know better, it could have been a small mountain range. It was, in fact, the distant call of the Citadel's massive towers and walls, which languidly became recognizable.

After entering the red gates outlining the Proliate and Magician territory of Rettengolo, the path became cleanly straight, lined with evenly spaced trees positioned with military precision. The white marble towers of the Citadel had been looming large for so long it seemed that the massive fortifications must be moving away from them at the same speed they were traveling forward.

Late on the second day a plump, waving form could be seen aggressively riding towards them screaming something inaudible.

As he violently wobbled closer, his words grew perceptible, "Did you decide to take a holiday?"

"It's Veli Pingius!" Ritari cried. As the horse galloped, Veli's spherical form gyrated up and down. Bellae winced at the thought of the weight repetitively bearing down on the poor horse.

"Did you silly wittle boys and girls get wost?" Veli Pingius said, laughing hysterically, not minding in the least that he was the only one amused by the endeavored joke.

"Is he always like this?" Vanalia asked.

"Goofy and funny? Yeah, pretty much," Bellae answered.

"It's nice to see you, Pingius."

"It's a relief to finally have you join us! We've been sending out scouting parties to try and find you! May I escort you the rest of the way to the Citadel?"

"We would be delighted."

As the excitement of seeing Pingius evaporated, they continued the monotonous ride. White banners and flags rippled angrily in the wind atop of the massive white stone walls of the Citadel. Occasionally, a fierce gust would slap them hard enough to reveal the blood red image of Tallcon.

"Wow!" Vanalia uttered in awe. "This place is huge."

"You could fit ten Liberums in this castle and still have plenty of room," Finn added.

Vanalia muttered something about not realizing such things could be built.

"Welcome, my friends, to the main gate of the Citadel!" Pingius explained.

Enormous crowds swirled erratically outside a massive entryway, above which hung a massive shield bearing the blood red figure of the phoenix god Tallcon.

"If the castle were under siege they would not only drop the portcullis, but that immense shield would fall to block the gate as well," Finn informed.

Figure 8: The one-time jewel of the Knight's extensive crown of castles, Cumhacht formerly served as the seat of power for the once dominant Independent Knights. The massive castle complex is now known as the Citadel and ruled by the Proliate and Magicians. Under the Knights it was renowned as a seat of learning with a string of universities and libraries. The former houses of learning have been transformed into temples and service areas by the devout Proliate, who see no need to look past the sacred books of their god Tallcon for knowledge.

"So, you would have to somehow get through that enormous metal shield, then the portcullis, and then the gate?" Bellae wondered.

"Yep," Finn said. "But remember, this is only the barbican, not even the main gate. Once..."

"The barbi-what?" Vanalia interrupted.

"The barbican is an extra outpost before the moat and the real gatehouse of the castle."

Lontas finally managed to catch up to them on an exhausted looking Klaufi, "The Citadel would be impossible to take."

"Nothing's impossible," Sorea claimed with a covetous look, her mind planning which siege engines she would employ and where.

"Why did the Knights ever leave this place?" Vanalia asked innocently enough, but the Knights exchanged tense glances.

An uncomfortably awkward silence arose, the kind that comes when a simple question has such a painful and complex answer that stillness seems the only response. Where could one even begin? Friar Isa? The massive defeats during the Dark War? The Proliate and their influence with the Magicians?

Veli Pingius broke the quiet, "We better start the long process of moving through the gates. They aren't letting anyone in without cataloguing who is here and why. Competitors in the Tournament have a separate check-in so…" he said, raising his eyebrows and nodding towards Vanalia and her family.

"Let's get you down," Friar said, reaching out to the girl.

"After the Tournament…is there anyway Vanalia might become a squire?" Svika asked Friar, tears welling up in his eyes. "I want her to have a good future."

"We would be delighted. We'll stop by the village after the Tournament to gather her things. I am confident Bellae will help her adjust to life at Liberum."

Bellae and Vanalia squealed and hugged.

"I don't know what this is about, but I'm guessing you want me to be sick with all the lovey-dovey, huggy stuff," Grym wheezed, his compressed head peeking out of her pocket.

"We're going to be great friends," Bellae said excitedly, ignoring Grym.

"We should go," Veli Pingius said, pointing to the horde amassed in front of the colossal gates of the barbican.

"Good luck. Make us proud," Svika said, holding Vanalia tight.

"Bye!" the girls said in unison, waving excitedly.

The Knights and squires joined the bottleneck outside the entrance to the barbican. Fierce looking Proliator warriors lined the path and aggressively eyed them with suspicion.

The massive crowds made Lontas feel dizzy. He longed to be reading a book in the library or gatehouse, traveling on a less terrifying, and infinitely safer, mental adventure.

A unique-looking man wearing a bright yellow robe laden with blue stars stood in sharp contrast to the stoic, red clad Proliators. He had a goatee sitting proudly below a conspicuous yellow headband. The man's black hair was pulled back into a long winding ponytail, tied at the bottom with another yellow band.

Veli Pingius answered everyone's unspoken question, "He's a student of Magic. The yellow means he's an Adjutant, just below the rank of Master Magician. Apprentices wear green and Novices dress in red."

"Good day, fine sir! Keep up the good work," Pingius bellowed, jauntily tapping the man on the shoulder.

The Adjutant Magician rolled his eyes and turned up his nose, yet continued yelling instructions in a practiced, but tedious voice:

"Horses and carts stay right. If you are walking in as a competitor, stay left, while *all* others stay in the middle. Continue through the main gatehouse. Once you enter the Citadel you *must* register. Competitors, go left; spectators, go straight; merchants, tradesmen, musicians, and others with business, go right."

"Those your wagons?" Two husky Proliate guards questioned.

"Yes," Friar answered. The guards nodded, seeming to appreciate his brevity.

"Competitors?"

"Yes."

"Those on foot to the left, your horses and wagons need to get wait in the longer line to the right so that they can be searched," the guard informed.

"Stay with the wagons and horses. Once you are through, catch up with us," Friar instructed the advance guard.

"What's wrong with Honey?" Finn asked as the large horse began to snort and rear-up.

"I told him we have to separate and he's not happy."

"Calm that horse now!" a guard yelled, menacingly pointing his spear at Honey. "I have the authority to terminate any threat to public safety!"

Bellae spoke urgently, *"Stop now! Let me see what I can do."* Honey immediately stood still, nodding with an impatient snort.

"Excuse me, sir," Bellae said, moving to stand in front of the Proliator's spear-tip. He cocked his head to the side and stared at the small girl who just calmed a massive horse with what he heard as humming.

"Can my horse please stay with me? She gets very nervous in crowds and, well, she is crazy strong. You seriously don't want her throwing a fit."

"We have strict orders…"

The second guard put his hand on his companion's arm and threw his head back to throng of onlookers now circling around the scene. "Look at this crowd. Do you really want to spill this horses' blood in front of them? It's such a large horse can you envisage how many spear thrusts it will take to bring down? Just imagine the mess and, more importantly, the crowd panicking and slowing things down. If the horse dies, we get stuck cleaning it up, filling out a report, and then the sergeant at arms comes, investigates us and the cause of the delay. Plus, if someone gets hurt in our territory you heard what happens to the guards respons…"

The first guard held a hand up to silence the second one and turned to Bellae. "Can you keep this beast calm and orderly?"

"Yes."

"Do you understand we will kill this horse if you cannot?"

"Yes."

The first guard waved her on with a huff of annoyance.

Friar, Pingius, the Liberum Knights, squires, and Honey quickly fused with the crowd of competitors before the Proliate changed their minds. They gradually crossed under the giant shield and a large metal portcullis of the barbican. The pace was slow, but eventually they passed through a second portcullis and rear heavy gate of the barbican before emerging onto a vast wooden drawbridge floating above a massive moat with rows of menacing wooden stakes and logs.

"What's with all the wood?" Bellae asked.

"Assuming it is not raining they use the wood to create a moat of fire. If it is raining, or once the logs burn out and the flames disappear, they can flood the moat with stored water," Veli Pingius proclaimed.

"Up there on the tops of the walls are some of the largest merlons in the world—those are the solid parts. The gaps between are the crenels."

"Amazing," Bellae murmured.

"The walls are huge," Lontas agreed. "They remind me of the path through the Northern Dwarves' mountain." Memories of the claustrophobic trail closed in around him and the world started to spin.

Instinctively, Bellae grabbed for her friend as he stumbled. His weight was too much and they both started sliding over the edge of the drawbridge just as Finn's powerful grip pulled them up to safety.

"You two okay?"

"I think so, thanks. You alright Lontas?"

"I got dizzy looking up at those walls," Lontas explained.

"That's the clumsiest kid in the world. Seriously, what's wrong with him?" Honey neighed.

"He got lightheaded, that's all."

"Just look straight ahead," she advised, feeling a little unsteady herself stuck with the massive crowds between the height of the walls and depth of the moat.

"Nice feet, blockhead," Jumeaux chided.

Bellae was about to reply when she noticed something wrong with Friar.

"What...where?" Friar mumbled, turning pale and looking as if he might vomit.

Bellae followed his eyes to the top of the massive walls where twenty red statues of Tallcon stood under hundreds of white pendants and flags with the same phoenix image.

"It can't be," Friar murmured.

Bellae managed to get Finn's attention and raised her eyebrows questioningly.

"There used to be statues of learned men up there: great philosophers, scholars, and mathematicians. They were a source of great pride for the Knights, and a reminder that only scholars obtain such recognition, not fighters. They are all gone, replaced with sculptures of Tallcon. The largest library in the world is..." Finn paused, a pained look creasing through his thick skin. "Well, used to be here. A lot has changed."

Friar mumbled something he had often told the squires, "Books are magical keys to open up worlds and change perspectives."

There are a lot fewer magical keys in the world, Bellae thought sadly.

Scroll 5: Humiliation-Invitation

"How long do we have to wait in this line to register?" Jumeaux wondered once they had finally made it into the Citadel only to come to a standstill in queue.

"As long as it takes!" his Knight Luchar growled.

I was just asking, Jumeaux thought, stung by the anger of the response.

"Excuse me," Friar said to a Proliator guard. "I heard the library was shut down. What happened to the building?"

"You mean the Great Temple?"

"The world's greatest library was converted…into…a…temple?" Friar asked incredulously.

"Of course, the greatest temple in the world to the one and only, Tallcon!" the guard bristled, as if a temple to Tallcon was the obvious use of such a space.

Friar's mind whirled, lost in pain and sorrow at the demise of so much stored knowledge. He felt like a shadow visiting from the grave, floating through a world that had changed beyond recognition and no longer held a place for him. The trip to date had been bruising. Punch after punch, kick after kick, reality had repeatedly knocked the wind out of them.

The squires were not feeling any better. The scale of the Citadel, its immense walls, and crowds of unfamiliar people were overwhelming. The excitement they had carried at the beginning of the journey had been slowly desiccated through the trials and battles of the previous days until transformed into a vapor, a fog that had long since evaporated. They were plagued with questions that had remained safely hidden by the great distance between the Citadel and Liberum. Where would they stay? How would they find their way around this massive place?

"Are you all right?" Svika asked, his family appearing suddenly.

"Vanalia!" Bellae cried out with a sense of relief.

"We're fine. Your familiar faces are a sight for sore eyes," Friar said.

Svika held up a piece of parchment. "We're official spectators!"

Vanalia was twisting side to side, gently twirling her dress with joy.

"I'm afraid the line for competitors is much longer."

"We'll let you get registered. Thanks again for this opportunity," Svika said genuinely.

"Bye," Vanalia said.

"See you soon," Bellae whispered.

As the family turned to leave, a group of five preteen girls moved to block their way. They postured in various poses of self-importance. Bellae felt a shiver of warning, the same sensation she gets before the Tilkeri Squad attacks Lontas.

The girls wore delicately embroidered satin dresses trimmed with lace and pearls. They oozed the delusional self-confidence of those who believe the world knew of their decided importance well before their conception and, therefore, had appropriately placed them in a wealthy, high-ranking family befitting their renown.

The tallest one had long brown hair, roguish eyes, and lips that quivered in palatine anticipation, "How are the peasants who wash the latrine supposed to do their job if you're wearing their cleaning rags little girl?"

The tall girl paused to let the full weight of her words bite into Vanalia's self-confidence. The girl's hands had grown soft from the absence of work, their minds quarrelsome from lack of discipline, and their heart's hardened from entitlement. Out of the corner of her eye the tall one confirmed the herd of girls, which served as her corrupt crowd backbone, were still there.

They were.

Each one snickering, providing the highly combustible fuel of group endorsement.

Vanalia's chin quivered in humiliation and tears swelled.

"Don't cry! Tears will make that *thing* you're wearing look worse, and then they might refuse to clean the shit bucket with it."

Vanalia's parents froze, the joy of coming to the Citadel vanishing, replaced by shame and inadequacy. Removed from their simple village, the brutal truth of their poverty was flayed open by the cruel knife of her persecuting remarks. A sea of people had formed a ring around them to add to their embarrassment.

Vanalia's sorrow and tearful response fed their zealous hunger to keep defacing her most valuable commodity, dreams. The fact that the thrill they felt now would soon invert into an empty cavity demanding more, did not enter the entitled girls minds.

"Honey, they're attacking Vanalia," Bellae called out intently.

Already annoyed by the crowds, Honey reared up and snorted aggressively. The girls screamed as hooves flailed ominously close to their faces.

"Bellae, restrain Honey!" Finn yelled. "This will not help!"

"Svika, take your family and go. We'll deal with these jackanapes," Sorea commanded as Bellae moved with unhurried reluctance towards the incensed Honey.

Finn smiled at Vanalia. "No matter what others tell you, know in your heart how beautiful you are. Always answer evil hearts with a smile. It annoys them!"

"Oh, that means so much coming from some tree-bark looking freak," the tallest girl rumbled.

"You shall find you don't have to bring down another to elevate yourself. In fact, it drags you down through the darkest of muds."

The girl pirouetted in her expensive dress before daintily raising her hands in a fashion pose. "I don't see any mud, bark-man."

"I was talking about your soul."

"Easy to say when you look like a tree full of bird droppings, you wacko!"

The girls laughed.

"That's quite original and amusing!" Finn chortled so loudly the girls stopped, looking at each other in bewilderment.

Ritari and Luchar locked their shields and strode in front of the girls, yelling for them to depart.

With the verbal sparring between the girls and Vanalia over the ogling crowd awoke to the realization that they had things to do and began to move en masse, pushing and shoving as they went in different directions with contrasting intent. As the spiteful girls huffed away, a new clamor arose.

What now? Friar wondered. His question was answered by the appearance of several Proliator warriors in red armor pressing through the mob on horseback. "This crowd needs to disperse, now! We have a message to deliver for HK. Anyone threatening the orderly disposition of the Citadel will be severely punished!"

"Get into lines, Knights!" Ritari ordered. "Stick together!"

"Honey, the mean girls are gone. Get in line with the others," Bellae pleaded.

"Too many people," Honey neighed, rearing up and jumping to the side. The horses' large shoulder struck Bellae, tossing her violently backwards. She spun around while tumbling wildly, only the mass of people managed to keep her upright, but her frail body was tossed, spinning and whirling, through the crowd.

"Calm that horse!" a Proliate guard screamed with genuine rage.

Grabbing mindlessly, Bellae managed to take hold of a stranger's cloak to keep upright and stop her floundering.

"Hey, let go!" the stranger yelled, slapping her hand and pushing her further into the multitude.

She fought to stay upright, knowing if she fell she would be trampled. Soon she found herself completely enveloped by the crowd. Having lost sight of Honey and the others, her small form continued to be tossed haphazardly around by the claustrophobic flood of people. More and more angry Proliate guards, affronted by the number of heathen visitors and indignant at the entropy before them, streamed onto the scene. Their presence managed only to heighten the panic.

"Honey!" Bellae yelled frantically. Her words were drowned within the clamor of exasperated comments of the throng. Despite a valiant struggle, her small frame succumbed to the anxious crowd and she was thrust further away from the others.

She felt herself thrown against an advancing Proliate warrior. Her face thrust against his cold, unfeeling armor.

"Can you help me?" she cried.

If he heard her plea, he did not acknowledge it. Spreading his arms out widely his large shield shoved her backwards as he barked orders.

Whisked further into the crowd by his shield thrust, she continued churning amongst the swarm of people. Her breathing quickened and her heart raced as panic towered within her. *I'm going to die!* her brain screamed as she was jostled back and forth, sometimes so tightly compressed she struggled to breathe, other times fighting to stay on her feet.

Finally, she felt some space behind her and she gratefully spun down a small side street away from the bustling crowd.

An odd feeling settled upon her and she turned to see an Elvish-boy staring at her. His eyes held a look of recognition and he waved jubilantly, but she was certain she had never met him. He had the typical brown skin with green and black streaks of the Elves of Creber.

"Hi, I'm Kainen," he said. "Looks like you guys stirred up a hornet's nest out there."

"We were just defending a friend. I'm Bellae."

The young Elf chuckled. "Of course I know who you are! In fact, when you were a baby my dad and grandfather carried you and led your siblings to Liberum and..."

"Enough!" a strong voice interrupted.

Bellae noticed two figures carefully watching her. One was an imposing adult Elf of Creber with a white wood bow slung over his shoulder and holding a large pole staff.

The other figure was hunched over and completely covered in a large, black cloak. At the sight of the hulking figure a chill ran through Bellae. She instantly knew she'd found the source of her previous feelings at the castle, in the graveyard, and in the mountainous trail.

That's the winged creature! She hesitated, *But something is different. It feels like him...yet it doesn't? Perhaps another one?*

Kainen interrupted her deliberation. "This is my dad, Kempe," he said, pointing to the muscular Elf. "He's fighting in the Tournament. We just came up from the Forest to meet our friend..." Kainen was hastily interrupted again as his father quickly closed the distance to place his hand on his son's shoulder.

Figure 9: After being knocked loose from her companions, Bellae is whisked away on a rolling tide of visitors within the Citadel. Eventually she stumbles down a side alley to be confronted by a large cloaked figure, a massive Elf, and young sapling Elf.

He doesn't want me to know who, or what, is under that cloak, she thought. For a reason she could not fathom muffled sobs drifted out from under the cloak.

"I'm sure this young lady has to get going," Kempe said in a deep voice. His piercing eyes sent a clear message, there would be no introduction to the cloaked figure.

"But Dad, you've known her since she was born, and her parents? You've known them even longer. In fact..." the boy stopped under the withering weight of his father's gaze and tightening grip. At the mention of her parents she was sure of hearing a deep sob from the cloaked figure.

Bellae failed to realize Kainen was about to say his father and the cloaked figure knew her parents well, instead she stared as the person beneath the cloak moved unnaturally. The figure's head swiveled and flexed at unusual angles. She could not see his eyes, but could feel his deep, penetrating gaze beneath a black fabric that covered some sort of bizarre mask.

"Bellae!" Finn's frantic voice wailed. Pivoting to find him, her eyes met a wall of people moving hurriedly by as Proliator guards continued to shout seething threats.

"You better go, young squire," Kempe encouraged, his eyes softening.

"Bye, Bellae," the boy, Kainen, said. "See you soon for our adventure!"

"What? What adventure?"

"Ignore him, for now, Bellae. You will find your friends if you head right through there," Kempe said, this time more gently.

Her desire to find Finn overwhelming her curiosity at the odd trio, she headed in the direction of his finger, splashing into the frothy crowd. Wave, upon wave of people flooded around her, tossing her about like rough tide.

"There you are my Inion!" Finn said, his words full of relief. He picked her up and protectively cradled her towards the others.

"Little tight around my neck!" he quipped.

"Sorry! I thought I lost you!" Bellae replied, finally feeling the ruts of his tough skin biting into her arms under her tight embrace.

"I'll hunt for you, my Inion, to the ends of the word!" he said. "Even if it meant searching forever!"

Finn moved through a line of Proliate warriors who had formed a ring around the Knights, Pingius, squires, and Honey. Bellae was relieved to have a little breathing room once within the ring of austere red-clad warriors.

As soon as Finn set Bellae down, Gimelli attached herself in a power hug, "Sister, do *not* ever leave me like that again!"

"I didn't do it on purpose!" Bellae wheezed through constricted ribs.

"Welcome back my young squire!" Pingius said joyfully.

The rest of the Knights walked up with similar relief.

"Did you lose one of your...group?" the frosty voice of a Proliator guard asked.

"Yes, but we found her. You mentioned something about a message?" Friar stated.

"Yes, HK," the guard said in a weary voice, as if the whole exchange bored him.

"Master Veneficus requests the pleasure of your company earlier than previously agreed upon." The soldier handed him a small scroll with a blue ribbon and a yellow star as its wax seal.

"Thank you, I shall read it later. We are quite tired from our journey."

"May I escort you to your camp?" the soldier asked.

"Actually, we would greatly appreciate that." Friar looked tired and desperate to get out of the crowd. "However, we still have to register. Could you help us get back in line for that?"

"Of course. I'll get you to the front, and once you register, to the Zenia."

"What's this Zenia?" Luchar seethed.

"The hospitality area for all the competitors in the Tournament," the Proliator huffed, as if he expected them to know that.

The Knights and squires waited as Friar and Veli registered them.

"So, initially there was a small wooden motte-and-bailey fortress here..." Lontas began, reciting the history of the Citadel from its humble beginnings. Most tuned him out, Jumeaux, however, was growing increasingly incensed.

"...of course, the original castle built of stone was much, much smaller than what we see today. It was constructed in..."

"Lontas!" Jumeaux howled.

Startled, and completely unaware others might not find such facts interesting, Lontas stopped his lecture.

"I understand that the blank expression on my face was not enough to clue you into the fact that I am totally disinterested in what you are saying, but I did expect the snoring to be a major hint!"

"Stop it, Jumeaux, that was interesting. This place has our Knight's history running through it," Bellae said, outwardly portraying sympathy, but secretly grateful for a change in subject. "I feel so bad about what happened to Vanalia."

"You should, you dunce!" Jumeaux barked with a little too much pleasure. "If you hadn't befriended her, and brought her along none of this would have happened!"

"Jumeaux? Seriously?" Gimelli protested. "Bellae was—actually all of us were just trying to help her and her family."

"That doesn't matter!" their brother replied. "The result is the result, she was humiliated because of *you*."

Finn placed his hand gently on Bellae's shoulder, "We cannot foresee, or control, every outcome in our lives, but our intentions absolutely make all the difference in the world. You did a good deed and she will make a wonderful squire!"

"Then why do they say no good deed goes unpunished?" Jumeaux asked sarcastically.

"A well intentioned action, even with a negative outcome, is a far better result than ignoring the chance to try and help."

Scroll 6: No, Training, Yes, Meeting

"What are you trying to pull, here?" Friar asked menacingly the next day. "This is our scheduled training time!"

The Knights and squires stood restlessly outside the competitor entrance to the massive coliseum where the Tournament of Flags would take place. The whitewashed travertine rock shone brilliantly in the early morning sun. A series of open arches, broken by columns, skipped their way around the massive four-story structure. Each floor was thirty-six feet high.

"It's your mistake, HK. There's no use accusing us. You can see the coliseum during the opening ceremony and get in some training time during the three Days of Celebration before the Tournament starts," a Proliator guard said sternly.

"I assure you, this was the time we were told to be here."

"I can *assure you* it is not our fault you missed your arranged slot earlier this morning! Our schedule clearly states this is the Proliate competitors' time."

"Convenient how you Proliate get extra training time and we get swindled out of ours," Luchar growled, his battle-axe shaking ominously.

"Watch your tongue, Ka-night," the Proliator taunted.

Friar quickly put a hand on Luchar's shoulder.

"Yes, keep your dog on a leash," the guard said, his eyes blazing.

"As wonderful as this conversation is, I wonder if we could at least unload the parts for our siege engines," Friar asked, pointing to the loaded down wagons.

"That, we can allow. Place them in the staging area, but stay away from the training zone," the guard said resentfully.

"Sorea, pick who you need to help unload. Ritari, take the rest and find the Proliator general in charge of scheduling. I want our practice times *written* down with *his* signature and seal. That message I received when we first arrived was from Veneficus requesting we meet earlier than previously stated and I, unfortunately, must go," Friar said.

"Please take someone with you," Ritari begged, skeptical of the Master Magician and his relationship to the Proliate.

Friar smiled. "As you wish. I choose Bellae." He preemptively held up his hand to silence the protests from Ritari and Finn.

Jumeaux rolled his eyes in disgust. *The golden child gets picked once again.*

Lontas, fearful of being without Bellae, took a step forward. His foot hit Lovag's and he stumbled, barely staying upright by performing an awkward, drunk-crab falling down a hill, sideways skipping maneuver.

"Boy, what in Tallcon's name are you doing?" a guard demanded when Lontas finished his bizarre lateral dance.

"He's just trying to stay loose. If you would let us practice, we wouldn't have to train out here," Friar said mockingly as the Knights chuckled.

Luchar put his rough hand over Jumeaux's about-to-erupt-mouth before he could fling an insult at Lontas.

A few minutes later Friar and Bellae were dodging between the seemingly never-ending stream of people on the teeming streets of the Citadel. Bellae tried to capture images of them as they passed. Sometimes she succeeded, but mostly they were just unfocused faces flowing briskly by in a rushing blur. She was hoping to see a Sprite or Fairy, but mostly caught glimpses of humans, Elves, and Dwarves bustling in indignant haste. The tension in the enormous castle was palpable as tens of thousands of different aspirations crashed, and objectives thrashed against each other in a massive wave of hurried uneasiness.

Friar was feeling at home and moving deftly. Abandoning the Citadel to the Proliate and Magicians had been painful. However, the Knights numbers had been devastated during the Dark War when everything that could go wrong, had gone wrong. Many Knights blamed the White Wizard, the malevolent ruler of the Dark Warriors, for cursing them, others blamed the incompetence of his father, Friar Isa.

The crowds mercifully began to thin once they veered down a small side street. Friar sighed, the world he knew was now nothing more than a series of tattered memories, fading more each day as the future trod mercilessly over them. "The House of Magic used to be the primary command center when the Knights ruled Cumhacht."

They finally came to a large, yellow limestone building. The deep-brown wood and black hinges of the door were framed by rampant ivy clinging to the walls and oscillating towards scarce sunlight. Occasional white or purple flowers poked out in friendly spots of color, otherwise encircled by truculent green.

Friar paused and pulled out two scrolls, one requesting his presence to meet Veneficus—that one had arrived at Liberum many months ago. He unfurled the second one, confirming to himself that it had asked him to come early.

"This is the right time and place," he said before banging a moon and star shaped doorknocker. Someone inside cleared his throat, quickly followed by muffled voices.

"We *can* hear you in there," Friar said, his annoyance growing in tune with his confusion.

"Come on in," someone finally said.

The door creaked open reluctantly, as if the tension in the room were creating friction. Stepping inside, they were met with grey stone walls with a series of archways, enigmatically closed off, each with an ornate symbol at the top of the arch.

Why have doorways with no doors? Bellae wondered.

A large fire roared in the fireplace against the far wall. The light was rather dim and provided by what at first appeared to be a series of odd, circular lanterns hanging from the ceiling.

Amazing! Bellae thought when she realized the untethered lights were, in fact, magically floating around the room. They moved almost lazily, bobbing slightly as if an invisible person were testing their weight. Bellae cocked her head to the side and stared at them.

They aren't lanterns at all. They're round and completely made of light.

Bellae gasped as one spun around to reveal a human-like face staring back at her from within the light.

"Paint a portrait, why don't you?" the enraged face challenged. "It'll last longer!"

"She meant no harm, fair Valo," Friar said, bowing to the light. He leaned over and whispered to Bellae, "Don't talk to, or make eye contact with, Veneficus' magical lights. They're called Valo, but didn't get the nickname of floating Crab Apples for nothing."

"She didn't mean any harm? Huh? Must be nice to walk around with nothing else to do but bother those of us who work *all* the time.

That's right, we literally work all the time! Want to know what we are doing at any given point in time? No need to stress your feeble little mind with cumbersome thought! We are *alwaaaaaaaays* hanging around Veneficus' office twenty-four-seven, day after day after day, year after year, decade after decade. All day and all night we spread light and joy!" the Valo light screamed. "Spreading light and joy!"

Light and joy? Friar snickered. *You spread little light and zero joy.*

"My name's Ignazio, by the way, not that you would care. A little tip for ya, the only people you should call 'fair' are princesses and judges. Do I look like either of those to you, Sir Simpleton?"

Bellae stifled a laugh and quickly averted her eyes before looking around the circular room. It had one large half-moon shaped table with numerous chairs strewn around it in no particular order. People from different nations stood anxiously on either side.

Bellae expected to see all sorts of unusual objects and creatures but it was bare except for scrolls and books strewn everywhere. Besides the

Figure 10: Bellae and Friar enter Veneficus' chamber and are surprised to find other high-ranking individuals from around Verngaurd waiting, as well as an unusual looking gargoyle statue and cantankerous floating lights called Valo.

barricaded archways the only decoration was a solitary golden sculpture of a gargoyle. It was sitting on a pedestal with its arms wrapped around both legs and its head down as if sleeping. An impressive gold bookstand sat in the middle of the desk.

With the heat from the fire and the large number of people staring at them, Bellae could feel sweat starting to form on her forehead.

"Hello, Fri…uhm, HK," a Northern Dwarf said. He looked immensely intimidating and regal. He was standing to their left as they walked into the room. His flowing red hair had a matching, and equally long beard. He held a menacing helmet topped with a crown. Two large red dragon wings and black horns splayed out from each side. He wore a red cape over glistening silver armor that had a picture of a red dragon in profile.

"King Abernan," Friar said. "It's wonderful to see you, but I thought I was meeting with Veneficus alone."

"I had the same surprise," King Abernan stated. "I should have known something was off with the second invitation."

"How so?" Friar asked.

"As soon as I saw the second invitation I thought it strange that it was written in different handwriting and not sealed with the blue ribbon and yellow star like the first."

"Both of mine *were* in Veneficus' handwriting and had his seal," Friar said, starting

Figure 11: Ruler of the dragon warriors, King Abernan strikes an intimidating pose. He wears the red armor of the Saatana division and carries the menacing Draak sword—its length covered in barbed spikes.

to feel like he had walked into an ambush. "Neither one mentioned a group."

To the left of the Northern Dwarf king stood three crude-looking people. They wore a motley assortment of clothes and armor. One was a human wearing silver and gold armor with four scimitar swords across his waist.

The second was an Elf wearing a brown cloak, with a large bow slung over his shoulder. The final member of the trio was a Dwarf who reminded Bellae of Pumilus.

"Good Morn' to you Vakava, Kelig, and Teyol. It's nice to see the leaders of the Rebelde Plains here," Friar said. The Rebelde Plains are known as a place where those with a free spirit, outlaws and outcasts, come together and live by a very rough code of conduct.

"Good Morning, Friar," the Dwarf said.

"Watch yourself, Vakava. Honor the edict to call him HK," a steely voice said.

"Loosen your armor, Lidenskap," Vakava, the Dwarf, stated indifferently. The other two rulers of the Plains rolled their eyes at the Proliate general.

"You would do well to hold your tongue until Veneficus arrives," the Proliate General Lidenskap decreed as a Valo levitated over to where the general stood.

"Oh, don't mind me. I'm happy to travel *all* the way to the back of the room to light up your unsightly face, Big-Deal-General Lidenskap," the Valo huffed before murmuring "General Know-it-all is more like it!"

Lidenskap shot a look of disgust at the floating light but said nothing, one seldom won when lured into a verbal quarrel with a choleric and loquacious Valo.

"Our second note also lacked Veneficus' seal," Vakava informed.

"All will become clear soon enough." Lidenskap's lips contorted into a smirk after the echo of his words finished their conniving tone.

As the glaring Valo floated closer to Lidenskap a flood of recognition came over Bellae. Abhac had introduced him near the flower fields when Soma had been hurt. *He is the general of the Proliate temple who injured Soma!* she thought angrily.

"You missed a spot when shining your red armor, general!" the Valo laughed. The other magic lights chuckled. Their spiteful humor made their pallid light flicker, and shadows danced across the ashen room.

To the left of the Rebelde Plains trio was a girl of stunning exquisiteness. The grace and beauty she exuded stopped Bellae in her tracks. She had smooth, bronze skin, completely devoid of any blemish. Her strikingly black hair was long and straight. There was a tumult of emotion and fire smoldering behind her piercing ebony eyes.

She was thin, but muscular, and wore a mesh-lace headscarf. Over her shoulder was a cloak lined with white fur from the valkea osolobos—the wolf bear of the north. She wore two short swords.

"Blessings upon you," Friar proclaimed to the girl.

"Blessing upon you and your house," her soft voice said tunefully.

"Hello, Princess Hamaza. How is Jaa?"

"Well, thank you," the princess answered.

Figure 12: Princess of the frozen tundra of the North, Hamaza is known for her beauty and athletic prowess. Like all women of Jaa, she is a fierce warrior.

Figure 13: Massive and vicious, the male warriors of Jaa are known as much for their mental toughness as their physical adeptness. They are seemingly impervious to the cold.

Standing behind her was one of the fiercest looking warriors Bellae had seen. His head was completely shaved. Tattoos marked his dark tan skin in a series of swirling waves and spikes. He held a guandao: a large weapon consisting of a four-foot long wooden pole and ending in a large, heavy blade.

Everyone turned as the door abruptly opened without a knock. A surprised Western Elf stood in the doorway.

"Bondi!" Lidenskap yelled happily. "Welcome to the ruler of the Western Elves!"

"Thank you," he replied cautiously. "I wasn't expecting this crowd for the first meeting."

First meeting? Friar wondered. *What's he talking about?*

Bondi strode into the room wearing a flowing and fluid silk outfit. The gold fabric made a gentle swiping noise as he walked. His skin was smooth and lacked the dark streaks and ridging of Finn's. His eyes were soft blue, and his hair was smooth and fine. His neck, hands and ears were littered with elaborate gold jewelry.

"Dverg and Dvergur! Nice to see you," Bondi said to the two ornately armored Southern Dwarves. They were much shorter than their northern cousins, with larger eyes.

"Dverg and Dvergur are two of the High Council members that rule the Southern Kingdom," Friar whispered. "Their gold plated armor is carved so ornately it's more art than protection."

"I know where Bondi gets his gold!" Bellae giggled.

Figure 14: Leader of the Western Elves, Bondi is known for his formal and ostentatious disposition. Copious jewelry will always accompany him. As with all Western Elves, he has a severe distaste for the Elves of Creber.

Figure 15: Members of the Southern Dwarf High Council, their country is so awash in precious gems and metals they routinely incorporate them into their battle-armor. The Southern Dwarves divide up into various clans depending on the mines they are from. Each clan elects members to their ruling council.

Friar raised his eyebrows in mock disgust, "The Western Elves have recently become cozy trading partners with both the Southern Dwarves and the expanding Proliate army. This has greatly increased their wealth."

"Welcome, lovely Herra Isanta!" the posh Dverg said.

All eyes turned to see a sleek Western Elf warrior stride through the door in black armor inlaid with gold. Her long black hair hung along her back. Her soft green eyes seemed to look straight through you.

"Did you bring your best Knight with you, Friar?" Lidenskap asked sarcastically of Bellae as he marched across the room. Before Friar could reply Lidenskap continued towards the gargoyle statue on the pedestal.

"You better not be heading for the gargoyle, you red peacock!" an angry Valo chastised.

Lidenskap ignored the comment and boldly strode up to the sculpture.

"Don't you do it!" another Valo warned.

Ignoring the floating lights, Lidenskap looked directly at the gargoyle, "Hey, where's Veneficus?"

Bellae glanced at Friar who shrugged his shoulders, equally confused by the sight of the Proliate general talking to a statue.

"I said, hey, gargoyle!" Lidenskap yelled, poking the statue with his finger.

"Now you've done it, you ninnyhammer!" a light screamed.

Figure 16: Sleek and skilled warrior from the Western Elves she prefers to use a seven-foot long halberd, but is a skilled archer. Like all Western Elves they do not carry the deep, bark-like skin of their distant relatives, the Elves of Creber.

Bellae squealed as the statue's head shot up before the whole figure precipitously stood, two golden wings spreading menacingly.

"Who wakes my slumber?" the statue demanded.

"It is I, General Lidenskap. I have need..."

"You have need? Are you my master now?"

"No, however..."

"I know what you seek impatient fool! You disturb my slumber in vain. Master is entering...entering...just...now!"

Just as the gargoyles' words ceased, Veneficus entered. The gargoyle fluttered upwards and slapped the general's cheek with lightening quickness before returning to its pedestal and stiffening once again into a motionless sculpture with it's head resting on both knees. The general flushed with embarrassment, but said nothing.

Veneficus' eyes locked with Friar's and he smiled. However, realizing the room was full, his grin instantly fell.

An uncomfortable silence once again packed itself stuffily around the chamber.

"Lidenskap, I told you not to bother the statue you red-twit!" an angrily hovering Valo chastised.

"Veneficus, nice of you to join us," Lidenskap uttered smoothly, ignoring the Valo's anger. "I'm glad you received my message to show up early and meet with *all* of us."

"I received no such message. In fact, I was still under the impression that this group meeting was not for another hour. I had planned to meet with Friar first...*alone*."

The Grand Master Magician was much taller than Bellae expected. His robes were blue and decorated with yellow stars. He had a large wooden crosier with an enormous crystal on top. His gray hair had a fine speckling of black. A thin blue headband wound around his forehead.

"When I discovered you had invited HK to come early for a private meeting, I took the liberty of informing everyone. We wouldn't want it to look as though you were showing favoritism towards HK and the Knights," Lidenskap said contemptuously.

"Blow-hard!" one of the Valo blurted, pretending to cover it with a cough. The other lights laughed scornfully and some made faces at the general.

Walking behind the half-moon shaped desk Veneficus chanted, "Avion, chairs!" The crystal on his crosier flashed and the chairs disappeared. "Ah, that's better, little more room seeing all the unexpected guests."

"You say unexpected guests," Lidenskap drawled, "but I say, guests of necessity."

"I see your point, general. However, we should all remember that the Knights have long defended Verngaurd. The best use of our time is to discuss how we can become more united. I thought it inappropriate to accuse Friar in a public manner without some warning. Throwing around baseless charges and accusations does not help Verngaurd secure its future."

"What charges and accusations?" Friar demanded, finally understanding why only his second note asking to meet earlier had Veneficus' seal. Lidenskap had written the other notes telling the participants to come early.

"Veneficus, it certainly sounds as if you are rooting for the Knights and not us," Lidenskap stated coldly, ignoring Friar's question.

"Actually, with evil rising everywhere, I do not consider this a time for any sort of cheering, nor do I consider it a time to pick individual sides. We, all of Verngaurd, need to unite. If you leaders do not put aside your differences and band together, Verngaurd will suffer under the plague of death known as the Dark Warriors and their leader, the White Wizard. The Knights have defended Verngaurd for centuries and deserve the benefit of the doubt."

Friar Pallium nodded in appreciation. Veneficus' words, however, did nothing to soothe his swelling unease.

"Here, here!" shouted King Abernan. His outburst drew several sharp looks.

Lidenskap stayed silent and let the weight of his glare radiate towards Veneficus, who calmly stared back in defiance.

A knock at the door broke the tension.

"Enter!" Lidenskap yelled.

Veneficus seethed, "You would be wise to remember that this is still *my* chamber."

Ailante, the head of the ruling class of the Elves of Creber entered and walked towards Bellae, with a cordial nod to Friar. He had piercing green eyes with gray veins winding through them. Various shades of green lined his face and body in streaks. His simple gray robes flowed elegantly around his stately stride.

"Welcome, Ailante," Veneficus said, purposefully standing in front of the upstart Lidenskap.

Bondi and Herra Isanta, the two Western Elves, glared crossly at the newcomer, their hatred towards their cousin Elf radiating fiercely. If he noticed, Ailante chose to ignore them. The second to enter was a Proliate guard. He saluted crisply before handing a large scroll and a small note to Lidenskap. After whispering, "The person you requested is outside and ready upon your command," the guard quickly left. The general read the note and smiled coldly.

"Anything you would care to share?" Veneficus asked.

"Oh, most definitely!"

Scroll 7: Bodies, Meet the Floor

"I will eventually share with you the contents of this scroll," Lidenskap said. "But, first, isn't it funny that birds of a feather stick together?"

"What are you talking about?" Veneficus asked impatiently.

"Whether you want to see it or not, the room is divided into two sides. One is fighting for, and the other against, Verngaurd. I see those promoting anarchy on one side of your desk: the Knights, Northern Dwarves, Rebelde Plains, Elves of Creber, and Jaa. On the other side we have those fighting for Verngaurd: the Proliate, the Southern Dwarves, Western Elves, and our two friends who just arrived, Emperor Fanga, ruler of Piscium, and King Tarha, sovereign of Ager."

"Absurdity!" King Abernan shouted.

"Preposterous!" Veneficus thundered.

Figure 17: The meeting in Veneficus' chamber has begun to disintegrate as dissension weaves its way within Verngaurd, dividing the countries in conflict. From left to right: Bellae—squire to Knight Finn of Liberum, Friar Pallium (HK)—ruler of the Independent Knights, King Abernan—Northern Dwarf ruler, Ailante—head ruler/Archerian of the Elves of Creber, Jaa Warrior—bodyguard to royal family, Princess Hamaza—first in line to the throne of Jaa behind her mother (the Queen), Veneficus—Supreme Master Magician, Lidenskap—ambitious General within the ever expanding Proliate Army, Bondi—ruler of the Western Elves, Herra Isanta—champion warrior of the Western Elves, Dverg—member of the Southern Dwarf ruling council, Emperor Fanga—thick and boisterous ruler of Piscium, King Tarha—ruler of the agrarian country of Ager.

"Take back that insult!" King Abernan bellowed.

"We are not promoting anarchy!" Friar yelled.

Despite their protests Friar thought it did seem like there were two sides, with Veneficus caught in the middle.

"Stop fanning the flames of unrest," Veneficus stated firmly. "This Tournament is a chance for solidarity. I believe we all aspire to a goal greater than any single person or nation, peace for our lands."

General Lidenskap smiled. "Those awake to Tallcon's omnipotence know there is an authority greater than any ruler or nation. We serve, *the* creator Tallcon."

"I'll serve you, ya nitwit," a Valo huffed as Lidenskap purposefully began unrolling the large scroll on the table.

"Serve the nitwit!" another Valo squeaked in a high-pitched voice before cackling.

Lidenskap shot the Valo a piercing glance.

"I meant I'll serve you some light my favorite, forceful, and may I say, quite ravishing, general," the first Valo said loudly before muttering, "What you really need is healthy serving of repeated smacks upside your head."

"What was that?" Lidenskap demanded.

"Nothing, nothing at all. Please continue your enlightening and magnanimous speech. I'm sure we'll all be riveted by what comes next!" the Valo said sarcastically as his fellow lights chuckled.

"Feel free to use my desk, general," Veneficus said, rolling his eyes.

"Thank you," Lidenskap answered, unaware of the second helping of sarcasm he had just been served. "The hour grows dark, and we all know the menacing forces amassing against us from across the Dark Sea, the Dark Warriors.

"However, our greatest danger is the storm threatening us from *within*. This map outlines the crux of the dire situation confronting us, but more importantly it clearly defines the traitors. A little help with keeping this scroll flat?"

"Ex agito hic!" Veneficus called out with a nod of his crosier. Four books suddenly appeared and began floating across the room before gently coming to rest on the corners of the scroll.

"Ah, thank you. Very useful indeed. This map shows all the nations of Verngaurd including significant cities. The "X's" represent Dark Warrior attacks. Several suspicious facts will quickly become evident.

"These attacks extend over great distances, but *only* in certain countries. The inverse is also true. We have *zero* attacks, that's right NONE, in the territories *currently* under the control of the Northern Dwarves, Elves of Creber, Independent Knights, or in the Rebelde Plains. The people of Jaa have only endured one single attack!" he said, pointing out each territory. A palpable tension permeated the room as each one of them studied the map.

"What are you implying, and what do you mean, 'territory *currently* under the control of the Northern Dwarves?' Are you suggesting it could be ever be under someone else's control?" Northern Dwarf King Abernan asked hotly.

"Yeah, what are you trying to say, big shot red-armor guy?" a Valo hissed.

Figure 18: General Lidenskap unfurls a map showing the unequal distribution of Dark Warrior attacks.

"Yeah, what's the matter with you, general?" another Valo chimed in. "I think this Proliator is itching to fight you, Abernan. You shouldn't take this…appalling…atrocious insult!"

"I would agree with my honored, distinguished, and handsome fellow floating purveyor of perpetual light," an additional Valo chimed in. "In fact, it is fair to say that it is an egregious insult from some strutting, egotistical, General Peacock!"

Veneficus rolled his eyes in disgust, obviously used to the constant bickering and snide remarks of the Valo.

"Don't stand for it. Get him Dwarf King!" another Valo agitated.

"Let me continue, please!" Lidenskap replied. "Any rational person would conclude there is something suspicious about the locations of the Dark Warrior attacks. Those of us from the Proliate Islands, Ager, Magicians, Western Elves, the Southern Dwarves, and especially the poor people of Piscium, endure repeated Dark Warrior attacks."

Several murmurs of agreement ran through half the room. Lidenskap yelled over the din, "It should be obvious that those without any attacks are aiding the Dark Warriors! There is no other explanation!"

Shouts exploded from both sides of the chamber. The massive Emperor of Piscium yelled loudest while banging his staff hard against the floor. "Here, here! How do you explain yourselves?"

Friar marveled at the anger raging through half of the room, counter-balanced by the stunned feeling on the other side from those accused of treachery, yet feeling deeply betrayed themselves.

"This is an outrage!" Princess Hamaza yelled. "You insult the character of the entire nation of Jaa. Veneficus?"

"There do seem to be irregularities in the attack patterns of the Dark Warriors. They are fighting a very different war than they did decades ago in what we should now regard as the *First* Dark War. As to the conclusion, I'm not sure…" Veneficus let his voice trail off.

"I will tell you what it means. It means we have sincere doubts about your loyalty to Verngaurd!" General Lidenskap accused, as a fresh round of protest arose from the delegates from Jaa, Northern Dwarves, Knights, Rebelde Plains, and Elves of Creber.

"This is outrageous!" Friar howled. "They devastated our ranks during the first Dark War and despite what your "X's" show, the Dark Warriors *have* been attacking *us* and *our* villages! This map is misleading and trying to divide us!"

Lidenskap rolled his eyes and scoffed.

"In fact, the Dark Warriors recently attacked our village of Kippe. Unfortunately we could not save it, and you took it over!" Friar shouted. "You had to see the carnage of the Dark Warriors on a village *that was ours!*"

Lidenskap smirked, "We will come back to Kippe later, but I have ample proof and evidence that was not the Dark Warriors threatening that village."

"Evidence? There can't be any to the contrary. I saw it with my own eyes! Please, listen to reason. Peace between the nations of Verngaurd is essential to our survival!" Friar said.

"Half of us want peace, half of you are creating havoc!" Lidenskap huffed. "Peace is *our* objective, it is *yours* that leaves one to question."

"Peace is not a destination to be traveled towards, it is a decision of how to live *on* our journey," Friar countered.

"If you truly want peace, you shouldn't ally with the Dark Warriors!" Bondi of the Western Elves shouted.

"Why would we even be in league with the Dark Warriors?" Friar asked exasperated.

"Your motivation, Friar, is obvious," Emperor Fanga shouted. "You formed an alliance with the Dark Warriors in pathetic hope of regaining your lost territory. You covet all our lands and those taken over by the Proliate that you hope to reclaim after the two of you defeat us. These so called Dark Warrior "attacks" on your territories are staged. I have seen them with my own eyes!"

Fanga wore a yellow cape and a gold crown studded with various pearls and jewels. He carried a large scepter topped with a simpukka shell, native to Piscium. In his other hand, he held a golden trident. A pepper-gray beard dangled down from a plump, fiery face. Piercing sable eyes told of a volcano of emotion bubbling below the surface.

Figure 19: Emperor of the embattled country of Piscium, Fanga is emotional, volatile, and extremely distressed by the number of attacks his country has endured at the hands of the Dark Warriors.

"What?" Friar yelled incredulously.

"I talked with a Proliator just this morning about the village of Kippe you mentioned. He said there was no evidence of the White Wizard or his Dark Warriors when they arrived. The attack was likely from your very own Knights whom they saw leaving the scene!" Fanga shouted.

"Outrageous!" Friar replied in total shock. "Why would we attack Kippe?"

"It was retribution for them signing on with the Proliate," Fanga scoffed and nodded to Lidenskap who went and opened the chamber door.

A terrified villager walked in awkwardly, his eyes widened in horror as they careened between the distinguished guests. His hands were curled up to his chest and his wrists and fingers flexed in contractures of fear. His robe was new and his body cleaned and better fed, but both Bellae and Friar instantly recognized him.

"Bardus!" Friar said. "Good, now we can get to the truth."

The shaky villager Bardus nearly doubled over in fear, but two large Proliate warriors pushed him forward while simultaneously propping him up.

"Whom did you see when your village was attacked?" Lidenskap asked.

"Min-min-mina-min!" Bardus stuttered, shutting his eyes against the compressive stares and oppressive stress.

"'Men! Many men,' he said! Not Dark Warriors!" Lidenskap stated with gloating delight.

"That is not what he sa…" Friar started but was cut of by Lidenskap.

"Let him speak! Go Bardus!" The villager seemed to shrink even more under the anger radiating towards him. "Tell us who attacked you!"

"N-n-n-n-no! D-d-d-d-dark-k-k W-w-w-w…"

"See! No Dark Warriors! He clearly said no Dark Warriors. Did you see the Knights there? Were the Knights at Kippe?"

Bardus nodded.

"Take him away!" Lidenskap bellowed as the two guards briskly escorted the trembling villager out.

"That was a sham!" Friar stated, anger wavering in his words.

"So, you were not there?" Lidenskap asked.

"Of course we were there! I already said as much, but only after the Dark Warriors had attacked. Bring Bardus back and let him answer without two of your guards manhandling him."

"He has answered enough questions. Can't you see how upset he is? You and your so called allies are the root of the problems, rotting Verngaurd from within!" Lidenskap shouted as most of the room erupted in arguing.

Not Friar. He was too stunned to speak anymore. *It's happening. We are being torn apart from within.*

As the din decreased, King Abernan, the Northern Dwarf King, pointed menacingly at Lidenskap and the Emperor from Piscium. "Are you trying to tear Verngaurd apart and start a civil war?"

"I am letting you know that we will defend our lands from abroad, *and* from within. It's not like the old days when we depended exclusively on the Knights for defense, we have a powerful army. If you are supporting attacks on my country, you better be ready for the consequences!" Emperor Fanga thundered.

"Be careful who you threaten, Emperor. There's a reason 'Dwarf' has "war" as the core of its name," King Abernan replied. "D-war-f. We are always ready for battle and your accusations and threats are wearing my patience thin!"

"No one has ever accused Dwarves of being thin," a Valo chided as the other lights laughed. The floating lights were shining brighter, feeding off the angst of the argument.

"So you admit to aiding the Dark Warriors?" General Lidenskap bellowed.

"I would sooner die than help those psychopaths. That said, if you endanger *my* Dwarves, it is *you* who will pay dearly! My Dragon Warriors and dragons will obliterate you!"

Before General Lidenskap or Fanga could reply, Ailante blurted out, "May I remind you that the sacred woods of Creber are stronger than any castle wall, and our Elven warriors fiercer than any other within its boundaries. No army has ever been more than a few yards inside our forest. This explains why the Dark Warriors will not attack us."

King Abernan scoffed, "I admit that your forest is impressive, Ailante. However, we Dwarves live in a fortress of rock and hot lava, with *dragons* guarding our skies. Our Dragon Warriors are unbeatable. It's obvious why we are unscathed. The only slimy creatures crawling within our borders are you Proliators."

Bellae moved in close to Friar while Grym and Borb stayed hidden. Friar looked down apologetically, deeply regretting his decision to bring her.

"Just because you Elves have a forest and the Northern Dwarves flying pet lizards, you have the audacity to accuse the Southern Dwarves of weakness?" the High Council member, Dvergur, blared. His voice was so full of indignation his voice shook.

"I am simply saying a predator naturally goes after the weakest in the herd!" Abernan replied.

"You must have fried your brain soaking it in the magma of your volcanoes if you think the Southern Dwarf army is weak!" Dvergur cried.

"Greed blinds and distracts you Southern Dwarves. Your armor looks fit for a girly queen on parade, not battle," King Abernan growled, drawing his vicious Draak sword.

"Good one!" the Valo floating above Abernan blared. "Don't take their crap!"

"What do you mean, girly queen?" Princess Hamaza of Jaa questioned. "We are ruled by a strong queen, my mother, and our expeditionary warriors are all *women*!"

Dverg ignored Princess Hamaza's comment and brandished his gold plated battle-axe. "You're just jealous because you live in worthless volcanic rock, coated in dragon shite that spews only fire, while our mountains shower us with unlimited riches!"

King Abernan retorted, "As much as I hate the Dark Warriors, they are not stupid. You may not like it, but the truth is Ailante was correct, the Dark Warriors are attacking weaker targets. The impenetrable Forest of Creber and harsh volcanic mountains protect us. This so called 'mystery' is nothing more than good scouting on the enemies part."

"Please, let us discuss this rationally," Veneficus pleaded. The furrows on his brow ran deep with concern. Few could hear him over the commotion. The revved up Valo were flying in circles casting more abusive comments than light.

One voice rose above the rest, Emperor Fanga of Piscium. His eyes were blazing, and his hand blanched from squeezing his trident so hard. "We bleed because of your treachery, and you have the audacity to accuse us of bringing this on ourselves?"

"Bring it, you hotheaded fish-monger!" Abernan screamed.

"Who are you calling hotheaded, you blowhard lizard-lover?" Emperor Fanga retorted.

"Nice one! Give it to him," a Valo encouraged.

Friar pushed Bellae back and drew his sword.

Suddenly, lightning flashed in the room and Veneficus began to grow. His desk screeched in protest as the Magician's expanding body thrust it forward. The ceiling bowed upwards as his head pressed against it. Finally he bellowed, "Cease, NOW!" The force of his voice shook the room and echoed fiercely. The golden gargoyle lifted his head and yawned, seemingly accustomed to his master's outbursts.

Veneficus towered above them holding out his crosier with its ominously glowing crystal. The hatred and anger in his face sent a chill of fear through Bellae. Dwarf King Abernan and the Piscinian Emperor ignored the Magician and locked weapons while continuing to hurl insults.

"My patience has run out! Leag uait!" Veneficus shouted. Everyone was instantly slammed to the floor save himself, the gargoyle, and the floating Valo. The room erupted in nauseating noises as bodies crashed to the floor in a mix of corporal thuds, clanging armor, and cavernous groans.

Bellae felt the air flood out of her lungs. It felt as if there were a million hands shoving down every part of her body, pushing, prodding, forcing.

Veneficus shrank to his normal size and began nonchalantly walking around the room examining each of the confined and struggling occupants as if they were flowers, and he on a garden stroll.

"Well, now. I had sincerely hoped this meeting would not need to be carried out with you pinned to the floor, regrettably unable to breathe. In fact, the room will be quite a mess to clean up if all of you suffocate to death. Actually...it would require an annoying amount of explaining as well."

"Yeah, what a mess that would be!" a Valo echoed excitedly.

"Plus, their deaths *would* be hard to account for!" another shouted.

The Valo, revved up by the fighting, began to float between and around those pressed against the floor, sometimes muttering insults.

"Princess Hamaza," a Valo uttered sweetly. "You are so beautiful, you take my breath away!" All the Valo laughed mercilessly.

"What? Too soon?" a Valo said. "Why aren't you laughing? Oh yeah, you can't breathe!"

Veneficus held up his hand for the Valo to be quiet.

"When…" Veneficus paused for dramatic effect, "…I decide to release you, we will have no more yelling. No weapons may be drawn in my chambers, ever!"

Coming to Bellae he poked at the two writhing mice laying next to her. "Interesting," he whispered, raising his eyebrows and screwing his face into a whimsical smirk.

Bellae and Veneficus' eyes locked, she tried to scream for help but couldn't move, couldn't breathe. She willed her eyes to communicate her panic. Flashing lights in a sea of darkness started dancing in front of her eyes. The scorching hunger to breathe burned through her lungs, but she could not answer their desperate plea.

Scroll 8: Relieved to Leave

"All right, then. Why don't I let you up and see how things go? Desino avta aon-leag uait," Veneficus said.

Choking, gasping, and panting filled the room as they fought to recover. Bellae sucked in air voraciously as she reached for her struggling mice friends. She slowly rubbed their backs as the fog of stars dancing in front of her eyes began to clear.

"You…okay…Bellae?" Friar panted, using his sword to prop himself up to a sitting position.

She nodded.

The expressions around the room varied from anger to fear except for one, the hulking figure that was the King of Ager. He was easily a head taller than the others in the room and stood with a contemplative

Figure 20: Hulking and mostly reserved, Tarha rules over the pastoral country of Ager. Known for their above average size and expertise in farming the warriors of Ager are fearsome when angered.

look, appearing to be solving a complex problem rather than recovering from a near death experience. He wore a simple crown, a cape around his portly form, and carried a large scepter with his country's symbol.

"Hysgegio!" Princess Hamaza huffed, her beauty sharpened by the bite of her anger.

Bellae could tell by the tone that it was not a pleasantry.

"I hope this ends any notion of fighting in my presence," Veneficus said in a motherly scold. "Now, I need everyone to kindly listen."

"That's right all of you! Keep quiet and listen to *the* one, *the* only, big-time master!" a Valo howled.

"Yeah, what's wrong you people? Shut up and listen up!" another floating light yelled.

"All of you are so impertinent and irreverent with your sniveling, yelling, and bleat-like bickering. You come into Veneficus' chamber and get all uppity? Of course he's going to knock you down. Just be quiet and listen already!" a third Valo stated. "Do you want to kiss the floor again? Huh? Do you? You guys like kissing the floor? You want me to call you splinter-lips? Do you…"

"The request for silence includes incandescent ignorami!" Veneficus bellowed.

The floating lights rolled their eyes and moved their mouths in silent mockery.

Grym sat up squeaking mad, *"That slime ball almost killed us!"*

"That's why you need to be quiet. Don't give him an excuse to finish the job."

Grym huffed but remained silent while Bellae put the two mice into her pocket.

"Trust me, I have been around an exceedingly long time, I know what will bring true peace to our lands," Veneficus said. "This Tournament must reunite the forces of Verngaurd. As leaders, that means *no* fighting! Does anyone have anything to add?"

"This is just what the White Wizard and Dark Warriors hope for! They want us blaming each other for their dreadful acts and fighting amongst ourselves instead of the real enemy," Friar said.

"Very wise, Friar. Anyone else?"

After a pause he continued, "No? Fine, then I will assume you can leave here and act like civilized neighbors until the truth comes out. Time will illuminate what's really going on with these attacks. I will endeavor to get to the bottom of who is behind them and, likely, clarify that it is Dark Warriors that are to blame!"

Lidenskap huffed, but did nothing else under Veneficus' glare.

"That's right big red oaf, keep your mouth shut or suck on floor dust!" a Valo whispered to the general.

"Everyone may leave my chambers except our fine representatives from the Independent Knights and Jaa."

General Lidenskap paused, desperately wanting to see the Knights and their allies held accountable for what he knew to be their treachery. He eventually followed the other delegates who were rushing in relief out the door. Ailante, the Creber Elf, gently squeezed Friar's shoulder before spinning to leave, accidently bumping into the leader of the rival Western Elves, Bondi.

Herra Isanta aggressively stepped forward to face him, blocking his way.

The three Elves, two from the Western Province and one from Creber, stood glaring at each other.

"A-hm," Veneficus said calmly, nodding ominously at his crosier. Not wanting to revisit the floor, they quickly hurried out.

When it was just the five of them, Veneficus looked at each one of his guests in turn: Bellae, Friar Pallium, Princess Hamaza, and her massive bodyguard.

"Thank you for staying. I trust you are all feeling well?" he said, his tone implying it was a statement rather than a question. "I would humbly ask that Princess Hamaza and her guard wait in another room so I may converse with the Independent Knights," Veneficus said, swinging his arm around to point at a door he had just made appear under one of the many stone archways oscillating around the chamber.

Doors on demand? Very cool, Bellae thought.

Princess Hamaza maintained her brash expression as she sauntered through. The door vanished immediately after they passed through, replaced by a normal appearing wall.

"Desino avta avion-chairs!" Veneficus chanted, making the chairs reappear. They were nondescript except for a mammoth and ornate one behind his desk. "Please sit."

As Friar and Bellae did so, he moved to the far wall where a tea set unexpectedly appeared.

"Magic is in my blood, so to speak. I love it as much as I hate clutter. If you really saw what was in here you would be amazed. Out of sight, out of mind, as they say," he said, offering them each a cup of tea. "Plus it saves on dusting."

Both accepted, but neither one drank the enigmatic green liquid with yellow clumps swirling around. Their stomachs lurched as Veneficus gulped the mysterious brew.

"Nationalistic pride is rearing its snake-like head, just like the ancient days before you Knights found your way to unite Verngaurd in order and peace," Veneficus said, sitting on the throne-like chair. "Of course, after your bitter defeats in the Dark War, all that changed. Now each country once again strives for dominance while we drown in the powerful run-off of their vanity."

He sat a moment before quickly rising and moving towards Bellae, "So this is the little wonder I've heard about? Talk to animals, hmm? Those were your mice I saw earlier?"

Bellae nodded.

"Lovely. You have a brother, do you not?"

"Yes, sir," she answered with surprising confidence.

"Wonderful. Is he here? Did he join you at the tournament?" Veneficus' smile was broad, but forced, and his voice had a sickly sweet tone that made Bellae wary.

"He is."

"Good. Good. I should very much like to meet him. What's his name?"

"Jumeaux."

"Wonderful. Jumeaux," he repeated. For several moments the two were locked in a silent gaze.

"Friar," the Magician continued, "I want to apologize."

"For what?" he asked cautiously, wondering which offense Veneficus was apologizing for. Was it letting him be ambushed at the meeting? Or, perhaps, almost killing him?

"Once I got wind of Lidenskap's true motives I asked to meet with you beforehand, to warn you. Obviously, he found out and invited the others to come early as well and seemed to spoil our chance to unite, developing a strategy together to defeat the Dark Warriors."

"I appreciate the sentiment. The correct path does not seem as clear to me as it once did. Perhaps I am fooling myself and the choices were never easy. Maybe the truth is I'm just wise enough to see more depth to the options now," Friar replied.

Veneficus chuckled. "I hate to tell you that age and experience do not always translate to solutions. Sometimes they just bring more questions. The decisions I make seem to have unanticipated consequences.

"Long ago it seemed like a good idea to help the Proliators mature into a great warrior society. I could see and feel their potential, waiting to be set free. Of course, then the Dark War broke out across Verngaurd and it turned out, militarily, we did need them.

"Somehow we ended up merging and my Magicians replaced their clerics. Seeing this fabled white city decorated in red, and the great library replaced with a *temple*? It's too much. I'm sick of seeing that pompous red phoenix everywhere." Veneficus paused, surprised he had shared so much with Friar.

After studying the map with all the X's for several minutes Veneficus spoke.

"The crucial and irrefutable fact is that we are on the brink of another Dark War. This time, however, we are teetering on the threshold of being torn apart internally by a disastrous civil war. The most disturbing fact is there have been sightings of the White Wizard. He did not appear during the first Dark War and we still almost lost."

"We saw the White Wizard near the Northern Dwarf Kingdom, albeit briefly. Outside the village of Kippe we saw a minotaur and several Watchers," Friar said. He thought about mentioning the Tacet-Vand and IleZuri, but something made him hesitate.

Veneficus' face scrunched in concern. "A minotaur and Watchers? The White Wizard actually appearing? That does not bode well. This time the White Wizard is throwing everything he has at us. By the way, I knew you didn't have anything to do with that village attack."

"Of course not. We failed to prevent it, that is a big enough burden for us to bear."

"How is it possible for their troops to appear and then disappear in such numbers?" Veneficus asked rhetorically, rubbing his tired eyes. "The amount of magic that would take…"

"Their Watchers and giant portals," Friar answered.

Veneficus contemplated this information but said nothing, so Friar continued.

"Using those portals to only attack some of the countries of Verngaurd while framing the others is sowing mistrust and anger. Just look at what happened here," Friar said. "We are going to do their work for them by killing each other."

"The Dark War…I keep forgetting we really need to start calling it the First Dark War, taught them our true strength when we stand united. Now they intend to divide us. Once we are at each other's throats, they will move from guerrilla warfare into a more traditional ground attack, picking off our fragmented armies one by one."

Veneficus paused as if watching the advance before his eyes. "The White Wizard of Ifrean is not to be underestimated in his cunning, or the ruthlessness with which he will use his Dark Warriors."

"I am happy to do my part. Here's to a defending Verngaurd!" Friar stated, raising his still full teacup.

"Excellent, Friar!"

Friar laughed.

"What is it?" Veneficus asked sharply, slightly offended at being laughed at.

"I thought that I was supposed to be known as HK?"

"I bet you can guess who thought up this 'HK' nonsense," Veneficus laughed, his face easing. "Friar. Might I have a word with you alone."

Bellae nodded and went outside.

"I wanted you to have this." Veneficus handed him a tattered book. "I managed to save it from the library when these Proliate bird brains started getting rid of them."

Taking the book, Friar read the title, "*A History of the Dark War* by Isa, Friar of the Independent Knights."

Tears formed in Friar's eyes as Veneficus spoke, "I thought you might appreciate having your father's book. Unfortunately, it seems we are doomed to battle the Dark Warriors again, and perhaps it will contain some insight to help us."

Friar nodded, breathless with gratitude.

Veneficus smiled kindly. The old Magician's expression changed before he continued, "Friar, I must tell you I have a strong feeling that Jumeaux and his family have some role to play in the coming conflict."

Friar looked at him surprised. "I have the same feeling! Visions come to me about them when I sleep."

Veneficus paused, studying Friar. He racked his ancient brain to remember the exact wording of the ancient prophecy. *It's the boy, the brother of the last animal talker that was the Chosen One in the prophecy. Isn't it?* He started to doubt himself, silently cursing time's power to smudge old memories. *Those blasted Ainmhi Caint are just devious enough to make it the less obvious choice, the brother of the animal talker.*

"Does Jumeaux speak with animals?"

"No, just Bellae."

"I see. You may have heard that we are nearing a critical shortage of the magic crystals we use in our crosiers, the mindre crystals. Once their power is gone, we will be helpless. Do you know about the prophecy and the Chosen One?" Veneficus asked.

"A little," Friar said cautiously, not sure how much he was *supposed* to know. His Elf friend Patuljak had warned him multiple times to try to keep the Chosen One moniker confidential.

"The Chosen One is presumed to be the *only* one with the ability to follow an ancient prophecy which will lead them to the long lost Macht Crystals. The Macht Crystals are sometimes called the mother crystals or power crystals because all magic flows through them—is born of them. With those supremely powerful crystals, we can recharge our mindre crystals and keep magic in the world. Only then can we save Verngaurd. After all these ages, I believe the time of the prophecy has finally arrived and the Chosen One to be Jumeaux."

"You do?" Friar said in surprise, thinking of the diminutive Bellae and emotionally fragile Jumeaux. *It is unfair burden for either to carry.*

Chapter Three

Red Rising

Scroll 1: New Vision, Old Memory

"Bring them into MY fold!" a voice boomed.

Bring whom into the fold? General Lidenskap thought. He recognized the thunderous voice, but could not place it. *Who is this?*

"Bring them into MY fold!" the voice exploded once again.

Am I falling? No, not falling, flying! Praise to Tallcon, General Lidenskap thought, unsure of what was happening. He could feel the wind rushing by as he soared over Castle Liberum. A smiling Friar Pallium was dressed in red robes and waving feverishly up at him.

What is he mouthing? Ah! Praise Tallcon. Yes, Friar, praise him.

The general flew over the new central tower, now retrofitted to be a chapel to Tallcon, his red phoenix figure emblazoned on it as well as the countless flags around Liberum. *It is the voice of Tallcon! How could I not instantly recognize it?* A small contingent of Proliate warriors intermingled freely with Knights in Liberum's bailey. The entire group waved up at him.

"General Lidenskap!" they yelled. Louder and louder, they shouted. He slowly descended. Nearing the ground they all began to pat him on the back.

"Little rough, men!" Lidenskap said, his body shaking forcefully.

"General Lidenskap!"

His eyes burst open and his hand went to his blood red sword. The Lieutenant shaking him stopped and backed up cautiously.

"Sorry, sir. You told me to wake you up for Morning Prayer before the opening ceremony this afternoon."

"Of course. Thank you," Lidenskap stated calmly.

"Your cheeks looks red, sir. Did you get sunburned yesterday?"

"No, I wasn't even outside…" *Wait, why does my face feel sore? I'm wind-burned. Actually, my back where the men were striking me hurts as well. That wasn't a dream! It's Tallcon's vision for the future!*

He froze. "That voice…I have heard it once before. The greatest day of my life!"

"Voice, sir?" the increasingly uncomfortable lieutenant asked. "My voice?"

Lidenskap, still in awe, waved him out and the soldier quickly, and happily, obliged.

"A message from you in a vision! I am humbled that you would once again speak to me Tallcon!"

Could it be? The Knights? A new strategy started forming in his mind as the lieutenant briskly shut the door.

Tallcon, I understand! We shouldn't fight the Knights—we should convert them. Give them a chance to repent for their sins and join us. United by Tallcon's love we will defeat the Dark Warriors and spread your message of hope to the world!

He dropped hard on his well calloused, knees. Warm vigor surged through his body as he remembered the miracle of Tallcon's appearance to him. It was decades ago when he heard the magnificent voice of Tallcon for the first time. An odd, paradoxical, mix of tranquility and excitement flooded over him. A small taste of the overwhelming emotions he had experienced that wondrous day, so long ago.

Lidenskap's mind was transported back to when he was a young man hunting a Tilkeri high up in the unforgiving mountains of the Proliate Islands. Clinging to a thin edge of a precipice, Lidenskap willed himself not to look down. He could hear the saber-toothed beast's breathing growing louder as he neared a sharp bend.

The beast is right around the corner. Remember your training, he told himself, trying to calm his breathing as blood dripped from several wounds. His spear had broken long ago during this long, rolling battle with the beast, so he clenched his sword with a purpose.

Knowing he was losing too much blood and sick of trying to anticipate when the beast would pounce, he decided to make a preemptive strike. Screaming, he jumped around the corner. Rocks tumbled off the slender path before plunging over the side of the cliff as his foot slid all the way to the edge. His right arm was back, ready to thrust his sword—instead, he froze.

Fire encased the suffering animal. The Tilkeri's head, with its dagger-like front teeth, thrashed in pain. His muscled body jerked in spasms of agony. Misery shone through its eyes, pleading with the young Proliate warrior to end its anguish.

Lidenskap looked around but could find no source for the flames. The creature howled pathetically while looking up at him in despair, struggling to comprehend what was happening.

Why do the flames heat the beast but not burn its flesh? he wondered. Cautiously he reached out his hand towards the flames. Several times he quickly withdrew it, expecting intense warmth or a snap from the beast. Neither came. Finally, he watched in awe as the red flames comfortably swallowed his whole hand. *It consumes the beast, but not me!*

"Follow me," a deep vibratory voice thundered, the same voice he had just heard in his vision.

Lidenskap jumped backwards. His heels skidded to the lip of the trail and his hands frantically pin-wheeled to keep his balance, dropping his sword in the process. Instinctively he turned to retrieve it and tumbled, screaming, over the lip of the overhang. Rushing air pelted his face with increasing vengeance. Gray and black rock hurtled past, faster and faster. He closed his eyes and prayed, *Tallcon.*

Instantly he began to slow, coming to a gentle stop. His eyes opened to find his body suspended high above the craggy ground, surrounded in a warm blanket of red light. It was not hot, but friendly and welcoming. *Tallcon's good fire of life!* he thought. *I understand the scriptures!*

After hanging there a moment, he began to rise, quickly finding himself back on the path staring at the head of a giant phoenix. Its penetrating eyes bored through his body, probing his very soul.

"T-t-tallcon, it's you! You cradled me to safety and make the Tilkeri burn."

"Follow me," the phoenix whispered in a hollow, raspy voice. Lidenskap was speechless, absorbed in holy wonder at the tranquility he was immersed within.

"Follow me," the phoenix said a third time. It boomed, "Unwaveringly!" before disappearing. As the flames surrounding his body left, a whoosh of cold mountain air slammed into him, knocking him to his knees.

"Come back!" he screamed. Answered only by his own echoing words, so cruelly tossed back by the cold-hearted mountain. He felt a deep sense of loss and sadness, his body ached, yearning for the warm caress of Tallcon's holy flame.

Looking up he saw a sword in the Tilkeri's lifeless heart.

Is that my sword? The color had changed from silver to a glowing blood red, but it was the sword he had dropped off the side of the mountain. Gently, he stretched out his hand and grabbed it.

The blood of Tallcon runs through this sword and colors it red.

The thought of his sword brought him back to the present. Lidenskap sighed deeply. His heart had a gnawing desire for the feeling of that day to return.

You saved me on that mountain. It must be the Dwarves and Elves who are the true source of betrayal to Verngaurd, not the Knights. Now, with the gift of your vision, I know how you want me to save Verngaurd from the Dark Warriors. Today, after the opening ceremonies, I will make the Knights see and feel Tallcon's power. They shall be forgiven and join us.

I will follow you, unwaveringly!

Scroll 2: Opening a Ceremony

Bellae itched in her new blue stola. The fresh and fancy clothes were appreciated, but the long pleated dress felt foreign and stiff. Her mice friends did not appreciate the small pockets, she could feel them squirming and chittering angrily. A few subdued lanterns lit the dusty grey-stone antechamber under the coliseum with a bored, yellowish light.

"I can't believe the opening ceremony is finally here," Gimelli whispered.

"I wish they would open the doors already," Bellae replied.

Lontas nodded his agreement.

"Why is Scelto leading us into the coliseum?" Jumeaux complained.

"It's tradition for a squire to lead the Knight's procession."

"Yeah, but why *him*?" Jumeaux asked. "I could have done it."

"He's the biggest squire we have at the Tournament, by far. It makes sense for him to carry the huge five foot banner," Gimelli smiled.

"Hey, Gimelli, wipe your chin," Jumeaux advised.

"Why? What's there?"

"A big gob of, 'I have a crush on Scelto' drool!"

"Be nice, Jumeaux," Gimelli pleaded telepathically.

"It's not my fault you can't appreciate my humor, sis."

"It's not funny."

"I agree! My sister having a crush on the clodhopper Scelto is NOT funny!"

Gimelli huffed, but said nothing.

"Why do we have to carry all these flags anyway?" Jumeaux complained.

"They call it the Tournament of *Flags* for a reason, boy," Luchar growled impatiently.

Everyone but Scelto carried two-foot long pennants. Both Scelto's banner and the pennants bore the Knight's symbol, a white dove flying over two crossed swords, all set over a single castle tower and resting on blue fabric.

Bellae turned back to see the Knights representing the three remaining castles: the Liberum Knights, Toil Shaor's Squad III directed by the sizable Veli Pingius, and, finally, the impeccably dressed contingent from Taiheart, the Chevron and Gyronny squads, led by Veli Falciss.

Figure 21: The Knight's symbol of a white dove flying over crossed swords and a castle stands for their role as defender of Verngaurd and enforcer of peace and tranquility.

Despite the stale and warm air, everyone was a bundle of nerves and excitement. A small bead of sweat started down Bellae's forehead. She contorted her lips to blow a puff of air up towards the descending sweat. Her effort managed to fling a tuft of hair up, but did nothing to stop the droplet from rolling down her cheek.

"It's stuffy in here, I hate sweating," Scelto lamented.

"What parts of you are sweating?" Jumeaux asked.

"My lower back and underarms…hey wait, why do you care?"

"Luchar told me the details of the sweat are the key to success."

"It's sweating the details are the key to success you dunce!" Luchar growled.

I know that, it was a joke! Jumeaux thought angrily.

Scelto rolled his eyes, but said nothing as Jumeaux huffed his displeasure at the lack of appreciation of his humor.

Shrouded in the shadows of the back wall Friar contemplated the future. *The Knights can never lose another battle. Our flag used to mean, Defender of Verngaurd and enforcer of peace and tranquility. It will again.*

He closed his eyes and listened intently to the beating drums out in the arena. When not being haunted by visions of Jumeaux or Bellae, his dreams were tormented with premonitions of desperate battles between his Knights and the Dark Warriors or Proliate. He was risking a great deal of the Knights limited resources preparing for a potential war. It was a chance he was willing to take to ensure the Knights were prepared. *Never lose again.*

"Do we get to hit someone today?" Luchar bellowed, breaking the monotony of shifting armor and undulating weapons.

"No?" Luchar responded to an inaudible answer. "Then what are we doing here? Are we going to dance with them? If so, who leads?"

"Come on, Luchar, give it a rest," Lovag said mirthfully.

"You're right, Lovag. You know me so well, I am, in fact, dying for a nice dance and then yearn for the hushed chatter of tea time," Luchar continued in animated fashion.

"Enough!" Friar bellowed. Luchar quieted as a few snickers ran through the hall.

A thunderous grating noise was followed by a loud crash as the large double doors in front of them slammed open. Loud cheers, blinding light, and fresh air rushed in from the coliseum.

It was time.

Scroll 3: A Walk, a Glance and an Insult

"Wait to lift your flags until *after* you exit through the door!" a voice yelled from the coliseum, barely audible over the cheering crowd and music. "I am the Proliator guard assigned to lead you around the arena floor and then back here, your designated spot for watching the opening ceremonies. Follow me!"

Confused and disoriented, the squires fought the dazzling light streaming though the open doors to see who was ordering them around.

"Friar?" Scelto cried out.

"Go ahead," Friar answered calmly.

They were unprepared for the intense sensory stimulation as they groped their way into the blindingly enthusiastic coliseum. Their ears were besieged by loud, pounding drumbeats accompanied by various string and wind instruments. Bright lights, conventional and magical, lit each of the four massive stories of the arena, each one packed with cheering and yelling spectators.

"It's bigger than I could have imagined," Bellae wheezed, her heart pounding as eighty thousand spectators stared down at her.

Thanks to an enchanted Huuto, an announcer's voice reverberated across the colossal arena, "The first competitors have arrived! The Tournament of Flags is officially open!"

"Raise your flags and follow me!" a Proliator in full armor yelled.

Bellae lifted and shook the pole she was carrying to unfurl the pennant and reveal the Knights' symbol.

"Wake up and move, you goober," Jumeaux growled. Bellae struggled to catch up to Lontas while anxiously glancing at the faces in the seating area.

A Proliator in red armor stood in front of each of the wooden doors ringing the coliseum. Each housed a different group of competitors from the other nations of Verngaurd.

"To honor their history as founders of the Festival, now called the Tournament of Flags, we welcome the Independent Knights, led by HK Pallium," the announcer proclaimed.

An exhilarating cheer rose from the crowd. Smiles spread like wildfire through the squires and Knights as a thrilling shiver ran through their bodies. Scelto raised his banner high and gave it a victory wave.

"Bellae!" a sweet voice yelled from the crowd.

The squire swiveled to see Vanalia frantically waving as Svika and a Proliator guard attempted to remove her from the bottom musician row. Her father looked embarrassed and self-conscious, but Vanalia seemed to be enjoying herself.

"Vanalia!" Bellae called out. The girls' eyes locked and exchanged an unspoken "nice to see you."

The Knights walked around the edge of the arena before ending up in front of the same door they had originally come through. The Proliator escorting them nodded to where the Magicians were sitting. A dazzling flash of light near the Proliate guard quickly turned into the form of a Magician standing right in front of them. Raising his hands he began to chant.

As he finished flag poles rose out of the top of the entire coliseum. Blue and white flags bearing the Knights' symbol shot up behind the section where they were standing. Blue shields with their symbol appeared on the wall directly behind them.

The doors to the left of the Knights crashed open to blistering cheers as massive men entered the coliseum. Bellae recognized one as the bodyguard to Princess Hamaza of Jaa. Spiked tattoos crisscrossed in intricate designs across their shirtless torso and the top of their shaved heads. Each of the towering men carried a huge flag with green waves representing the northern lights behind a white Inukshuk and a yellow star.

"Next we welcome to the Tournament of Flags the wonderful contingent from up north, Jaa! The Royal Bodyguards are followed by Princess Hamaza and her amazing female warriors!" A monumental roar went up that eventually settled into a rhythmic chant of "Jaa, Jaa!"

Figure 22: The green waves gliding across the Jaa flag represent the northern lights, the Inukshuk represents their spiritual culture, and the yellow star represents the hokumua, or first star (others in Verngaurd call it the North Star).

The flowing grace of the alluring women warriors stood in stark contrast to the intimidating bulk of the men. The women wore white fur caps with red veils flowing over their faces. Strong Ko mountain stones, found exclusively in Jaa, dotted the fur of their hats. Smaller stones were woven into reinforced silk to form a strong and flexible chainmail-like armor. They each carried the guandao, a sizable weapon consisting of a long wooden pole ending in a monstrous curved blade.

"Wow, those warriors are huge!" Jumeaux said in quiet awe.

"They're the bodyguards," Bellae whispered. "Friar said the females of Jaa are the ones who fight out of country. Men fight exclusively in defense of their homeland *in* Jaa itself. The only men who can ever even leave Jaa are the Royal Bodyguards when the princess or queen leave their country."

Know it all! Jumeaux thought, staring at the menacing bodyguards.

Princess Hamaza came last wearing a crowned helmet with no veil, allowing her large, voluminous eyes to bore into Scelto. She smiled and gently inclined her head in acknowledgment of him. He managed a weak smile.

Everyone in the auditorium noticed, and Gimelli found herself feeling green with jealousy. Nauseated, she felt fatally self-conscious at her appearance compared to the princess.

Scelto, surprised by the attention and dumbfounded at his swirling feelings, strained his eyes to track the princess with as little movement of his head a possible.

"She's beautiful," Jumeaux said, shamelessly watching her progress around the arena.

After traveling around the coliseum the men of Jaa stood to the left of the Knights, while the female warriors took center stage.

"What's going on?" Lontas asked.

"Not sure," Bellae answered.

For the first time since they entered the coliseum, quiet settled on the crowd as the twenty-four female warriors lined up in two rows of twelve.

Hamaza nodded and music boomed from the first row of the coliseum, led by a fast drumbeat and joined by shrieking string instruments. Abruptly, the female warriors began a series of synchronized acrobatic moves. Their first was to jump up, extending a sidekick with their left leg while simultaneously slicing their guandao in a slashing arc, cutting through the air just inches above the head of the warrior to their right before slicing around and under their own extended leg.

In midair, they contorted into a synchronous twist, landing together in a squat with their right legs forward and their guandao slicing down in front of them. The crowd exploded as they continued to distort and contort their bodies into unimaginable positions while wielding the guandao absurdly close to their neighbors.

"Those blades are close enough to cut hair!" Lontas joked.

"I know, it makes me nervous!" Bellae admitted.

For a finale they sprinted towards each other, one side flipping headfirst over the other. Behind the bodyguards from Jaa, flags and shields bearing their countries' symbol appeared courtesy of a Magician.

As the women returned to stand behind their banner-waving countrymen, Princess Hamaza again made a point to let her eyes linger on Scelto.

"Hey, Scelto. Why don't you go out there and flip around a bit. I bet she would be really impressed," Jumeaux laughed.

"Be nice," Bellae chided.

"Clam it, little Sis," Jumeaux returned. "Why don't you and your blundering boyfriend Lontas go out there and trip all over yourselves?"

"Don't be mean!" Gimelli pleaded.

"You're just jealous Scelto is staring at that fantastic looking princess," Jumeaux stated telepathically.

"You can't see his eyes."

"I don't need to. But don't worry, a dull, simple squire like you has nothing to worry about from a vivacious, drop-dead gorgeous princess."

"Jumeaux!" she protested, the verbal salt her brother had thrown stung her jealously wounded heart.

Untamed and exhilarating music took over the arena as the group from Piscium entered.

"The economy of Piscium is based on the ocean. Other than the dreaded pirates, they are the only sailors of oceans in all of our beloved Verngaurd," the announcer proclaimed.

"They are best known for their passion and quick tempers," Lovag added.

"Why didn't we get to pick a song or put on a fancy show?" Lontas wondered.

"I don't think we were told," Bellae replied.

The Piscium army, made up of the Retiarian and Suoli Divisions, wore uniforms of pale blue and bright yellow. They energetically marched into the coliseum with little to no order to their ranks carrying blue pennants with yellow shells, spears, and tridents.

"Their armor looks like bluish-green fish scales," Jumeaux commented.

Lontas cleared his throat, "Their distinctive simpukka armor actually is made from the tough dried mussel shells of the same name, which are found only off the northern coast of Piscium. Because they weaken over time, they are soaked and baked with a thin iron coating. What's interesting about…"

"Too much information, book-boy," Luchar interrupted. "They have iron-covered, blue-green, fish-scale armor. That's *all* we need to know!"

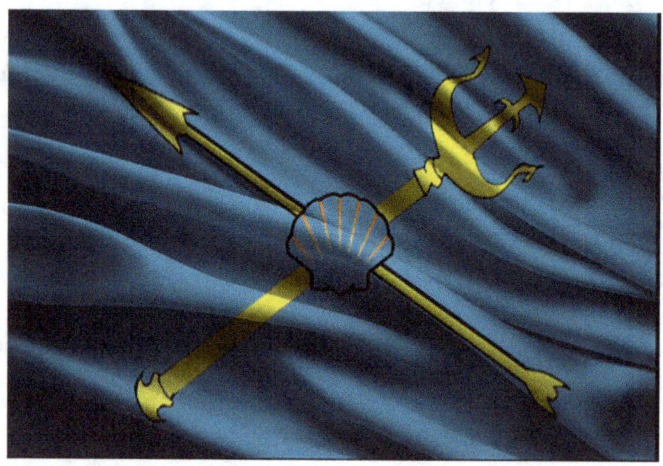

Figure 23: The flag of Piscium pays tribute to their beloved sea with a shell and trident as well as their militaristic style by a crossed spear. They are the only true sailors of Verngaurd save for a small band of pirates.

Lovag chuckled as Lontas turned crimson with embarrassment. "Sorry my squire annoyed you with seeds of knowledge."

"I forgive you…this time, but you two book-addicts better keep those useless factoids to yourself."

The Retiarian helmet had a fin-like crest down the center. On the left arm they wore a large spiked manica or armored shoulder and arm guard, and they carried weighted nets and six-foot long tridents. For close-in fighting they carried their infamous anclas with three curved, and razor-sharp, triangular tips that can as easily rip flesh as they can disarm an opponent.

Figure 24: Piscinian warriors within the Retiarian division are known for their long tridents and weighted nets. Besides their distinctive blue-green simpukka armor they wear a large manica (shoulder and arm plate armor).

The Suoli carry a shield with the bottom portion splaying out like the tail of a whale corseting down with reinforced netting. Their weapon is an iaculum, or disemboweling spear. After a leaf-like blade its shaft has several large backwards-facing barbs to rip and pull flesh when withdrawn.

Figure 25: Piscinian warriors within the Suoli division are known for their fearsome iaculum (disemboweling) spears. Besides their distinctive blue-green simpukka armor they carry a large shield, its shape paying homage to a whale's tail.

Yelps and shouts of excitement were rampant in their ranks as they danced more than marched around the arena. They appeared more like kelp gyrating and bobbing in rough ocean waves than a disciplined army.

As the Piscinians took the center of the arena, several gestured angrily towards the Knights causing Luchar to seethe and mumble obscenities. The tempo of the music became more brisk as did the Piscinian's gesticulating movements.

The crowd cheered and swayed to the infectious music. The announcer, obviously taken by the melody, began to chant and hum.

"Even this announcer guy is in tune with the Piscinians," Jumeaux said. "We should have come up with a catchy tune and snazzy dance for when we marched out."

Emperor Fanga raised his arms in triumph as his soldiers danced zealously to the edge of the arena.

"Not sure how they can top that euphonious rhythm and aesthetically pleasing performance, but here comes…"

Scroll 4: Farmers, Crebers, Don't Kill a Squire

"…the men of Ager!" the announcer proclaimed.

There was a noticeable letdown across the arena as the rollicking music and wild dancing of the warriors of Piscium ended.

"Watch your head, men of Ager! Ha, ha!" the announcer continued. "They are at least a head taller than the rest of us and two to three times the size of Dwarves! Their leather breastplates are adorned with the symbol vita, or symbol of life. Our agrarian friends supply a good portion of Verngaurd with grain, vegetables, and meat. Ager warriors use heavy broadswords and an adaptation of their threshing flails, an armored pole flail."

"Threshing flails have a five-foot wooden pole connected by a chain to a two-foot pole and are used to separate grains from the husk," Lontas stated. "The weaponized version has armored spikes. Sometimes…"

Figure 26: The rich chocolate brown color of the Ager flag recalls the life sustaining soil for this agrarian society. The tri-arrow symbol they call vita, represents life in all its many forms.

"Enough!" Luchar growled. "Lovag, it's your responsibility to stop your squire from spouting useless facts!"

"Yeah, thanks for stating the obvious, La-la-lontas," Jumeaux admonished.

The towering men wore leather helmets with hair accents or horns from a massive ox-like beast they call a trompe.

The a cappella chants of the Ager combatants grew louder as they marched past the Knights. Scelto rolled his neck tensely at the sheer size of them. Their emotionless faces stared straight ahead as they filed past.

"The last warrior, walking by himself, is Ager's champion, Campesino," Finn whispered. "He and Ritari *hate* each other."

"What happened?" Bellae asked.

"Not exactly sure. I know there was something about repeated run-ins when Ritari was out on patrol, and then Ritari went to negotiate with Ager and had a brawl with Campesino."

Bellae looked at Ritari and even through his helmet she could see the animosity in his eyes.

"I am pretty sure he's banned from Ager," Finn said, chuckling.

Figure 27: Formidable beasts of burden, Trompe are known for their incredible strength. Their hides are used for the thick leather armor of the Ager warriors and its horns used in both weaponry and medicine.

The colossal six foot eight inch Campesino carried two pole flails in one of his enormous hands. His sandy brown hair flowed down past his shoulders, but stopped short of his portly abdomen. He had a long beard of the same color.

"Here is King Tarha!" the announcer stated, regaining some of his previous enthusiasm. The king was a hulking man whose body slouched under the weight of his girth. He wore the same dark brown colors as the others but added a flowing cape and a gold crown. He carried an impressive gold scepter with engravings including Verngaurd, the three suns, and the ubiquitous Ager symbol, vita.

Once they had made it around the arena floor Campesino parked his monumental frame in the center of the coliseum. With ruthless precision he began to wield the two armored pole flails. They whizzed

Figure 28: Massive champion of Ager, the hulking Campesino is deadly with both the pole flail and sword. Like most warriors of Ager, he is much taller than most other Verngaurd inhabitants.

within fractions of an inch of each other and his head, as they flew subserviently in his hands.

Walking back to rejoin his countrymen he stopped and pointed to Ritari. "You!" he yelled with Agerian curtness.

A mixture of laughs and cackles ran through the arena. Ritari coolly stared straight ahead as the section behind Ager was magically adorned with shields and flags representing their country.

"Now we have the Elves of Creber," the announcer indicated in a suddenly, and obviously, monotonous tone.

Figure 29: The lush, life-giving greenery of their beloved Forest of Creber is illustrated with the rich emerald color of their flag. The Edelia Arbor Breith is a humongous tree in the center of their forest and is the first tree of the forest. They call it the tree of their nation. It is roughly translated into Tree of Life and represented in the center of their flag.

Any tension was transported away with the melodic and serene string instruments of the Elves. The stately and graceful warriors strode out with easy elegance. Their pennants had a green background with a silvery-white tree.

"The ones in front are Varna, the defenders of the sacred forest. They do not wear metal armor because they are one with the forest, the trees are their shields," Finn whispered wistfully.

Their brown skin appeared harsh and coarse and was streaked by deep, dark grooves colored in a combination of black, green, and gray.

"All their weapons come from the forest," Finn declared. "All birth trees have an uhri, or a completely smooth vestigial branch. It's the only wood Elves ever cut. Once shortened it simply re-grows without harming the tree. It is one of the forest's many gifts.

"The first weapon is a pole staff. Next is a Kama, or sickle weapon, made from the top portion of the tuima bird's beak. Finally, of course, is the ornate white wood bow.

"The next group is the Pretes or priests. They head up our festivals and important ceremonies like the unification, christening, the conaisc…"

"Wait. What-what?" Bellae asked.

"Sorry," Finn said, bubbling with excitement. "The unification happens when an Elf is born. The Pretes must connect us to our arbor breith, or birth tree."

He said "us," Bellae thought. *He still has a connection to his forest.*

The three Pretes marched serenely behind the Varna. They wore long hooded robes with green and gold leaves woven into them.

Finn continued, "In the christening you endure a series of trials to determine your place in the forest. You can be a defender of the forest, a Prete, a Hintel/builder, or rarely an Archerian."

"Here come their rulers, the Archerians," the announcer said in a lukewarm voice.

"The conaisc is a complex marriage ritual joining the couple to one arbor breith tree and separating the other to be used later, usually by one of their children. Two Elves and spirits bound to the soul of a birth tree, becoming one," Finn smiled as his thoughts drifted to Gleoi Dea.

After the Elves marched around the arena, six of the Varna stood in the center of the ring. Three drew their bows and loaded them with staggering speed and efficiency. The other three pulled out a series of circular targets.

Lontas traced an imaginary arc from the end of their bows to the seats in the coliseum. The audience in those sections squirmed at the arrows pointing their way. Visions of blood and pain filled Lontas' head and he felt the world start to spin.

"You all right, Lontas?" Bellae asked at the same time one of the Elves yelled, "Release!"

Three of the Elves threw up a string of circular disks and the others shot them down with blistering and meticulous precision. Bellae was vaguely aware of activity in the center of the arena as Lontas limply fell to the ground.

A series of screams and gasps rang through the arena as Bellae and Finn knelt to tend to Lontas.

"They shot a squire!" someone yelled from the crowd.

The six Varna anxiously rushed over to Lontas. "What happened?"

"He's fine. He just got dizzy," Finn informed them.

"Those cursed Elves shot a boy!" another from the crowd shouted.

Bellae could feel every eye in the arena boring into them. Beads of sweat sprang up on her forehead.

"Hmm," Lontas moaned, trying to sit up. He suddenly froze. Realizing he was the center of attention for the entire coliseum, he fell back again. The crowd let out another gasp as one of the Magicians flew down to the arena floor.

"Nice job, knucklehead. The crowd thinks the Elves shot you," Jumeaux gushed, rudely kicking Lontas' foot. "We are going to have to start a "LRC," a Lontas Retarded Counter. This is a big number one."

The Magician had a young looking face but gray hairs flowed alongside black in his long ponytail. His blue robes billowed as he came to rest on the arena floor.

"Has this boy been shot?" he asked, his eyes scouring the Elves accusingly.

"No!" an Elf exclaimed. "This stripling fainted."

The Magician looked skeptically at Lontas. Seeing no injury he shook his head in disgust. Mumbling to himself, he flew back up to the top of the stadium.

"This just in, folks, no one was shot. Seems as if a squire was just a little dizzy. Poor kid," the announcer said sarcastically.

"You can do it, Lontas. Get on up," Bellae said gently.

"Stand up, you putz," Jumeaux chided.

Lontas closed his eyes and wished for a hole to suddenly swallow him up.

All but one of the exasperated Elves walked away. The other stared at Finn. Bellae recognized him from the alleyway after she had been separated when they first arrived. He was Kempe, the brawny Elf she had seen with his son Kainen and the hulking creature under the black robes.

"Finn?"

Bellae swiveled in time to see a glimmer of recognition flash in her Knight's eyes. "Kempe?" Finn uttered, stepping out of formation. "You've gotten big!"

As the two approached each other Finn chortled, "You've gotten *really* big!"

The two embraced as a flood of long lost memories bled across their minds, flashing quickly, but vividly, as only childhood remembrances can. The sights, sounds, and smells came flooding back: walks in the woods, playing and roughhousing, laughter, crunching leaves, the fresh outdoors.

"Come on Kempe!" a disgruntled Elf called, his words heaving Finn and Kempe back into the present as their old memories vanished, replaced by the sights and sounds of the coliseum.

"I'll find you after the Opening Ceremony," Kempe promised.

An ear-piercing clamor of instruments ruptured as two sets of doors slammed open. Two melodies competed against each other for dominance, creating a wretched cacophony.

"Oh, no!" Friar cried out.

Scroll 5: Don't Kill Each Other-N vs. S

The musicians of the Northern and Southern Dwarves each played with increasing intensity. Both sides determined to outshine the other, neither willing to back down. The resulting cantankerous music blistered the ears.

"Wow, that sounds horrible," Bellae mouthed.

To add to the chaos both Northern and Southern Dwarf combatants emerged from adjacent doors and instantly began hurling insults.

"This should be interesting," Finn smiled.

"More like catastrophic," Friar added.

"See, the crowd already forgot about you!" Bellae said. Lontas took a deep breath and nodded gratefully.

Grym and Borb popped up from her stola. *"Lovely, just lovely music!"* Grym squeaked.

"I have to admit, it makes being scrunched into this tiny, rigid dress pocket so much more tolerable," Borb added spitefully.

"Stay out of sight, guys, there could be trouble," Bellae advised.

"Please welcome to the Tournament..." the announcer said, unaware of the confusion below, "...the assembly from the Northern Dwarves. You can see three colors representing their three military branches."

The stunned crowd watched the two groups of Dwarves glare ominously at each other as the horrendous music screeched on.

"Does the announcer have crap in his ears and a bag over his head or what?" Jumeaux buzzed. "Hey, look down here genius!"

"The Northern Dwarves are led by the Saatana Division clad in red," the announcer continued. Their eyes glimmered menacingly behind their intimidating helmets with red dragon wings and black horns. Their chest plates and pennants held a Red Dragon over a silver background.

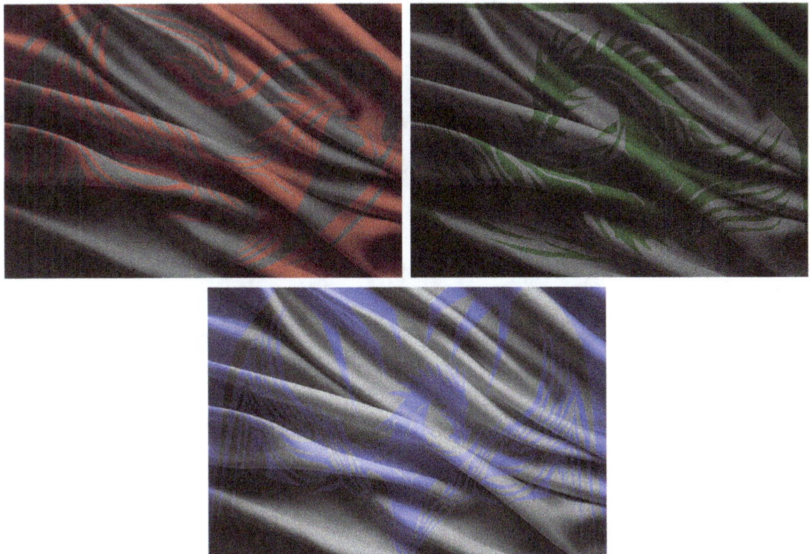

Figure 30: The Northern Dwarf Army is divided into three distinct factions representing the three dragons (Saatana, Vioma, and Kirvella) that share their mountain home. Each carries a like-colored flag. The red armored Saatana (dragon trainers and infantry), the green Vioma (infantry and air force), and Blue Vasama (special forces).

A dozen Vioma Division Dwarves came next wearing green tunics and carrying green pennants, both with dragon emblems. The squires instantly recognized Abhac, the Aer Ridire dragon rider they met in the flower fields, who had guided them out of the mountain pass.

There were only three of the elite Vasama Division wearing white tunics with a blue dragon. Their helmetless heads had long braided hair with blue dragon scales down their length.

The obtuse announcer continued, "They are led by King Abernan and are responsible for training the Saatana dragons that…huh? What? Oh, I see!

"It seems we have a double entrance problem…who was the idi…?" the announcer's voice trailed off before continuing. "Let's also welcome the Southern Dwarves led by their High Council…they…uh," he fumbled.

The Southern Dwarves formed lines and continued taunting their Northern cousins. The short, stout mining Dwarves of the south evolved enormous eyes courtesy of living underground excavating metals and jewels. Their square noses turned down, forming a natural filter in the dusty and dank condition of the mines. Their helmets, armor, and shields were richly decorated with gold inlay and a generous helping of jewels. Their tan pennants had depictions of precious jewels and metals encircling an axe and sword.

"Bloody fools!" Luchar shouted, moving towards the Southern Dwarves.

"Let the Proliate handle this!" Friar said firmly. Luchar growled, but reluctantly stepped back. To add to the unrest the contingent from Piscium began chanting impromptu slurs in support of the Southern Dwarves:

"It's the Northern Dwarves! Our clue?
They smell like Dragon doo!
You have to admit,
You reek like dragon shhhh-grit!
Northern Dwarves are dense,
Their armor doesn't make sense.
Blue, red, green, which color to choose?

Figure 31: Always anxious to remind the world of their wealth, the Southern Dwarves flagrantly display various jewels and precious metals. Demonstrating their perceived military prowess, they also display an axe and sword.

Doesn't matter, they will lose!"

Scattered howls of laughter could be heard around the arena. Half of the Northern Dwarves broke off their stare-down with the Southern Dwarves and turned towards the Piscium contingent who continued their derisive chant,

"Beat a path,
To take a bath.
Hope you don't drown,
Before the Southern Dwarves take you down."

Without warning, two green Vioma dragons stocked with Aer Ridire riders dropped precipitously out of the sky. They dove startlingly close to the ground, forcing the Southern Dwarves and Piscinians to dive and jump out of the way. The green dragons flew in a crisscross pattern before circling ominously overhead. One spewed fire into the air with a fearsome shriek as the Aer Ridire riders chanted menacingly.

Several Piscinian warriors stood back up and instantly began yelling obscenities.

"Shut your mouths or I'll do it for you, you ocean-loving scum!" an Aer Ridire rider shouted from the back of one of the dragons.

The Southern Dwarves immediately formed a shield wall and began advancing towards the Northern Dwarves. Just when it looked like the two sides would come to blows, several squads of Proliators swarmed them. The specifics were inaudible, but choice words could be heard from all involved.

The skies abruptly filled with dozens of griffins carrying Magician riders, each with a crosier pointed at the Northern Dwarves' dragons. The griffins have the head of a fearsome bird surrounded by a lion's mane and massive wings. Their large front talons opened and closed menacingly. Their back half was that of a lion, complete with tail and claws. The blue robed Magicians were yelling at the Aer Ridire to leave. Under commands from their riders, the Vioma dragons quickly flew higher, vanishing into the depths of the sky.

Figure 32: Griffins have the head of a fearsome bird surrounded by a lion's mane and massive wings. Their large front talons are a menacing weapon, while their back half is that of a lion, complete with tail and claws. They are exclusively trained for battle by Magicians.

"Uhm, sorry for the confusion," the announcer stammered. "Let's move on…uh, who's next? The Rebelde Plains? What? Oh yes, first the shields and flags."

Behind both Dwarf contingents shields and flags appeared. With an uneasy peace restored, the Proliate soldiers, and griffins with their Magician riders, withdrew.

"*Now,* the Rebelde Plains," the announcer stated. "Their warriors march under a simple blue flag." As he droned on, obviously reading scripted words, another skirmish broke out amongst the Dwarves.

"Friar!" Luchar yelled, his eyes wide with anticipation.

"Hold!" Friar shouted as Luchar drifted longingly towards the fray. The Draak swords of the northerners could be seen clanging against the heavy axes of the south.

"We have a blood alliance with the Northern Dwarves!" Luchar declared, his teeth gnashing. "Let's get in on this!"

"Friar, perhaps…" Ritari started.

He stopped as three Magicians landed next to the battling Dwarves. Spectacular flames and intense heat burst out of their crosiers, soaring into the air.

"Something's coming…oh, amazing!" Bellae trilled. "I never thought I would get to see the winged horse!"

The whooshing of wings was quickly followed by gasps from the crowd as Veneficus flew down to the arena riding his Pegasus, a white horse with large silver wings and a silver feathered mane and tail.

"Desist and listen!" Veneficus thundered. "Protocol will be followed at this Tournament! The Magicians and Proliate will see to it. We are not afraid to use extreme force. Test us and you will regret it."

The two groups of Dwarves separated and started picking up dropped banners. The flames from the staffs of the Magicians ceased, and they disappeared.

"Do *not* make me return," Veneficus cautioned before flying into the sky.

"All right," a heavily annoyed announcer sighed. "Can we please continue?"

Figure 33: Widely regarded as one of the most majestic creatures in the land, only a single one exists at any given time. The Pegasus is highly guarded by Veneficus. The current one is called Runor.

Scroll 6: Rebels, Western Elves, and Opening Speeches

"The pure blue flag of the Rebelde Plains symbolizes freedom and autonomy in all facets of their life," the announcer stated in an apathetic voice. "The ruling triumvirate runs their politeia, which is a countrywide democratic meeting to discuss the political issues of their nation."

The Rebelde Plains warriors wore a jumble of different armor of questionable caliber and received more taunts than applause for their ragtag appearance. They took great pleasure in the jeers, sauntering with renegade swagger.

Figure 34: Known as outlaws and outcasts, the Rebelde Plains prizes liberty and independence. The plain blue flag is unencumbered with anything but those ideals.

A mix of Elves, Dwarves, and humans marched in random order. A few held their flags overhead, but most had them leaning indifferently against their shoulders. The Proliator guard leading them looked embarrassed, as if he had drawn the short piece of straw.

"Uhm…you might want to turn around there, chum!" Jumeaux cried out.

The Proliator looked up to find himself walking around the arena alone. A chuckle went through the crowd as the Rebelde Plains participants ditched their escort and romped to the center of the ring.

"Apparently, these big shots don't feel the need to walk around the arena like everyone else!" the announcer rebuked.

Once there, they haphazardly tossed down their flags. Swaying to the beat of fast music, the warriors began to juggle and toss their weapons with surprising accuracy. Maces, swords, and axes were flung, twisted and spun across their bodies and the arena. After several minutes they formed a circle.

Suddenly, every weapon burst into flames and they began tossing them to the man across, and one over from them. Like a homicidal wheel, the burning weapons seemed to spin in a circle of fire. The loudest cheers of the night went up. Even the slighted Proliator guard seemed enthralled enough to forget his humiliation. As quickly as the flames started, they disappeared.

"The flames were prestidigitation!" Lontas cried, noticing several Rebelde Plain's Dwarves in the corner with loitsia sticks.

"Thanks for, once again, stating the painfully obvious you dunce!" Jumeaux rebuked.

After making their way to their designated area, blue shields and flags materialized behind them.

"Welcome the Western Elves!" the announcer proclaimed. "Centuries ago they left the barbarously primitive Forest of Creber and settled the Plain of Dunn, becoming highly civilized with impressive cities. Their Black Tower is an architectural legend."

The Elves of Creber bristled and booed at the notion of the Western Elves "becoming civilized" after leaving their "barbarously primitive" forest. However, loud cheering from the crowd mostly drowned them out.

Figure 35: Although a solitary tree gives a nod to their previous woodland existence, the Western Elves are supremely proud of their city life—especially the architecturally complex Black Tower of Dunn. Their warriors are excellent archers and proficient with a halberd.

The black armor of the Western Elves was lightly inlaid with gold. They carried modified halberds with black pennants showing a golden bow strung with an arrow pointing straight up. Within the bow to the left was a tree and to the right the Black Tower of Dunn. Their steps were graceful and self-assured as they glared at the Elves of Creber.

Bellae recognized the jeweled Bondi, the leader of Western Elves, and his silk outfit from their meeting with Veneficus.

The Western Elves were taller and fairer of skin than the Elves of Creber. They had hints of streaks, but few bark-like fissures and no deep ruts. They gathered into two lines on either side of their leader.

Bondi threw a six-foot long pole high into the air. The Elves unslung and fired their bows so precisely that the arrows landed on opposite sides and ends of the stick, spinning the pole around. The cheer roaring through the crowd turned into a collective gasp as the Elves instantly fired again, making it spin faster. A final volley of arrows hit the rotating stick so it stopped and fell into Bondi's hands. The Elven warriors performed a series of summersaults, landing in a pyramid formation with Bondi gesturing grandly.

"A more impressive display of archery I would say," Bondi glowered to the protesting Elves of Creber. "Plus, we managed to avoid shooting any children!"

The crowd exploded in applause. As they made their way to the side of the arena, shields and flags with their black and gold colors went up.

Scelto's shoulders and back ached and he adjusted his large banner. In the hours since the Knights had entered, nighttime had fallen, but the darkness had been kept at bay by torches and magical lights illuminating the arena.

Without warning, all light was extinguished, plunging the coliseum into total darkness. A surge of flames exploded from the center of the arena. The heat forced many of the front line competitors to turn their heads away. A lone figure was briefly outlined against the flames before the blaze disappeared and the lights returned.

"Greetings!" he boomed using an enchanted Huuto. Piercing eyes sat within a square face and above a horizontal jaw. A thin silver outline of a Phoenix adorned his blazing ruby chest plate and a blood red cape flowed over his shoulders.

"I am Storlax, Proliate High Commander of the armies of Tallcon. Welcome to *our* Tournament of Flags, refrain from calling it by its old name, Festival. Competition starts after three holy days to honor Tallcon's pietistic day." Storlax rigorously looked around the arena as if gauging the integrity of every person there.

"Every inhabitant of Verngaurd knows of the Dark Warrior attacks and the peculiar happenings plaguing our peaceful existence. Any of you rogue nations caught aiding the Dark Warriors will be dealt a swift and terrible retribution. I don't care what you think you have done for this land in the distant past," Storlax said, glaring at the Knights.

Figure 36: Intimidating and fractious, Storlax is devout to Tallcon and dedicated to leading his highly trained military. He is the overall Proliate leader, or High Commander.

His eyes then landed sequentially on the representatives from the countries of the Northern Dwarves, Jaa, Rebelde Plains, and Elves of Creber, as if they too were to blame for the recent invasion of Dark Warriors.

"This guy is a bunch of fun with healthy dash of cheer. They should call him 'Chuckles the Psychotic Jester' or something," Jumeaux said as the others giggled.

"We, *the* caretakers of Verngaurd, are the protectors of the weak and oppressed!" Storlax growled, his face growing more hyperbolized.

Lidenskap! Bellae thought as the tall Proliator moved to stand next to his High Commander.

"Nonhuman instigators better watch out!" Storlax shouted to a roar of disapproval from many in the crowd. "I am specifically referring to the Elves, Dwarves, and all the reprobates from the Rebelde Plains. All cesspools of corruption will be purged!" he yelled, as fresh calls of condemnation mixed with cheers from Piscium and Ager.

He seemed not to notice or care, "I look around and see no King Kuningas or any Fairies or Sprites from Cappadocia. Why? Those nonhumans are up to no good, that's why. I can…"

Lidenskap tapped Storlax on the shoulder and whispered. The High Commander looked annoyed, but nodded.

"I meant no offense to the law abiding Southern Dwarves and Western Elves!" Storlax added.

"Oh, I absolutely believe him! He's totally not racist!" Jumeaux scowled as the High Commander continued.

"However, we must come to terms not only with the menace from abroad, but the treachery within. I…" Lidenskap put his hand gently on his Commander's shoulder, but Storlax flung it off and continued despite the loud boos from the Northern Dwarves and Elves of Creber.

"I have no doubt the Dark Warriors are being helped by one or more of you as they ravage only *certain* countries. There can be no other explanation but treason against Verngaurd!"

Veneficus flew down on his Pegasus, landing just behind Storlax.

Thinking of his vision from Tallcon, Lidenskap began to sweat. *Tallcon wants us to find a peace that includes the Knights.* He could see the dread mirrored in Veneficus' eyes.

"Let's promote peace, High Commander," Veneficus whispered.

Storlax snarled and continued his rant. Veneficus magically silenced Storlax's Huuto and the rest of his tirade went unheard. The High Commander appeared not to notice as he continued his muted rant for several minutes. The contorted rage plastered on his face drawing a few snickers as his mouth flailed in noiseless anger.

Once his tirade finally concluded Veneficus nodded to the announcer who quickly began speaking as Veneficus flew off, "Get ready for the last competitors, *your* Warriors of Tallcon!"

A steady drumbeat echoed around the coliseum. The center of the arena was once again engulfed in darkness save for a massive fire.

"Something's coming out of the flames!" Lontas shouted.

"Seriously, Lontasia? Of course there is, we can all see that you…" Jumeaux was cut off by a glowering Luchar.

Scroll 7: Red Vibration: Magic Oration

The heat could be felt throughout the coliseum as a blazing tower of flames reached nearly one hundred feet high. The blaze vanished and a fiery image of a Phoenix shot out of the dying embers into the night sky.

The light returned to reveal an impenetrable shield wall of Proliate warriors.

Hectic drumbeats intensified, followed by a loud guttural yell and a blistering series of maneuvers by the Proliate fighters. They moved with such precision it appeared they were tied together. Their massive merja spears peered menacingly above their shields with perfect spacing.

"Repetition to the point of habit can lead to abstraction. Relying too much on routine puts a strangle hold on creativity," Friar told his Knights. "Many great battles were won when Knights took initiative

Figure 37: Simple but intimidating, the Proliate flag has an outline of a phoenix representing their god, Tallcon. Red representing the Sanctus or Red Guard, silver for the Ultor division of their military.

without waiting for a direct order. The Proliate are so engrossed in habit and apprehension that they would wait for a command to breathe."

The Proliate continued to perform movements with meticulous timing. Scelto's eyes widened in terror as their formation swept ever closer.

"Hey now," he whimpered as their spears came within a few inches of his face.

"Picking on a squire? Try that with me and I will smash your head in!" Luchar snarled.

"Not so subtle sign they hate us," Finn seethed.

Wordlessly, the Proliate withdrew to their section of arena as red and silver shields and flags appeared behind them.

"That was quite the speech by Storlax," Ritari whispered. "He blames us for the Dark Warriors and practically declared war on us."

"I know," Friar replied. "The Proliate's hostility towards us is increasing. The extent of the Dark Warrior's cunning ability to manipulate the situation so that we look guilty is painfully apparent. Let's meet with the Veli after this is over. The three days of celebration will give us a chance to shore up some confidential planning."

"Pingius should have informed us of the scope of the Dark Warrior's attacks in and around his territory," Ritari stated.

"At this point blame doesn't help. We need to accept our own failures and try to fix the problems before us."

Suddenly a white light streaked up into the night sky, silver sparks trailing behind. It looped high above the coliseum before rapidly approaching the center of the arena.

"It's beautiful-l-l!" Gimelli purred. "But, what is it?"

Before anyone could answer, the dazzling light came to a stop twenty feet from the ground. The glow faded so sedately it was hard to tell exactly when it disappeared and a figure materialized, hovering effortlessly above the arena.

"I am Supreme Master Magician Veneficus," his voice boomed. "We are honored to host this competition with the Proliate. As High Commander Storlax mentioned, these are uncertain, trying times, which is precisely why we must come together. Humans and non-humans, those being attacked by the Dark Warriors and those who are not, must join forces.

"I feel invigorated as I look upon Verngaurd's diverse flags and shields coming together as one community. Reconnecting over the next several days is the only way we can meet this emerging threat to our way of life. It is wise to never forget the past. Let us thank the Knights for their long history of defending us!" Veneficus shouted. Light clapping ran throughout the stadium before quickly ending.

"Let us now praise our famous warriors and hosts who are battling so bravely against the current Dark Warrior aggression, the Proliators!" An enthusiastic round of applause erupted through the arena.

"Take the next few days to greet old friends and make new ones. Enjoy the festivities!" Veneficus stated, before floating towards the Knights.

He stopped above Jumeaux. "Hello, dear boy," Veneficus said, the words of the old prophecy rattling in his mind. *So this is the Chosen One?* he thought, sensing the turmoil, contempt, and insecurity churning within the boy. *Excellent, most excellent. He will serve me, and, of course, Verngaurd well.*

Overwhelmed, Jumeaux just nodded. His heart thumped with pride and exhilaration at both the attention he was receiving, and the power of the Magician.

Veneficus levitated downward, leaning over he clasped Friar's hand. "We have to come together," he whispered. His eyes were shining and his face smiling with optimism. With a flash, he was surrounded in cool light and shooting back into the sky.

The spectators gave a standing ovation as the trail of light disappeared amongst the twinkling stars. The competitors ringing the arena made a glorious sight. The many colored flags fluttered in the cool night breeze and armor glistened in the pale light. A hush settled on the arena as everyone soaked up the palpable feeling of calm and something else, an elusive feeling, felt by all, but recognized by few. Hope, in the fledgling form of a wisp of optimism delicately fluttered around on the applause of the arena, but if carefully nurtured with understanding and effort, it could grow.

"Thank you for coming," the announcer declared. "A celebratory reception will be held in the greeting area though the doors to the north. Good night!"

The formerly tidy and homogeneous groups dispersed, splattering the various colors of the different nations and turning the arena floor into a kaleidoscope.

Once Veli Falciss, Veli Pingius, and Ritari were together, Friar spoke. "We can hope Veneficus' words of peace will win over the countries of Verngaurd, but we need to be realistic. After my meeting, and what High Commander Storlax said, we need to be ready to deal with the division ripping through Verngaurd. The sad truth is we will likely have to fight some of the nations of Verngaurd before the Dark Warriors."

"The Dark Warriors want us tearing each other apart, making their conquest of Verngaurd easier," Ritari said.

Veli Falciss nodded, "Fighting each other will weaken our ability to battle the Dark Warriors. However, the alternative is to roll over and be obliterated! Knights never capitulate."

"It's hard to blame the Proliate for their aggression," Veli Pingius said. "The Dark Warriors are incredibly calculating and convincing. If I didn't know better, I would think we *were* guilty."

"The Proliate have been a threat to our way of life well before this mess with the Dark Warriors," Falciss sneered. "I'm just glad you're finally willing to deal with them."

"They have been our allies…"

"Allies only on paper!" Falciss snorted.

"Perhaps, but I would still prefer not to fight them."

Veli Pingius' stomach rumbled as servers offering appetizers walked by. He gave a nervous smile and patted his robust abdomen, encouraging patience.

Noticing Friar's meeting, Bellae pulled Lontas against the crowd. "We need to hear this."

Lontas winced at the visions of the other times he followed Bellae: war dogs, prickly bushes, winged demons, falling off a bridge towards certain death, ghosts, and possessed librarians. "No more adventures!"

Bellae said nothing but continued dragging him closer. They concealed themselves behind Pingius' imposing form as a thunderous rumble echoed from his stomach. Lontas looked at Bellae and they tried not to laugh at the cacophony of hunger pangs echoing from his gut.

"We better move, I think he's going to explode," Lontas joked.

Bellae choked back a laugh in her sleeve.

"Any thoughts on my contingency plan for the Proliate?" Friar asked.

"Good location, good plan. After the hostility of today, we should start getting ready," Veli Pingius said, willing the silent Veli Falciss to agree so his stomach could find fulfillment at the reception.

Friar smiled. "The preparations to stockpile reserves and necessary props were begun over six months ago."

"Six months? Amazing!" Pingius exclaimed. "You listened to the visions you mentioned?"

Veli Falciss huffed. "How do we know the visions aren't from the White Wizard trying to lead us astray? Plus, your plan seems better suited for charlatans and cowards. We need to stand toe to toe with our enemy and beat them *like* Knights. Have we given up on everything we stand for?"

Veli Pingius spoke before Friar could answer, "What news of our allies? You had question marks besides some of the nations on your battle plans."

Bellae thought back to the war maps in Friar's office. *I saw those!*

"The loyalty of some of our "allies" is uncertain, which could unhinge our best laid strategies. The leaders of our most trusted friends have started their own preparations.

"I have spent many sleepless nights playing out different scenarios. To your point, Falciss, there is simply no way we can stand directly in front of the full Proliate army and survive against their overwhelming numbers. If we are forced to fight them we need to hit hard and fast, forcing them to the bargaining table so we can deal with the Dark Warriors together. Obviously, this plan is complex, but…"

"'Obviously complex,' is the only true thing you have said," Falciss interrupted. "Your strategy is too circuitous. Too scripted."

"You're correct, trying to anticipate the chaos of battle can be a recipe for disaster. However, if we come together and work hard, we have a chance. The 'coward's way,' as you put it, is our *only* prospect for victory. I refuse to offer our brave warriors up for slaughter to placate your pride."

Falciss crossed his arms and silently looked off in the distance.

"If an internal war comes to Verngaurd we will not fail from a lack of preparation or training, that I can promise you." Friar began to walk away then stopped, "That said, at the end of the day, Knights stick together and I expect you to follow my bloody orders."

"HK!"

Recognizing the voice, Friar groaned and immediately changed course.

Scroll 8: Knight's Night Invite

"HK!" the voice rang out again.

Closing his eyes and grumbling, Friar slowly turned, "Hello, General Lidenskap."

"Good evening!" he said, striding energetically. "A glorious opening ceremony, wouldn't you say?"

"I suppose," Friar answered, taken aback by the unfamiliarly kind tone in the general's voice.

The general swallowed hard, even under the direct guidance of Tallcon, being nice to Friar and the Knights would take extraordinary effort. *I can and will follow Tallcon's command. I follow you.* Forcing a big smile he continued out loud, "I would like to apologize about what happened in Veneficus' chambers. I should not have accused you."

"Thank you?" Friar said, still struggling with Lidenskap's new and inexplicably cheery disposition. "Anyway, I would have appreciated knowing that the other groups were entering to their own music and performing in the center of the arena."

"As the 'grandfathers' of the Tournament we thought you would want to enter as you did in the ancient days," Lidenskap answered, waving his hands in the air dismissively. "Anyway, I have come to present you with another request to join me…what?" Lidenskap yelped as two small forms scurried between his feet.

Bellae dove on the ground in front of the general before he could stomp on her friends.

"Sorry, sir," she said, her face reddening. She quickly hid what she picked up behind her back.

"Bellae?" Friar questioned.

"My…" she hesitated, not wanting to advertise what she was concealing, "I was chasing, er, dropped and lost…I apologize."

"Were you chasing your two pet mice?" Lidenskap asked, smiling.

Bellae turned a deeper shade of red and hid her head. "Yes, sir." She gently put Grym and Borb in her stiff pocket. Scelto and Gimelli ran up, looking self-conscious, as if it were their fault Bellae's mice ran off.

"Squires, could you excuse us?" Friar asked.

"No, please, stay. I want all of you to come to a Pietistic Day Ceremony tomorrow morning. It's only about an hour."

Friar feigned a smile, "We would be honored."

"All Knights and squires are welcome as my personal guests," he stated, still smiling and shaking his head joyfully. Friar and Bellae were stunned at the change from his previous gruff and pompous attitude.

"I assure you nothing would please my Knights more, unfortunately, they have training first thing tomorrow. Perhaps Captain Ri…

Friar turned to see his captain had abandoned him. Twisting the other direction he noted the Veli had deserted him as well.

Friar turned to see Lidenskap staring at him with a hopelessly optimistic grin which seemed absurdly out of place on his normally stoic face. Bellae swayed a bit as her mice friends squirmed. *The squires will have to be offered up,* Friar thought.

"Ah, these young squires and I will be delighted."

The squires inwardly groaned while outwardly spreading sham smiles.

"Wonderful!"

After several uncomfortable moments of silence, the smiling Lidenskap left. *Unite them in Tallcon,* he reminded himself. *Follow Tallcon. Praise Tallcon.*

"Well, that was interesting," Friar stated. "I cannot fathom what brought about his sudden change." *He is definitely up to something. All we need is more hidden agendas!*

"You're not mad, about the mice?"

"How could I be mad when your rowdy mice saved me from going to some boring Proliate ceremony by myself?"

Ritari contritely meandered back.

"Thanks for leaving me hanging!" Friar chastised, mostly jokingly.

"Into any battle, on any day, at any time, against any odds, you have all of me. However, I leave the political conversations to you!"

"Blessings upon you! Good evening!" Princess Hamaza said in a melodic voice as she sauntered up.

"Blessing upon you and your house," Friar replied.

Scelto was leaning forward, floating under the magnetic pull of her gaze while Gimelli was suffocating on a thick fog of envy.

"It is nice to see you again," Princess Hamaza said, nodding towards Bellae. "You made quite the impression in Veneficus' office. Our trainers, especially our master trainer, Seestya, are interested in your ability to speak with animals." Turning back to Friar she continued, "I would like to invite a few of you to see our kotatu in exchange for a chance to talk with the girl who can converse with animals."

"We would be most appreciative of the opportunity," Friar stated.

"If it is convenient, the girl can speak with the trainers tomorrow, by herself, and a few of you can come the day after?"

"We would be most honored," Friar responded.

"I will see my new little friend tomorrow at the Jaa kotatu."

"Blessings upon you and your house," Friar responded. They all watched as the princess left, flanked by two incredibly intimidating bodyguards.

"Does *everyone* know about your mice and ability to speak with animals?" Gimelli wondered.

"Apparently. What's a kotatu anyway?"

"They started back when we held the Citadel and it was known as Cumhacht. Each country had a kotatu, or consulate, as a home away from home. Bellae, I apologize for volunteering you to speak with their trainers, but I did not feel right denying the princess."

"It's fine," she lied, nervous about what sorts of things they would ask her.

"Turns out our three days of "rest" will be busy in…whoa!" Friar exclaimed, teetering precariously over a little boy who had latched onto both his legs.

"I'm gonna become a Knight," his small voice chirped. The boy was ten, but half the height of someone his age. His disheveled brown hair sat over large, protruding brown eyes. He wore a pale blue and yellow Piscinian cloak. His skin was darker than the average Piscinian. A slight bluish, almost black discoloration lingered around his mouth. His grip seemed weak to Friar given how hard he was struggling.

"Sumar, son, leave the busy Knights alone," his embarrassed father exclaimed.

"It's fine," Friar said, gently patting the boy's back.

"He's excited because his grandfather, Martello…"

"Martello was an amazing Knight!" Friar exclaimed. "He's buried at Liberum, not far from my father in fact."

"My older brother filled Sumar's head with thoughts and dreams of being a Knight like his grandfather." His sad gaze affirmed what his heart could not bear to put into words, the boy was too sickly, too small for such an ambition.

"When can I be a Knight?" the boy asked. His somewhat dull eyes smoldered with flawed hope, the absurdity of which, his young mind could not yet grasp. Friar looked at the boy's father, but he simply turned away with the hint of tears in his eyes.

"You have to get older first," Friar replied, returning the boys gaze sympathetically.

"I'm really strong." Stepping back, the boy pulled back his sleeve and flexed his anemic bicep muscle.

"Very strong!" Friar agreed. "You keep up the good work, son."

"Okay" the boy said, suddenly seeming to tire.

"Here's your salt," the father said. The boy promptly began to suck on the salt cube as they walked away.

"There's something you don't see everyday," Scelto said.

Scroll 9: Knock, Knock-Floor

"Jumeaux, get up or I'll hit you so hard your senses will meet your attitude!" Scelto threatened the next morning.

"He drives us crazy, but he's still my brother," Gimelli said. "Come on, Jumeaux, we have practice. Early to rise and hard work mean success!"

"Actually, it's the bigger, faster, and stronger who are successful, no matter what time they wake up. Although, I will say a good night's sleep is key. Hence, and by that reasoning, I need more sleep," Jumeaux said.

"Please J, we have to get to the coliseum for practice," Gimelli pleaded telepathically.

"Everyone else is ready," Scelto huffed. "Get your lazy tail up or…"

"Knock, Knock," Jumeaux interrupted.

"Jumeaux, don't!" Gimelli implored telepathically.

"No, it's important." A smug smile spread across his face. "Oh, c'mon! Knock, knock."

"You better get up after this," Gimelli whispered. "Who's there?"

"Sore."

"Sore who?"

"Sorea and Finn can prepare for the tournament themselves, so I can sleep!" Jumeaux laughed, wriggling on his bed.

"We listened to your pathetic joke, now get up!" Scelto demanded.

"Just get ready and let's go," Lontas said.

"Great advice from the guy who spends half of his life falling on the floor."

"That was just plain mean," Bellae complained.

"Just one more. Knock, knock."

"Last one?"

Jumeaux nodded. "Knock, knock."

"Who's there?"

"Sell."

"Sell who?"

"Scelto has a big fat head! Ha-ha!" Jumeaux laughed. Scelto dove at him, but in avoiding Gimelli, overshot the bed and crashed onto the floor.

"What? Can't take a joke, big guy?" Jumeaux said, standing up and jumping on his bed.

Scelto moved forward, every muscle in his body taut with anger, but Jumeaux was too busy laughing to notice. Time seemed to slow to a crawl for Bellae. She watched as Jumeaux's face seemed stuck in a howling laugh. His dark eyes glistened against his gaunt frame. Scelto's face contorted in rage as he lunged. His right hand caught Jumeaux's chin.

There was a loud "crack" and Jumeaux's thin frame instantly spun around, bounced off the bed, and then thudded limply to the ground.

"KO'd in one shot!" Lontas cheered. "Nice, Scelto!"

Gimelli scolded him with an exasperated look while shouting, "Scelto! Really?" She gently cradled her twin brother's head. "Get some water, Bellae!"

"Is he okay?" Scelto asked, flushed with a mix of embarrassment and exhilaration.

"He's knocked out, but breathing with a strong pulse," Gimelli answered.

"I'll go tell the Knights why we're late," Scelto said sheepishly.

Scroll 10: Clandestine Meeting Meets Shock

Three powerful men gathered for a confidential meeting in another part of the city. Veneficus, General Lidenskap, and Emperor Fanga from Piscium stood in the soft candlelight of a deserted hallway.

"While Friar and the Veli are distracted here at the Tournament, your Proliate warriors should destroy the Knights in their castles. Once they are shattered, distribute their wealth to those of us who have toiled for centuries to furnish them with gold," Emperor Fanga seethed. "We all know the Knights and their allies have to be the ones helping the Dark Warriors. Destroying them will disrupt the Dark Warrior's supply lines, forcing them to leave."

"This dangerous scheme would have far reaching implications. I think you are underestimating the Knights *and* forgetting how they served Verngaurd for centuries," Veneficus answered.

"*You've* forgotten the Knights' abuses when they set themselves up as Kings and bled our resources dry," Emperor Fanga declared. "One central power controlling all the military is not healthy! You have to admit those blasted Dark Warriors did us one favor. The Knights have been circling the outhouse since they were thrashed in the Dark War!"

Veneficus frowned, "It has been centuries since the Knights abused their power when they were ruled by kings. Since they changed to the Friardom they have protected our land faithfully."

"Some scars take more than a few centuries to heal. Plus, they didn't protect us during the Dark War. The Proliate saved us then, and they're shielding us now!" Emperor Fanga said angrily.

Veneficus scowled, disturbed by the residual power of transgressions, even ones executed generations ago, to leave a film of resentment that clouds the ability see beyond those bygone wrongdoings. "It seems a bit unfair to let trespasses so far removed from our current times scatter their critical effects through distant generations and onto today."

Normally extremely critical of the Knights, General Lidenskap shook his head slightly as the voice of Tallcon vibrated in his mind—breaking apart his will to join Fanga in condemnation of the Knights of past and present. *I must follow Tallcon.*

"With my country besieged, I can offer *no* forgiveness. We fight for our very survival!" Fanga raged.

"I understand you are angry, Fanga," Veneficus said. "However, can't you see the Proliators have stepped into the role of the Knights? Even as we speak they expand their influence into every corner of Verngaurd."

Lidenskap bristled at the comparison, "The crucial difference between the Knights and the Proliate is that we serve a higher purpose, Tallcon, and are thus incorruptible. Plus, unlike the Knights, we encourage each nation within Verngaurd to maintain their military. The Knights sought to keep you weak and at their mercy.

"While the Knights have done some good, there can be little doubt they were prone to periods of momentous abuse. With no guiding force like Tallcon, they were easily, and frequently, led astray. I…"

Lidenskap paused, his eyes suddenly moving to stare distractedly forward, as the voice from his vision came flooding back, "Bring them into MY fold!" *As you wish Tallcon.*

Clearing his throat and focusing on his two companions once again he continued, "It has been revealed to me that the Knights need to come within our confederacy, under Tallcon. Therefore, I will convert them."

Emperor Fanga banged his scepter hard against the stone floor. "General, what has gotten into you? You have been the most vocal champion for annihilating the Knights! You have forced them to scurry into three measly holes they call castles. The lands they are supposed to protect are too vast for their dwindling numbers. They are all but finished and now that you have them on the run you want to pull back?"

General Lidenskap made a move to talk but was cut off by the continuing harangue of the boisterous Fanga.

"Do not forget, it is the people of Piscium that suffer most at the hands of the Dark Warriors. The Proliate policy of slowly taking over Knight Territory because of the Dark Warrior threat has been working perfectly. Now, with the Knights on their last leg and the end in sight, you want to convert them? Outrageous!"

"This is quite the change. What happened general?" Veneficus asked.

"Tallcon came to me with clear instructions," Lidenskap said calmly, with no hint of uncertainty angling off his words.

Emperor Fanga scoffed in disgust.

"When I was younger I physically touched the hallowed flame of Tallcon. I have no doubt, and follow Tallcon's will without hesitation. If he tells me to change my position on the Knights, I will do so and won't apologize to anyone!"

Veneficus smiled, "This path will certainly spare us of unnecessary bloodshed within Verngaurd and leave us better prepared for the Dark Warriors."

"Exactly!"

"What about High Commander Storlax?" Emperor Fanga demanded. "He has got to still be pushing for war with the Knights."

"Unfortunately, he is," Veneficus stated. "However, these are dangerous times, and if we misstep and rush into civil war, all of Verngaurd will fall to the Dark Warriors."

"What will you do if they do *not* convert?" Fanga asked.

"Tallcon wouldn't ask if it wasn't possible," Lidenskap replied. His smile belied his thoughts. *If they do not convert, we will resume our plan and obliterate them.*

Scroll 11: No Turning Back

"What's going on here?" General Lidenskap thundered.

As he approached, Friar Pallium, Veli Falciss, Veli Pingius, the Knights, and squires stood toe-to-toe with a dozen bristling Proliate guards outside the coliseum entrance. The early morning first sun highlighted the outrage on both sides.

"General? Good morning. Sir, the Knights insist they are supposed to practice now, but they're not on my schedule!" a Proliate guard said.

"Who's training now?"

"Our soldiers."

"They leave immediately and the Knights practice!" Lidenskap growled. Turning to Friar he calmly asked, "Ready?"

"We are," he said, grabbing the wincing Bellae, Gimelli, and Scelto-all three greatly regretting being in the blast radius of the general's invitation at the opening ceremony. "Thank you for your assistance. There seems to be a recurring mix-up with our scheduled training time."

"It won't happen again," Lidenskap said sincerely.

"Have fun at the ceremony! Sorry we can't join you!" Finn called out sarcastically.

Bellae turned to see his mocking smile. Crann neighed while Lontas waved warmly.

"Uhhh-brown-nosers-ugggh," Jumeaux mocked in a fake cough, but he opened his mouth too wide and the shrieking pain from his formerly struck jaw instantly made him regret it. *Jerk! Scelto can't take a joke!*

Bellae, Gimelli, and Scelto gawked at the pristine, whitewashed buildings of the Citadel as they walked.

"The university once stood right there," Friar reminisced sadly. "The library used to be where the temple is now."

Gimelli grimaced.

"What is it?" Bellae asked. "Sad the university is gone?"

"No, it's your rutabaga-head brother harassing me telepathically. His jaw hurts and he's complaining about Scelto's punch."

"I can't believe you girls are related to him," Scelto declared.

"You've mentioned that once or twice," Gimelli smiled. "But you shouldn't have hit him."

"The Great Temple in our wondrous Citadel is quite a marvel," Lidenskap said. "I hope that you young squires will appreciate the building for what it is, not what it was. Open yourself up to experience our life of service. Who knows, you might even be moved in your soul to consider Tallcon."

He paused to gauge each of their responses while silently praying, *Tallcon, open their hearts, especially Friar's.*

They moved out of the surrounding buildings into an extensive courtyard sprawling around the towering Great Temple like an emerald moat. Stone benches sat below groups of white and red flowering trees throughout the pristine plaza.

"The Great Temple!" Lidenskap announced proudly.

"It's unbelievable!" Scelto exclaimed. The other squires stared open-mouthed at the impressive building.

Massive columns lined the entire circumference. Between each pair of pillars immense red banners fluttered in the wind, making the silver outline of a phoenix appear to fly.

"They are the Red Guard or Sanctus Division of our army," Lidenskap said of the men standing as still as statues throughout the square. "They are responsible for guarding our temples."

"Are you in charge of the whole army?" Scelto asked in awe.

"Storlax is the overall commander. I am proud to say that I have recently been promoted to be leader of the red Sanctus. There is a separate commander for the silver or Ultor divisions."

"I have to admit, General Lidenskap, I'm impressed," Friar said.

"Yes!" Lidenskap replied with vigor. "We have done extensive remodeling…"

"No," Friar interrupted. "I was referring to your army. You have made massive changes."

"As with everything, it is Tallcon's will. We had the right ruler at the right time. King Udistus was brave enough to follow Tallcon's visions. The unfortunate events of the Dark War served as the final ingredient to make us an elite fighting force."

"You have a king?" Scelto asked.

"Not any longer. Our military rulers now serve the role of governorship."

Only when they neared the temple did the massive number of stairs required to get to the door became apparent. Neat rows of immaculate Red Guard warriors lined the path to the gates, each holding a red pennant with Tallcon emblazoned upon it.

At the top of the stairs they found themselves on a marble landing which led to a gigantic wooden gate embossed with ornate gold and silver figures. The gate was impressive, but also a bottleneck causing throngs of people to queue behind it.

"Everyone must check in at the front tables," a Proliate guard explained. "Once the group ahead of you is through the Tunnel Glanha, the doors will open, and you will be allowed to enter. Once in, you *cannot* turn back!"

Bellae was squeezed between Gimelli and Lidenskap. His cold armor felt good as the heat from the crowd grew. Time seemed to slow to a standstill as the pressure from people pushing from behind increased, while the impatience of those towards the front swelled.

Friar caught sight of a face moving quickly out and back from behind a column. *Is that... Tacet-Vand, the wizard who protected us from the Watchers?* He looked to the squires for confirmation, but they were too bored standing in line to notice.

Tacet-Vand's face popped out and gestured something before disappearing once again.

Did he just signal me to watch my back? Friar desperately scanned the crowd for him. Time crawled as they sluggishly inched forward, but the wizard did not reappear.

When they finally reached the check-in the shocked guard's jaw dropped, "General? You could have used the back entrance. I apologize..." he sputtered.

"It's fine, son. I have guests, so I had to use this entrance."

"Your group is next," the guard stated. "Remember children, once through the gate, there is no turning back."

"Why would we turn back?" Scelto wondered aloud.

"You must endure the storm before enjoying the rainbow, you must survive the nightmare before appreciating serenity."

"Uhm, Friar?" Gimelli questioned.

Before he could answer a loud wailing screech signaled the massive doors of the gate were opening.

The guard cackled, "It's time for your souls to be cleansed!"

Scroll 12: Cold/Terrifying vs. Warm/Serene

BOOM!

The massive gate shut behind them. They instantly felt transported to a different world, their eyes immersed in darkness and their bodies hurtled into the frigid Tunnel Glanha. Faint candles made feeble attempts to break the murkiness of the long hallway they found themselves within. The candles' orange glow cast long and peculiar shadows down the seemingly endless passageway, causing the bizarre heads carved in relief along the walls to bob a macabre dance.

The blood of Finn flows in this, Bellae thought, rubbing her Inion Medallion. *I can do this.*

"Shall we?" Lidenskap asked calmly.

Bellae grabbed Gimelli's arm as she, in turn, grabbed Scelto's hand.

Gimelli felt a bolt of excitement course through her body at his touch. She couldn't help flashing a giant smile despite the fact he seemed obliviously unmoved.

After a short distance the floor became uneven and each step resulted in an obnoxious crunch followed by a disgusting ooze.

Gimelli put her arm around the whimpering Bellae, "What are we walking on?"

"No questions, just engage yourselves in this experience," Lidenskap offered.

Left to their imaginations the substances on the floor mutated into crushed bones, intestines, bugs, dead creatures, and other terrifying objects.

Bellae began to shake from a mix of fright and the dropping temperature. After what seemed like a mile walking on the gory floor a deafening thumping noise, like thunder, startled them from overhead. Soon, a wailing and whirring sound erupted from within the walls themselves.

Crunch-ooze! from underfoot.

Boom, boom! from overhead.

Whiiiiiiiiiiiiiir! from the walls.

Wherever they turned, darkness prevailed, broken only by poorly lit islands of terrifying images of teeth, claws, horns, inhuman faces, and piercing eyes from carved figures. Scelto ran his hand down the furrowed brow of one of the sculpted beasts. His fingers accidently slid into its mouth and pushed down.

A click echoed through the hall, quickly followed by a gusting howl from the mouth of the statue. Startled, Scelto jumped backwards, pushing Gimelli into the beastly face on the opposite wall.

"Sorry! You okay?"

"Fine, thanks," Gimelli replied sweetly, despite quietly rubbing her sore back.

"You might want to move away…" Lidenskap began, just as another blasting screech pierced the air from the face Gimelli had fallen into.

Drowning in the sensory assault of this strange world they were submerged within, the squires huddled close.

Grym pushed his head up, *"This is lovely, just lovely. Could we ask who decorated? Maybe bring some of this charm and appealing ambience to Liberum?"* Bellae felt for his head, but the sarcastic mouse had already retreated to the safety and warmth of her pocket.

"Let's keep moving," Lidenskap suggested.

"How much longer do you think this is?" Gimelli whispered.

"No idea, I can't see the end of this horrific tunnel."

After what seemed like a long time, but was actually just a few moments, Lidenskap finally spoke the words they had been waiting for, "We have come to the end of Tunnel Glanha!"

Lidenskap stepped on a special stone and, after a click, torches burst into flames, lighting giant brass doors. A relief carving of a giant beast stretched across them. Its mouth opened so wide it appeared you could fall in and be swallowed. Massive teeth raged from under its curled lips. Gaping eyes peered with a crazed look. Sores and scars littered the sculpture.

Lidenskap stepped forward, depressing another tile on the floor, which was quickly followed by an additional click. The two massive brass doors creaked and moaned open by themselves, splitting the horrific face in half.

"How did these doors open?" Friar asked, examining them thoroughly.

"This is just the beginning of what you are about to experience. Beyond these doors are wonderful things!" Lidenskap said, walking through.

With bright light flooding in from the other room they squinted and stumbled forward. The beastly doors behind them closed with a crash. Finally escaping the howling, rumbling, and cold darkness of the Glanha tunnel, they were flushed with a sense of tranquility, warmth, and peace.

Instantly several young boys wearing red pointed hats and robes began cleaning the gunk off their boots.

Don't look down to see what you were walking on, Bellae told herself.

"These boys helping us are Novices, just starting their studies to become Magicians. Now we purify our hands," Lidenskap stated, handing them each a gold coin and walking towards a row of large metal cylinders.

The platinum cylinders were etched with an elaborate phoenix rising from flames. The bottom of the cylinder had a box with a slot on top and a spout below.

"General," a Novice said with a slight bow. Another Novice held a large bowl under the spouts.

Lidenskap put a coin in the slot and a dark red liquid poured out.

"Amazing," Friar said, as the general washed his hands in the crimson fluid.

The same Novice handed him a red towel to dry his hands. The others took their turn before Lidenskap motioned for them to follow him into a massive room where a dozen green robed teenage boys spread their hands out hospitably.

"Welcome General Lidenskap and guests," they said with a bow. "Please enjoy refreshments, and whenever Tallcon's spirit moves you, enter the celebration chamber."

"After being a Novice for five or more years they graduate to Apprentice and these green robes," Lidenskap said. "After a few more years they become an Adjutant. You will see them shortly wearing yellow hooded robes with blue stars. After six more years they can advance to Master Magician."

"I love the light and warmth," Bellae whispered.

"This is definitely better," Gimelli whispered back, gazing at the numerous torches and chandeliers throwing off radiant light. Women in white robes strummed on harps and various other string instruments creating a serene environment.

Several Adjutants came by with glasses of red liquid. As General Lidenskap grabbed one, Friar feverishly shook his head.

"Would you squires care for one?"

Heeding Friar's warning, they politely declined.

"Just as well, it takes some getting used to, but it has wonderful healing properties," he said, sipping the red concoction. Bellae's stomach lurched at the site of something floating in the liquid. She had to re-swallow her breakfast when she saw the general chewing, *What's with all the chewy liquids around here?*

"Are girls allowed to become Magicians?" Bellae asked.

"Of course!" the general answered with a burst of enthusiasm. "Are you interested?"

Friar could see Lidenskap mentally salivating after his prized squire as she mumbled something about not being sure. She looked so full of potential draped in the naive innocence of youth. The idea of her as an old woman seemed impossibly far away, yet, he only had to remember his own fleeting childhood to realize it happens in a blink of an eye. *Squire, your future is so uncertain,* he thought. If it is possible to mentally send hope and compassion to another, he did so to her at that moment.

Four silver statuary versions of Proliate warriors with red capes billowing behind moved of their own accord on a round platform within a large gazebo-like structure. Five hollow glass columns with large flames burning within held up a red circular dome over the figures.

"How do they move?" Scelto asked of the spinning Proliate statues.

"A bit of magic, a bit of ingenuity," he answered, smiling. Bellae was amazed at how relaxed Lidenskap appeared. She felt a similar sense of calm. After the terror of the Glanha tunnel, this room seemed like paradise. A lantern went off in her head, *They make you feel afraid and cold so you can feel warm, calm and appreciative of this place!*

Looking around the room she saw nobles, Magicians, Kings, and Emperors gilded in gold standing next to peasants with tattered clothes.

A loud horn abruptly sounded. "The Horns of Infula," Lidenskap said. "It begins."

Scroll 13: Independence or Independence?

They shuffled with the rest of the crowd through a series of doors flanked by Adjutants clad in yellow and smiles before entering a giant oval auditorium. Massive rows of seats descended to a central stage built out of solid marble. An elaborately decorated podium stood at one end of the platform while an intricately engraved silver phoenix sat at the other. Two red staircases descended on either side of the altar.

They followed Lidenskap through jostling crowds down to the front reserved seating where ornate wooden chairs were carved with various themes based on Proliate warriors, Magicians, and Tallcon.

"Look up!" Lidenskap smiled.

The squire's jaws dropped at the series of colossal arches curving to support the massive dome above them. Thousands of different Proliator battle scenes and images of Tallcon were painted, creating a canopy of art.

"Could this be the great reading room?" Friar asked.

"Once, long ago," Lidenskap stated apathetically, clearly indicating the building's history should be relegated to the past. "The ceremony will be led by special Master Magician clerics. I can't wait for you to hear the amazing Hassu-Palvella singers!"

"Nice crosier," Gimelli said to a thin, balding Magician sitting next to them.

"Thank you! Each one is unique and hand carved. Are you interested in becoming a Magician?"

"Maybe," Gimelli replied, more out of politeness than intent.

"The top holds the mindre, or lesser magical crystals we use to create magic."

"The staff and crystal are beautiful!"

"You're very kind, just don't touch the mindre crystal!" the thin Magician said anxiously. "It will burn you savagely."

A hefty, black haired magician leaned forward, "The mindre get their power from the Macht or power crystals."

"How often do you need to rejuvenate them?" Friar asked.

The Magicians laughed, "Right now, we can't! The Macht crystals were stolen some thousands of years ago from Veneficus."

"I can't imagine anyone stealing from him," Bellae shuddered, remembering her forceful introduction to his chamber floor.

"Deceit from someone trusted is the most unwelcome and powerful of surprises," the thin Magician answered.

A Novice came down the aisle with a leather strap around his neck supporting a rectangular wooden box. "Incense sticks!" he called out as the sweet smell of cinnamon filled their nostrils. "Would you sponsor some for the altar?"

"Of course," Lidenskap replied, handing him several gold coins.

"Thank you, sir," the boy replied gratefully, placing ten sticks into a golden box.

"Cinnamon is used in the ceremony to commemorate the miracle of Tallcon's regeneration. In his eternal life cycle he uses cinnamon, myrrh, spikenard, and twigs in his nest of rebirth," Lidenskap recalled happily.

Friar couldn't help staring at the inexplicably agreeable and cheery general. *I cannot yet imaging his ulterior motive.*

After the throngs of people had finally managed to find their seats, the arena was plunged into darkness and the Horns of Infula sounded once again. Magical flames burst forth along the cordoned off staircases highlighting several Novices in red robes carrying "T" shaped wooden poles. Each one supported two semitransparent, white banderoles sporting the image of a silver phoenix. The fluttering of the translucent cloth gave an ethereal quality to the figures.

Apprentices robed in green and vigorously shaking long metal rods covered in large bells followed the Novices. The squires could feel the vibration from the bells resonating deeply within their bodies.

Adjutants emerged in yellow robes carrying boxes of cinnamon, myrrh and spikenard. The Novices set the airy images of Tallcon in stands around the altar. The Adjutants placed the aromatic gifts into four ceremonial brass plates. The entire group then sprinted up the stairs to the left of the squires.

As they disappeared, four massive Proliate warriors emerged carrying what looked like a gigantic gemstone resting within a sedan chair upon their shoulders. The men unloaded the radiant stone and a dozen Master Magicians immediately descended upon the altar. Four lit the aromatic offertory fires on the brass plates. The other eight began to chant.

"That's our most sacred possession, the sanctus kivi—the residue from Tallcon's miraculous rebirth. It is unbreakable and, as you can see, glows of its own accord," Lidenskap whispered.

One of the Magicians made his way to the podium.

"Prast!" Friar whispered contemptuously.

"Isn't that the cleric who came to Liberum and told Friar to change his name?" Bellae whispered.

Gimelli nodded.

Fragrant, pungent smoke from the offertory plates tentacled its way into the crowd in looping spirals from the altar as he spoke. "I am Master Magician and cleric, Prast. Welcome to those joining us due to the Tournament of Flags. This is a great opportunity for any heretics to embrace the faith of Tallcon."

Subtle, Friar thought.

"Today I will talk about independence. Many of you likely take its definition for granted. I challenge you to throw off preconceived notions about the word and hear, not just listen, to my words.

"Independent is a common word we all use. Some even have it in their name." While he stopped short of mentioning Independent Knights, it was implied.

"True, unbridled, independence is being lifted up by the all-powerful Tallcon. He transports you from all cares, worries, and pain!"

Leaning forward, his knuckles blanched as he squeezed the podium and raised his voice, "If you believe in his power, his rebirth will become your rebirth! True independence! This life is but a brief test of worthiness, if you would just believe and follow…" he paused and raised his hand to the crowd which shouted, *"True independence!"*

"In giving yourself to Tallcon you gain eternal life and a peace!"

"True independence!"

"The Hassu-Palvella singers," Lidenskap breathed, as white robed figures surrounded the altar. A male and female singer in red robes made their way to the podium. Prast moved back, swallowed by the white robes of the singers. Strings and percussion instruments began to play soft and tranquil music.

The lady in red robes began to sing. The first part was higher pitched, full of dynamic energy and melodious. The second was slow, deliberate, and cast with a low pitch. The result was hypnotic.

"All I need is to…*submit to your will."*

"All I am called to do is…*submit to your will."*

"In times of darkness I…*submit to your will."*

The male singer took over the first part of singing and the white robed singers took up the chanted refrain.

"Here is my heart …*Tallcon give me courage!"*

"Here is my mind…*Tallcon give me truth!"*

"Here is my body…*Tallcon give me your strength!"*

"Here is my spirit…*Tallcon give me your will!"*

Prast returned to the podium, "You are the sword of Tallcon on earth. If you are weak, he is weak. If you are disciplined and battle ready, he is empowered, True Independence!"

Suddenly, the beat seemed to be coming from all around them. As the strength and tempo began to quicken it shook their bodies to their core. Armored Proliate warriors stood up and began chanting,

"Glory in battle is…FOREVER!"

The female chorus sang, *"Cleos!"*

"Honor in this life is…FOREVER!"

"Timay!"

"Tallcon is…ETERNAL!"

"Aionios!"

A warrior painted completely red stepped forward. His body shook with the kind of passion available only to youth with zealous faith, "You are *red fire*!"

The other Proliate warriors joined him for the last two words, *"Red fire!"*

The string instruments stopped, leaving only a deep pounding of the drums, *Boom! Boom!*

"You are unstoppable!"

"Unstoppable!"

Boom! Boom!

"You will spread Tallcon across Verngaurd!"

"Across Verngaurd!"

Boom! Boom!

"You will never lose!"

"Never lose!"

Boom! Boom!

Everyone in the temple rose to their feet. The squires followed but only the wide-eyed Scelto seemed moved by the ceremony.

Prast shouted, "Did you ask to be born?"

The Warriors responded, *"No, it was Tallcon's gift!"*

"Did you ask to be strong?"

"No, Tallcon graced me with his power!"

"Did you ask for consciousness?"

"No, Tallcon shared that gift with me freely!"

"Do you ask to die?"

"No, that is Tallcon's to bestow!"

"We all die. Today, tomorrow, a hundred years from now. What do you ask?"

"To live with honor, give glory and praise, and join Tallcon in rebirth!"

"Boy, talk about flare for the dramatic. These guys are certifiably..." Grym squeaked. Bellae quickly pushed his head below the top of her pocket and smiled awkwardly at the Magicians who seemed annoyed at the interruption and repulsed by a mouse in her clothing.

"It is Tallcon who breathed his life-giving fire into our pathetic, fleshly receptacle. It is a temporary home for our spirit. We must constantly battle to overcome the weak desires of the flesh to nurture the everlasting soul. Death is a mindless savage that destroys indiscriminately. All become equal in this final event, as it does not distinguish between the mighty and the weak."

A gasp ran through the crowd as a massive metal statue of Tallcon magically floated across the temple.

"Behold, Tallcon!" Prast yelled unnecessarily, as every eye in the temple was already transfixed. Many continued to chant or openly cry.

While Friar's face scrunched with skepticism, Scelto seemed completely mesmerized. Friar leaned towards Scelto, "Pomposity, when combined with large egos, is a toxic concoction that often blocks ones ability to truly see, to truly hear, and truly love."

Scelto nodded almost imperceptibly, obviously tuning out, or completely ignoring Friar's sagacity.

Suddenly, a burst of flame and smoke shot out from behind Tallcon's statue. The smoke cleared to reveal Veneficus. He shouted, "Suotuisa!" A bluish light arced over all those on the floor of the temple. "Leiskahdus nielaista," Veneficus bellowed.

The crowd cried out as an explosion of flames engulfed the entire altar and everyone standing on it.

"Peittya!" Veneficus yelled. The crystal on his crosier flickered a reddish-orange but nothing happened.

The Magician sitting next to the squires gasped, "His mindre is failing!"

Veneficus' eyes flushed with panic. Grasping the crosier with two hands, anger rushed over his face, and he yelled "Peittya!" This time, everyone on the floor of the temple disappeared.

Abruptly, there was a loud whooshing sound and the flames collapsed to one center point on the ground. From that spot a flaming image of Tallcon burst up towards the ceiling. As it collided with the decorative roof, a burst of sparks exploded and rained down on the crowd.

Chapter Four

Battle Begins

Scroll 1: Unexpected Boost to Hope

"Does Bellae *have* to see the Jaa trainer, Seestya, alone?"

"Yes, but don't worry, she can take care of herself," Friar said, looking closely at Scelto. "What did you think of the ceremony this morning?"

"Impressive. The temple was awesome!"

Friar paused, choosing his words carefully. "It's important you realize that passion, however genuine and intense, is not equivalent to truth."

Bellae came out from the Zenia barracks before Scelto could reply.

"Are you and your mice ready?"

Bellae nervously grabbed Friar's hand. "Now, we are."

"Good luck!" Scelto encouraged.

Friar anxiously paced outside the doors to the Jaa kotatu as the hours sludged forward, each passing moment increasing his concern about his young squire.

"How was it?" he requested apprehensively as Bellae finally emerged.

"Not bad."

"Any details?"

"They made me have Borb and Grym do a whole bunch of tricks. I can tell you, they weren't happy!"

"How many people were there?"

"There were ten trainers and a few mystics. Then they brought in some nice animals and asked me to talk to them. Then, things got weird—really, really weird!"

"What happened?"

"They asked me to talk to a whole bunch of strange stuff."

"Like?"

"Rocks, jars, and food! I told them I couldn't, but they insisted I try."

"That is quite peculiar! I am so sorry, but thank you for representing the Knights so well. By the way, was Princess Hamaza there?"

Bellae shook her head.

"Scelto will be pleased he did not miss her!"

Bellae nodded and giggled.

"Glad you two are having a good time, but you promised us food, lots of food, if we did tricks for those dimwitted halfwits!" Grym complained.

Bellae laughed at her angry friend.

"What in the world is going on with your mouse?"

"Hungry!" Bellae managed between laughs.

Seeing her simple, yet profound, joy allowed hope to seep through the cracks of his mental wall of fear and doubt about the future.

"Ah, let's go fix that. They should be rewarded for their service to the Knights. I think this is the first time in our long history that mice have served us, much less been honored!"

"Can we go say 'Hi' to Honey and Crann, first?" she asked.

"Not unless you want me to fall out of my skin from starvation," Grym squeaked.

Bellae laughed again, so irresistibly that Friar found himself joining in.

As long as the world has laughter, there's still hope!

Scroll 2: Whose Got What Spirit?

"Welcome Scelto, Sorea, Bellae, and Gimelli to the Jaa compound for your tour," Seestya said the next day.

"Blessings upon you!" Scelto said, with a slight bow to Princess Hamaza who was standing next to the Jaa trainer.

"Blessing upon you and your house," she replied, her eyes locked on Scelto. "How has your training been?"

Gimelli let out an audible huff but instantly regretted it.

"Very well, thank you," Scelto answered quickly.

"Hamaza!" a grating voice screeched from behind a set of double doors with two circular viewing ports.

Seestya and Hamaza rolled their eyes.

"Get back in here now!" the voice shrieked.

Gimelli paused under a pang of sympathy, realizing that even a princess has problems.

"My mother, Queen Antiopay," Hamaza said with a forced smile. "I have 'vital' business I must attend to. Therefore, I will leave you with Master Trainer Seestya."

"Nice to see you again, Bellae," Seestya declared after the princess left. "Thanks for yesterday."

"You're welcome."

Seestya motioned for them to follow him to the back of the large antechamber. The shirtless Seestya wore loose-fitting black pants. The tattoos on his back rippled as his muscular body moved with surprising grace. His head was shaven save for a single ponytail braided down the back. "Have your mice friends calmed down?"

"They're fine," she giggled. "But, they definitely did *not* want to come back!"

"I can understand that. Anyway, welcome again to the Queendom of Jaa's consulate or kotatu," Seestya said, pointing to a stone sculpture. "You can see from our Inuksuk statue and decor that we make it our home away from home."

"That statue looks like a person," Gimelli said of the two vertical stones with four horizontal stones resting on them. The top horizontal stone was the longest and looked like outstretched arms. The "head" was a small vertical stone on top.

"Good observation! Inuksuk serve many purposes in our culture. They symbolize the spirit of our people and serve as a conduit for our ancestors to make contact with us. They are also useful landmarks during winter white-outs."

"What are those creatures?" Bellae asked, pointing to a painting showing a brutal scene. There was a massive beast covered in white fur with a broad face like a bear's, but with a long snout complete with massive protruding fangs. It had a long bushy, wolf-like tail and razor sharp claws swiping at another fearsome looking creature covered in thick wool displaying equally long fangs. The wooly creatures' front legs ended in claws while its hind legs ended in hooves.

Figure 38: Fearsome creatures of the North, many call these beasts the wolf-bear. Known for their strength and savagery, they dominate the frozen tundra.

Scelto ignored the trainer as he caught a glance of Princess Hamaza arguing with her mother through the circular apertures of the doors. He stared at her beauty as Seestya continued.

"The big creature, a valkea osolobos, is attacking the torahammas, the fanged sheep of the north," he explained. "My people have tried, and failed, to domesticate those sheep for thousands of years. We have pastoralists who occasionally manage to get their wool and milk. The pay is amazing because their milk is a scarce delicacy, but it's dangerous...sometimes deadly work."

"Scelto!" Gimelli said as Seestya began walking away. "Come on."

"Huh? Oh," Scelto replied, blushing slightly.

"Were you listening?" she asked.

"Uh, yeah. It's called an Inuksuk or something?"

Shaking her head Gimelli and Scelto followed the others and Seestya down several hallways, eventually moving through a set of double doors into a room full of armor and weapons. "Our armor is made from tightly woven silk around innumerable small pieces of native Ko stones. This makes it lightweight but strong."

"Uhm, no offense to you, Sorea," Scelto muttered bashfully. "But why do only Jaa women fight?"

Seestya laughed heartily. "Have you ever seen a woman defend anything she holds dear?" Seeing that the guests were not satisfied, he continued.

"Men born in the north are produced *from* the tundra. We are connected to our land in ways you cannot fathom. The gods formed men from the sacred northern dirt, so they fight only grounded to our land, within our country. A few select Royal Guards are able to fight out of country, but only to protect the queen and princess. The women of Jaa, on the other hand, were made from the drifting boreal clouds, and can drift and fight wherever the wind takes them."

"It's just, you guys are...so big," Scelto added.

"When you slam your open palm down on the surface of water, it hurts and creates a large splash. If you focus the power of your hand by turning it perpendicular it slices through the water without pain or much splash. Sometimes throwing your weight around as the biggest or strongest isn't an advantage. Adapting strategy, using agility and speed, that's our way."

"What about your healers?" Sorea asked. "I hear they play an important role in your culture."

"Our healers are mystics who concentrate on what we consider the most important elements of our earthly existence, the mind and spirit. The ground reclaims your flesh and bones, but your mind and spirit live on forever."

"I heard your warrior initiations are ferocious," Sorea stated.

"True. Initiates tread water in a freezing lake as an offering to the water spirits. If they are virtuous they survive. If deemed unworthy by the water spirits, they die."

"Your warriors can die during initiation?"

"We lose as many as are needed to prove our worth. It is a sacrifice we are delighted to make so that our cold water will be stocked with fish."

They could hear the clanging of metal on metal and grunts of exertions while following him through another set of doors. The room was full of Jaa's female warriors working with different trainers. All were covered in sweat and breathing hard.

After watching the training for several moments Seestya became restless, continually looking off to one of the doorways.

"Everything okay?"

"Unfortunately, they want you to meet *him*."

"Him, who?"

Without answering Sorea, he took off with long strides forcing the others to jog to keep up. After winding through several small corridors they entered a substantial, but congested, room teeming with containers of every size and shape. Each one seemed to be filled with unusual looking substances, some bubbled over, while others frothed. A lone man wearing a white robe stood on a colossal ladder so tall, his head brushed the towering ceiling. Although the room was silent he bobbed and bounced as if a melodious tune was prancing within his balding head.

His gyrations stopped and, mumbling to himself, he began inching down the rickety ladder. At the bottom he finally realized he had company and started vigorously clapping. "Guests? Visitors? How gloriously, wonderful, and sublime!"

Time had whitened the remaining hair on his head and beard, and furrowed his skin, but not dulled the dancing sparkle in his dark eyes. His broad face wore a perpetual smile, coiling with a hidden energy that seemed to make his many wrinkles less preeminent, if not less noticeable. Tattoos sat prominently on all exposed areas of his dark skin.

"Let's start with a joke, shall we? How many Proliators does it take to light a torch?"

"Unfortunately, we don't have time for jokes. Let me intro…" Seestya began.

"Be quiet you mountainous gruff!" the old man interrupted. "You trainers wouldn't be so irritable if you put on a shirt and stopped shaving your head—freezes your sense of humor! Now, how many Proliators does it take to light a torch?"

"I'm not sure?" Gimelli answered tentatively.

Come now, come now," he said, bouncing up and down expectantly. "Fine, it takes as many as are ordered to do so! Get it? They won't do anything without an order!"

"Funny," Gimelli offered kindly.

"You know, laughing is the traditional way to show you think something is funny. Let's try another. How many sea-loving Piscinians does it take to light a torch?" He paused as the squires looked questioningly at each other.

"Twenty! One to light the torch and the other nineteen to sing, dance, and stumble around with their ale bragging about how they could have done it better because of all the salt in their veins!"

When he stopped laughing he continued, "How many Magicians does it take to light a torch?" This time he didn't wait for an answer, "One hundred! One to say the incantation and ninety-nine to complain and boast how their crosier would have cast a brighter flame!"

"Enough 'jokes!' This is Ystinen, our resident mystic and healer turned scientist, and, most regrettably, wannabe jester. Knight Sorea, and squires Scelto, Gimelli and Bellae are here learning about Jaa."

Ystinen suddenly looked concerned and began looking around several of the crowded benches frantically.

"Are you okay, Ystinen?" Seestya asked.

"I had a scroll I wanted to show you, but, on second thought, I better not. It was *tear*able!" Ystinen laughed hysterically while the squires and Sorea glanced questionably at their trainer guide.

Seestya shook his head.

"Get it? Tearable," at this he made a twisting motion with his hands as if tearing a scroll, "versus terrible as in bad?" Seestya seemed genuinely disappointed at their failure to laugh. "Well, apparently I have a group of grim tragedians in front of me."

"Why were you up on the ladder?" Bellae asked, desperate to change the subject.

"To get a different perspective, of course. Looking at a problem from a new angle can help you see a previously hidden answer."

"Or break your neck," Seestya mumbled.

"Do you know each of you have a spirit guide?"

The squires and Sorea shook their heads.

"Well, if you want to learn about Jaa culture, let me do a spirit reading on each of you."

"Actually, I was just about to take our guests to..."

"Nonsense. You first young man." His expression becoming intense while motioning for Scelto to come forward, "Close your eyes and relax."

With surprising speed the old man grabbed a pouch out of a hidden pocket and withdrew a white powder. After chanting a few sentences he blew the dust directly into Scelto's face.

"Hey!" Scelto coughed.

"Stay still boy!" Ystinen ordered, before continuing chanting. Scelto's body and expression suddenly froze, as if magically solidified.

The girls screamed as a ghostly, blue saber-toothed cat rose out of the immobile Scelto.

The spectral beast roared loud and long before dissolving into tiny glistening flecks that drifted down, finally being reabsorbed into Scelto's body.

Ystinen clapped and smiled, "Wonderful!" He then began chanting again until Scelto started moving.

Figure 39: Scelto is having his spirit guide revealed by the unique mystic man of Jaa, Ystinen, as Master Trainer Seestya, Bellae, Gimelli, and Sorea watch.

"What…?" Scelto sputtered.

Ystinen placed his index finger over the squire's mouth. "You, young man have the heart of your spirit guide, a saber-toothed Tilkeri. You're a natural warrior and a born leader. You will fight and win many battles over your extensive life. Okay, done. Next!"

Scelto stumbled over to the others, "I remember coughing and then…nothing. What happened?"

"No idea, actually," Gimelli whispered.

"Since you feel the need to share," he pointed to Gimelli. "You're up."

He once again chanted, blew the powder into her face and she became motionless. An ethereal and yellow flaming orb rose from her. Two sparkling wings shot out from the orb and began beating furiously. The winged sun rose to the ceiling before exploding into thousands of glittering stars that drifted down until dissolving back into her.

Gimelli took a deep breath as Ystinen spoke, "You are the rarest of gifts to the world—warmth of a sun and wings of optimism! Where you tread, hope and light will follow."

"The suns are swimming across the sky, informing us time is moving forward. Therefore, we, regrettably, should move on," Seestya pleaded.

Without warning, the mystic began to mumble to himself, something about the suns. "Yes! Time. Of course we have it! As long as you can say there isn't, or there is, there is indeed always time left in your life for a quick experiment!"

"We truly do not have time for…" Seestya began, interrupted by Ystinen.

"Ah-ah-ah! You are right, we don't have time to ignore the chance to learn and expand our minds! Well said trainer Seestya!"

Grunting, Seestya shook his head, resigning himself to the mystic's antics.

Ystinen's eyes sparkled with excitement as he pushed on the squires shoulders, "Down on the floor youngsters. That's the way, down you go! Lay on your backs…perfect! Not you Seestya, you old gruff. Go put on a cloak and you might not be so stressed and grumpy. Anyway, just stand back and keep quiet. I want *the children's* opinions, whose thoughts are not yet jaded by learned negativity, still awash in creativity and wonder!"

"What of Sorea?" Gimelli asked.

"That's okay, squire!" Sorea said quickly, grateful to be left out of whatever was coming. "I'll just hang back and observe."

The aged man shuffle-sprinted to the back of the room and quickly lit two candles. Setting one of them down he moved back up the ladder with surprising speed. He balanced the candle precariously on the top rung before descending.

Grabbing the candle he left at the bottom he hastened to stand over the three squires. "Now youngsters, tell me what you see," he asked, bringing the candle within a quarter of an inch of their faces. "Huh? Come now, come now," he said bouncing up and down with energy and mumbling something about using their intelligence.

"A candle," Scelto answered. "A very close candle," he added as they laughed more out of a disquieted anxiety than humor.

Ystinen seemed annoyed that they hadn't guessed what he was thinking. "What else. Move beyond the obvious and tell me more about it."

"It's hot?" Gimelli ventured, nervously eyeing the wavering hot wax threatening to trickle on her face.

"Yes! Yes, it is hot. Outstanding," the mystic said.

Sorea muttered, "Hot when you have some crazy guy shove a candle right in your face."

Seestya nodded his head at the Knight's comment and rolled his eyes, "Try living with this crazy mystic!"

"Come, come. What else?" Ystinen prodded, giving the two adults a disparaging glare.

"It's really close," Bellae said, giggling.

"Really, really close," Gimelli added, laughing.

"Yes, yes! So move beyond that, is it bright, dim, or dark?" he asked.

"Very bright right in front of your face," Gimelli added.

"Ah, correct. Now, look. Look there. Go on, look, look!" he said, finally removing the teetering candle and standing to the side while passionately pointing to the candle on top of the ladder near the ceiling.

"Might as well join you," he said, creaking his way down to the floor in front of the squire's feet. "Come, time is wasting. It is a beautiful day, and I have lots of discoveries to make. Look at that candle near the ceiling and tell me what you see!"

"It's far away," Bellae offered, between gusts of laughter.

"Exactly…and?" he challenged, resting his arms behind his head just below their feet.

"We can't feel any heat when it's so far away," Scelto stated.

"Yes. Good boy, good. Now take it further, think. Do these two examples remind you of anything?" the man asked. He groaned as he stood up to a chorus of complaining joints. His body had yielded too much to age to move with same rhythm as his spry mind.

"Think about what we have learned. The closer source had bright light and gave off warmth. The farther source did not give off much light and no warmth. What does it remind you of?"

He slowly paced back and forth, willing them to understand. After what seemed like forever to the mystic, but was only a brief moment he continued, "Think about what this situation reminds you of! Think outside and the sky!"

Gimelli sat up.

"Yes, girl, do you have it? Imagine there were three close candles!" he said.

Gimelli smiled, "Our three suns and the stars!"

"Yes!" the mystic cheered. "Doesn't the close-up candle remind you of one of our suns? Big, easy to see, and gives off heat. Isn't the far away just like a star, being small and no heat?" he asked, raising his arms expectantly.

"Yes, yes. Fascinating," Sorea stated, guessing what he was hoping for.

"Well, yes. Fascinating is the perfect word for such a wonderful discovery," he said clapping. "Therefore, our 'stars' are simply other suns, just extremely far away! There you have it, understanding our world using intellect! Something to think on as crotchety Seestya here drags you away. I can see the impatience growing and bloating inside him like grain left in water. You overgrown spoilsport!"

Seestya gently lifted Bellae and Gimelli up with obvious power. Scelto scrambled up on his own accord.

"Let's continue our tour," Seestya encouraged hopefully.

"Wait, wait, wait! I haven't finished with the spirit readings, neeeeext!"

Seestya grunted in displeasure.

"Relax, this is the last thing!" the mystic said cheerfully.

"Then we can go?" Seestya pleaded.

"Of course!" the mystic replied.

Sorea gave Bellae a gentle nudge. "Okay, kiddo, show us what you've got."

"Ah, the youngest," Ystinen said, as the old man blew the white dust directly into Bellae's face after chanting a few sentences.

"She's not moving, but nothing's happening," Scelto observed.

Ystinen's face contorted into an agonizing expression before he too seemed to solidify.

"They're both frozen! Is that supposed to happen?" Sorea asked after a few uncomfortable moments.

"Are they breathing?" Gimelli wondered anxiously. "Have you seen this before?"

"No, I've never seen Ystinen freeze, or no spirit come out of the person before. In faaaaaaaacccccccttttt…" Seestya's speech ebbed as his body, and time itself, slowed.

Panic exploded in Gimelli's mind as she tried to look back to her sister, but could barely move as everything and everyone seemed stuck in painfully slow motion.

Without warning time seemed to speed up again as an explosion of color blasted out of Bellae. Containers and supplies were thrown aside as Ystinen hurtled backwards. His fragile body slammed into the wall before crumpling to the floor. The large ladder fell, knocking down even more containers as it crashed to the ground. Luckily the candle on top went out.

With the room still teeming in a fog of brilliant color, Gimelli rushed to her motionless sister, "Bellae! Please answer me!"

A loud twang sounded, quickly followed by the colors that had spread across the room rushing back to surround, but not be reabsorbed by, Bellae. With a thunderous clap the cloud of color exploded out again. Every unbroken container in the room shattered, the walls bowed out and the door blew off its hinges as everyone, but Bellae, was thrown to the floor. The colors rushed back, and into, Bellae.

Slowly, dust and debris settled as those on the ground moaned and whimpered.

"Anyone hurt?" Seestya asked, cautiously standing.

"I don't think so. What just happened?" Sorea asked.

"Not sure. Ystinen? Ystinen, what happened?"

Bellae started moving and Gimelli jumped up, enveloping her within a relieved hug.

"What in the world?" Bellae asked of the destruction.

"Don't worry about it, are you okay?"

Bellae nodded.

Gradually Scelto and Sorea rose and made their way across the rubble to the old man.

"You injured, mystic?"

"Never seen…like that. What is she?" Ystinen moaned. "Red, orange, yellow, green, blue, indigo, and violet. So much uncertainty, so much pain, so brief…is that the future? Can it be changed?"

"What are you talking about?" Sorea asked anxiously.

"She's…something different," Ystinen whispered.

Gimelli bristled. "What does that mean?" she asked defensively, embracing Bellae tightly.

"What it means," Ystinen stated, "is that even a wise old mystic sometimes needs to know when the universe is telling him to walk away and let the future become the present, and hope that someday, someone will be around to know our present, as the past."

"Okay, seriously, what just happened, and what is that gibberish supposed to mean?" Sorea asked angrily.

"Absolutely, no clue! I have no idea what is going on!" Seestya yelled.

"I need rest—headache," Ystinen said. "Leave."

"Not without some answers!" Sorea demanded.

"Now!" he shouted with surprising force. "Leave now!"

"Let's go," Seestya ordered. "When he gets ruminative like this, he won't be telling us anything else."

"Shouldn't we make sure he's okay?" Gimelli asked as they made their way through the open doorway, carefully walking over the broken door.

"Definitely not! That old man blows himself up at least once a week with his experiments."

They began walking down a hallway as a dozen Jaa warriors rushed towards them.

"You okay?" one of them asked.

"Yes, just Ystinen again." Seestya answered.

Several of the warriors rolled their eyes while moving to the broken door and mumbling, "Not another explosion!"

"Is someone going to tell us what happened back there?" Sorea asked. "Or what he meant about Bellae?"

"Honestly, I don't think even Ystinen knows. I have never heard of anything like this occurring before."

Seestya led them through a series of back hallways, finishing up at the entrance. He pulled on a long yellow cord and distant bells could be heard ringing.

He stood in stony silence until a door opened and Princess Hamaza entered.

"Did you have a good time?" she asked graciously.

"Yes, although something unusual..." Gimelli started.

"They learned a little about our culture, and enjoyed our hospitality," Seestya interrupted.

"I am delighted to hear it. I will see you at the Tournament tomorrow," she said, letting her gaze linger on Scelto.

Profoundly perplexed and deeply unsatisfied by what happened with the mystic, the three squires and Sorea left. Bellae walked self-consciously with her head down, aware of the intermittent questioning glances from the others. It was not a new sensation, she had absorbed thousands of interrogating gazes around her ability to talk with animals.

However, it did not make the scrutiny any less unpleasant.

Scroll 3: Thorn of Consciousness

"What's wrong with Gimelli?" Friar asked Sorea when they returned from the Jaa consulate.

"It was an odd visit and we met an especially unusual mystic who gave the squires spirit readings. Bellae's was...bizarre to say the least."

Friar tried to hide the concern itching to spread across his face at the mention of Bellae. "Is she okay?"

"Bellae is fine. Although, as I think about it, the thing that probably bothers Gimelli the most is that we ran into Princess Hamaza," Sorea said, raising her eyebrows.

"I did not see her attraction to Scelto coming."

"I don't think anyone did."

"Gimelli, with me," Friar said quietly. He wanted to find out more about what happened to Bellae as much as cheer up the young squire. As the two walked through the bustling streets of the Zenia, Gimelli recounted the unusual events with Bellae and Ystinen during the spirit readings.

Friar simply nodded.

"You don't seem surprised or angry!"

"Your sister speaks with animals, not much surprises me about her," Friar said, however, he was also thinking about her potential role as the Chosen One. He was becoming more convinced it must be her, not Jumeaux. *How could Veneficus be wrong though?*

Gimelli was unnerved and could tell Friar was hiding something, but said nothing.

He finally turned down a side street filled with peddlers packing up their carts for the day. After weaving though the merchandise and produce that littered the path, they approached an iron gate with vines desperately clutching its length.

"The Knights will never be called shrewd in their negotiations with the Proliate when giving up Cumhacht, but the Proliate agreed to maintain a few gardens, and let us keep this!" Friar said, producing a key and brushing back a frisky vine slinking over the rusty keyhole.

That's a loose definition of maintain, Gimelli thought, glaring at the overgrowth.

The gate protested with a loud screech, straining its rusting parts and pulling against the extending vines wrapped around its feet. As the vines stretched thinner their leafy arms waved increasingly hopeless encouragement for the plant to hold together.

SNAP!

The two stepped over the vines' broken body slumping dejectedly on the stone steps.

"This courtyard is beautiful," Gimelli gushed of dwarf trees and flowers of every shape, color, and style. Inside the white walled enclosure it felt secluded and protected from the bustling world and its swirling troubles.

Gimelli inhaled deeply, enjoying the flood of fragrance permeating the garden. "The smells are amazing!"

Friar smirked.

Turning her head to the side Gimelli raised her eyebrows questioningly.

"When I was little we joked that flowery fragrances are earth-bred, pollen-wed, and sun-fed."

The squire smiled, but was enjoying the beautiful aroma too much to laugh.

"Not much of joke, but the point is that the end result, for flowers or people, takes teamwork. The Knight family, your team, is behind you and your sister, whatever may come."

"Thank you."

"I hated the allegations thrown at my father. No matter what he did, or didn't do, he was still my dad. This was my refuge growing up. The soulful colors of a garden can wash away the darkest gloom!"

After a moment reliving the old memories he continued, "When you're young time passes slowly, and you feel as if you'll never get to adulthood. Somewhere along the way the days became dizzyingly long and complicated, but the years begin to melt away with alarming speed. Then, you wake up old, with more memories to chew on than days to make more."

Gimelli nodded, enjoying the calm that permeated the garden.

"Ah!" Friar said, rushing over to a symphony of colored roses dancing in the quickening breeze, which circulated their distinctive scent.

"The rose is wonderful, yet it does have thorns to prick your skin, and, if you pluck it from the earth and place it in a vase, it will die."

Gimelli stared at Friar, unsure of exactly what he was getting at.

"People, like flowers, have metaphorical thorns, or failings. This rose could be likened to Princess Hamaza…" he hesitated as Gimelli laughed.

"So you're saying Princess Hamaza is a beautiful flower with thorns that could hurt Scelto? Plus, she won't last, especially if you pluck her out of the ground?"

Gimelli and Friar laughed deeply.

"Cut me some slack, I came up with this on the spot. Anyway, I was trying to say that some live only by their beauty, some by defensive 'thorns,' and some by both. You have the rare gift of unlimited joy, so don't become discouraged or let your sunshine be weakened because of what someone else thinks or does."

Gimelli laughed even harder.

"What? Horrible analogy?"

Gimelli stared dubiously at Friar while still laughing.

"Honesty is okay."

"Yes!"

"I swear, here and now, no more flower analogies, ever!" Friar declared.

"I have to agree," a voice startled. "I am a firm believer in the evils of plant-life analogies."

They turned to see the tall figure of Veneficus standing behind them, one hand leaning against his crosier, the other gently stroking his grey goatee.

"Veneficus! What a pleasant surprise," Friar said. "Will you sit?"

"Ah. I think we all should, long day and all that. Well, more accurately, short on time, long on problems," he said, chuckling as the three sat down. "I should thank you."

"Really, why?"

"I loved the gardens of Cumhacht. If you Knights had not insisted they keep a few, this place would be a giant statue of Tallcon! I come here now and again for a brief taste of peace."

"Glad I could help. I didn't know you had a key."

Veneficus raised his eyebrows expectantly and nodded towards his crosier.

"Oh, of course."

"It helps when you can appear wherever you wish. Anyway, the conversation around here is a little one-dimensional these days. It's all, Tallcon this, Tallcon that, and Tallcon the other thing. It's not nearly as stimulating without you Knights, the University, and the library." Veneficus sighed and leaned forward on his crosier. "When I think of Verngaurd I feel like I am staring at a giant hourglass of destruction."

"What do you mean?"

"Unless we can stop the sands of war and disconnection which are now pouring through the neck of a civil-war hourglass, I fear Verngaurd will be plunged into darkness."

Friar and Gimelli silently considered his words.

"We have to find a way to turn the hourglass over, and reset the balance of Verngaurd. That starts with a great Tournament," Veneficus said, his face suddenly souring.

"What's wrong?"

"I thought I saw someone today who could destroy our goals for peace, Tacet-Vand."

Friar's eyes widened in surprise before his face fell, "I have something to tell you. We met him near Kippe."

Veneficus smiled, "I already knew, but assumed you had your reasons for not telling me. Once, an eternity ago, Tacet-Vand and I were very close."

"What happened?"

"We strongly disagreed on how to use magic for the world. He did not want me to use it to protect and guard the world. I don't trust him, and I would encourage you to be skeptical of his motives."

Friar paused, taken aback by a description of the wizened wizard that seemed at sharp odds with his opinion and experience. "He did save us from the Watchers."

"Perhaps to throw you off of his true motives? I have fallen victim to his deception in the past." *He incited those disloyal and upstart Ainmhi Caint!* "The pain of his betrayal still stings. Sometimes what is presented as a favor will, in the future, be turned into a debt."

Friar shook his head. "Can't anything be simple?"

"A precious few things in this world are absolutely simple, and they should be treasured absolutely," Veneficus said. "I feel like I have experienced and studied enough for a hundred years, yet the answers are thousands of years down the line. Solutions seem to move forward, just out of reach, always producing more questions."

"It does seem like the more we learn the more questions that arise," Friar stated.

Veneficus nodded approvingly.

"That said, even though it is true we can never completely scale the giant mountain of enlightenment, that does not mean we shouldn't try, shouldn't keep fighting, striving to learn more, to discover more. The heights of knowledge that we climb do benefit those that come after us as we ascend a little higher," Friar said.

Veneficus' expression turned increasingly harsh as Friar was speaking. However, his face softened as he abruptly used magic to cut a rose stem at its base. Surrounded in a gentle blue light, it tenderly floated towards him. He paused, staring at the barbed stalk. "Although each life has the potential for beauty, we carry too many thorns, just like this plant. Thorns of regret for decisions made and chances lost. Barbs of sadness at those who have betrayed us, or, pricking deeper, those we have lost. Perhaps the one that pierces deepest is the thorn of consciousness for those that are awake to the world it is a painful flower to grasp.

"The soul of the world is only manifest in a precious few. It is those burdened with such encumbrance that must keep our world on the right track. Humans get reliably stuck in their own perspective, blinding them to the reality of the universe."

Feeling overwhelmed at his words, Friar and Gimelli remained quiet. *Aren't you human?* Friar thought, but dared not ask.

After a long pause the Magician continued, "Na Cearcaill is once again barreling down on us."

"Na Cearcaill has been mentioned to us before. What exactly is it?" Friar asked.

A look passed over Veneficus' eyes. Was it anger? Was it sorrow? Regret? Friar wasn't sure.

"It is an endless cycle that has washed over Verngaurd countless times," Veneficus finally stated.

"Can it be stopped?" Friar asked.

Veneficus stood up, shaking his head, "I honestly don't know. Well, that's my breath of serenity, back to work."

"Good night," Friar said.

Veneficus chanted until his form became swallowed by blinding light, disappearing.

Friar's mind exploded with questions. *Has Veneficus lived through, survived, Na Cearcaill before? How old is he? What exactly does "endless cycle" mean? What will happen to us during this Na Cearcaill and why did he not want to talk about it?*

Turning to see Gimelli staring at him Friar forced a smile, "Let's keep this talk between us."

"Okay. In spite of the plant-as-a-princess analogy fiasco, I do appreciate your support and this time in the garden."

"I apologize for my imprudent words, and I appreciate yours. Although, if you were paying attention, Veneficus himself *did* use that rose, i.e. a plant, to make an analogy! Maybe, I *was* on the right track."

Gimelli laughed, "Maybe, but, either way, I will absolutely never look at flowers the same way."

Scroll 4: Anticipation

Later that night the flames of the candles surrounding Friar's papers shivered above small nubbins of wax. He rubbed his tired eyes before refocusing on the list of events for the next three days just as a knock on the door startled him.

"Come in."

"Hello, Friar," Ritari stated, looking a mix of exhaustion and exhilaration.

"Trouble sleeping?"

"You're one to talk!"

"Fair enough. How're the Knights doing?"

"Let's just say if Luchar keeps sharpening his battle axe it's going to be see-through!" Ritari laughed, taking a seat across from Friar. "The others are nervous, but at least they're resting."

"Since I'm awake, it's hard for me to chastise them. Sometimes the anticipation is heavier to bear than the actual event."

"Are you worried?"

"Actually, I'm feeling optimistic. Our talent is well distributed throughout the Tournament. I will oversee the Knights from Castle Liberum and the two Veli will do the same for theirs.

"Here's the schedule. I have written the names of our competitors. I only wrote down the Knights from the other castles if we had no one competing in that event."

Ritari read:

Order of Events
Tournament of Flags
Citadel Coliseum

Day One:

I. Opening Observance: Presided over by Veneficus: *Everyone*

II. Races-sprints: *Sorea, Finn, and Lovag*

54 yards; 109 yards; 218 yards; 436 yards

III. Archery:

-Skill: *Arquero, Finn, and Sorea*

-Distance: *Lovag and Arquero*

IV. Combat:

-One-on-one:

-Sword: *Ritari*

-Open (any weapon): *Luchar, Sorea, and Finn*

-Hand to hand (no weapon): *Luchar and Ritari*

-Equestrian (held at stables): *Lovag and Arquero*

Day Two:

I. Mechanicians:

A. -Projectiles/siege engines:

-Distance: *Sorea and Finn*

-Destructive force: *Sorea and Finn*

B. -Sappers: *Taiheart and Toil Shaor*

II. Squad battles: *Taiheart and Toil Shaor*

III. Dragon Battles: *Pantteri Squad*

IV. Strength Tests: *Ritari and Luchar*

Day Three

I. Races-Distance run: *Finn, Sorea, and Arquero*

II. Weapons demonstrations/skill: *Lovag, Sorea, Finn, Ritari, and Arquero*

III. Mystery weapon (participants given weapons to fight with):

-Individual: *Luchar and Sorea*

-Group: *Knights from Taiheart*

IV. Awards and Closing Ceremony: *Everyone*

Ritari flipped it back, "Looks good. I wish there were more combat events for Luchar. The busier he is, the safer it is for the rest of us!"

"Agreed! Since you're here, I need to tell you about a letter I received from Storlax and the League of Magicians demanding a total ban on prestidigitation. They say this "false magic" is a corrupting influence that weakens Verngaurd. They implied the White Wizard developed it for his Dark Warriors, totally ignoring the fact their allies, the Southern Dwarves, are its creators and main users."

Ritari scoffed. "They fear it because, with the Rebelde Plains using it, their lackeys, the Southern Dwarves, don't completely control it. If it comes to war, we will slam prestidigitation down their throats on our way to running them over!"

Friar laughed. "Exactly what I feared. I thought you might ride the fence on this issue."

"Are you going to send a reply?"

"No good could come from it. I'm not worried about the letter, but I *am* anxious about the Dragon Battle. You?"

Ritari laughed, "Only a fool picks a fight with a forty-five foot fire-breathing dragon. On the other hand, part of me is excited, and we are ready for a fight."

Friar sighed, "There's a reason the Knights eventually banned this event. It's bad for all involved. It perverts the relationship between the Dwarves and dragons. I think the Proliate brought it back simply to see dragons injured or killed, and to spite the Northern Dwarves."

"It does seem that way."

"I am surprised the Northern Dwarves allowed it to resurface," Friar said, his face scrunched up in anxiety.

"Me too. I wish we would have thought to ask them about it when we were in their territory," Ritari replied.

Friar nodded until a devious smile spread across his face, "What about you and your buddy?"

"My buddy?"

"Your chum from Ager, Campesino," Friar said, trying to act innocent.

Ritari scoffed, "Either that dunderhead's leather pants are chafing his privates, or he has something seriously inflexible stuck where it shouldn't be."

At breakfast the next day few of the sleep-deprived Knights managed to eat. Most had to be content calming the butterflies churning in their otherwise empty stomachs.

Bellae pushed her food around, resisting the temptation to pat her empty pockets, *I can't believe Friar made me leave my two friends behind.*

"Knights!" the young voice of Sumar cheeped. The boy they met at the opening ceremonies from Piscium hobbled towards them. His disheveled hair, gaunt and dark complexion made him easily recognizable.

"Sorry to interrupt your breakfast, but he wanted to say hi," the boy's father said.

"Any relative of Martello is always welcome," Friar said kindly.

"See, Papa, I told you they would remember me," Sumar gushed. His body looked sicklier, the bluish discoloration around his mouth darker, and his skin tauter.

"He didn't sleep very well," his father said, seeing them stare at his son's frailty. "Come, Sumar. The Knights need to get ready."

"I'll be cheering for you," the boy said weakly.

"We'll look for you in the stands. You be ready, we may need you out there big guy," Friar said.

The boy's eyes sparkled with excitement while his father's narrowed in deep appreciation.

Bellae thought she saw the hint of tears in Luchar's eyes before he quickly put on his helmet.

"What are you staring at, squire? It's dusty in here," he growled. "Let's go hit someone…really, really hard!"

Scroll 5: And So, it Begins-Sprint

"On behalf of the Magical League and the Proliators, welcome to the Opening Observance!" Veneficus boomed, floating in the center of the arena. "Seeing the vibrant rainbow of colors that is Verngaurd's many countries coming together is more beautiful than the Storten Flower Fields!

"This is the last time we will all gather until the closing ceremonies. Let us remember this competition is a sign of friendship and unity. Do your best and good luck!"

Gripping his axe longingly, Luchar scoffed at the mention of friendship and unity.

Magicians and Proliate flooded the arena floor, "If you are a registered competitor for the foot races, report to us. Everyone else, go to your waiting area. Only one assistant per competitor and the head of each country may stay."

Friar took out his list of events. "Okay. I need Sorea, Finn, Lovag, and their squires!" he shouted. "Everyone else from Castle Liberum, to the holding area!"

"Luckily, I recently took up needlework so I'll have something to do while rotting in our hole!" Luchar bellowed.

"The Proliate will run this like a military drill," Friar told Finn, Sorea, Lovag, Bellae, Gimelli, and Lontas. "You must be ready and vigilant. These sprints will be happening one right after the other. They will have four to six heats for each race before the final."

"That's the line-up. Take it or leave it," the Magician in charge of sprints said after handing the copy back to Friar.

"Having all seven Knights racing against each other in the first heat? You have got to be kidding me!"

"It's a mere coincidence."

"Please! You're saying it's chance that the first heat has only Knights except for one Proliator, Velox? Oh, and by the way, Velox is widely regarded as the fastest person in all of Verngaurd!"

The Magician rolled his eyes and walked away.

"This is a scam and you bloody know it!" Friar screamed, his words bouncing deafly off the back of the Magician's blue robes.

"It's an obvious attempt to get the Knights out early," an Elf of Creber stated.

Friar nodded gratefully to the sympathetic Elf.

A short time later all three Knights from Liberum, and two each from Taiheart and Toil Shaor, lined up at the starting line next to Proliate speedster, Velox. The Magician who had just been "talking" with Friar cast a spell to protect against an unfair start. A wall of green appeared along the length of the starting line.

"If you start early, this wall will spark red and shock you!" he declared with a little too much pleasure. "The blue wall at the finish line will record the top two finishers."

Falciss shook his head angrily, glaring at Friar as if this was somehow his fault.

"I understand your frustration."

"They see us as weak, pushing us around and rubbing our nose in it!"

Veli Pingius smiled while quickly wiping the side of his mouth to salvage a few of the crumbs that had narrowly escaped digestion during his breakfast. "At least we have a good chance of winning. We have seven, and they only have one!"

"Wake up you fulsome! We're competing against *Velox*, favored to win *all* the sprints!" Falciss growled.

"One does not *always* have to be negative," Pingius offered, smiling and shaking his head indifferently.

"The Tournament of Flags is about to start!" the announcer proclaimed to loud applause. "The first event is heat one of the fifty-four yard race!"

"On your ready. Prepare. Go!" the Magician shouted.

The competitors took off just as the green wall dissolved. Finn bolted into the lead. Velox was second, followed by Sorea. They sprinted hard across the field. As they neared the finish line, Sorea and Velox moved even with Finn. Slowing down on purpose, Velox dropped back.

"Finn will win!" Bellae yelled excitedly.

With an effortless burst of speed Velox shot ahead, easily plunging through the blue finish line first. Thirty yards above the arena enormous blue letters magically declared the winners:

"Heat One, Fifty-Four Yards:

Winner: Velox-Proliator

Runner-up: Finn-Knights"

"AH!" Veli Falciss huffed, his exclamation of disapproval lost under the din of cheers and cries of, "Tallcon, Tallcon!"

"Whew, you were right Falciss. That guy's fast," Pingius said, undaunted.

"Everyone but the top two finishers, who advance to the finals, go to your holding area!" a Proliate yelled. "Those competing in heat two line up now!"

Finn, Sorea, and Lovag jogged over to Friar and the squires. Finn was holding a metal version of a phoenix attached to a small chain. "Second!"

"Great job, Finn," Gimelli and Bellae congratulated.

"Hold onto that phoenix charm, it's your ticket into the finals," Friar said.

Veli Falciss mumbled while gruffly pushing his competitors towards the Knights' holding area. Pingius shook hands with his Knights. "Good job. Let's go see if they have snacks in the holding area. You must be famished!"

With little time between each race the Proliate and Magicians kept up a blistering pace.

"Calling all competitors in the fifty-four yard sprint final. Turn in your winning Tallcon markers and get to the starting line!" a Magician said angrily.

"That's me!"

"Good luck, Finn!" Bellae called. "You can do it!"

He trotted off, handing the dangling image of a phoenix to the inexplicably irked Magician who pointed to his lane.

"In the final we have, Velox!" the announcer stated to a huge cheers. He proclaimed the next eleven competitors: one each from Piscium, Ager and the Rebelde Plains, three other Proliate, two Elves of Creber, and two from Jaa before ending with Finn.

"Good luck," Finn said to Hradur of Jaa.

She seemed surprised. "And to you." Leaning close, she whispered, "One of us *must* beat Velox."

"That would be nice!"

"On your ready. Prepare. Go!" the Magician yelled.

The runners exploded off the starting line as the magical green wall dissolved.

The four Proliate jumped out front. Hradur of Jaa was next, followed by Finn. Halfway through the race Finn began to gain on the front-runners.

"Come on Finn!" Bellae yelled, jumping and cheering. He and Hradur continued to move up as they neared the blue-walled finish line.

"And the winner is..." the announcer proclaimed. "...the winner is...looks too close to call. Let's wait for the magical wall..."

Giant blue letters proclaimed the winners as the announcer screamed the results, "The winner is Velox! Second is Finn, and third is Hradur!" A huge cheer waved through the arena.

Lidenskap trotted out on the field with three large ribbons, "Congratulations, winners!" He draped the first-place red over Velox, the silver over Finn, and the blue on Hradur.

"As a note, the award ceremony at the end is for the overall individual champion and team winners," the announcer stated. "All other awards will be given immediately after the event to boost efficiency."

Scroll 6: And So, it Begins-Shoot

"Finn, you're up next and then Arquero," Friar stated, as Sorea prepared to shoot first in the initial archery competition.

"Each of your arrows or bolts have been magically tagged and your hits will be scored automatically," a Magician explained. "Any direct hit will cause the bird-shaped targets you will be shooting to fall."

He nodded to other Magicians who began using their crosiers to make thirty-six bird-shaped targets magically change from wood into what appeared to be live birds flying in zigzag patterns through the sky.

"Each competitor has thirty-six bolts or arrows and five minutes to shoot as many targets as possible. Once I give the command to start, the red wall in front of you will dissolve and you may shoot. If you shoot early your projectile will ricochet back and hit you. We are *not* responsible for stupidity-related deaths! On your ready. Prepare. Go!"

The magical red wall disappeared and Sorea fired.

"You can do it, keep cranking!" Finn encouraged. Although smiling, the strain on Sorea's face was obvious as she repeatedly wound up her crossbow, a huge speed disadvantage compared to her bow shooting competitors.

"All the Knights are going first *again*?" Falciss bellowed.

"Think of it as a challenge to overcome and adapt. If we let adversity discourage us, we have already lost," Friar stated calmly. "Finn placed second in the fifty-four yard race, Sorea third in the one hundred and nine yard race, and two of your knights have third in the other two races. Given the competition and extra obstacles, not bad."

"Considering this used to be only for Knights, these pathetic results are..." Falciss abruptly stopped, realizing Friar had walked away.

"Thirty-three hits out of a potential thirty-six bolts for Sorea of the Independent Knights," the announcer said to a mix of cheers and boos from the crowd.

Sorea and Gimelli trotted over, passing Finn and Bellae heading for his turn.

"Great job," Bellae stated.

"Thanks. I ran out of time to get those last three bolts off. Go get them," Sorea encouraged. "Why are they booing?"

"The Proliate believe there is no honor in archery."

"No honor in concentration, endless practice, skill?" Arquero said defiantly.

"I know, I know. They feel killing from a distance gives no glory to Tallcon," Friar said.

"Pretend they're not booing, but chanting, 'You! You!' As in, 'You're the best!'" Gimelli laughed.

"So we have a five-way tie. Sorea, Finn, Arquero, Kempe—an Elf of Creber, and Herra Isanta—a Western Elf all managed thirty-three hits," Friar informed.

"What now?" Finn asked.

"A shoot off. You will all compete at the same time to see who can hit the most hippogriff-shaped targets."

"Winged horse targets? Really?" Finn smiled.

"Hey, they get points for originality!"

"We have to be smart about this," Arquero interjected. "From what we have experienced so far, they will likely put us next to each other to compete for the same targets. Let's agree that the person on our left will go for the targets on the far left, the one in the middle targets the middle, and so forth."

"Excellent," Friar nodded.

"Hello Kainen, Kempe!" Finn greeted as the father and son Elves approached.

"Good luck," Kempe, the muscular Elf, said.

"Bellae! Nice to see you again," Kainen smiled.

"Hi," she answered, remembering when she had met the young Elf, his father, and the hulking figure hidden within a full body cloak who had given her such an odd feeling.

"After the competition, do you want to come to our camp? I can introduce you to the other Elves, and we can get to know each other better. We're going to spend a lot of time together very soon!"

"Uhm." Bellae was so taken aback by "spend a lot of time together," she couldn't think of a better answer.

"Ready your bows and crossbow," the Magician said.

"Well, just know you are welcome any time," the young Elf Kainen smiled.

Bellae returned an awkward grin as the Magician continued.

"Do not fire until I say and the red wall disappears. Remember, only head or heart shots bring the hippogriff targets down." He nodded to his colleagues controlling the targets. The winged horse targets seemed to come to life and began careening around in all directions.

"Take your ready. Aim. Fire!" he yelled. The red barrier vanished and all the competitors fired instantaneously.

Thhhhhhwwwwwwwwwwtttttttt.

Four arrows and one bolt loosed. Five targets went down, six left. Finn and Kempe were the first to loose their second arrows—two more hits. Sorea was just finishing cranking her second bolt back as the other two competitors shot and hit. Sorea shot and a target fell.

"Ten targets down, one left!" the announcer proclaimed.

Finn and Kempe shot. Both arrows flew simultaneously into the heart of the last target. The non-Proliate crowd cheered as the winged horse turned back into wood and fell lifelessly to the ground.

"Soooooooooooo close!" the announcer shouted. "We'll have to wait for the magical scoreboard to see who won!"

Glittering letters flashed above the arena:

"Winners: Finn-Knights, Kempe-Elves of Creber. Tie for First.

Second: Herra Isanta-Western Elves.

Third: Arquero-Knights."

"Excellent, competition," the normally crusty Magician said.

"Congratulations, Kempe!" Finn said.

"You too, brother! We'll see you later."

"Bye, Bellae!" Kainen, said, smiling broadly. "We're going to have the best adventure together!"

Bellae scowled. *I seriously wish I knew what in the world is he talking about.*

Book Two

"Regretting not signing up for the archery distance competition?" Arquero asked.

"Yes. I can't believe they only let you compete in seven individual events," Finn replied. "I better head to the holding area before the Proliate attack me."

"No one has said anything, yet," Friar winked. "I think they're getting used to you competing in everything."

"Worth a try! I'll hang out until they say something."

"Listen carefully, competitors," a Magician shouted. "We created a magical obex barrier to hold your arrows at their highest point and register the distance it would have gone. Bows only, no crossbows. You each get three arrows and twenty seconds to shoot.

"Everyone competing will be given a numbered metal phoenix. Please line up in that order." As he finished, the Magician handed Finn a metal phoenix with the number one, "Good luck."

"Line up! Let's go!" a Proliate yelled.

Shrugging, Finn ran to the line with Bellae close behind. She smiled as Finn nocked his ornate long bow.

Finn stood well behind the line as the red barrier dissolved and the Magician shouted, "Go!"

Finn rocked his whole body backwards, before jumping towards the line and releasing the arrow. It flew high and fast. A green light sparked around the arrow as it stopped at its highest arc, caught in the magical obex net.

Green letters appeared in the sky next to the arrow:

"Finn, Independent Knights

410 yards."

"Here, Finn," Bellae said, offering his second arrow. He turned from the suspended arrow waving in the sky and quickly shot two more.

The same happened for all competitors. Their best shot hung in the obex with their name and the arrows distance magically floating above.

"The results for the distance archery competition are: First place; Kempe, Elf of Creber!"

As the announcer proclaimed the champions, their wining arrow lit up and spun around as their name flashed in the sky. "Second place goes to Lovag of the Independent Knights and Third place, Finn, also of the Knights."

"Arquero, you were fourth, take the third-place blue ribbon. I shouldn't have competed," Finn said.

"I couldn't…"

Finn held up his hand prohibiting Arquero from protesting, "I shouldn't have participated, looks like a Western Elf had dropped out and that's why there was an extra competitor spot."

"Thanks, Pointy!"

Thunderous drumbeats exploded across the arena, quickly followed by a loud wail from the announcer, "Get ready for *combaaaaaaaaaaaat!*"

Scroll 7: Unleash Thunder

Ritari burst out of the holding area, adrenaline surging through his body.

"Ready?" Menas, a Knight from castle Taiheart, asked.

Before he could answer, Veli Pingius yelled, "I've got it!" The Veli's body jiggled in silent waves of rippling protest as he bounced towards the Knights waving a scroll. "We just received the combat schedule! Ritari, you face off against Campesino first!"

Veli Falciss joined them. "Annihilate him! I saw Campesino up close, that Agerian is huge, but also way overweight. Move around, make him miss and he'll tire!" Turning to Menas, "You fight second, against Mester. He's been the Proliate Red Guard champion for three straight years. Once again, they're trying to get Knight competitors out early by putting you against the best opponents in the first round. Don't give them the satisfaction!"

Slipping on his black helmet Ritari lowered his head. Menas hit it several times on each side, "Go unleash thunder!"

Ritari grunted and headed off to battle. He moved directly across from the large warrior from Ager. The diminutive Magician serving as judge stood between the two mountain-like men, his neck craning upwards, eyes darting nervously between them.

Campesino was simply colossal. His shoulders and chest bulged, but they were out prominenced by his portly abdomen. His blonde beard flowed onto his leather chest protector.

"Listen, you will respond to my commands..." the frail looking Magician stated, trying to act tougher than he felt. "...or I will zap you to the frozen lakes of Jaa where...you will drown."

"The first one to land ten major blows wins. The One-on-One Sword Combat rules dictate that you can only use a single sword and shield. Your bodies will be enchanted so that the blows will hurt but can't slice, dice, or kill."

"We can do without that enchantment. Can't we Ree-tar-dee?" Campesino mocked.

"You're half-right, farm-boy! I can do without it because you won't touch me."

"E-e-e-nough!" the slight Magician squeaked. "Neither of you can go without the enchantment!" He pointed his gnarly looking crosier with a clear blue crystal at Ritari, "Alio contego caeruleum!"

Ritari grunted as a sudden pressure squeezed his body from all sides. As quickly as the sensation came, it left, and he exhaled loudly. The Magician grabbed a thin club, "I have to test the spell." Trembling, the Magician looked abashed, "Do *not* retaliate."

He whacked Ritari in the chest. The club sprang back with a burst of green light. The Magician's arms were vibrating wildly while Ritari was unmoved.

"It wor-r-r-rksss," he said, his voice quivering from the impact. "I forgot to mention there is recoil when you strike your opponent. Also, weapon on shield, weapon on weapon, and mild blows will shower green sparks. If the hit is strong enough to score a point, Campesino's hits will flash red, and Ritari's score with blue." He repeated the ritual on Campesino before giving a thumbs-up to the announcer.

"Now, get ready for *combaaaaaaaaaaaat*! We start with a feature fight. Ritari of the Independent Knights versus Campesino, Champion of Ager! These two heavyweights could just as easily been battling in the final!"

"Remember, I will transport you somewhere unpleasant if you ignore my commands," the Magician threatened, his face partly obscured by the crosier he held up defensively. "Ready! Fight!"

"I don't care if that Magician put a blocking enchantment on you, I'm going to split you in two!" Campesino yelled.

He lunged at Ritari and struck hard with his sword. Ritari easily raised his shield, angling it to deflect some of the blow's power. A shower of green light blasted up. Both men hesitated, surprised by the magical shock waves from the blow.

Ritari moved deftly, constantly circling and moving, first away and then towards Campesino who was growing increasingly frustrated. Ritari deflected some of his opponents' massive sword blows with his shield, others with his sword. After several minutes of relentless strikes, Campesino's sword began to lower slightly.

He's tiring, Ritari thought.

Feigning negligence, Ritari stopped moving and stood straight up to lure his opponent in. Campesino lunged with surprising speed and Ritari was barely able to bring up his sword to meet the blow. A massive shower of green flowered as the two swords crashed together. Ritari's center of gravity was too high, and the force sent him stumbling back. Nearly falling over, Ritari tried to bring his shield up for protection while bending his knees for support. Both were too late and Campesino took advantage.

With his arm already vibrating from the massive sword blow, Ritari felt a crushing impact on his breastplate as Campesino used his shield to slam into him. It felt like he had been hit by Luchar's war hammer. A hail of red sparks shot up as Ritari had the air knocked out of him.

"A hit by Campesino!" the announcer yelled.

"Don't get careless, Ritari!" Knight Menas yelled.

Campesino raised his sword high, and on the way down spun around, slamming it into Ritari's right side. Once again, red sparks flew.

"Two to nothing, Campesinooooo!" the announcer quickly proclaimed.

Emboldened by his success, Campesino threw down his shield and began swinging ferociously with a two handed grip on his sword.

Ritari's center of gravity and stances were back in balance and he was moving well, making Campesino work hard until the large Agerian's adrenaline started to diminish.

With his opponent breathing heavy and feeling overconfident, Ritari went on the attack. He started high. Blow after blow at shoulder level or higher, forcing Campesino to keep his arms above his head to block. With sweat pouring from under his helmet, Campesino began to backpedal. However, unlike Ritari's steady movements, his were becoming choppy and cumbersome under the burden of fatigue. Ritari began a blistering combination of attacks, alternating high-low, left-right, all to keep the pressure on his tiring opponent.

Ritari lunged, pretending to overextend himself. Campesino took the bait and flung his massive weight straight at Ritari, who deftly recoiled, moved to his left, and began slashing precise attacks all over his opponents exposed right side. Several blasted out as blue sparks.

Campesino whirled around to defend himself and raised his sword for a powerful overhead blow. The fresher Ritari moved with stunning quickness and slammed his sword up into Campesino's, pinning his arms up. Simultaneously he threw a jumping knee that caught his opponent under his left rib cage. It was powerful enough to make Campesino grunt in pain and stumble backwards as blue light sparked.

High above the competitors, Ritari's name and score of "6" flashed in blue. Campesino's name and score of "2" flashed red.

Campesino recovered enough to lumber forward. With a fresh adrenaline surge boosting his spirit, Campesino's blows were once again heavy and accurate. Ritari was all too happy to oblige, circling and weaving, carefully deflecting his blows with as little energy as possible.

"Campesino is making a comeback!" the announcer proclaimed. "Ritari's lead is only two, six to four!"

As the announcer's words began to fade, so too did the drained Campesino. He brought down a hard overhead blow while pushing his weight forward in a desperate, but off-balance attack. Ritari easily dodged his charge and began a series of punishing blows, many scoring hits. Ritari's tenth scoring blow crashed into Campesino's side with such force the huge Agerian started falling backwards. Ritari leapt, dealing a punishing jumping sidekick for good measure.

A series of boos rang out from the arena as the hulking figure of Campesino crumpled to the arena floor. Ritari reveled in the crowd's angst, raising his hands triumphantly.

"Your victory token!" the scrawny Magician yelled, handing Ritari a silver image of Tallcon. Raising his crosier, he yelled, "Desino avta aon alio contego! The magical shield is gone, so don't go throwing yourself on a sword. We'll find you when it's your turn to fight again."

"You probably ruptured his spleen, you oaf!" Tarha, King of Ager, yelled, waving his gold scepter wildly close to Ritari's face. "That side kick was cheap!"

"If your boy thought he signed up for basket weaving, he was wrong," Ritari said icily.

"You insolent…" the King began.

"Tarha!" Friar interrupted. "This is combat! We all know Campesino wasn't asking for cooking advice out there," Friar said as Ritari and Menas laughed. "Go see to your man and stop embarrassing him with all this caterwauling."

Still fuming, the King stopped his tirade and walked to his fallen warrior.

Scroll 8: Finals: That's *Got* to Hurt

"Slaughter that Proliate for me," Menas yelled, still upset at barely losing in the first round to Proliate Champion Mester by a score of nine to ten. Ritari nodded while heading out of the holding area, followed by Friar, Luchar, Finn, and their three respective squires.

"Planning on it!"

"Welcome to the One-on-One combat finals!" the announcer proclaimed. "First up, we have the Sword Finals pitting Ritari of the Independent Knights versus Mester of the Proliate Islands!"

Once the cheering died down he continued, "In the Open Finals we have Finn of the Independent Knights versus Hystum of the

Southern Dwarves. The Hand-to-Hand Competition pits Luchar, another Independent Knight, versus Fawr of Ager.

"If you want to see the Equestrian Finals find a Magician and they will transport you to the stables where Arquero of the Independent Knights is battling Marchoga of the Rebelde Plains."

"Pretty impressive to have four Knights in the finals," Finn said.

Friar beamed as Ritari and Scelto headed towards a large contingent of Red Guard Proliators standing in a semi-circle around Mester, each one holding a red banner of Tallcon.

Mester was several inches shorter than Ritari but even more muscular. He had a silver outline of Tallcon on his red chest plate and wore the traditional helmet of the Proliate with its intimidating flat winged front and red horsehair running in an arc down the center. He stood, zealously pivoting his sword in concentric arcs around his body.

As Ritari and Scelto stepped closer, the Red Guard moved to completely encircle them.

"What in the blazes do they think they are doing?" Friar lamented, running towards the wall of Proliate surrounding his Knight and squire.

"Let's head over to the open finals," Finn suggested to Bellae. They walked briskly towards a waiting Magician and Hystum. The Southern Dwarf was half as tall and three times as wide as Finn and decked out in elaborately decorated armor. A double-sided axe hung on his back. Hystum was swinging an ominous weapon that looked like a grappling hook, an adaptation of a tool the Southern Dwarves use in deep mining.

Finn carried a similar flying star weapon of his own design. One end of a thirty-foot rope held razor sharp blades in the shape of a star, the other a metal grappling hook. Currently he brandished his telescoping dagger, its finely sharpened tip able to telescope in and out.

"Looks like there is some controversy regarding the sword competition. Apparently the Knights are complaining, *again*. So, let's start with the Open Finals between Finn and Hystum," the announcer said.

"Oh, my," the magician assigned to that event remarked. He stopped leaning on his crosier and stood at attention. "Come closer, looks like you fight first!"

Bellae followed Finn towards Hystum and the Magician.

"All right. I need a clean battle. Follow my instructions. Finn, step up, quickly now! Alio contego rubrum! If you score a hit, it showers red." He repeated the process for Hystum in blue.

"I'm going to chop you into firewood, bark-boy!" Hystum threatened. "While I'm at it, I think I'll cut off those freakish, pointy ears!"

Bellae shuddered while gasping, "Be careful, Finn,"

"Don't worry, I've already defeated the best fighters in this competition," Finn laughed. "Trust me, this seriously won't end well for him."

She smiled nervously before scurrying out of the circular area set aside for the battle.

"What's that? A toothpick?" Hystum asked, laughing at Finn's telescoping dagger.

Finn ignored the comment.

"Fight!" the Magician yelled.

The lighter and more agile Elf floated around the stocky and heavily armored Dwarf.

"What are you planning on doing, a windmill interpretive dance or fighting?" Hystum yelled.

With the Dwarf laughing, Finn thrust his telescoping dagger. Hystum raised his shield just in time to deflect it as a sizzling sound and green light radiated off. Finn reversed direction while constructing a mental grid in front of the Dwarf and repeatedly shooting out his telescoping dagger, each one forcing his heavily armored opponent to block the relentless attacks in a new location.

Sweat began to drip from under the annoyed Dwarf's helmet. He stopped swinging his grappling hook and concentrated on frantically deflecting the relentless stream of strikes.

"He's trying to wear you out, you dumb oaf! Attack that bark covered aberration!" the Dwarf's assistant yelled.

"Fancy, imbecilic fairy dancer!" the frustrated Dwarf muttered, letting the grappling hook fly. Finn easily batted it away and laughed.

The enraged Dwarf re-coiled the grappling hook with surprising skill. Hystum let loose a side arm throw with such power Bellae squealed. The grappling hook entwined around Finn's telescoping dagger.

"Got it!" the Dwarf yelled triumphantly.

Finn began to pull, and a game of tug of war commenced. The two lowered their center of gravity and shifted their weight backwards in a struggle for supremacy.

Bellae jumped when a hand landed on her shoulder. "Oh, Friar! Hystum hooked Finn's telescoping dagger."

"Don't worry, Finn's nice and relaxed. To control one's emotions and remain calm is the path to victory. Pain breeds fear, fear generates panic, and panic leads to defeat."

Suddenly, Finn lowered his hips and shot backwards, pulling the heavier Dwarf towards him. The infuriated Hystum retaliated by leaning back forcefully. Finn instantly threw his telescoping dagger and the attached grappling hook straight towards Hystum. With the counter weight gone, the Dwarf dropped his weapon and stumbled backwards, flailing wildly in an attempt to gain his balance.

Bellae sighed in relief, "Finn was setting him up!"

Friar nodded.

Bellae finally felt herself relax as Finn fought with almost careless ease, one born to fight who had trained everyday to hone his natural skills.

Friar sighed, *What trials and tribulations await you, young child?* Despite having no control over the future, Friar felt intensely sad and guilty for any coming afflictions on his youngest squire.

"The greatest obstacles we face are often those battling from within, rather than external," Friar said to her. His words caused her to take her eyes of Finn and focus on him.

"Whatever comes your way in the future, always remember to take a deep breath and steady your resolve. The black vapor of fear can easily tentacle its way into our brain, marinating its poison over our resolve and courage until they become lame."

Bellae, still worried about Finn, closed her eyes, wishing away all the Chosen One and "future adventure" nonsense she kept hearing about.

"I did not mean to add to your stress," Friar added, gently holding her chin until her eyes opened. "Have courage, and don't let the fight be over before it even begins."

Bellae nodded gently, Friar flashed as genuine a smile as he could muster before they both turned back to the fight.

Finn pulled three throwing daggers from his belt and launched them in quick succession while charging the faltering Dwarf. This forced Hystum to block the projectiles while backpedaling. Hystum barely managed to pull out his battle-axe as Finn closed in rapidly. Merely holding his battle-axe seemed to embolden the Dwarf who stopped backing up and swung his axe in slashing arcs.

Finn easily dodged the attacks, but began backpedaling.

"Get him! He's on the run!" his assistant hollered.

The Dwarf rattled forward in his ostentatious armor. Finn backed up a few more steps and then sprinted towards Hystum. The Dwarf swung his axe wildly. Finn crouched and leapt into a soaring front flip. The battle-axe sliced just under Finn's head as his momentum carried him forward. For one brief moment Finn was upside down, his head about half of a foot above Hystum's. While there he reached down and ripped the Dwarf's helmet off his head. Hystum instinctively dropped his axe to reach for his disappearing helmet.

"The Knight just front flipped over the Dwarf!" the announcer screamed incredulously.

When Finn landed the two warriors' backs were opposite each other. In one smooth motion Finn swung the Dwarf's helmet with both hands while twisting his hips to add power. The helmet slammed into the right side of the Dwarf's head. A splattering of red light shot forcefully out from the center of the blow as Hystum's head slammed onto his ornately armored shoulder.

As his head bobbed back up slobber sprayed out from his wobbling mouth. Finn immediately moved in with a jumping, double kick. His right leg pounded into the left side of his opponent's face and red light exploded out, while the left hammered his shield and flashed green.

The blows sent the Dwarf reeling backwards and his shield rattling to the ground. Finn landed, bent down, grabbed his opponent's shield and sprang towards the staggering Dwarf while rotating his body in a violent spin. As his body completed a three hundred and sixty degree revolution, he smashed the shield into the Dwarf's face, lighting up another shower of red.

Figure 40: Finn is battling Southern Dwarf Hystum in the Open Weapons Finals. As with most competitions involving the Knights so far, Finn was forced to fight the strongest opponents first—this does not bode well for Hystum.

"A flying three-sixty shield hit! That's *got* to hurt!" the announcer exclaimed.

Finn arched backwards until he was fully curved in a bridging position with his right hand on the ground for support. With his left hand, he grabbed the Dwarf's previously dropped axe. In one fluid motion he shot forward into a somersault pummeling Hystum's badly bruised face with a blow from his own axe. Even as the red sparks splattered, Finn spun to his left, slamming the axe into Hystum's lower right leg which shot forward and across his body sending the Dwarf tumbling.

With lightning speed, Finn launched the axe into Hystum's falling body three times before the Dwarf hit the ground. Each one eliciting a grunt and red sparks. Finn drifted back as the Dwarf shook his head and groggily attempted to stand.

Finn instantly let loose his flying star. The sleek iron weapon pounded into the magical shield, which softened the blow, but still sent the Dwarf's head snapping backwards. Finn re-coiled his weapon and struck over and over again until the Magician jumped between the two, his crosier raised menacingly towards the Elf, the crystal on top gleaming angrily.

"Enough! You have sufficient hits to win two times over!" He tossed a red victory sash at Finn. "Congratulations, you won," he added contemptuously.

"Finn of the Knights wins ten-plus-plus-plus, to zero! He's your Open Weapon Champion!" the announcer stated.

"Great job, Finn!" Friar yelled over a chorus of boos. "Imagine what the crowd will do when we win the next two bouts!"

Scroll 9: Prepare Yourself for Pain

"Up next, the brutal Hand-to-Hand final with no shield spell, no metal armor, and no weapons!" the announcer said. "Fawr of Ager has to be nervous after Knight Luchar's previous victories which included three knockouts and an opponent's leg broken in multiple places!"

"He's the one who should be nervous!" Fawr yelled, gesturing rudely towards the announcer.

Fawr was similar in size to Campesino, but fifty pounds heavier. His face was broad with a wide bulbous nose and eyes set so deeply they were shrouded in shadows giving him a haunting look. While the man from Ager's mind thrust out abundant overconfidence, his abdomen managed to protrude even further, expanding pregnantly from ale and meat pies.

Luchar, wearing a woven white shirt with a large panther embroidered upon it, growled and ran straight at Fawr, who braced himself and prepared to punch. As Luchar neared the much taller opponent, he stopped and with surprising agility ducked his head down so that his chest rested on his bent knee. As Fawr's powerful roundhouse punch whiffed through the air over his head, Luchar shot his body upward, until his right elbow slammed into Fawr's nose. Since Fawr was leaning forward, the blow was devastating.

Fawr's head flew backwards, sending blood spraying out in a massive arc from his shattered nose. Fawr swung wildly even before his head had recovered enough to look. Luchar deftly stepped to his left and slammed three punishing kicks into Fawr's right leg.

Howling in pain Fawr brought his right fist hammering down toward Luchar, who brought both arms up into an "X" shape, blocking it easily. Luchar then swung his left leg in a roundhouse that slammed into the damaged area on Fawr's right leg. Yelping in agony, Fawr stumbled backwards.

Luchar took time to wind up before slamming his left elbow into Fawr's already bruised right leg. Fawr instantly collapsed. As he did, he managed to clock Luchar in the face with a punch. The damage was minimal, as Luchar tucked and rolled completely out of the much larger man's reach.

"Get him to the ground and strangle the life out of that blasted Knight!" Fawr's attendant yelled. Luchar stood at a safe distance and let Fawr hobble up with blood flowing freely from his nose.

"You should have stayed down, Jumbo," Luchar growled.

Fawr staggered forward. Laughing, Luchar easily circled away. Howling, Fawr flexed his muscles in frustration. His broad nose looked more freakish each moment as it continued to swell and rain down blood on his already red splattered chest and abdomen. Fawr coughed and gagged, forced to swallow some of the viscous and sickly sweet blood draining down his throat before spitting up the rest.

Several times Luchar faked an attack, carefully watching Fawr weakly prepare for a takedown. Acting as if he were going to dance around, Luchar relaxed his guard and shook out his arms to draw his opponent in. As Fawr put his head down and charged Luchar introduced his right knee to his already fragmented nose. A sickening "crunch" was quickly followed by Fawr gagging on the fresh stream of blood charging down the back of his throat. He dropped to his knees gasping for air as a deluge of blood showered from the unrecognizable, flaccid mess that once passed for a nose. Coughing out a stream of blood Fawr tried not to vomit as his shattered front teeth surfed out on the red ichor retreating from his mouth.

Seeing no stop signal from the Magician, Luchar launched a front kick, mercifully aiming away from Fawr's devastated face and towards his abdomen.

In a panic, Fawr lurched up and backwards just as Luchar unleashed his kick. Luchar's foot slammed into Fawr's groin, instantly crumpling the large man as a gasp rose up from the crowd.

The Magician observing the match immediately jumped in, "Illegal kick! Groin strike! Disqualified!"

"That was an accident!" Luchar yelled. "I should have aimed for his battered face!"

"Rules are rules. You're disqualified. Remove yourself from this arena now!"

"Idiot Magician, this is ridiculous!" Jumeaux yelled.

"Stay out of this, boy!" Luchar screamed.

What? Jumeaux thought. *I was trying to help. Like I care if you win!*

In the blink of an eye the shields of six Proliate guards surrounded the Knight and squire, pushing them towards the Knight holding area.

Luchar obliged but continued muttering insults.

"Fawr wins! Luchar is disqualified for a despicable low blow!" the announcer said cheerfully.

"This is absolutely ludicrous!" Friar lamented. "I want to talk with Veneficus."

"I can assure you, we have his authority. Your lack of character as an institution came through loud and clear with that blatant kick to the groin!"

Friar put his hands on top of his head and bit his lip. "You're baiting me, hoping I'll throw a fit and get ejected."

"No, of course not," the Magician said unconvincingly.

"Blatant cheating like that will always lead to disqualification! Good riddance to that cozener Knight!" the announcer taunted. "Fawr wins!"

"That's right, move along, cheater!" one of the guards herding the Knight and squire towards the holding area scowled, adding a shove.

"That's it!" Luchar yelled, charging the mouthy Proliate. He slammed into the guard's heavy shield, pushing the surprised warrior back. Luchar grabbed and violently twisted the shield with the Proliator's arm strapped in.

The Proliator screamed, squirming to avoid his arm breaking. As his howl of pain subsided, a massive number of Proliators descended upon the Knight and squire. Luchar continued raging despite the sea of guards washing over him.

Eventually, a bloodied Luchar was lifted and carried out, kicking and screaming. Jumeaux thought it best to close his eyes and play possum. His strategy of going limp and letting himself be hauled away to avoid any pain seemed to be working. Both were unceremoniously thrown into the Knight holding chamber.

"We'll be outside in case you get any ideas!" a Proliator yelled.

Luchar shot up, spitting blood, but the door had already slammed shut. Ranting and raving, he strode in a storm to the opposite end of the room. The Knights and squires crowded Jumeaux, gazing expectantly.

"He was disqualified for cheating, but…" Jumeaux said to loud gasps. He began to sweat as they closed in upon him, each squabbling for their question to be answered.

"Give him some room. Even Jumeaux needs to breathe!" Gimelli said, smiling at her brother. He did not return it.

Show off, Jumeaux thought. *I get abuse from Luchar trying to help, and then everyone suffocates me when I try to talk, and now my sister's being sarcastic!*

Spurred on by the perceived slights, Jumeaux recounted the story including the accidental kick to the groin.

"He had it won!" Lovag lamented, looking back at the bellowing Luchar. "All the bruises and blood came from the Proliate?"

Jumeaux nodded, "Fawr never really touched him."

The healer Sanar was carefully trying to negotiate a way to help the bloodied Knight.

"Give him a few minutes," Lovag instructed the healer while thinking, *Maybe a few hours.*

Back in the arena Ritari and Mester, were completely encircled by a ring of red Proliate except for Friar and Scelto.

"Why are they doing this?" Scelto asked.

"They're trying to intimidate Ritari. Also, with his red armor, Mester's movements will be masked against their wall of scarlet. It's abusive and unheard of."

"Can't Veneficus do something?" Scelto inquired.

"He tried, Storlax overruled him. Nothing else to do but fight."

Mester was making the equivalent of several jab combinations with his sword. In their scouting they had noticed he tended to fall into predictable patterns. Friar smiled, he knew what was coming. After several parries, the Proliator began his anticipated heavier strikes. Ritari easily deflected them while quickly backpedalling and waiting. Finally, Mester threw a hard overhead thrust.

Ritari deflected the blow by making a half circle with his sword and moving to the side, guiding Mester's sword downward before slamming it hard to the ground. Ritari instantly thrust upwards and smashed his sword into the helmet of the Proliate. A stunned Mester recoiled as blue light erupted.

Figure 41: Against Friar and Veneficus' protests, the Proliate have surrounded Ritari in a sea of red as he battles Mester for the Sword Championship.

Ritari sliced his sword towards Mester's head again. This time Mester blocked it with his shield and in one fluid movement thrust his sword towards Ritari's chest plate. Ritari slammed his shield into the approaching sword while bringing his own sword over the top, stabbing towards Mester. Mester arched back to avoid the thrust, spun around and tried to slice Ritari's legs.

Ritari smashed his shield downward and laid his weight on Mester's sword. The torque on his arm was so great that Mester fell to his knees and dropped his sword. To coerce Ritari off his sword, Mester slammed his shield into Ritari. It noisily rammed into his chest and Ritari exhaled sharply as red light burst forth.

Mester raised his shield for a second strike. As he did, Ritari struck first with his own shield. The force of the blow forced the weaponless Mester to roll away.

"There's no honor in defeating an unarmed man," Mester chided. "Give me my sword and we'll settle this with true glory!"

"There is supreme honor in disarming a fellow combatant and more than enough glory in finishing him. Prepare yourself for pain!" Ritari seethed, kicking away the fallen sword before going on the attack.

Mester bravely tried to defend against his attacks but Ritari mercilessly used combinations of shield and sword strikes to pummel him as nine blue lights flashed in rapid succession.

"Ritari is victorious ten strikes to one," the announcer stated to anemic pockets of applause. "Also, this just in, Knight Arquero is the victor in the equestrian battle."

With no fanfare, Ritari received his red victory ribbon, "I guess they wanted the other guy to win!"

"I think you may be right," Friar answered.

"Did you even break a sweat?" Scelto asked, squinting at Ritari's forehead as he removed his helmet.

"It's there, you're just too short to see it!"

They received rousing applause entering their holding area.

"You know I softened him up that Proliate Peacock for you," Menas declared.

"Oh, totally!"

"All of you did great today! I mean *all* of you," Friar said, looking at Luchar. "I have never been prouder of the Knights!" Everyone erupted into applause and howls of celebration.

"Get cleaned up and relax. Everyone but those working on the siege engines remember your curfew! I will be checking each and every cot."

A bright light flashed and a young Magician appeared, transporting two others.

"Falciss and Arquero are back! Congratulations equestrian champion!" Friar declared as the two embraced. The Magician rolled his eyes and disappeared.

"We heard two of the three combat victories were ours."

"Actually, we won all three matches. Even without a red ribbon, Luchar won that fight."

Falciss raised his eyebrows, moving closer to Friar he whispered, "See, with our superior training we can stand toe-to-toe with anyone! If war with the Proliate comes, let's lose your overly complex plan and get some old-time, smash-shield combat."

Friar chuckled, "I appreciate your faith in our troops. However, even a swarm of mindless arrows can take down even the mighty and spectacular Pegasus."

Falciss scrunched his fierce eyes, "Well, at least think about it."

Scroll 10: What a Crowd Likes

"Friar! What do we do?" Ritari screamed.

"Where are we?"

"What? We're getting slaughtered! The Dark Warriors and the Proliate are about to overrun us!"

The clanging of metal on metal, the crash of projectiles against the shattering castle walls, and the screams of the dying all exploded around him.

How did I get back to Castle Liberum? Friar thought, dazed.

"They've breached the walls!" Luchar yelled, just before several Proliate spears sliced through his body. He went limp, a massive blood trail followed his crumpling body to the wall walk as hordes of Dark Warriors and Proliate streamed over the battlements.

"Protect Friar!" Ritari yelled.

A handful of exhausted Knights encircled Friar as the enemy closed in around them. One by one the remaining Knights were annihilated, squirting blood and splattering entrails until Friar was bathed in them. The last to fall, a wide-eyed Ritari, slouched at Friar's feet, his body covered in oozing wounds.

"Noooo!" Friar howled as dozens of enemy weapons hurtled towards him. Suddenly, everything but the black clouds hurtling across the sky froze. Panting heavily, Friar stared into the bloodthirsty eyes of the motionless attackers, their bodies and weapons forming an impromptu, razors-edge cage.

Two fiery eyes appeared in the dark swirling clouds as a raspy voice boomed, "Na Cearcaill has been unleashed! Death is coming for you, and for all!"

A strike of lightning was followed by war cries from the encircling enemy as they unfroze, exploding into movement. Friar's howl of pain joined their voices as dozens of weapons skewered, pierced, and carved into him.

He shot out of bed screaming, quickly checking his body, surprised to see no wounds or blood. Despite the lack of injuries he grunted in agony, struggling for breath due to the searing pain. *How could that be just a dream if the pain is real?*

The discomfort slowly dissolved as his confusion increased.

"Death is coming!" a voice hissed.

"Who's there?"

Only silence greeted him from the empty chamber. *Am I still sleeping? Am I losing my mind? Are these visions a chance to see, and change, a desolate future?*

He knew the next few months would decide the fate of not just the Knights, but the whole world.

Friar entered the crowded arena and unfolded his schedule to review the day ahead. He was ecstatic with yesterday's victories, but discouraged at the hostility propagated against them. His Knights were constantly put in the least advantageous spots and the crowd had been mostly venomous. No bridges were being built as he and Veneficus had hoped.

Day Two:

I. Mechanicians:

A. -Projectiles/siege engines:

-Distance: *Sorea and Finn*

-Destructive force: *Sorea and Finn*

B. -Sappers: *Taiheart and Toil Shaor*

II. Squad Battles: *Taiheart and Toil Shaor*

III. Dragon Battles: *Pantteri Squad*

IV. Strength Tests: *Ritari and Luchar*

"You okay, Friar?" Sorea asked.

"Fine."

"Truly? Your furrowed brow looks as if you're trying to hold up the weight of the world."

Upon seeing her, his face softened into a grin. As smiles often do, it spread up, and freed his forehead from its wrinkle generating worry. "I really am fine. I had trouble sleeping because…of all the excitement. How late did you stay up finishing your siege engines?"

"Let's just say Finn, Gimelli, and I never met our long lost friend, sleep!"

"Good morning!" Finn said, jogging effortlessly towards them.

"You're cheery for being sleep deprived."

"Time enough for sleep later! I have some unexpected news after the way they stacked the day against us yesterday."

"We get to go last so we will know what score we have to beat?" Sorea said hopefully.

"Better! We go first."

"What a shocker."

Just then, Ritari showed up with Bellae, Jumeaux, and Gimelli.

"Good morning!" Gimelli said brightly. "We're ready for another round of victories!"

"She's absurdly cheerful for staying up last night helping get the siege engines ready," Ritari said.

"It's a sickness," Jumeaux said sarcastically. "Try being her brother."

"Sleep is boring," Sorea said. "Staying up all night working on machines of destruction is a blast!"

"Welcome back," Veneficus yelled, soaring into the center of the arena on his winged-horse. "Yesterday was wonderful. It was great seeing so much camaraderie among the different nations of Verngaurd!"

"He must have been watching a different competition," Ritari commented.

"Today will be another great day," Veneficus continued. "We start with the mechanicians. After that we have the sappers, squad battles, the Dragon Battles, and …"

At the mention of "Dragon Battles" an immense roar of approval exploded from the crowd, drowning out the rest of his words.

"I guess they like the idea of us fighting a dragon," Ritari said.

"It would seem so," Friar replied.

Scroll 11: Nice Try

"Why do we have to use Proliators to power our siege engine?" Sorea protested.

"The Magical League will only allow the bare minimum of you obstreperous Knights out in the arena," a haughty Magician decreed.

"Seriously? Do you even know what obstreperous means?" Friar questioned. The Magician, however, had already walked away.

"They think we're going to cheat?" Sorea raged.

"Apparently."

"There are tons of Proliate, Piscinians, and Agerians around their siege engines!"

"I guess they're not obstreperous!" Friar smiled.

"So not funny!" Sorea huffed.

"Let's welcome our five mechanician teams!" the announcer said. "The Knight's will start. The Proliate have two entries. Piscium and Ager are the last two competitors."

A few snickers ran through the crowd at the site of the far less sophisticated Piscium and Ager siege engines.

"The Knights have five minutes to fire their first projectile," the announcer proclaimed. "Each team will have three shots. Those sitting at the end of the coliseum can relax as the Magical League constructed an obex or magical wall that will catch the projectile and register distance."

A Magician standing next to the Knights shot a fireball out of his crosier, "Go!"

"Move it!" Sorea yelled. The Proliator guards who "volunteered" to be the literal guinea pigs to power the trebuchet began running as fast as they could in large wooden wheels attached to the siege engine. As the massive wheels turned they raised the counter weight of the trebuchet via a system of pulleys.

"See how the weighted end of the arm is so much shorter?" Gimelli informed Bellae. "Sorea and Finn have the longer arm five times the length of the shorter one on this counterweight trebuchet. Sorea worked all night to get the sling and its release pin just right."

"How much weight is in the wooden box?" Bellae asked.

"Sorea insists the counterweight is at least one hundred times the weight of the projectile."

"Better hurry up Knights, just one minute left to fire!" the announcer chided.

"Can we aim our boulder at his booth?" Finn quipped.

"Release!" Sorea yelled, too wrapped up in layers of concentration to be amused.

The heavy stone rumbled into action, hurtling though the air, slamming into the magical net. A sizzling sound erupted as green light swallowed, and then harmlessly lowered the rock to the ground.

The space where the projectile hit flashed, "1,233 feet."

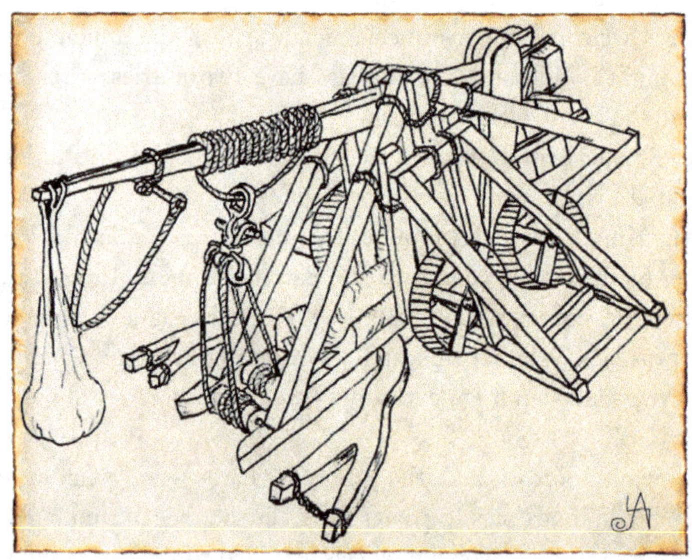

Figure 42: Sketch of the Knight's counterweight trebuchet.

"Great job, Sorea," Finn congratulated to sporadic applause.

After a few minor adjustments the Knights added fifteen feet to their distance.

"Next up, we have the Proliator Mechanician Divisions. The distance to beat is one thousand two hundred and forty-eight feet. They have two entries for us and will fire them simultaneously," the announcer informed.

The first Proliator entry had a series of stair-stepping platforms on either side. Each platform had two Proliators manning a large crank to pull down the trebuchet's arm and lift the counterweight.

Their second machine had a series of massive spoked wheels, like gears, to lift and then hold the counter-weight. With a loud groan, both machines burst into action. A high-pitched squeal replaced the groan as the arms of both machines whipped upwards.

The large rocks careened forward, violently colliding into the protective net and making a sound like water on a hot pan. The green light of the obex enveloped, and brought the projectiles safely down.

A round of applause exploded from the audience as the wall magically flashed, "1,249 feet" and "1,250 feet."

Sorea muttered obscenities as the Proliate dashed down from their machines, formed up ranks and marched from the field with terrifying precision.

"Looks like the Proliate are satisfied with just one attempt. Who can blame them after that impressive double performance?" the announcer cheered.

"I'm really starting to hate that guy," Sorea muttered.

"They only beat our distance by one and two feet!" Gimelli lamented.

A Proliator ventured close to the Knights cocking his head to the side disparagingly, "Nice try."

Finn quickly stepped in front of the enraged Sorea, "Thank you and congratulations," he said with a false smile.

"Let it go and concentrate on winning the destructive force competition next round."

She exhaled sharply but nodded.

"Next up is Piscium," the announcer informed.

Their machine was a traction trebuchet. Instead of a large counterweight, soldiers pulled down on ropes to propel the projectile. A long wooden beam sat on a fulcrum with a sling for the projectile on one end and a wedge-shaped piece of metal with hundreds of strands of rope tied to the other. When the pale blue and yellow clad warriors of Piscium pulled down on the ropes, they provided the force for launching the projectile.

"Those soldiers would be cut to pieces in a siege," Sorea stated.

"Easy targets," Finn agreed.

Once their projectile was loaded, their officer gave the signal, and the Piscinian soldiers pulled down on the ropes. The boulder flew with surprising force, but their best score was only six hundred and forty-five feet.

The counterweight trebuchet from Ager used a sizable wheel with a series of cogs to raise the weight. This helped prevent slipping but made the cranking painfully slow and inefficient. The incredibly large warriors of Ager moved at a steady but plodding pace. Their best score was eight hundred and seventy-five feet.

"The Proliate win first and second, the Knights are third!" the announcer declared.

Figure 43: The primitive traction trebuchet of the Piscinians.

"Now that's nifty," Gimelli said, as a semitransparent grey wall of conjured stones magically rose in front of the newly positioned war machines.

"I have to admit, that's cool," Finn agreed.

"We only have four teams in the destruction competition. Each will fire a single shot at the magical obex, constructed to look like a castle wall, which will read a score from zero to ten. If two or more teams score the highest destructive score, ten, they will compete in a second round. The Knight mechanicians get to go first..." the announcer stated.

"Figures," Sorea said coldly.

"...the team from Ager is next, followed by the Piscinians. The last to fire will be a single Proliate team."

"You are pushing the weight ratio and threatening the integrity of this machine," Finn warned.

"It will hold," Sorea insisted, willing the machine to stay together.

With an unhealthy groan, the trebuchet sprang to life. The colossal rock hurtled forward, hissing as it slammed into the conjured wall, blowing it apart. Virtual fragments of rock flew everywhere. An audible gasp of wonder went up from the crowd.

"Yes!" Sorea shouted as the fake shards reigned down, only to disappear once they touched the ground or audience.

The enchanted wall instantly repaired itself as magic safely lowered the massive boulder to the arena floor.

"A perfect ten to start the competition!" the announcer stated.

Finn climbed down after examining their trebuchet. "Sorea, the arm is showing a few splits. It should hold together to fire again, but I couldn't guarantee it."

"Let's hope we don't need it."

Instead of a trebuchet, Ager launched an impressive catapult. Its large rock smashed into the wall at a spot much lower than the one from the Knights. They seemed pleased as the artificial wall exploded and a score of "8" flashed.

"What's that thing?" Bellae asked, as Piscium prepared its machine.

"It's an onager, it's like a catapult but based on the power stored in twisting rope, like a ballista," Finn stated.

The onager creaked into action and its powerful arm slammed into a wooden crossbeam as the projectile hurtled forward, scoring a six.

The Proliate team wasted no time in firing their gigantic trebuchet.

"Those guys are always in such a hurry," Gimelli noted.

"They do seem to have a fire lit under their arse," Sorea laughed. "I can't imagine it won't score a ten." Her eyes scanned their trebuchet, hoping it had another shot left in it.

Focusing back on the Proliate's machine she shouted, "Their sling is not set right! It will release early."

Sure enough, their stone released well before its full arc and the stone toppled at an awkwardly high trajectory. Despite releasing early, their shot did enough damage to the wall to score a seven.

"The Knights win. Ager is second and the Proliate third," the announcer stated in a deflated tone.

Sorea, Finn, and Gimelli cheered wildly. Bellae stood motionlessly, regarding a winged figure fluttering above the rim of the arena. It quickly flew behind the wall. Despite her tough talk to Lontas, after all the weird creatures they fought to on the way to tournament she felt a chill at the sight of the creature.

Why is it following, but avoiding, me? she wondered in frustration.

"Nice try," Sorea said sarcastically as the Proliate marched out of the arena. The one who had said the same thing to her could only look down. Another soldier mumbled something about the Knights tasting the Proliate's diezmar siege engine soon enough.

Scroll 12: Is Forever Enough?

"Rest up before the Dragon Battle. Make sure you're drinking lots of water," Friar urged the Pantteri once the Knights of Taiheart and Toil Shaor left for the squad battle. "Listen to your captain, Ritari *will* lead you to victory."

"Won't you be with us?" Bellae asked.

"No. The Magical League is insisting I sit in the stadium with the leaders of the countries competing in the Dragon Battle."

"Oh," Bellae said anxiously.

"Finn and Lovag, your horses will be brought up for the battle. No, Bellae, they can't come inside now. I already asked!" Friar said preemptively.

Bellae's expression melted into disappointment.

"Come on, let's head over here," Finn said, leading Bellae to an empty corner and sitting down. She lay with her head across his lower legs.

"What's wrong my Inion?"

"Something doesn't feel right," she said rolling over to face him.

"Fighting a forty-five foot long, fire-breathing dragon isn't supposed to feel right!"

She scowled. "I keep hearing the howling pain and anger from the dragon we heard on the way here. What if you fight that psychotic one?"

"I'm a Knight. Fighting's what I do," he said, playfully tousling her hair. "How about a story to take your mind off this needless worry?"

Bellae nodded.

"I've told you most of the stories I remember from growing up in Creber...there's one I haven't told you about three wood nymphs. One brutally cold winter, when summer's heat was a nothing but a tantalizingly distant memory, the gods of Verngaurd moved to the southern heavens to be closer to the three suns. Huddling for warmth they decided to demand a race for entertainment.

"So they ordered the tree nymphs of Creber Forest: Drysia, Oreia, and Karya, to race from earth to the gods to prove their loyalty and keep their status as demigods of the forest. To motivate them, the gods decreed that the order they finished would determine which section of the forest they would get to look after.

"As Drysia, Oreia, and Karya set off from the Forest of Creber, a cry of pain rang out from some injured trees. Oreia and Drysia ignored it and bolted into the sky. Karya went over and nursed the damaged trees back to health. When she was done she took the time to encourage each barren and sleepy tree, reassuring them that soon enough warmth would once again enter the world.

"Oreia finished the race first and Drysia, second. The gods cheered and the nymphs picked the best sections of the forest to live in and protect. Finally, an exhausted Karya crossed the finish line. The gods chastised her for being lazy and indifferent. She said nothing but looked at her sister nymphs to come to her defense. They stayed silent. Disgusted, she quietly looked down while given the dark and dank part of the forest. She did not complain but worked hard to improve her appointed woodlands. Who really won?"

"Karya, the one who helped."

"Exactly!" Finn said. "There's a tremendous difference between a victory the world will recognize, like in a contest, and the more important victory of spirit and heart. I know I don't have to worry about you. Like Karya, you will always do what's right."

A small tear ran down Bellae's cheek.

"Oh, come on! The story wasn't that bad."

"It's not the story," Bellae said, closing her eyes and releasing a stream of tears. In her mind she was listening to the hideous howling of the dragon in the mountain. "Finn, if something happens to any of you…"

"We'll be fine. Don't get too caught up in the anxieties of the future and forget to enjoy the here and now.

"Remember, you will carry a part of me in the Inion necklace and in your heart forever. Is forever long enough?"

Smiling through tears she answered, "Forever sounds about right."

Chapter Five

The Metal Hits the Scale

Scroll 1: Time to be Annoyed

"You are moving to a new dressing area so Master Veneficus can enchant your weapons," a Proliate Red Guard announced.

"What?" Luchar bellowed. "He can kiss my…"

"Let the man finish!" Ritari thundered.

"The enchantment is *required,* as a precaution, to make sure there are no magical augmentations on your weapons. Plus, it allows the Magical League to count your hits."

"Wait a minute!" Luchar roared. "He's putting an enchantment *on* our weapons to make sure there's no enchantment *on* them?"

The guard shrugged his shoulders. Since Friar was sitting with the Magicians, they had no choice but to follow the Proliator as he led them through a series of small tunnels and chambers.

"This is your new dressing area. Veneficus will be here shortly. I'll wait outside," the Proliate said.

The new chamber was long but narrow. Luchar stood closest to the door, muttering insults and occasionally bashing his helmet. In his perpetual state of anger, he considered the scars on his helmet a sign of genuine affection.

Ritari stood as a silent buffer between Luchar and the rest of the Pantteri. His eyes blazed unblinkingly forward, playing out the coming battle in his mind.

Sorea visualized repeated blows from her tallons striking deep and drawing equal parts blood, and howls of pain.

Finn sat with his eyes closed, and his mind clear as he strummed a melodic tune on the string of his bow.

Lying on his back, Lovag propped his feet up on the wall. Despite his calm appearance, his mind was a burst of activity as he mentally walked through innumerable situations and planned his response.

Several Red Guard finally entered. Everyone stood but Finn and Lovag who were lost in thought. Ritari signaled for Bellae to rouse them before speaking, "Where's Veneficus?"

"He's waiting for you in the warrior gathering area directly under the amphitheater! Why did you move?" the guard asked accusingly. "We've been looking for you!"

"What? Another Proliator told us to come here!"

"Where is this supposed 'Proliator'?"

"Right outside."

"Try again."

"You dirty, fire-worshiping red snakes calling us liars?" Luchar yelled.

"If you want to forfeit, we will inform Veneficus," the Proliate retorted.

"Forfeit?" Luchar barked, his voice shaking with rage. "Why don't we fight you first, then the dragon?"

"Enough!" Ritari said. "Just take us to him."

"Ahhh," Luchar huffed.

The Knights moved through an even longer series of poorly lit underground passages. They were thoroughly disoriented by the time the Red Guard finally pointed to a small doorway. The Knights and squires filed in with the Proliate close behind.

"Line up here."

The Pantteri obliged.

"I thought Veneficus was waiting for us?"

"He was, but obviously left because you weren't here, deciding instead to take an unsanctioned tour on some misguided escapade. I'm sure he'll be back shortly."

Luchar growled but lined up with the other Knights in the middle of a large and poorly lit stone room. Straining eyes could pick out the form of at least fifty unlit torches along the walls while only ten fought impotently against the darkness. The air hung stale and unmoving, except for what their adrenaline and excitement could stimulate.

More mental games, Ritari thought. *Trying to disorient us and keep us in the literal dark.*

The Knights continued to wait while the Red Guard stood as still as statues. After several minutes, Ritari yelled, "At ease! Veneficus is obviously detained."

"Hey, you need to..." one of the Proliate began, but thought better of it as the Knights and their squires dispersed around the room.

BOOM-BOOOM-BOOM! A series of loud crashes reverberated through the traumatized roof. The Knights shot up and drew their weapons.

Ritari looked at the Red Guard who continued to stand motionless. "The first Dragon Battle has begun!" he said, sheathing his broadsword.

Several cheers could be heard above as fine bits of dust rained down from the abused ceiling. Loud howls of a dragon in pain were followed by shouts and orders from the soldiers battling it.

Wave after wave of loud booms rocked the ceiling.

"Will it hold?" Jumeaux finally asked.

Before anyone could answer their ears were assaulted by a piercing shriek from the beast above.

"The dragon's out of fire," one of the Red Guard said in a steely voice.

A series of desperate and explosive moves by the dragon viciously rocked the ceiling as the room once again filled with flakes and rubble, slowly wafting down from the battered ceiling.

Ritari knelt next to the terrified Jumeaux, "Not feeling so confident now that we are close to fighting the dragon?"

"I guess not."

"Problems separated by time and space, almost never seem intimidating. It is only when we come face to face with the situation that we see its true size and significance."

"Sorry I was bragging about seeing the dragon."

"Take a deep breath, remember your training and you'll be fine," he said with surprising kindness.

Immediately after the howling stopped a massive thud rocked the ceiling, quickly followed by a violent explosion of applause.

"One dragon down!" Luchar cried. Shouts of joy from the soldiers as well as the excited, but muffled, voice of the announcer could be heard above.

"The one time we want to go first, they make us wait directly underneath the bloody action!" Sorea said crossly.

"All part of their twisted mind games," Ritari said, glaring at the Red Guard.

After what seemed like hours Master Veneficus entered with an additional pair of Proliator soldiers.

A carefree laugh from Master Veneficus pierced the festering tension in the room. It seemed inappropriate for the life and death situation at hand, and dampened the adrenaline flowing through the Knights' veins. Seeing their expressions, his face turned solemn and eyes apologetic, "Are you ready to battle your dragon?"

Scroll 2: Time for Bad News

"Congratulations on your tournament successes so far. You have added to the prestige of the Knight's already illustrious history." Veneficus' words were met with icy expressions from the impatient and aggrieved Knights.

"Yes, well, let's get you ready to battle your Saatana dragon. The Piscinians already defeated Pallens, and the Proliate will fight Furasta shortly." After looking around pensively he leaned forward, "Your Saatana is named Hullus." The Knights looked unimpressed and continued their silent stares.

"I can see the name doesn't mean anything to you, but this, unfortunately, is bad, extremely bad," he said, shaking his head with a melancholy look wrinkled on his already wizened face. "Normally thirteen to twenty Northern Dwarf handlers can control a Saatana dragon. Hullus, his name means madness by the way, required thirty-five and that scant seemed enough. He makes the other dragons look like puppies. The audacity of bringing such a creature to the Tournament is outrageous, to my thinking, but it's too late to find a replacement.

"How about some advice? First, dragons are not weaker on their underbellies. It makes no sense for a flying creature to have an unarmored abdomen when it's exposed during flight.

"There is a small vulnerable area between the smaller neck scales and the larger scales of the thorax. The second area is where the wings attach," he said, winking. He hunched forward expectantly, his wide eyes foraging for appreciation.

"Thank you for the information. We are grateful for your guidance," Ritari said, indifferently.

Satisfied, Veneficus took a few steps back and straightened, "Now, this is simple. I will utter a spell to detect any enhancements on your weapons. I know you would never cheat, but I must check. All must be fair at the Tournament, mind you."

"Oh, of course," Luchar huffed sardonically. "We've been feeling the equitable love all Tournament!"

"Please place all your weapons within the circle," Veneficus said, ignoring the comment. "If you forget even one dagger the stadium will prohibit you from entering and you will fight shorthanded!"

A thin circle of white marble with gold etching began to glow brilliantly on the floor. Veneficus chanted quietly and a complex design appeared within the ring. The symbol resembled a warped triangle with its three arms flowing into quarter moons, and symbols representing the three suns. The Knights hesitated.

"If you wish to call off the fight…" Veneficus said, letting his voice trail off while innocently shrugging his shoulders.

"All right. All right!" Ritari hissed, as if he were trying to convince himself that laying their weapons down was acceptable. Reluctantly, the

Figure 44: The enchantment symbol in the holding area of the arena.

Pantteri Knights and squires spread out around the glowing circle. Not only did they consider it bad luck to disarm on the eve of battle, they didn't trust Magicians. However, no one wanted to be thought a coward and four of the Knights placed their weapons in the circle.

Luchar remained welded to the floor despite the weight of every eye in the chamber upon him. His heavy battle helmet made it impossible to see his expression.

"Ahem, *all* of you must place your weapons in the circle!"

"You know I never get bad feelings about battle, but get Friar in here," he replied. "That Magician is hiding something, I can sense it."

Offended, Veneficus glared, his crosier raised.

Ritari quickly jumped forward, "Please let me handle this. Antagonizing Luchar will only result in his weapons hurtling towards your head."

Veneficus eyed Luchar distastefully. "He is violently impetuous, isn't he? All right. I want you Knights to be able to fight your dragon so I will let his insult slide."

Play off his impulsiveness, Ritari thought, straining to withhold a smirk at his scheme. Forcing a sullen look he said, "Luchar, there's no dishonor in withdrawing. After hearing what Veneficus said about Hullus, if the Saatana seems too much, we can collect our weapons and…"

Luchar let out a menacing growl and pushed past Ritari, "Not fair!"

He angrily placed his battle hammer and battle-axe inside the circle, letting them clank loudly.

"You know I'm no coward!" Luchar scolded, his eyes glued on his weapons, willing them back to his side.

Ritari's guilt at goading his friend did not make his thoughts clearer. He justified his actions for the honor of the Knights.

"Excellent Pantteri," Veneficus said. "DO NOT attempt to touch your weapons until told to do so! The consequences to your health would be grave."

Veneficus held up his crosier and stretched out his other hand in front of him. Closing his eyes he began to chant, "Quaero enchantments effrego lemma si exsisto illic."

Something hidden beneath the lines of age and concentration in the Magician's face reminded Bellae of the meeting in his chamber when he slammed them helplessly to the ground.

A bright light rose up from the floor, casting an outline of the design up to the ceiling. The weapons glowed pallid blue and clattered as they rose three feet off the floor. Veneficus chanted, "Vanda!" and the weapons began to whirl around and around with increasing speed. Red sparks sizzled each time they bisected the white light emanating from the ground.

Bellae closed her eyes to quell her growing nausea and avoid the flickering light and sparks. Jumeaux was the only one inching closer. He carefully studied Veneficus' expressions, in awe of his power. *Who else could order the Pantteri Knights to disarm, and then put on a spectacle like this?*

Veneficus startled everyone by shouting, "Desino avta aon vanda ili quaero enchantments effrego!" The weapons stopped. He started whispering, and the light changed from white to purple and filled the entire circle. His grey goatee glimmered and his eyes glowed in the pale reflected light.

Bellae noticed a puzzled look on the faces of the Red Guard. *Is he doing something different to our weapons?* Just when Bellae couldn't stand it any longer Veneficus yelled, "Desino avta! Arvosana!"

He slouched and let his arms and crosier fall towards his sides as the weapons plunged down, rattling loudly on the marble floor. As the clanging subsided, the purple light seemed to slither up like smoke. The emblem on the floor faded until completely disappearing.

"Done! Well now, that wasn't so bad, was it? All weapons are clean from enchantment and …"

"What did you do? Don't tell me you just screened for enchantments!" Luchar interrupted, waving his hands wildly at the misting purple smoke wriggling aggressively around him.

Veneficus raised his eyebrows and tilted his head back indignantly, the crystal on his crosier glowing menacingly.

"Luchar, hold your tongue!" Ritari growled. "My apologies, Supreme Master." Although he had the same thought, it is not wise to anger any Magician, but especially this one.

Bellae shuddered at the painful memory of being slammed to the floor under his magic, and slowly backed away even though she knew it would do no good if Veneficus sought revenge.

The Magician nodded slightly, "Your reputation precedes you, Luchar. However, I understand your frustration giving up your weapons. Therefore, I can forgive this second lack of discretion. Before I was interrupted I was going to say that I also marked each weapon with the Arvosana Enchantment, for scoring. This way, when you strike the dragon, it will be automatically recorded.

"We can then determine who won in the fastest time and with the fewest number of hits to decide our Dragon Champion. Also, these scores will help crown the overall Festival Champion. Now, pick up your weapons. These Proliators will lead you up to the arena when it's time. I…" Veneficus stopped abruptly, turning towards a sound hidden deep within shadows at the back of the room.

"What, who…" Veneficus said, his crosier throwing out a bright band of light. "…is that Fino?"

"What are you doing in here?" one of the Proliate screamed while dashing towards a Magician sprinting along the back wall.

"I saw Tacet-Vand!" the Magician screamed as he bolted through the door.

The Pantteri looked up to see a gaunt—to the point of looking sick—Master Magician darting out of the room.

"You know Veneficus decreed there can be no Magicians down here!" another Proliate bellowed while in hot pursuit.

A concerned look spread across Veneficus' face. "Fino will regret disobeying my orders! His being here is troubling me, however, not as much as the notion Tacet-Vand might have been down here as well. I apologize for the interruption and will double check to make sure no one tainted your weapons with…"

A new group of Proliate stormed into the room. "Veneficus, you are *urgently* needed in the arena!"

"Of course. I just need to check…"

"Sir, Emperor Fanga is literally strangling a few spectators from the Rebelde Plains because they insulted his Piscinian warriors. Large crowds of soldiers from both countries are descending on the scene and itching for a fight. High Commander Storlax is threatening to kill everyone."

Figure 45: Gaunt looking Magician Fino was caught in the holding area despite explicit instructions from Veneficus.

Understanding Storlax's bellicosity Veneficus' eyes instantly widened. He quickly chanted a few words and immediately disappeared.

"These weapons have a foul stench," Luchar growled, picking up his axe and sniffing it. "Either Fino or Veneficus did something to them!"

"What choice did we, and do we, have?" Ritari answered. "Does anyone wish to forgo the battle?"

Despite their uneasy feeling, no one said anything.

"It's no fluke that we drew the fiercest dragon and fight last!" Luchar declared.

"They have been stacking the odds against us all Tournament!" Sorea added.

"Finn, what do your Elvish eyes see?" Ritari quizzed.

"Something with these weapons seems off, but it could be the enchantments? I don't know."

"Please, Ritari, speak to Friar before the battle," Bellae pleaded.

"Be quiet, half-pint!" Jumeaux yelled viciously. "The Magicians wouldn't do anything to hurt us!"

"All squires would do well to hold their tongues!" Ritari growled. "No more doubts, no more discussion! We are Knights and we fight with *no* fear!" Just as he finished speaking a ferocious roar and heavy-footed thumping boomed overhead.

"The second Dragon Battle begins!"

Scroll 3: I Shall Look Upon You

The Knights tried to relax despite the battle raging overhead between the Proliate and the second dragon, Furasta. Bellae curled up next to Finn as the floor above creaked and moaned, occasionally shedding tears of dust. Finally, a deafening thud was followed by a passionate cheer.

As the last resonance of the crash faded away, Bellae's eyes shot open and her entire body tensed. *The Knights are next,* she thought. It felt like the world was rushing by, and her body was plummeting in a free fall.

She closed her eyes to fight a rising nausea. She hugged Finn and he gently rubbed her back as the seconds slowly ticked by. The arena became relatively quiet save for a loud scuffing sound and the jingle of chains as the Northern Dwarves hauled the dragon's carcass out of the arena.

Eventually total silence and tense suspense settled on the waiting Knights and squires, who were gripped in an odd mix of anticipation and boredom.

THUD, THUD, THUD!

The floor overhead cried out in thunderous groans as it bowed fiercely enough to send a jolting vibration through Bellae. A terrifying roar blasted above them, joining rattling chains, desperate shouts, and nervous applause.

"Knights!" a new and tall Proliator guard boomed. "Those dainty sounds overhead would be your dragon, Hullus," he said, smiling slyly while pointing towards the exit. "It's time."

The Knights and squires followed him through several tunnels before climbing a set of stairs and coming to a darkened entrance area that would directly lead out onto the arena floor.

"You guys running low on torches or something?" Luchar asked sarcastically.

"Enter the arena through that door," the tall guard stated, ignoring the question.

"Knights to battle!" Ritari yelled, holding up his black spear. His eyes seemed to glow red with hunger for combat. The Knights shouted loudly in reply.

"Are you okay?" Finn whispered to Bellae.

"Just worried," she managed.

"Pantteri to victory!" Ritari shouted as he followed the Proliator into the arena. Lovag, Sorea, their squires and Jumeaux went through next. Luchar waited impatiently in the doorway while Finn lingered, pretending to adjust his armor.

"Ah, my little Inion. Everything will be fine. I doubt this dragon is any worse than Luchar on a bad day. In fact, his breath probably smells better!"

"Finn! Be serious! Talk to Friar, or have Veneficus come and check your weapons. That Fino guy looked frail and frightening."

He paused and stared at her as if painting each detail of her face into his mind. "I hope you choose your own path and make your own destiny in life as I have tried to do. However, there are times when you can't escape the world. You can only deal with what is directly in front of you. There is nothing in Verngaurd that could make me leave my fellow Knights right before battle," Finn said, his green eyes sparkling with anticipation.

"Be careful," Bellae entreated, trying to be supportive despite her doubts.

"I swear, I shall look upon you when this is over," he answered.

Bellae smiled and wiped away a small tear.

"Come on pointy ears," Luchar cried. "Let's get it on!"

Bellae held on briefly before Luchar bellowed an impatient grunt.

"Got plenty of tricks up those Elvish sleeves of yours?" Luchar challenged with a smile—at least what would pass as a smile for him. The excitement radiating off his face was barely contained by the helmet he now slipped on.

The tall guard poked his head through the door, "Now would be the time to exit!"

"We're coming!" Luchar growled.

"Let's go, Inion, my daughter," Finn whispered with a genuine smile that warmed her heart.

She noted his face turn grave as he headed towards the door where Luchar was intent on having them walk through together. Luchar excitedly slapped the muscular Elf on the back, "Time to fight, brother!"

Bellae watched her Knight get swallowed by the brilliant light streaming in from the coliseum. Her heart skipped a beat and screamed for her not to enter.

Oh, just shut up doubt! Whatever the future would bring, she would stand by Finn.

She reluctantly plunged into the blinding light of the arena. Palpable heat seized and squeezed her tightening lungs. The unhindered din seemed deafening after growing accustomed to the muffled roars and shouts from inside the waiting area.

The dragon's fire, Bellae thought as a terrifying blast of heat pressed up against her. She saw Lovag mounting his horse, Behalen. The edgy horse bucked up on its hind legs as a barbarous growl ripped the air and shook her very soul. There was a vibratory quality to the dragon's roar as air passed through the gill-like slits that serve as its nostrils. Lovag calmly stroked the horses' mane and whispered into his ear.

Bellae froze as she suddenly became viscerally aware of the creature. The emotions of the dragon washed upon her like a tidal wave of frothy hate. It slammed into her gut and she doubled over, her legs suddenly feeling heavy and weak. She felt frozen in a nightmare, unable to move.

Terror tingled its way through her spine, forcing her entire body to shiver in anticipation of seeing the dragon. Bellae finally managed to stand up, her eyes rising towards the fearsome roars. Thankfully, a triple squad of Proliator guards had formed a towering shield wall in front of the Pantteri Knights, blocking her view.

Suddenly, the guards turned their heads away in a grimace of pain as a rush of flames came skirting over the top row of the shield barrier. The fierce heat wormed its way through the strength of their shields and armor. Bellae caught her breath as another wave of intense heat blasted her.

"Compared to the other dragons this one is way larger, more menacing and definitely full of more rage," the announcer murmured in horror-laced excitement.

"Bellae!" Gimelli shouted. "Get to Crann! He's panicking!"

Crann and Finn. The thought focused her racing mind and gave her strength. Taking a deep breath, Bellae forced her wobbling legs to move towards the horse. With each step her movements gradually became more natural.

Crann's fear was palpable as he bounced up and down in repeated, jittery cycles. He thrashed his head wildly as if trying to shake off an invisible attacker.

"Crann, I need you to fight for Finn," Bellae told him as placidly as she could. *"You can defeat this beast."* The words seemed hollow and she felt like joining him in protest, but realized their best chance for survival was teamwork.

Crann stopped bouncing but stomped his feet and stared with wide-eyed intensity in the direction of the dragon. Bellae was aware of the terror within Crann, but she could also palpate the bordering determination that was starting to wall in his panic.

"You keep Finn safe!" Bellae instructed, trying to keep her own boiling emotions contained. Crann's upright brown mane quivered as he lowered his head. She leaned forward until their foreheads touched. *"Be strong, move quick, and trust Finn."*

Bellae grabbed Crann's reins and led him to Finn who was busy loading his hailstorm weapon with its spring-loaded blades. Bellae saw only strength and determination in Finn's eyes. His movements were as smooth and steady as always. He climbed on Crann and smiled down at her. "Thanks, dear Inion. Crann, old buddy, don't worry. We'll win," he said, patting his horse's flank.

Just then a ferocious blast of fire plunged over the Proliate shield wall. A collective gasp went up from the crowd as the Northern Dwarf warriors shouted commands and violently attempted to control the extreme dragon. Cheers from the crowd had given way to awe at the fierceness of this dragon.

"See you soon. Remember your promise," Bellae said, trying to smile despite the tear sliding from the corner of her eye.

"I *will* see you afterward," Finn said with calm resolve. The two mounted Knights rode up to the other Pantteri who were lined up directly behind the Proliate shield wall. Lovag was on the far left sitting on Behalen. Ritari, Sorea, and Luchar were next on foot. Luchar was bobbing back and forth while pounding his fist against his breastplate and shouting, "Knights!" Finn took Crann to their place on the far right.

"Remember your training, Pantteri," Ritari shouted above the din. "Don't bunch up. Attack and move. Find and exploit weaknesses. Keep to the basics, but don't become predictable. Protect yourself and watch each other's backs. If someone's in trouble, distract the demon. Work together, coordinate attacks, and use diversions to play off one another.

"Lovag and Finn, send a steady stream of hurt from those bows." Nodding to Sorea he added, "Rain down a storm of bolts. It's a way for us to wear him down from a distance. Remember, the dragon's reserve of fire oil will eventually burn out. Once his naphtha runs out we must act quickly, before it regenerates."

A piercing bellow of anger cracked out of the dragon. A rattling of chains followed with an occasional "twang" signaling the dragon had tensed out the irons holding him to the arena floor. The Northern Dwarves in charge of the dragon could be heard screaming desperate orders. At least two had been helped from the arena, their scorched, steaming armor now blackened. Flames shot violently across the top of the arena as the dragon's head flailed wildly from side to side. The crowd recoiled in horror but was protected by a magical shield.

"You filthy son of a mongrel! I'll rip your bloody heart out!" Luchar roared in response. "What do you think, Finn? Do you see any danger in that beast?" Luchar laughed, ecstatic for battle after all the waiting.

"I'm sensing a bit of peril," Finn quipped. In reality, his world was a blur of menacing red and orange.

"Bellae, here, now!" Scelto yelled. The other squires motioned to her from behind a short stone barricade. Another palpable blast of heat clawed at her back, but she did not turn to see the flames, continuing to run as fast as her wobbly legs would allow. Reaching them, she fell into Scelto arms and he held her.

I will see Finn again. There's always a way to win, she tried to reassure herself. Yet, she could feel the unsettling panic blaring in Scelto's racing heart.

"Two dragons came into the arena, two dragons are deaaaaaad!" the announcer yelled as the crowd let loose ravenous applause and catcalls. "Let's get ready for the final Dragon Baaaaaattllle!"

"The Pantteri squad of Knights from Liberum will fight…" a distinct cheer rose from the crowd. Bellae scanned desperately for Friar Pallium, but there were too many people moving and screaming in the sea of colors, banners, and shields "…they fight one mean Saatana dragon, HULLUS!" A deafening roar went up from the crowd.

"Bloody swine, cheering louder for the dragon are you?" Scelto shouted. Sparked by the anger ascending within him, he gently released Bellae and stood up.

"Listen up squires, forget about the crowd and get in this battle. Behind us we have weapons, bandages, and water in case our Knights need them. However, unlike a real battle, we absolutely cannot go to them. The rules are clear during the Dragon Battles. Knights will have to come to us, near this magically protected barricade, before we can assist them. No one, I mean no one, goes out there without my approval! Don't do anything that will get us disqualified."

As Scelto finished a small voice inside each of the squire's head yelped, *Who would want to go out there?* They all stole furtive glances at the others to see whether they held the same dread. The prestidigitation dragon conjured up by the Dwarf Pumilus hadn't prepared them for this.

The announcer's voice roared over the din of the coliseum once again, "After a fierce performance defeating their dragon, the current leader for Tournament Champion is Proliate Red Brigade Commander, Fenik, with ten thousand seven-hundred and thirty-four overall points!"

The crowd bellowed again which seemed to enrage the dragon as it returned an ominous roar. The squires could see flames shooting high into the air. The profile of the Knights shone black against the orange-red flame of the dragon's fire.

"Knights, get ready!" the announcer screamed.

Ritari raised his spear and the five warriors shouted, "Knights!"

Friar, where are you? Bellae thought.

"Brave Proliator Guard, disperse!" the announcer instructed.

The Proliate broke apart with lightning efficiency and speed. Half sprinted around Lovag while half circled around Finn. To Bellae's surprise, the orderly retreat ended behind them with their captain standing next to Bellae.

Sensing her fear, he forced a smile, "Don't worry, miss. Grand Master Veneficus put an enchantment on this section and the stands. The dragon can't get you or them."

It's Crann, Finn, and the Knights I'm worried about, she thought.

Bellae appreciated his kindness, but it did little to stay her dread, especially with black scorch marks all over his once gleaming red shield. The steam rippling out from it performed wavy, meandering dances.

She moved her hand forward, but stopped short of touching the shield when she felt the intense heat still radiating from it.

"The last Dragon Battle has begun!" the announcer declared emphatically.

Scroll 4: Dragon Bleeds, Armor Burns

"Release the dragon!" the announcer yelled.

The three dozen Northern Dwarf warriors released the chains holding Hullus and sprinted out of the arena, dragging the shackles behind with a loud metallic rattle.

For the first time, the squires had a full view of the beast. It was fire-red save its dark green tongue framed by serrated teeth the size of daggers. Rows of large, spiked scales lined the side of his face and neck. A large horn stuck up menacingly from its snout and three from the sides of its head. Two hook-like horns curved on the top of its head.

Foul smelling poisonous drool dripped onto a razor-sharp projection below his chin. His tan ears were flaps with scalloped ends that

Figure 46: Hullus is a giant amongst giants, regarded as one of the largest Saatana dragons to ever live. These fearsome dragons are perpetually foul-tempered, and notable for their slit-like noses that allow for smoke and toxins to escape as they breathe fire.

resembled miniature versions of its enormous wings fluttering above the massive back needed to support them. Smoke could be seen billowing from the fluttering, gill-like slits it used to take in air and vent its toxic vapor when breathing fire.

Hullus stood up on his hind legs showing a well-armored abdomen, as Veneficus foretold. His legs were muscular but lean and ended in large claws. Suddenly, he crouched low and rotated his wings forward until a claw-like horn at the top of each wing pressed firmly to the ground. Both pairs of legs and the wings flexed in unison, sending the dragon exploding upward. The wings quickly took over with massive pulsating beats.

Bellae's heart lifted. *Maybe he'll fly away!*

BOOOOOM, TSSSSSSSSSTTTTTTTT! A shower of sparks rained down on the arena as he hit the magical shield preventing escape. The dragon, along with Bellae's hope, plummeted to the earth in a painful roar. He shook his head and stood up while roaring with a terrifying mix of pain and frustration.

Ritari barked orders and the Pantteri sprang into action. Lovag urged Behalen into a hard run to the left while loading and firing his heavy bow. Finn sprinted Crann to the right, firing three arrows at a time from his saighead, or triple arrow, bow. Sorea stayed in the center and dropped to one knee to fire her crossbow.

Figure 47: The Knights move in as their dragon battle finally begins.

Zwing! One of Lovag's heavy arrows struck hard into the inner wing of the dragon's right side causing Hullus to screech in fury and pain. He rose up on his hind legs and pounced towards Lovag, who wheeled Behalen towards the opposite edge of the arena through an adrenalin fuelled sprint. The dragon growled furiously at missing Lovag and released a scorching burst of flames at the retreating horse. Behalen's tail was singed, but they were otherwise no worse for the wear.

As the dragon lurched towards Lovag, three arrows from Finn, who had swung around behind the dragon on Crann, found their mark in its lower neck.

Just then a longbow shot from Lovag glanced off the dragon's head.

"How did that not penetrate?" Lontas yelled.

"Must have hit the scale wrong or something," Scelto added.

"Lovag doesn't miss like that."

The dragon turned toward Ritari and Luchar who quickly came together to join shields in front of Sorea.

A crossbow shot from her, and another heavy bowshot from Lovag hit right between the dragon's eyes and glanced off. Three arrows from Finn were the next to carom off.

A tense murmur rose up from the dismayed crowd at the ricocheting shots.

"What's going on here, Veneficus?" Friar thundered.

"Where's Fino?" Veneficus asked.

"What? Why? Who's Fino?"

"Where is Tacet-Vand?" Veneficus thundered.

"What's happening?"

Veneficus didn't answer but scoured the crowd. *No Fino, but there's Tacet-Vand! He is here!*

The aged wizard shook his head menacingly at Veneficus.

Back in the arena, Ritari motioned to Finn. He first held out five fingers spread as widely as they could, then pointed to the dragon, and finally, his own eyes.

"Come on Finn, make it work," Ritari pleaded. "Nothing else is getting through."

"It's a blasted Magician's curse, that's what," Luchar growled ominously. "Either Fino or Veneficus sabotaged us. Let's try a flying pincer and let it taste our blades."

Ritari nodded just as the dragon let loose a hoard of flames straight towards them. Ritari and Luchar squatted in unison.

"AHHHHHH," they bellowed as the heat roasted their interlocked shields and a portion of their exposed backs. Heat and smoke lazily danced from the metal, its casual nature strangely out of place in the hectic tension of the arena. The two singed Knights heard and felt the draft of more arrows and bolts flying overhead, each one harmlessly bouncing off the dragon.

Despite the massive thuds of the rumbling dragon growing infinitely louder as he charged, Ritari and Luchar held their ground.

"Come on!" Luchar shouted, swaying side to side in anticipation.

"Hold…hold," Ritari repeated.

"Come on!" Luchar thundered again.

"Hold."

BOOM-BOOM-BOOM-BOOM!

The ground trembled harder as the pace of the dragon quickened.

The crowd gasped just as Ritari finally yelled "NOOOOOW!"

With lightning quickness both Ritari and Luchar took three fleet steps, Ritari to the left, and Luchar to the right, before diving high in the air. Their outstretched shields landed first, then their heads, and finally their backs as they somersaulted forward and sprang to their feet. Luchar left his shield lying on the ground and grasped his battle-axe with two hands. He swung with enough force to fell a large tree. The blade ricocheted off the dragon's scales, sending a fierce quiver reverberating through Luchar's body.

The crowd gasped in disbelief and alarm.

"What are you made of, fiend?" Luchar challenged.

Veneficus stood up, apprehensive about the ineffectiveness of the Knight's weapons. Tacet-Vand had disappeared and he still did not see the sallow Magician, Fino.

"Do something!" Friar screamed.

Veneficus yelled a series of enchantments meant to remove any magic protecting the dragon or hindering the Knight's weapons.

Ritari dropped his shield, grasping his spear with two hands he charged like a man possessed. The crowd held its breath as he drew closer. With a fierce yell he slammed the blade forward. After chinking through scales it squished deep into the flesh of the dragon.

"It worked!" Veneficus exclaimed as he, and the crowd, let out a sigh of relief at the success. The beast howled and reared up, ripping the flailing Ritari into the air as he desperately held onto his spear.

As Luchar reached for his shield the dragon's wing swung forward and knocked him to the ground. With a powerful flick of his massive head, the dragon flung Ritari skyward, forcing him to release his spear and land hard on the ground. Hullus jumped closer while tucking his chin down. By quickly raising his head, he used the horn on the top of his snout to scoop Ritari from the earth, tossing him skyward like a rag doll. Ritari landed harshly on dragon's spiked spine.

Arching his neck rearward, the dragon managed to pin Ritari against the spikes running down his back. Ritari groaned as the air rushed out of his lungs and the spikes dented into his armor. The dragon bounded up and down on his front legs trying to dislodge the spear stuck into his flesh while squeezing the life out of Ritari.

His breath nearly extinguished, Ritari began to see a kaleidoscope of flickering lights on a growing background of darkness. After riding around behind the beast, Finn stood up on Crann's back while swinging his flying star weapon that Ritari had signaled him to use. The star-shaped blade whizzed around on the end of a thick rope. Finn released and it flew towards the head of the dragon. The crowd gasped, as it almost hit Ritari who was now limply dangling in the grasp of the dragon.

It missed.

Finn urgently gave commands to Crann who headed straight for the dragon's right front leg. Crann came within a few feet of the beast before abruptly stopping. Finn jumped, flying feet first through the air at the side of the dragon while re-throwing his flying star weapon. He made a few adjustments in midair, and the star sliced into the dragon's right eye. Finn kicked off the dragon's side and vaulted backwards, somersaulting away from the dragon. Crann had turned around and Finn landed hard in the saddle, now facing backwards.

"Teigh!" Finn yelled, holding on tightly with his legs. Crann bolted forward and Finn wrenched his flying star. The dragon howled in pain-filled rage as the star slurped towards Finn. Chunks of the dragon's eye scattered in all directions, followed by vitreous fluid. A large, fleshy, ocular glob still clung to the star. As it whizzed through the air, trails of mucous, stringy eye residue, strands of optic nerve, and blood followed. The dragon's trembling spasms of agony released Ritari and, unconscious, he fell flaccidly to the ground. The dragon nearly stepped on him several times before moving backwards in anguish.

A burst of indiscriminate fire engulfed Ritari's limp body. Lying on his stomach, his armor mostly protected him from the flames pouring over his immobile body. Unfortunately, his helmet was gone and the crowd gasped as Ritari's armor and hair burned. Horrified, Bellae started towards him.

"He's too far away for us to help him!" Scelto yelled, grabbing her.

Bellae strained to see through her tears. The noise, the heat, the stress, and apprehension were too much when she was also burdened by the feelings of rage and pain radiating from the dragon.

Finn reached the sizzling and smoking body of Ritari just as he began to regain consciousness, groaning and coughing weakly.

Finn jumped off Crann, "I got you, buddy."

"Hot," Ritari croaked in a hoarse voice.

"Dragon fire usually is."

Finn sliced open his water skin, dousing Ritari's hair. Luckily, only a small amount of the dragon's oily naphtha had fallen on his head and the flames sizzled out. Finn tipped the rest onto the fasteners of Ritari's body armor, which, unfortunately, had the dragon's naphtha oil sprayed on it, making it impossible to extinguish. Using the empty water skin as a glove he unfastened the flaming hot armor while the dragon continued to howl and shake his head in uncontaminated rage.

Ritari managed to sit up as Finn coaxed the dented, and still flaming, armor off. The back of his head was burned an angry red and his hair stood in blackened clumps. The skin of his body suffered less from burns, but tingled from having been roasted inside his armor. "My sword," Ritari said weakly.

"Your sword, unlike your hair in the back after the flames, or your wits after hitting your head, is one of the few things you still have left! Let's get you to the squires and out of this fight."

"Not a chance, pointy!" A burst of energy surged through Ritari's scorched body at the idea of being removed from the fight.

"All right, big guy. But when this is over you have to tell me who does your hair. It looks absolutely fantastic," Finn laughed.

Ignoring the searing pain from the back of his head Ritari stood up, "Very funny."

As Finn approached, Crann neighed nervously, eyeing the wounded and wrathful dragon stomping ever closer.

Scroll 5: Eye See You

Finn grabbed his bow and quickly put three arrows into the dragon's leg before getting astride Crann. He continued slamming arrows into the dragon's body in an attempt to divert attention from Ritari.

It wasn't working.

The dragon sensed weakness in the armor-less Knight. The other Pantteri sprang into action to protect Ritari. Luchar's axe bit deeply into the dragon's back left leg. Blood surged out, spraying his armor with a series of tings, *plink-plink-plink-plink.*

He followed it with two more blows, each leaving cavernous gashes of sliced flesh. The ground around Luchar quickly became drenched in dragon blood, each slash bringing a fresh shower of green gore lapping out. The dragon blasted flames at Luchar. He quickly dove out of the way in a series of somersaults staying just out of the fire.

"Don't get hit with the naphtha oil!" Finn yelled. "It will not extinguish."

Sorea abandoned her crossbow and sprinted towards the dragon while it was distracted with Luchar. Jumping, she vaulted off the dragon's right front leg, and then used the back of her tallon blades like climbing piolets to scale up to his wing. Finally, she used the base of the wing as a fulcrum, swinging onto his back. Once there she swayed from side to side viciously slamming the tallon blades strapped to her forearms into the dragon's flesh. Hot, green ichor now coated her body and the dragon's backbone as she carefully avoided the impenetrable row of spikes running down his spine.

Each bite from the tallons sent a shock wave of pain through the dragon, who began zealously fluttering his wings in a vain attempt to dislodge Sorea. When that didn't work, he started stomping wildly to buck her off. She dropped down and held onto a large spike with one hand while furiously stabbing with her other. The dragon stopped bouncing and shot fire arcing across the arena in frustration. Sorea stood up and moved forward to find a fresh area to attack. Sensing her movement the dragon arched his head back.

His massive skull slammed into Sorea, sending her whipping backward. After bounding several times off the dragon's back and tail, she landed limply on the hard earth ten feet behind the dragon, flaccidly rolling another five.

Gimelli immediately jumped up. One of the Proliator guards deftly moved forward and grabbed her. "I know it's customary for you to help your Knight in battle, but you absolutely cannot assist them unless they are near this barricade."

"My Knight just got knocked out and I'm going to help!" Gimelli shouted.

"Hands off the lady!" Scelto yelled, grabbing the Proliators hand and flinging it off.

A dozen Proliate quickly surrounded them.

"We admire your fighting spirit, but do not dishonor your Knights by getting them disqualified," the captain declared.

"Ridiculous!" Scelto shrieked, realizing there were too many guards to overcome.

The dragon fell onto his left side, writhing in pain. Its body had green blood oozing over the red scales where Sorea had gouged its flesh with her tallons, and Finn had shot it with arrows. Blood dripped from his legs, thanks to Luchar. The dried blood covering his face constantly received fresh recruits as more continued to percolate out of the shredded right eye socket. His wings had lightning bolts of blood charging down them, courtesy of Lovag's arrows.

Suddenly, he whipped his tail around and caught Luchar in the abdomen just as he started towards the dragon. The blow sent him somersaulting onto his back. His battle-axe went flying end over end and the air shot out of his lungs as he landed with a hard *thud.*

The dragon bellowed and got back to his feet. Lovag had ridden in an arc and was continuing to shoot his heavy bow, repeatedly hitting the dragon's wings. Sorea lay unconscious twenty feet from the rest of the Knights.

Ritari was still shaking the cobwebs out as sweet oxygen continued pumping into his formerly deprived brain. He found his shield and drew his broad sword out of its scabbard. Luchar was just catching his breath as well, grasping his battle hammer he stood and ran towards the dragon.

The dragon turned towards Ritari, before abruptly thrashing his tail in the opposite direction just as Luchar was swinging his hammer. The hammer and tail met in mid-air. The weight and momentum of the dragon easily overwhelmed Luchar and the hammer shot back into his helmet with a reverberating, *gong!*

Luchar flipped head over heels several times before landing limply on his back, his helmet indented into his head. The metal split apart and the edges were biting deeply into his flesh, releasing a torrent of blood over both the twisted silver of his helmet and his unconscious head.

A taciturn silence gripped the stunned crowd watching the fierce battle. A brief spurt of flame nuzzled out of Hullus' mouth as smoke swirled angrily from his slit like nostrils.

"It appears his ability to produce fire is extinguished!" the announcer declared. "This will give the Knights a little break before his naphtha regenerates."

The remaining three conscious Knights quickly moved to form a line in front of their fallen comrades. Finn, riding Crann, was on the right. The armor-less Ritari stood in the middle, his face contorted

Figure 48: The battle has been brutal. Only three Knights remain standing and they are determined to protect the two unconscious Knights.

in wide-eyed anger. Having shot the last of his arrows, Lovag sat on Behalen with his curved scimitar sword.

Finn leaned down to whisper. Ritari's nod was barely perceptible. After briefly talking with Lovag, Ritari screamed, "KNIGHTS!" and charged towards the dragon. Lovag's Behalen paused for a moment before taking off in a sprint while Finn and Crann waited.

The dragon attempted to generate fire but couldn't and howled in frustration. His one good eye bounced between Ritari and Lovag as they charged. Finn started swinging his flying star as Crann began stealthily trotting towards the dragon's left, trying to get in range of the dragon's remaining good eye.

The dragon fiercely snapped his massive fangs at the fast approaching Ritari. Missing, his forked tongue shot out menacingly. Two streams of brightly colored poison sprayed out from either side of his tongue. Ritari dove to the ground and rolled to his left, safely under the jets of venom. Springing up with amazing agility, Ritari contorted his heavy frame and rapidly swung his broad sword upward, slicing off the tip of the dragon's tongue. An immense gush of dark green blood and viscous poison flooded out in pulses from the stump as Ritari went to work on the dragon's right leg and chest.

Just then Lovag vaulted off Behalen onto the back of the beast and began chopping wildly with his sword at the base of the dragon's right wing.

As the dragon roared, Finn unexpectedly leapt off Crann's back, swinging the opposite end of his flying star that held a three-pronged hook. The rope wrapped around the beast's neck before the hooks dug in-between the scales. Finn swung onto to the beast's chest and instantly began to scale up the dragon's neck. He grabbed his dagger and stuck it deep into the dragon's upper neck for leverage while pushing off hard with both legs, flinging himself backwards and upwards. In midair he grabbed his hailstorm and shot it at the dragon's remaining good eye. Diamond-shaped blades sprung out of the weapon and slammed into the flesh of the dragons face, ripping and tearing as they sank deep into its tissue. Three pierced the eye, again sending showers of intraocular fluid shooting in all directions to join the downpour of blood.

The Saatana howled and brought his right leg slashing blindly up through the air. Just before Finn could land on Crann's back, the bleeding claws of the dragon's right leg ripped into Finn's side. The force sent him flying fifteen feet through the air, spinning, and tumbling wildly as his flaccid body sailed swiftly and rudderless. After a gasp, a heavy silence settled on the arena, all previous excitement thudding to a somber stop.

The now blind dragon crouched, his ears rising and turning to listen. Upon hearing Finn's frame thud, the dragon limped his way towards the sound where the body landed.

"Wow. Three Knights down," the ruffled announcer proclaimed.

The deep and labored panting of the dragon could be heard as it struggled towards Finn. Bellae's eyes widened in horror while the rest of her body froze. Within the terror clutching her mind she repeatedly screamed, *No!*

The dragon kicked Ritari aside. He rolled about ten feet before skidding to a stop. His sword and shield scattered, and he looked for them through dazed eyes.

The dragon seemed to be ignoring Lovag who had nearly hacked his right wing completely off. The generous blood supply to the wing displayed itself and was spurting out massive volleys of blood. Despite being completely drenched in the sickly green gore Lovag ignored the gushes and continued his unremitting blows.

Finn moaned as Crann swung around to keep an eye on both the dragon and his beloved Knight. Gently, but firmly, Crann nuzzled Finn's gore soaked side, urging him with increasing desperation to rise as the revenge-minded dragon limped closer and closer. His wing-like ears peaked high, listening intently to the labored breathing of Finn, the person who had blinded him.

A burst of movement on the arena floor energized the crowd reeling in a mix of awe and alarm. Bellae had bolted from behind the barriers and was sprinting towards Finn.

"Here, foolish girl!" the stunned Proliate captain roared.

"NO!" Gimelli shrieked in horror. The Proliator guards surrounding her and Scelto had not thought it necessary to watch over the diminutive Bellae.

"Let me get my sister!"

"One girl out there is quite enough!"

An enormous gasp shot out from the crowd as Bellae stopped between Finn and the dragon, stretching out her arms. Like a single drop of water outlined against a tidal wave, she held her ground. Blackened eye sockets oozing dark green blood stared lifelessly at the young squire. His ears and slit like nostrils searched for Finn as green blood and frothing poison poured out of his tongue-less mouth.

Veneficus made his way down through the crowd to the edge of the seating area as the dragon continued his methodical limp towards Bellae. The beast seemed to be sliding over the pool of green blood oozing and dripping from its mangled body rather than walking.

She wanted her own revenge for injuring Finn and yelled, *"Stop! You will not hurt him anymore!"*

Bellae felt nauseated by the beast's pain, which had begun to replace his dimming anger and hunger for revenge. She struggled to control her queasiness, but she couldn't turn off the dragon's suffering.

Ritari had found his sword and ran, hacking fiercely at the beast's side. The dragon had resigned himself to death and ignored the pain streaming from his wing and side as the two remaining Knights desperately chopped. The dragon thrust his mangled head towards Bellae and snorted. Black and gray wisps of smoke shot from its gill like nostrils and swirled around her head. Bellae contorted her nose in disgust as the putrid acid smell burned through her senses.

It was a strange sight that had everyone in the coliseum mesmerized: the miniature form of Bellae inches away from the bleeding and disfigured face of the massive dragon.

Bellae stared at the naked agony in front of her. A stream of hideous information ripped into her senses as she felt and talked to the creature. The amount and depth of the communication was too much for her to manage. Her eyes scoured his mangled face. The coagulated black sockets where the eyes had once been were still spitting trickles of fresh, green blood. Worse than the physical suffering was the mental affliction. Torture, hate, heartache, steamed off the beast and into her mind and heart. Her mounded feelings of revenge melted to sorrow.

Figure 49: Overwhelmed at the site of her injured Knight, Bellae sprints out to stand in front of the massive dragon. Although her will is strong, her size appears preposterous compared to the immense dragon intent on revenge.

Someone has been tormenting this beast. That is why it was howling in the mountain.

"Help that girl!" a spectator yelled.

"I'm about to!" Veneficus replied at the bottom of the coliseum's seating. He grabbed a nearby Magician's crosier. Now with two staffs of power he jumped over the railing. While free falling he chanted and flames began shooting out of the bottom of both staffs, propelling the Magician through the air towards the girl and the dragon. He shot across the arena and slammed into the startled Bellae and dragon's snout. She went careening to the ground, while the bloodied head of the dragon smacked to his right, releasing a yowl of pain and surprise. The conjured flames stopped and Veneficus gently landed. He quickly moved to stand between the girl and bloodied dragon.

"No!" Bellae shouted, now laying face down on the ground, weeping and gently swaying side-to-side, overwhelmed by the information from the dragon.

"You will not hurt this child!" Veneficus thundered. He stood with both arms fully raised, each one holding a crosier high into the air. He crossed his arms, bringing the staffs into an "X."

Bellae turned to see Veneficus' back. The dragon snorted something only Bellae understood.

"Don't. Plea…" Bellae started, but was interrupted by Veneficus' shouting.

"Faire incende!" As he finished the words, narrow bursts of blue light exploded out from the crystal atop each staff.

"NO!" Bellae yelled, just as Veneficus began uncrossing his arms and Hullus began a tongue-less roar.

Scroll 6: Everything Will Be Different Now

The streams of scalding light arcing out from the Magicians' crosiers met the dragon's neck. Its fierce howling abruptly stopped, replaced by a vile sizzling and a disgusting gurgle as the dragon's head wobbled slightly before lopping forward, severed clean off. The blackened edges oozed a smoky char and the sickly scent of burnt flesh hurtled around the arena.

Veneficus quickly put both staffs together in front of his body and shouted "Orbis proteger contego!" A large sphere of blue light burst around Veneficus, Bellae, Crann, and Finn. The dragon's mutilated head crashed into the magical shield, bounced, and slid off to the side leaving a bloody trail smeared across the magic shield. The dragon's body, headless and covered in blood and gore, fell forward, striking the sphere of light before crumpling unceremoniously against the blood soaked dirt.

Bellae's soft sob was the only sound in the war torn coliseum. Lakes of blood and islands of fire joined the crumpled heaps of bodies littering the arena.

"Veneficus saved her!" the announcer shouted, breaking the silence.

The crowd erupted in cheers, "Veneficus! Veneficus!"

Gimelli was the first to reach the outside of the shield. Seeing her, Veneficus shouted, "Desino-avta!"

The shield dissolved. Gimelli paused at the gruesome site before rushing towards her sobbing sister. Bellae's legs were floating in a lake of Finn's blood and her torso draped across his mutilated body.

"I told you I would see you when it was over," Finn whispered. Bellae slowly sat up to look into his eyes. He abruptly winced in pain before coughing and spurting a shower of pink, frothy sputum over his face. A stream of bright red blood bubbled out of the corner of his mouth, coursing down the channels of his rough skin.

"But not like this Finn. Not like this," Bellae sobbed, surveying Finn's broken and bleeding body. Deep gashes arched across his mangled chest and left side, each slash remorselessly formed by the dragon's claws.

"Don't forget me and take good care of Crann."

"No! You CANNOT die!" Bellae boomed with a burst of energy born of desperation.

"I wasn't given a choice. Trust me," Finn said weakly, managing a faint smile.

Sanar, the Knights' healer, burst through the ring of Proliator guards forming around the grisly scene as spectators rushed the arena floor.

"Finn!" he yelled, instantly triaging his visible injuries.

Moving a blood-soaked piece of shredded leather armor, Sanar froze in despair. Finn's lower sternum and left ribcage were fragmented into powder and his bark like skin totally removed. The lower lobe of his left lung had been wrenched out and his spleen obliterated into red puree. Arterial spasms meant for the blood-rich organ sprayed aimlessly. The healer looked at Bellae and shook his head.

"It's not fair!" Bellae cried.

"No," Sanar whispered. "It's not." He took out several cloths and began applying pressure to the larger wounds.

"Don't bother, Sanar," Finn said, his frail smile disfigured by red streaks and splatters of blood staining his teeth. "We all know how this story ends."

Sanar nodded and patted Finn's hand. "I'll leave you with your squire."

Panic-laced thoughts exploded in Bellae's head, futility thrashing against her skull. She could feel the inescapability of Finn's demise closing in as if literal physical walls were slamming around them. Bellae searched greedily for something, someone to help. Her eyes landed on

Figure 50: Bellae clings to Finn, the only father she has ever known, with equal mix of dread and despair.

Veneficus. Picturing him flying through the air and instantly killing a dragon she screamed, "Fix him!"

Despite the commotion around the arena Bellae suddenly felt immersed in total silence and everything receded to slow motion as Veneficus' head languidly lumbered back and forth like the unremitting march of a pendulum. His head slowly ground to a halt and fell to his chest, humbly admitting defeat in the face of death.

With all these people, with all their strength and power, surely someone can help. Her eyes landed on Finn and saw his mouth moving. Closing her eyes, she willed the sound to return. Like a rolling wave off the ocean, the noise came smashing back into her senses and her eyes shot open.

"…it's all right. We all die, and I'm ready."

The weakness in his voice scared her. "There's *nothing* all right about you dying!"

Finn closed his eyes as his mind drifted to the Forest of Creber. He suddenly found himself lying in the cradle at the base of his arbor breith. Beams of nutritious sunlight streamed down, dancing on the ground under the direction of the wind-nurtured fluttering of leaves. It was autumn, and golden leaves lazily swayed downwards as the breeze gently cradled them to earth.

His birth tree, sensing his impending death, desperately reached out. Finn felt himself connect with his tree as their spirits embraced for the last time. A warm sense of familiarity and peace descended upon him. For a brief moment he saw through his tree, looking up to see the clouds stepping gracefully across the sapphire dance floor of the seemingly endless heavens.

Suddenly, his birth tree began shedding leaves like tears, rustling a goodbye as they fell faster and faster. The massive pile of leaves quickly blanketed him in complete darkness as he crashed back into the pain of the present, his eyes opened and locked with Bellae's. Pale glass tears streamed down her cheeks before splattering on his rough and bloodied face.

"Bellae," Finn whispered weakly. "Do one last thing for me. Surprise me as you have with so many things, and accept my death."

"I can't," Bellae sobbed.

"My hands are holding you now and my spirit will embrace your heart forever."

His body felt cold, numb, and unjustifiably heavy. Realizing he would never stand again, his eyelids snapped open with a force born from an acute apprehension of death as pink frothy sputum volcanoed out of his mouth from agonizing spasms of pain. For the first time Bellae recognized fear bubbling behind his eyes.

His once strong muscles were impotent to fight against the weight of gravity pressing down and the toxic concoction of blood and fluid flooding in to suffocate his lungs. After decades of breathing rhythmically and unconsciously, he became acutely aware of his agonal respirations which were now pained and desperate.

Fighting against the mounting pressure around his chest he gasped. His eyes flickered before closing for the last time. His hand slowly fell from hers. Flinging herself down she clung to his shredded chest, willing his torso to rise.

It did not.

Bellae barely felt Gimelli's arms as they wrapped around her back.

Rubbing her Inion medallion, she braced herself as the reality of his death collapsed upon her, momentarily stripping her lungs of breath. Through closed eyes, she felt the world spinning out of control. As her consciousness faded to black she thought, *Everything will be different now.*

Scroll 7: Garden Blues

Sitting in his favorite garden in the middle of the Citadel, Friar clasped his head.

Finn's dead.

The hours since his demise were an odd elixir to swallow, at once feeling like an eternity, yet so vivid it felt like he was perpetually watching Finn's last breath.

"Would you prefer company or space, dear friend?"

"Veneficus?" Friar said, his eyes red with fatigue and sadness. "Company. Please."

As the Magician sat down, Friar looked up at the pitch-black sky, broken only by glimmering stars and several moons, each one seemed to be struggling as they tread through the thick, sludgy darkness. Perhaps it was Finn's death, but Friar had never realized how lonely, isolated, the moons and stars looked swaddled within the swarthy cold of night.

"I didn't realize how late it was."

"That may be more profound than you realize."

Friar looked at him critically.

"Someone is tearing Verngaurd apart, and the time to stop this plot is quickly shrinking." Veneficus rested his crosier against his shoulder before continuing. "For the first time in a great while I feel lost and just plain tired. I have been battling some threat or crisis for…well, forever. Can't we have peace? Just for a change of pace?"

Friar was taken aback by the Magician's frankness and how old he appeared. "Do you think it's the White Wizard?"

Veneficus sighed, "Could be. However, I saw Tacet-Vand in the arena during the Dragon Battle."

"What?" Friar's head was spinning. *Tacet-Vand? He seemed so sincere.* "Did he sabotage my Knights? Was it Tacet-Vand? Fino?" he asked, anger leaking through the cracks of his exhaustion.

"I don't know. I'm not even sure if I can beat this White Wizard, or if we can defeat his Dark Warriors. The most troubling question is, have I ever been helpful for the cause of Verngaurd?"

Friar looked with new fondness upon the wizened Magician and his openness. "We would be lost without you. It's amazing to me that such a powerful and long-lived person as you could be filled with self-doubt."

"Time does not fix all problems and age does not always bring peace or answers, that much I know for certain."

"I was kind of hoping it would."

"Occasionally the passing years will clarify a problem, however, mostly time has a way of simply smudging old feelings and memories as new experiences color the past."

"The White Wizard said something else when he briefly appeared to us. He mentioned that our destruction would not just come from abroad, but from within," Friar said expectantly, hoping Veneficus might have some insight.

"I see," the Magician said.

Friar waited, continuing only when it was clear he would say no more, "Do you know the White Wizard well?"

"I did. Now, I do not. In the future, I will know him as well as I know myself."

Friar paused, hoping the Magician would elaborate on his baffling statement. He did not. Instead, the aged enchanter continued staring straight ahead.

"Well, thanks for removing the blocking enchantment and saving Bellae."

"Ah, nothing else to do. I'm embarrassed I let the Proliate bully me into these Dragon Battles. I must balance diplomacy with my own beliefs." Veneficus motioned up and down with cupped hands like a scale. "What scares me most is that despite my magic I don't know who sabotaged your Knights."

"You're sure it wasn't Fino? My Knights saw him slinking around suspiciously in the waiting chamber," Friar said.

"With binding truth enchantments he swears it wasn't him. In fact, he states he was there trying to find Tacet-Vand!"

Friar felt bewildered. The Wizard had seemed so sincere.

"I sincerely doubt Fino has the skill to overcome my truth spell. Could be another Magician, Tacet-Vand, the White Wizard…someone else? I don't know if a Watcher possesses enough magic to create such a blocking enchantment." Veneficus shook his head, "I'm just sorry Finn died."

"Thank you."

"It seems like our enemies are multiplying and getting harder to recognize. Speaking of which, I hate to add another burden upon your grief but…"

"Go ahead," Friar sighed, dreading more bad news.

"It's Patuljak, the Master Elf."

Friar cocked his head to the side in genuine surprise, thinking back to the night the Master Elf had brought Bellae to Liberum. "My interest is piqued."

"Surely you know he has a long history of mistrust against Magicians. Reliable sources report he has turned the Elves of Creber against us and is inciting the Northern Dwarves. Many think he's colluding with the Dark Warriors…"

"What?" Friar interjected, standing up in indignation. "Never! He served with my father in the Dark War!"

"I understand your shock, but people change and sometimes a common enemy unites bitter rivals. I believe he joined them to help overthrow Magician and Proliate alike. I know you have heard stories circulating that the Elves of Creber and Northern Dwarves are aiding the Dark Warriors. Their ring leader is Patuljak."

Friar scoffed at the thought of his dearest allies helping the Dark Warriors.

"Please sit," Veneficus said. "I know this is a sensitive subject after the meeting in my office where you were accused of similar indiscretions. I know *you* would never betray Verngaurd, I am less certain about your allies. We both realize the world has been turned upside down, and we must scrutinize each fact, and every reactive decision, for potential consequences."

Friar nodded and sat down.

"If you hear something about Patuljak, let me know. Let us make a pact to stay better connected as we sort out the truth for the good of Verngaurd."

"Agreed," Friar said. "What about the rest of the Tournament?"

"That depends on you and your Knights."

"I hate to continue, but would loathe leaving. I've been around long enough to know that whatever decision I make, there will be plenty of critics."

"Experience has taught me to listen to opinions, mindfully consider constructive critiques, but blatantly disregard spiteful criticism."

Friar laughed.

Veneficus turned serious, "Whenever faced with different paths, the sweat and tears born from our decision will flow back around and sparkle with the glimmer of regret on the trail we forsake."

"Well said. I shall put it to a vote and let my Knights decide if we finish the Tournament or leave."

Veneficus paused, "I shall delay the games for one day. This will allow you to assess your options and do what's best for your Knights."

"What about the Proliate?"

"They'll complain at first, but then spend extra time praying in temple," Veneficus said, rolling his eyes.

The two embraced before Veneficus magically disappeared.

Exiting the garden Friar jumped, startled by a gruff, "Hey!"

A short but stocky, robed figure huddled in the shadows. Friar put his hand on his sword while scanning for other potential attackers.

With slumped shoulders the dejected figure slowly moved into the torchlight.

"I'm so sorry," the sobbing voice said, pulling back his hood.

"King Abernan?" Friar hardly recognized the Northern Dwarf leader without his armor and fierce expression.

"I made a deal with demons and it cost you a Knight and me three dragons!" he bawled.

"What do you mean?" Friar asked, taken aback by this ferocious warrior-king openly weeping. King Abernan took several slow deep, sobbing breaths before speaking.

"High Commander Storlax of the Proliate came to me with his silver tongue, telling me that if we provided three dragons for the Tournament they would remove Temple Palvoa and Aon Intinn from our borders and leave our lands alone."

Friar nodded, *Now I understand why they agreed to provide their precious dragons for this tournament.*

"You saw when visiting the Storten Flower Fields how the Proliate encroach on our lands. I let selfish and prideful aspirations overcome my common sense. I betrayed you, my people, and our beloved dragons," the king said, tears still streaming down his face.

"Finn was an amazing Knight. I think he would be proud to have died to assure the safety of all of your people and dragons," Friar said.

King Abernan's face contorted in rage, "The dirtbag Storlax recanted on his promise because of what happened with the dragon you fought! He said we defaulted on our agreement by bringing such a psychotic dragon, rendering the pact useless!"

Friar shook his head, "That is incredibly unjust!"

A small tear rolled down the rough Dwarf's face as a mask of sorrow descended upon his features. "Of course I grieve for your Knight, but I cry just as hard for the loss of three dragons as well. They are just as much a part of our family as any Dwarf. Never again. I swear on my life, never again will a dragon fight except by our side in battle!"

Scroll 8: AnFilleadh/To Return

Stunned by King Abernan's revelation and reeling from Finn's death, Friar felt frozen to the ground. Try as he might, there were too many problems swirling around for his mind to recede into peace.

He looked wistfully in the direction of the Xenia barracks, but knowing there was no chance his thoughts would ever quiet enough to encounter sleep, Friar headed back over to the coliseum lost in thought. Without remembering how, he suddenly found himself standing before the massive arena. Looking up at flowing rows of arches and all the architectural grandeur, Friar shook his head. Even this marvel of construction could not shine brighter than the fog of despair left by Finn's death. Slowly, he moved towards the back entrance.

"Halt!" a stern voice called out, startling Friar.

"I am an old man, unable to bear many more such shocks this night," Friar replied.

Several stern Proliate warriors moved out from the shadows.

"No one else is allowed into the coliseum."

"I am Friar Pallium of the…"

"We know who you are, HK."

"Very well, then you realize I have a dead Knight in there. I just wish to see his body and say goodbye in my own way. There was too much chaos after his death."

The front two guards looked at each other, neither one wanting to be the one to deny the aged ruler of the Knights, yet equally reluctant to defy their direct order.

Seeing their hesitation Friar spoke, "I promise, I just want to say goodbye to him. I shall be as quick as my heart allows." Despite himself, a small tear ran down his cheek. Too much emotion, too much uncertainty.

"You absolutely must be out before first light," a guard replied.

Friar nodded and passed between the first two Proliate as they stepped aside. A third guard motioned for Friar to follow. They crossed through several corridors, winding through drab passageways.

Finally they arrived at an ominously large wooden door. Melodic chanting could be heard on the other side.

"The Elves are in there…a lot of them. Not sure what you will be interrupting, but behind there lies your Knight," the guard said with surprising tenderness.

"Thank you," Friar said, nodding kindly. As the guard turned and left Friar paused outside the door, his hand hovering a few inches from the fawn colored wood. The fear of disturbing their funeral rites paled in comparison to the ominous dread of seeing Finn's lifeless body. The heartbreaking scene of Bellae clinging to her beloved, but fractured, Knight would haunt him the rest of his days.

He recalled Veneficus' analogy of the hourglass of destruction and couldn't help imagining the sand of despair descending to clink at the bottom of the hourglass, covering both the base and hope in equal measure. The barely audible plinks of sand stood in sharp contrast the grave significance of time speeding forward towards an uncertain, but certainly precarious, future.

Counting down, counting down…

Without knocking Friar gingerly pushed open the door. The creak alerted several within the room who looked up. He was grateful to see a handful of gentle, welcoming nods. Finn's bare body rested on top of a large catafalque. The decorative wooden framework was surrounded by dozens of Elves. Ailante and several other ruling Archerians stood solemnly to the left. Various hooded Prete were chanting in the middle, and obviously overseeing the ceremony. To the right stood the burly Elf Kempe with a variety of other anguished Elf warriors.

Sanar, the Knight healer, walked up to Friar and whispered, "It is good you came."

Friar nodded and they grasped forearms.

"The Elves are chanting their interment prayers, and have been for a couple of hours. They started right after I cleaned his body. Once they are done, they will prepare him for transportation and burial," Sanar stated.

Friar squeezed the healer's shoulder in thanks and continued to stare at Finn. His lifeless eyes had been left hauntingly open and his normally chestnut skin appeared pallid and drained. Innumerable flaps of skin were carefully puzzled together, but the gruesome tracks marking the dragon's grisly slashes were achingly evident, ghastly reminders of the massive trauma his body had endured.

The melancholy chanting was hypnotic, making the scene seem even less real. *How can Finn be dead?*

A chill went down Friar's spine, for the first time he noted the raw iciness of the room, and instantly recognized an old familiar, but disconcerting, feeling settling upon him. Friar was intimately familiar with death's icy grip. He had repeatedly become acquainted with it as a small boy during the Dark War, quickly learning death did not swoop in for a fleeting moment, hastily seizing life before hurriedly scurrying off.

No.

Death enjoyed lingering, making itself known in the form of frosty fog, mockingly gloating a raw coldness upon all in the blast radius of its preordained victory over life, a conquest unfairly guaranteed from the moment of birth.

Looking at his own aged, wrinkled skin and slightly bent fingers he could feel death smiling at him from within the hovering chill. His lungs suddenly tightened and he imagined hearing death's promise, *One way or another, in battle or by time, you will soon join your dead brother. You are mine. You have always been mine.*

Standing before his Knight's stripped body, death itself was laid bare, pulled from the shadow of the mundane to stand with naked swagger, awash in power and comfortably smothered with the boastful confidence of one destined to ceaselessly win.

Friar smiled. What else could he do? He knew how many years had passed in his life, death was coming for him sooner rather than later, *In battle or naturally.*

"Whatever 'naturally' being extinguished from consciousness means. Seems there's nothing 'natural' about that."

"What?" Sanar asked, jolting Friar with the embarrassing knowledge he had spoken his last thought aloud.

"Nothing, just listening to the chanting."

Sanar nodded, but obviously unconvinced.

How did Finn die before me? Friar thought. *Our bodies eventually decay when enough sands have passed through the hourglass of our lives. Eventually even the strongest mind crumbles into dementia when enough years have marched past. Only our soul remains for us to control as we travel through life, and I shall continue to guard mine, such an irreplaceable treasure should be well protected.*

Friar looked up to see Ailante standing in front of him with a puzzled expression, while his ears were ringing within the blaring silence which had, at some point during his internal deliberation, replaced the mesmerizing chanting, "Sorry, what?"

"I said that the Ullmhú, the initial preparation, is complete. We are ready for the AnFilleadh…" Ailante said, stopping to think. "That is a hard word to translate into the common tongue. It means something like the preparation to return. It is the second phase of our burial rites. I thought you might want to say a last goodbye before his body is made ready and wrapped."

"Of course, and thank you," Friar said, joining Sanar beside Finn's body.

Friar gently ran his hand along the side of Finn's cheek. Leaning down to Finn's ear he whispered, "I will join you soon enough, brother, friend, warmhea…"

The rest of what he had intended to say vanished in unanticipated sobs. Unable to speak any more of what was in his heart, Friar kissed Finn's forehead, several tears landing where Bellae's had struck hours earlier, and suddenly, he began to sway, the room unexpectedly reeling. He gratefully let several Prete guide him to a chair.

"Thank you," he said, wiping his tears. "I just need to sit a minute."

Through tear-blurred eyes, Friar watched the Elves bring out an enormous, ornately carved vat. Others carried over small, but still highly decorated, containers. One by one they dumped the contents of the smaller vessels into the large one while stirring. Some were thick and viscous while others flowed easily.

"What are you mixing?" Friar asked.

All the Elves stopped and stared, confounded at the question.

"I apologize if that is inappropriate to ask?"

"The AnFilleadh includes a recipe developed a millennia ago. It is a part of the preparation to return our bodies back to our Edelia Arbor Breith—you might know it as the Tree of Life," a Prete explained.

"Friar is a dear friend, we can explain some of what we are doing, but certain parts must remain our secret," Ailante said, walking over to help Friar up.

"We first coat his body in a thick fluid that will preserve it for travel yet still be nourishing to the Edelia Arbor Breith. It contains several resins from various species of trees in our forest, as well as honey, and numerous oils."

After the ingredients were fused, the hefty liquid was generously applied to Finn's body. Once it congealed they began covering his corpse in various leaves.

"We use a precise combination and ratio of various plants and trees that keep out moisture and air while conserving the body. The ones you may recognize are reed palms, spider plant leaves, death lily petals, and tillandsia blades," Ailante explained as the Prete worked tirelessly and meticulously.

Once his entire body and face, save for his still open eyes, were covered in the various plants they brought out a thick linen and began lovingly wrapping him.

"So, all too soon my friend, it ends and you are prepared to go back to the beginning," the muscular Kempe said when they had finished covering everything but the eyes with linen. Tears streamed down his roughly skinned face.

"It is customary to have a family member close the eyes, the last part of the AnFilleadh," Ailante said, squeezing Friar's arm for support. "Kempe is the closest thing Finn has."

Several Prete approached the massive Elf warrior, gently handing him various leaves and some linen. Kempe tenderly closed Finn's eyes for the last time before placing the plants over them, and finally adding linen. He spoke first in Elvish, and then repeated the final saying of the AnFilleadh in the common tongue, "Your life did emerge, light and soul pithily surge, and now, extinguished, return to submerge."

Scroll 9: Decision Dues

"I know you're injured, exhausted, and grieving, but we need to decide if we stay and finish the third day, or leave immediately to bury Finn," Friar said to the two Veli, Arquero, and the four remaining, heavily bandaged, Pantteri Knights early the next morning.

"We stay and fight," Ritari answered, his dressings soaked in weeping serosanguineous fluid and blood from the back of his burned head.

"Of course we fight!" Luchar bellowed, his head also heavily bandaged.

The remaining Knights nodded.

"I think that's what Finn would want," Friar said, turning to his corpulent Veli. "Pingius, send word to Veneficus that we will finish the tournament and thank him for a day of rest."

After Veli Pingius trundled out the door, Sorea stood up on wobbly legs, her concussed head pounding. "What about Finn's body?"

"Sanar cleaned it and the Elves prepared and wrapped it in linen for when we leave. Finn made it clear he wanted to be buried in the Forest of Creber."

"What about our weapons not working while fighting the dragon?" Ritari asked angrily. "Those bloody Magicians need to pay!"

"I had a long discussion with Veneficus. Could be Tacet-Vand, the White Wizard, or a rogue Magician."

"Veneficus is the rogue!" Luchar bellowed, wincing at the excruciating pain in his heavily bandaged and pounding head.

"I personally saw him stand up and throw out desist enchantments. After he did so, your weapons began to work," Friar said. "Plus, if it was Veneficus or Fino why did the first few shots from Lovag and Finn penetrate? If they had done something your weapons would not have worked from the start. No, this was not Veneficus."

"It had to be that scrawny Fino," Luchar said, this time bowing down to the painful thumping in his skull, and speaking more quietly.

"Veneficus questioned him with a truth enchantment, it was not him."

"That's it?" Sorea wondered. "How about an investigation and punishment? That blocking enchantment cost Finn his life!"

"I understand and share your anger, but trust Veneficus to find and discipline the culprit. For now, go rest and prepare yourselves. Make sure you are checking in with the healers."

The Knights filed out leaving Friar and Veli Falciss.

"You saw all three dragons," Falciss said. "Compared to Hullus, the other two dragons were babies. It was no coincidence *we* drew that monster and had a blocking spell working against *us*."

"I agree. Someone is trying to alienate us, but what would you have me do?"

"I can't answer that, but I don't trust any Magician, including Veneficus."

"I trust him. Now, more than ever, we must believe in our friends."

"Hello...your excellence," Veli Pingius murmured. Surprised at how nervous he was, his stout eyes darted about the cold and sparse chamber of the Supreme Master Magician.

Veneficus looked up expectantly and the Proliate guard accompanying the heavyset Veli gently pushed him forward.

"You can give your message now," the guard whispered.

"Ah, so I can. The Knights will fight your excellence."

"I am a Magician, not a foreign head of state my fulsome Veli. Do not address me as your excellence."

"Of course, your... Supreme Master."

"I am glad you decided to finish the Tournament."

Pingius nodded enthusiastically.

"Anything else?"

Shaking his head, the Veli slowly backed out of the room.

Tart memories blurred with raw visions of the future, causing Veneficus to pause and close his eyes. His head fell heavily to his chest, pulled by a coalescing of deep exhaustion and cavernous concern about the future.

Several normally scornful Valo floated towards him, a hint of worry in the shadows of their expression, "You okay Master?"

The ancient Magician looked up with a hint of tears in his eyes. "Na Cearcaill is coming again?"

"Uh, yeah boss," a Valo answered.

"Yeah Master, you know it!" another stated.

"It always comes?"

Several Valo turned their normally snide faces, true concern brewing within their magical light.

"Yeah, that's kind of what the whole eternal cycle thing means," one said.

"I don't really want to see this world end. I am quite fond of many living within it."

"You... sure you're okay boss?" another ventured.

"Only I can stop the coming darkness," Veneficus said, although it came out dripping with just enough doubt the Valo wondered if it was a question.

"Sure, that's the party line at least," a Valo who had just floated over added.

"I stop the darkness!" the Magician said with burgeoning confidence.

"That's it Master! Get a little of that zesty crossness we have learned to love!"

"Why do I have to be in this position? Why do I have to be the one to save the world from itself over and over again?" Veneficus said, his eyes looking imposingly at the Valo who had gathered around him. "It is inequitable!"

"Oh, yeah, totally unfair!" a Valo chirped. "How horrible for you to have pretty much unlimited power and immortality. That does sound like a real poignantly pitiable existence!"

The fire within the Magician's eyes seemed to reignite, causing the Valo to slowly bob backwards.

"What boss? I said you are all-powerful and such…"

"How many of you Valo are left?" Veneficus asked.

"There are just twelve of us."

"Only twelve?" Veneficus asked.

"Uh, yeah, that's what happens when you lose your temper and occasionally blast us to oblivion!"

"Hi everyone, Bellae's still snoozing," Gimelli said, sleepily entering the squire's barracks at the same time Friar and the Knights were discussing whether to stay.

Scelto approached, "Hey."

"Hey, back at you," she replied. Scelto gave her an awkward hug.

"It's chilly in Bellae's room," Gimelli said, grabbing an extra blanket. "I better get back."

"Let me know when she can take her mice back," Lontas said as the two mice chittered a rebuke, upset at being away from Bellae for so long.

Gimelli smiled, "I know they miss her, but she should rest more. Thanks for taking care of them."

"Trying to," Lontas replied worriedly.

"Did you sleep at all, Gimelli?" Scelto asked.

Shaking her head she saw Jumeaux still lying on his cot. "Come see Bellae with me."

"Friar said if we leave or stay this would be a day of rest, and she's asleep. Sooo…no."

"At least get up and get on your clothes," Scelto chided.

Jumeaux carefully set his clothes on his cot and then stood on them. "I did it! I got *on* my clothes!" he said, raising his hands in triumph.

Gimelli shook her head.

"What? That's funny. Listen, Sister Sunshine, Scelto told me to *get on* my clothes so, I'm *on* my clothes," he laughed.

Gimelli departed crying as Scelto moved forward. "You know, Jumeaux, we try, really we do. Sometimes you're just too much to handle."

"It's a joke!"

"A joke? Your sister's exhausted from grief and one of our Knights is dead. Finn, by the way, always went out of his way to defend you when no one, and I mean no one other than Bellae was. Either put your *clothes on*, or get out and don't come back," Scelto said, his voice tired and distant.

I know that Finn's dead. People deal with things differently, Jumeaux thought. *Say it to them,* a voice within him called. *Tell them you're hurting too.*

He said nothing. Instead he succumbed to sulking, and feeling completely alone, content to slide deeper into a darker seclusion while putting on his clothes.

Scroll 10: Warning

Bellae's eyes fluttered. She couldn't tell if she was fighting to stay asleep or struggling to wake up. Emotions and memories flashed into her consciousness before submerging, quickly replaced by another.

flash Veneficus smiling, laughing.

flash The Knight's weapons spinning in purple light.

flash Sickly Fino fleeing the waiting chamber.

flash Kneeling in a pool of Finn's blood.

flash Sorea flying through the air limply.

flash Finn's blood-stained smile.

flash Luchar's dented helmet and bleeding head.

flash Pink sputum shooting out of Finn's mouth.

flash Ritari hacking at the beast.

flash The dragon's fire, anger, and garbled words, spoken only to her through a tongue-less mouth.

flash Finn's last breath, letting go of her hand.

A familiar voice frantically broke the pattern of reflections, "… much time! Please wake up!"

The blurry image of a young Elf gradually came into focus. "Kainen?" It was the young Elf she had seen several times since arriving at the Tournament.

"Your sister will be returning soon and can't catch us here."

"Us?"

"This is Arend, the Eaglian who has been watching over you."

"An Eaglian? They're real?" she asked, but the familiar sensation in her gut answered the question. "I knew you were no demon!"

A squawking laugh pierced the air, "Thanks…I think. It's nice to see you again. I'm really sorry about Finn."

"Thanks," she said while staring in wonder at the half-human, half-eagle before her. "I didn't know Eaglians were real."

"We have kept ourselves hidden for centuries. Now, it's time for us to emerge. The hour is dark, and we will fight."

His majestic white head had a fearsome yellow beak above a human chin and torso. His beautiful brown wings were imposing despite being folded over. Two feathered thighs dove backwards before angling forward into massive talons. Two smaller wing-like ears framed his fearsome yellow eyes.

"Why have you been following me, but never really showing yourself?"

"I swore my life to protect you at all costs, but…"

"Time for explanations on our quest…"

"Wait," Bellae interrupted. "Why do you keep saying we're going on an adventure or quest?"

"Tell her about the prophecy," Arend suggested.

Figure 51: Finally revealed to be a mysterious and reclusive Eaglian, the winged creature stands before Bellae. Cloistered in their giant redwood forest for centuries, they were largely forgotten. They will stay hidden no longer.

Bellae took in the majestic Eaglian and tuned out the beginning of Kainen's refusal.

"...will eventually become clear. For now, know that we're watching over you. Arend had strict orders not to make contact unless your life was threatened, like at the cemetery. We don't want the Evil One to know the Eaglians are joining the coming war for the world."

"War for the *world*?"

"I know you have many questions, but we only stopped by to inform you Tacet-Vand, through IleZuri, told us something horrible will happen late tonight or early tomorrow, and he will not be able to stop it. This means we will likely see you sooner rather than later as the fabric of our world begins to shred under Na Cearcaill. Be prepared, but tell no one about us or any of this! Just be ready."

"For what?"

Kainen sighed. "When it happens we'll be there for you and your true journey begins."

A thousand questions burst through her mind, but fatigue and sadness won out as they briskly turned to leave, and she quickly descended into restless sleep.

Scroll 11: Seriously Low Blow

A scratching commotion from outside stole its way though the deeply disorienting, misty-maze of sleep, and continued long enough to tickle Bellae's weary brain awake. *Has the Eaglian returned?* she thought excitedly.

"Bellae," Finn called out. "Hello my Inion."

Bellae's face lit up in a smile, it was amazing to hear her Knight's voice.

"Bellae."

"Finn!" Bellae meant to scream, but it came out friably mute and tired. Her disoriented eyes fluttered open to see Finn smiling and waving. Motioning her to come. She closed her eyes and willed her body to rise and move towards her beloved Knight. Sitting up caused her brain to protest and spin.

Flopping backwards she opened her eyes and smiled at Finn. He continued to stand immobile, grinning and gently motioning for her to join him.

"Finn?" Bellae said, a hint of fear and truth leaching into her question. A brief warning flashed in her mind before reality crashed hope down around her, cratering out deep despair.

Finn is dead! her brain screamed. *Finn's dead?* She knew in her heart he was, but part of her coveted for him to be standing in front of her. Her drained brain struggled to come to terms with the image of her Knight, the shallow knowledge he was dead battling the cavernous desire for him to be alive. As Finn's form melted to reveal the grotesque, ghostly form of a Nishi, tears exploded out of Bellae.

"That's it, cry you wretched girl," the Nishi howled, moving right up to Bellae's bawling face. "Weakness oozes out of your scabby body like pus from an infected wound. Why are you so tired? You weren't the one who fought the dragon. Only a feeble and spineless coward would lay in bed too weak to come at my bidding!"

The spirit floated up, positioning herself horizontally over Bellae with her deep-set eyes glaring their anger from just a few inches above her face.

"You still cannot fathom the horrors about to befall you! However, all is not lost. Come with me to hasten your death and shorten the inevitable suffering! Don't you want to join your Knight in death? You can 'meet up with him.' Let me relieve your profound frailty."

Bellae's tears slowed and she sniffled her nose.

"I need an answer weakling."

Sobbing faintly Bellae slowly pulled down the sleeves of her cloak. "Suck on this!" she cried before violently waving her forearms though the floating ghost.

The spirit howled, her form turning to mist and disappearing as Bellae's talisman arm guards sliced through her head.

"Why *am* I so tired?" Bellae asked the now empty room.

Maybe it's because my sleep keeps getting interrupted, she thought. The idea somehow seemed funny to her and she laughed hollowly before falling back into slumber.

Scroll 12: Dragon Hangover

"That's it. It's okay to wake up," Gimelli said.

Bellae's eyes opened groggily. She quickly scanned the room, thankful the Nishi was gone. However, she felt a tinge of sadness that the Eaglian and Elf had left, but their words of warning still weighed heavily on her.

"Sit up and drink."

"Luchar, Sorea, Ritari?" Bellae asked, holding up her hand to stop the cup.

"They're bruised, battered, and burned, but up and about!"

Bellae took a drink. The liquid was cozy, warming her from the inside as it moved into her stomach.

Pausing, she glared suspiciously at Gimelli. "Luchar's really okay?"

"Yes. He proved he has the hardest head in all of Verngaurd. It took them forever to get his dented helmet off yesterday!"

"Yesterday?"

"It's almost noon of the next day."

"Sorea and Ritari?"

"Sorea has bruises but otherwise seems okay. She will still probably not wear a helmet. The back of Ritari's head is scorched but otherwise he is fine. The healers have managed to make a pad for his helmet. He otherwise seems good."

"Grym and Borb?"

"Both fine, Lontas is watching them."

"Where's Crann?" Bellae shouted. "He has to be so sad." Sliding out of bed she instantly felt light-headed, wobbled, and dizzily sat back down.

A gentle knock on the door interrupted them.

"Come in!"

Lontas and Scelto entered carrying hopeful smiles, Sorea followed carrying a tray of steaming food. Bellae's stomach growled fiercely, the sight and smells reminding her she was past due.

Bellae stood up, steadied herself then smothered Lontas in a warm hug.

"It's great to see you awake," he blushed.

She nodded, but resisted telling him about the Eaglian, Elf, and their terrifying prediction. *He will feel silly he didn't identify the creature as an Eaglian.*

Sorea placed the platter on the table before accepting a tentative hug, groaning at the pressure on her sore ribs. Her head was bandaged, and you could see a massive bruise stretching all the way down to her swollen eyes in a raccoon-like mask. "Please, eat."

Despite the growl from her stomach, Bellae headed for the door, "I must get to Crann and…"

Scelto gently held her. "Hold on there, Miss Brave. You stood within a hair's breadth of one of the fiercest dragons the world has ever seen. But right now, you need to sit and eat."

"I'll go with you when you're finished," Gimelli said.

Bellae felt weak and allowed Scelto to guide her to the table where she quickly began devouring the food.

"Not too fast," Gimelli mothered.

"So tell me everything," she said between ravenous bites.

"After you blacked out, the crowd swarmed the arena floor to touch the dead dragon and see Veneficus. I didn't want them trampling Sorea, so Friar came to be with you and I went to find her," Gimelli said.

"I found Behalen and Lovag covered in disgusting green goop, and then we made our way to you," Lontas said. "One of the Proliators started carrying you off the field, but Ritari went nuts, furious that someone besides a Knight touched you. After Friar stopped him from killing the Proliate, Ritari got you out of the crowd."

"You should have seen Luchar's smashed and trashed helmet!" Scelto declared.

"The blood was flowing fast, but his mouth was running faster," Sorea laughed, holding her side in a combination wince and smile.

"He went nuts when he saw Finn's dead bo..." Lontas stopped and looked away remorsefully. Through the awkward silence Bellae scanned their stricken faces, pained with loss, and sorry Finn's death had been brought up.

"What did Luchar do when he saw Finn's body?" Bellae whispered, the smoothness of her voice implying permission to talk about his death.

"Let's just say he put on quite a show," Sorea finally said.

"That's putting it mildly. We're used to seeing him upset, but this was a whole new level of insanity!"

"Yeah, he wouldn't even listen to Friar!" Scelto added, his eyes wide. "He hurt several Proliators before Veneficus magically immobilized him."

"Luchar has one response to every emotion. Anger, sadness, and happiness all come out as rage. That rampage was his way of crying for Finn," Sorea affirmed.

How had I reacted? Fainting? Bellae thought, a little embarrassed. She remembered the excruciating pain of the dragon but her memory hit a wall when trying to recall the conversation. It had all seemed so clear earlier, now it was fuzzy. With a full stomach the aching hole in her heart seemed more painful. The emptiness born from Finn's death could not be filled even in a room satiated with people.

"I *need* to see Crann."

"Okay, let's go."

"After that, I need to see Grym and Borb as well," Bellae said.

"Sorry, but I need a spot of rest," Sorea said, holding her head.

Gimelli resisted the chance to lecture her about wearing a helmet, deciding to save that for later.

"The worst part of butting heads with a dragon is the hangover."

Bellae could feel Crann's outrage as they moved closer.

"Something's wrong," she shouted, rushing ahead of Gimelli. She felt her way towards Crann and crashed through the stable doors to see four stable mates wrestling with her beloved horse.

A warm rush of rage rose up in her. "Release him!"

The four stable mates felt the ropes slacken as Crann stopped fighting.

"*Took you long enough,*" he neighed.

"*Sorry, just woke up*," Bellae said, taking off the reins.

"Hey, those took forever to get on!" a stable mate said angrily.

"*They left me in these since yesterday!*"

"These have been on all night!" Bellae yelled.

A look of surprise scaled their faces. It deepened when Ritari and Gimelli showed up. "Problem?"

"Four, actually. If they don't leave, would you mind teaching them what Knights do to liars and shirkers?"

"Shirkers? This beast has wronged us!" one shouted incredulously.

Ignoring the outburst, Ritari slowly drew out his sword, accentuating the disheartening screech until the stable mates disappeared.

Ritari and Gimelli stood guard as Bellae groomed and fed Crann. Afterwards she held his head until he fell asleep.

"I don't think I could stand it if you had died too," she whispered to the sleeping horse.

"Bellae, you have a visitor," Gimelli said kindly. She stood aside and the large Elf she had seen several times entered.

"May I talk to you?" he asked as Gimelli quietly shut the door.

Bellae nodded.

"We have met before, but to remind you, my name is Kempe," the Elf said moving forward tentatively.

"When we were young Finn used to always shake his head and chastise me when I tried to talk him out of leaving our forest, our home, in search of some great adventure and larger world that only he could see in his dreams. He was always so hungry to explore and find out more about the world. He began to detest his connection to his arbor breith…our birth tree."

The large Elf paused, a hint of tears glimmering in his brown and green eyes. "He would also tell me, 'You're missing the power of the acorn for the clutter of the forest.' I never understood what he meant until I saw you crying over his dying body. He was trying to tell me not to miss the importance of the small things in life, they are the things that really matter—the acorns of our existence grow into the strongest of forests, full of love, friendship, and hope.

Bellae put her head down. Despite the fresh wave of sadness, at least for the moment, she felt all out of tears.

"The world is always a little too small for an exceptional dreamer. It certainly was for the likes of Finn."

Bellae's tears oozed out at his last comment.

"Anyway, I just wanted to let you know his loss is devastating for many of us from Creber. He was one of a kind."

Bellae wanted to say something but nothing sounded right. *Thank you? Yes, he was great?*

After a few awkward moments the massive Elf turned towards the door, pausing on the way out, "Know you are in our thoughts. I will leave you to your grief."

Despite her long sleep and the commotion of the stables and street outside Bellae nestled into some hay and felt weary as she wiped away her tears. Her eyes fluttered to resist, but succumb to the quieting notes stirred up by the dust playing their silent dance within the murky sunlight of the stable. Eventually her eyes closed and she dropped into slumber.

She awoke to find Crann standing over her protectively and Friar Pallium sitting near the door.

"Hello, Bellae. I hope you slept well."

"I did, thanks."

"I didn't wish to wake you, but wanted to be the one to tell you we'll be participating in the final day of competition. We all felt Finn would want us to finish."

"I know he would."

"Friar, a messenger from Veneficus," Ritari said from just outside the door.

"Send him in. It seems this stable is the place to be!"

Wearing yellow robes and blue stars, a nervous looking Adjutant walked in, timidly handing Friar a small scroll.

"Thank you."

The boy muttered something like, "Ya-certly," presumably a mix of "Yes" and "Certainly."

With each word Friar's smile broadened. "Leave it to Veneficus."

"What?" Bellae asked.

"Veneficus is thanking us for continuing the games despite our great loss. He also wants to do something special."

"What?"

"You'll find out tomorrow."

Scroll 13: Are we Ready?

The door to the holding chamber under the coliseum squealed open the next morning. "Knights and squires, this way," a Proliator guard commanded.

"All of us?" Arquero asked.

"Everyone follow the Proliate," Friar said, grinning broadly.

"Friar," a voice whispered after the rest of the Knights, Veli, and squires had left.

Ili-Zuri quickly left the shadows to appear in front of Friar. He wore a large black cloak over his armor.

Glancing to make sure they were alone he spoke softly, "Tacet-Vand had *nothing* to do with the blocking spell on the dragon. He also wanted me to tell you that the first real deaths of Na Cearcaill have already happened."

"What?" Friar asked, aghast.

"I can tell you no more."

"Why? Why act so mysterious? Why not tell us more?"

Ili-Zuri looked down remorsefully, "Some magical bonds, even a powerful wizard can't overcome."

"Friar?" a voice came from within the arena.

"Coming!" Friar yelled. By the time he turned back around Ili-Zuri had already reclined into the shadows.

As Friar left the darkness of the holding area to join the Knights clustered right outside the door the crowd erupted in applause. He gently moved towards the front of the cautious Knights and squires. Curious, but unsure of what was going on, they followed their leader towards Veneficus levitating in the center of the arena.

Raising his hands for silence, Veneficus began, "Over this Tournament we have grown closer, learning to stop focusing on differences and celebrate what we have in common. The Knights agreeing to finish the Tournament despite the devastating loss of one of their own, symbolizes the courage and resolve of the inhabitants of Verngaurd.

"We have to, and we will, come together to defeat any and all enemies!" he said to a deafening roar of approval. "Let us turn the tragic death of this Knight into something constructive, something healing, a harmony across our lands.

"There is one last task I must attend to before we open the final day of the Tournament," he said, drifting down to earth.

Black flags and shields magically appeared where each country's own colors had just been as the arena floor became inundated with competitors from all of Verngaurd.

"Welcome, warriors of Verngaurd! We stand together, united in our spirit and resolve!" Veneficus said smiling. "I would like to bring back an ancient tradition of the Knights one last time. When a Knight died a charmed pin called a kalma-kunnia was given to the oldest child. Sired deep in the forges of the Northern Dwarves of magic metal supplied by Magicians it was indestructible.

"When anyone in Verngaurd saw the kalma-kunnia, great honor was bestowed upon the wearer. Their parent was a hero who gave their life for our future. Such a gift has not been given in over a century. But today, that changes," he said as the bandaged Ritari and Sorea parted to open a path. Tears blurred Bellae's vision as Veneficus approached.

"Desino avta," he said, his voice no longer amplified.

He knelt to be eye to eye with her. "As his Inion it is fitting that this gift goes to you."

He pinned the award on her cloak and the two embraced warmly as the stadium erupted into cheers.

Veneficus released her and chanted something inaudible, immediately flying upwards. "If you are not too tired of applauding, let the third and final day begin!" he said, his voice amplified again.

A great cheer erupted as the Knights circled Bellae to congratulate her. She pulled up her cloak to get a better view of the mysterious silver medallion with a yellowish glow. It consisted of two rhomboid shapes with the one on top slightly askew, making it look like a small box with the lid open.

Bellae felt dizzy at the constant stream of hands, congratulations, and faces of warriors from the different nations passing before her. After what seemed like hours the crowd began to thin.

Her Knight dies and she gets all this attention? Jumeaux huffed enviously.

"Let's begin! Competitors in the distance run assemble!" Veneficus said, still levitating above the arena. All the shields and flags turned back into their nations standard colors.

BOOM!

A loud crash from the northern part of the arena rocked the stadium. Magicians had blown apart the northern gate, which now lay in splinters. Bloodied Proliate Red Guard and a few Magicians stumbled into the arena. As they moved closer it became apparent that many were carrying dead or injured people. Blood was so ubiquitous in the ghastly scene that it was hard to tell whether the blood was theirs or from those they carried.

"STOP! Listen to us!" One of them yelled fiercely. He coughed, sending an eruption of blood from his mouth. Shaking his head he added, "Everyone stop!"

Book Two's revolutionary tempest came storming into Verngaurd, a forbidding forewarning of the cataclysmic conflict and heartbreak on the horizon as the mysterious time of Na Cearcaill gains momentum. Our journey proceeds as we slip from beneath the rune Hagalaz, ending as it began: "Even tumbling within the world's massive times of change we struggle to see beyond our own insignificant moment, unable to comprehend the boundless ebony bookends of eternity, which do not even bother to acknowledge our insignificant time."

Figure 52: All previous goodwill quickly evaporates as battered Magicians and bloodied Proliate warriors stream into the arena carrying countless dead and assisting numerous wounded civilians.

Too often we allow the cursory moments of our lifetime to melt our time into the tedium of habits and banal activities of day-to-day living. Outwardly refusing to admit how loath we are of the challenge of change, instead, we prefer to live within the treacherously thin, fraudulent bubble of a status-quo world. The world has the unwelcome, unauthorized habit of dishing out abominable challenges—some small, others life and death, that require us to fight, or be washed away in the gelid, pitiless sands of eternity.

Figure 53: Our excursion through Book Two withers as we prepare to tumble upon the blood soaked battlefields of Book Three and beyond. This rune woodcarving was found on the third wooden chest in the Far Forest of England. For Verngaurd, and those you encountered in the first two books, Rune Uruz prepares to unleash the brutally raw and untamed struggle coiled to encase the world within the ferocious power of a world at war.

Figure 54: Carved under the lid of the third chest discovered in the Far Forest of England is an etching of Uruz Reversed. This symbolizes the monumental missed opportunity Verngaurd had to avert disaster and come together. This failure upsets the precariously balanced equilibrium of primal power and intellect/reason. (Aside on Runes: of the 24 Elder Futhark Runes nine have no reverse form or meaning {including the first two runes we have encountered—Jera and Hagalaz.} A reversed rune can equate to an opposing view to the upright rune, or it can indicate looking at the meaning of the upright rune in a different light).

Figure 55: In Book Three the inhabitants of Verngaurd come face to face with the realization of just how short on time they are, as the hourglass holding any chance of peace in Book Two empties into the primal battlefield of Book Three beneath the Rune Uruz.

www.ingramcontent.com/pod-product-compliance
Lightning Source LLC
Chambersburg PA
CBHW060540310726
48982CB00009B/1322/J

* 9 7 8 1 7 3 2 1 4 9 9 4 6 *